SWORD

STORM OF FIRE AND BLOOD

Taylor R. Marshall

Saint John Press
MMXVII

This book is a work of fiction. Any references to historical events, existing locations, or real people, living or dead, are used fictitiously. Other names, characters, places, and events are the creation of the author, and any resemblance to actual events, locations, or persons, living or dead, is coincidental.

Copyright © 2017 Taylor R. Marshall

All rights reserved. In accordance with the U.S. Copyright Act of 1976, no part of this publication may be reproduced, distributed, or transmitted in any form or by any means, including photocopying, recording, or other electronic or mechanical methods, without the prior written permission of the publisher, except in the case of brief quotations embodied in critical reviews and certain other noncommercial uses permitted by copyright law. For permission requests, write to the publisher, addressed "Attention: Permissions Coordinator," at the address below.

Saint John Press
800 West Airport Freeway, Suite 1100
Irving, Texas 75062

Printed in the United States of America
Acid-free paper for permanence and durability

ISBN-13: 978-0-9884425-9-7

Cover design by W. Antoneta, Mitchell DeSouza, & Jose Luis Virviescas
Book and map design by SisterMuses

Please visit Sword and Serpent on the web at: www.taylormarshall.com

For my daughter Margaret Grace Carol:

*Deus, qui beatam Margaritam Scotorum reginam eximia
in pauperes caritate mirabilem effecisti:
da, ut ejus intercessione et exemplo, tua in cordibus
nostris caritas jugiter augeatur,
per Dominum nostrum Jesum Christum, Filium tuum,
qui tecum vivit et regnat in unitate Spiritus Sancti Deus,
per omnia saecula saeculorum. Amen.*

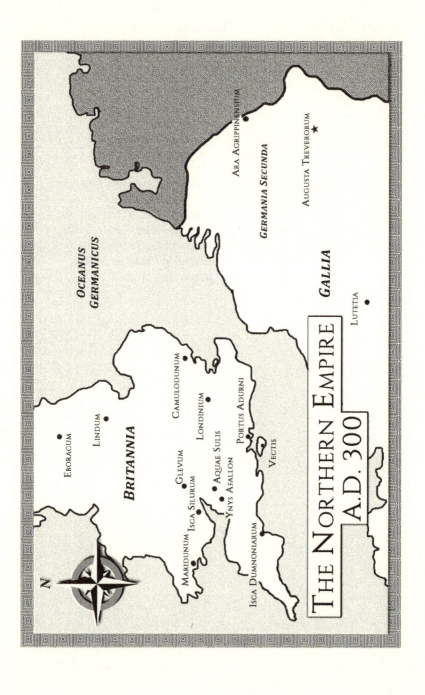

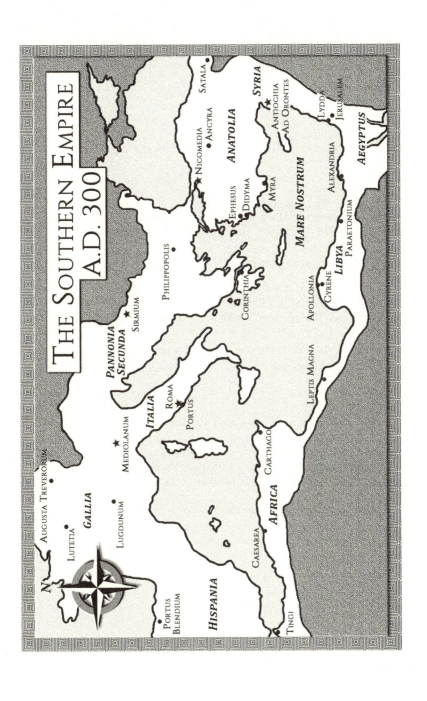

The Roman Tetrarchy
A.D. 295-303

Under the tetrarchy, Rome was divided in half, East and West. Each half was ruled by a senior emperor or *Imperator*, titled *Augustus*, and his "heir," or junior emperor, who was titled *Caesar*.

The Eastern Empire	The Western Empire
1. Diocletian *Augustus* (Husband of Prisca Alexandra)	1. Maximianus *Augustus* (Father of Maxentius)
2. *Caesar* Galerius (Uncle of Maximinus Daia)	2. *Caesar* Constantius Chlorus (father of Constantinus)

Eventually, Maxentius and Constantinus, the sons of the two Western tetrarchs, would fight to become the sole emperor of the West. Constantinus defeated Maxentius at the Battle of Milvian Bridge in A.D. 312, and subsequently legalized Christianity with the Edict of Milan, issued in February, A.D. 313.

In A.D. 325, he defeated Licinius to become the sole Roman Emperor.

PROLOGUE

Didyma, Anatolia — October, A.D. 300

Casca fumbled his way along the narrow *via sacra* leading to the Didymaion, his steps uneasy on the loose stone of the path. All day the clouds had been building, dark and ragged, and now the very heavens threatened to open over his head like an omen of doom warning him away. Thunder rumbled faintly in the distance, echoing among the hills, and Casca hastened his pace. But the track had not been well tended, and the more he hurried, the more his sandaled feet slipped in the gravel and dusty soil.

Is this the service I am called to perform? he thought, dark thoughts swarming in his heart like smoke. No. He should be attending the great feasts, mingling with the courtiers whose power and privilege Diocletian held in his hand, not pattering down some track like a miserable goatherd or doddering devotee of the god.

The thought of going to the Oracle made him feel queasy. He had never cared for such matters. Ever since he had spied on the Mysteries in Satala as a boy, he had worn his piety like a toga, proper and official, but quickly discarded in private. Gods and invisible powers that he could not see, could not judge, could not influence…such things terrified him. Like that girl

Sabra, who had been a priestess in Cyrene. She had always made Casca feel like his skin was crawling with ants or spiders.

The only god Casca could care about, the only god he could adore, was the one who had ordered him to seek the Oracle, and discover her counsel.

Casca let out a bitter breath.

Why didn't Diocletian ask his own haruspex to find the Oracle? Isn't that what he is for?

He shifted the belt on his traveling tunic and tugged his cloak a little closer.

Perhaps he was not thinking clearly. Perhaps this was not a curse, but an opportunity. He, and only he, had been trusted with his Divine *Imperator*'s message. He, and only he, would be trusted with the message of the gods.

It was, in fact, a marvelous honor. Not something to run from or fear, but to embrace. He would go to the Oracle and return in triumph, bearing the word of the gods, and Diocletian would realize once and for all that his counsel should be trusted in all matters.

"Aren't the gods silent?" he had asked Diocletian, when his *Imperator*, still enraged by Jurian's treason, had commissioned him with the task on their voyage back to Anatolia.

"We shall see," the Emperor had answered.

Casca could not help but hope that they still were, and would stay that way. Preferably, for good.

But if they broke their silence—if they broke it for *him*, Casca…what honor would he not find in Diocletian's eye?

Off to his right, a small statue of a faun nestled among the overgrown foliage, probably to mark some bush sacred to Artemis. He snorted and passed it without any gesture of reverence. Then, not three paces past the shrine, he turned his ankle on a loose stone.

He stumbled and fell to one knee, hissing in pain as another stone bit through the tender skin. Prying the stone free, he watched with morbid fascination as the dark blood beaded out of the cut.

That's what you get for disrespecting the gods, he told himself.

He pushed himself to his feet and continued down the path, limping a bit now from the pain. His hand fluttered nervously at his side, and he twisted it tight in the folds of his cloak. Here the boughs of the trees hung low over the path, so low that he had to duck to pass beneath them. As he straightened, he almost screamed aloud, because there, coiled in the branch of the tree just over his head, a black viper lingered, its wide, unblinking eyes intent on his face. They were uncannily blue, Casca realized, almost opaque, as if they saw both nothing and everything at the same time.

One hand clapped over his mouth, barely breathing, Casca edged up the slope on the side of the path, steering well clear of the snake. As soon as he had passed it, he slipped and slid back down onto the path.

Thunder rumbled again, closer this time, with an eerie reverberation among the stony hills. Casca passed a *kouros* and hesitated. The terracotta statue watched him with its lidless eyes, like the viper in the tree. For a long moment it stared down at him, and he stared up at it, too nervous to blink. Finally, sucking in a bitter breath, he made a hasty gesture of obeisance and hurried on his way.

The *kouroi* appeared more and more frequently, as if they were marching away from the temple in silent meditation. And then the path widened out, and he found himself standing in the shadow of the great Temple of Apollo.

It was staggering, he had to admit. The massive *peripteros* was flanked by rows of stately columns, as if it were a grove of smooth, straight trees. The white stone, stark against the darkened sky, seemed more like a warning than an invitation. And it all seemed utterly deserted.

Casca sidled toward the columns, his gaze constantly sweeping the grounds, desperate for the sight of another human being. But it was all utterly silent, until, faintly, he heard the burbling of a spring.

He passed through the *pronaos* and stopped for a moment,

puzzled. There was no entrance to the inner court of the temple, but only a high window through which he could glimpse the shaggy heads of laurel trees. The sound of the spring was louder here, but he couldn't immediately see a way inside.

He turned to the left and traced the wall to a narrow passageway, sloping down between the high walls of the *cella*. It was so close that it felt breathless, and it smelled of stone and damp and ancient air. He followed the tunnel, his heart pattering uselessly in his chest, and saw an opening into the *adyton* up ahead on his right. Stepping out of the passage, he found himself in the grove of the god.

In the midst of the laurel trees bubbled a clear spring, and a great bronze statue of Apollo presided, brooding, over the sacred space. Casca held his breath. Somehow it seemed a profanation to exhale.

A smattering of raindrops fell on his head and he cast a resentful glare at the overcast sky. Perhaps it would be better to seek shelter while he was still dry, but where, in all this open space?

He turned a slow circle, then stopped as his gaze lighted on a huge set of stairs leading up to a second level. Cautiously, with more fear than he cared to admit, he eased his way up the steps and found himself facing three doors, all identical, all unremarkable. He frowned as he looked them over, then shrugged and passed through the left hand door.

Inside, the room was dark. There were no windows, only a round hole in the ceiling that admitted a single shaft of gray light. In the far corners, bronze braziers held red embers, and the spice of incense lingered so heavily in the air it almost choked him.

"Pilgrim," came a woman's voice from somewhere in the shadows. "What do you seek?"

Casca reeled backward. A woman, her dark hair unbound and disheveled, stepped into the shaft of light. And there she stood, chin almost touching her chest, and stared at him. Her eyes were red-rimmed as if she had been weeping, and they held a haunting vacancy, as if what she saw was not the reality in front of her.

Casca's mouth flapped open. He'd spent his entire journey here longing to see another person, and now that he'd found one, all he wanted was to run away.

The heady smoke wound around and through him, dizzying his thoughts and blurring his vision. His eyes watered and he swiped distractedly at them.

"I thought the god was silent," he said in a hoarse whisper.

The priestess lifted her chin the barest fraction of an inch. "Is that why you have come?" she asked. "To test him?"

Casca mutely shook his head, but then, doubting whether she could actually see anything, he said, "No."

There was a silence, long and terrible, pressing about his ears like being submerged too deep in water. Then the priestess spoke, but her voice was low and harsh, deep as a man's and endless as thunder, "The gods cannot speak so long as the just are on the earth."

Casca shuddered, his knees watery, hand trembling treacherously at his side. He twisted it in the folds of his cloak and bowed his head, begging for release, cursing Diocletian for sending him on the god's errand.

Then the priestess said, in her own hollow voice, "What is it you seek?"

He licked his lips. "Answers. But—" He faltered. If the gods were silent, why should he bother asking? But perhaps she would give him a message anyway. Casca had no interest in facing Diocletian as a failure, with no advice from the gods for his god. "There is division in the Empire," he said. "I seek the path of unity."

He hoped that was specific enough, but what experience did he have with these things? For perhaps the hundredth time, he wished Diocletian had sent someone else.

The priestess sucked her breath in through her teeth. "Division...unity," she said, repeating the words in an endless chant that thudded in Casca's mind like a hammer stroke.

Then suddenly she shuddered violently, as if she were caught in a nightmare. Casca stepped back, every hair on the back of his neck standing straight on end.

"The way lies over the sea. The standing stones watch the stars and wait for the coming of the king, whose hand will draw the sword. He will take it up and lay it down again, and the stone shall become the king stone. The blood of the stone shall adorn the banner of the king. Unleash the storm of fire and blood and the red dragon will rise."

The priestess staggered back and fell to her knees on the stone. Her body shivered uncontrollably and her breast heaved, but her face in that eerie light was still, too still. Casca stared at her, torn between revulsion and fascination, and despair riddled with contempt. Would she say something else, or would he have to return to his Divine *Imperator* with nothing but a lot of nonsense to mock him? Were those in fact the words of the god, or were they the priestess's own ravings, her own lunatic nonsense?

At last, she lifted those haunted eyes to his face. "Your answer," she said, her voice hoarse.

"What am I supposed to do with that?" he asked. "You speak riddles to me, and I need answers." He took a step toward her. "Interpret it for me!"

The priestess blinked slowly at him, as if aware of his presence for the first time. "What I have seen, I have seen," she said. "It is for you to understand. Or for him."

Casca realized he was shaking—with fear or anger or both, he couldn't tell. "I can't go back to him with that," he said, his voice low. "Don't you understand? I can't. Stand up. Why are you looking at me like that? Give me something else. Give him something else!"

He reached a trembling hand toward her but she started to laugh, and the sound of that laughter was more horrible than her awful eyes and her frenzied convulsions.

"Begone," she said, the word snaking out in a low hiss. "And I will give you something else. You. Just for you." She leveled her finger at him. "You walk the way of blood. Take care you are not drowned in it."

Casca turned and fled with her laughter echoing in his ears.

1

The Tyrrhenian Sea — October, A.D. 300

The gentle slapping of water against the hull of the ship whispered a rhythmic lullaby, like something Jurian's mother had sung to him, long ago in the hot and moon-drenched nights in Lydda, a home he only remembered in moments like this. Moments of half-sleep and peace.

He rolled over in his bunk and squeezed his eyes shut. He hadn't thought about his mother in a long time, either. Not since…not since the look on Varro's face as the sword came down—that smile of joy. He thought at the time that maybe he could see his mother in that moment, that she had come to take Varro home at last.

There's fire in the darkness, a beast of fire and rage. Rome will run red with blood, blood poured out on the bones of the rock, and so much fire…

A storm of fire and blood.

Jurian shuddered, but he could barely feel his body as the words wound through him, around him, binding him.

The rock holds the steel and will hold it again, but first it must pass through fire and over the sea…

"I know, Mother." His voice sounded far away, like a lonely cry on a rocky hillside. "I'm going, can't you see?"

The rhythmic pulse of the waves rocked him.

He saw a woman's hand. Slender, pale, with nails like pearl. His mother's hand? He couldn't tell. The hand gripped the hilt of a sword, a plain, unadorned hilt with a long crosspiece—a hilt he would recognize anywhere. The woman twined her other hand around it, and he could see that Excalibur stood point-downward, the tip just touching cold, bare rock. Behind the woman's white dress, a star-strewn sky, and pillars of stone.

The stone shall become the king stone, she said, and the voice was not his mother's. This voice was different, low and sweet and with a cadence like falling water. *The blood of the stone shall adorn the banner of the king. Rise, the red dragon.*

The woman's hands lifted, the sword's point shimmered in moonlight. And then, still-faced and silent, she drove it straight down into the stone.

Jurian came to himself with a cry of pain. He sat up, fighting for breath, sweat chilling him. He rubbed the back of his neck with a shaking hand, then scrubbed it over his face. Green sunlight shimmered through the porthole and fell on the hilt of his sword, which lay in its sheath on the small wooden chest nailed to the floor beside Jurian's bunk.

"What?" he said to the sword. And then, before he realized what he was saying, "I don't fear you."

"Nor should you," said a gruff, booming voice from the doorway. Jurian started and then swung around with a wide smile. Menas folded his arms and raised the eyebrow over his one good eye. "Talking to it now, are we?"

"No. Just…" Jurian shuddered again. "I've had strange dreams."

Menas nodded slowly, and the ghost of trouble crossed his face. "As have I."

Jurian sat up straighter. Menas had been the *Christophoros*—and Jurian felt that, even with just one eye, he could see more clearly than most who had both.

"What kind of dreams?" he asked. His eyes tracked back to the sword. "About…"

Menas laughed. "No. That's not my business," he said. "I have dreamed of storms on the river. Storms and darkness, and the water swirling red like blood around my legs."

Jurian swallowed hard. He didn't need to ask what Menas meant by "the river." It was the river he'd carried the Child across, all those years ago. What could it mean, if the river were a river of blood?

Menas waved a hand. "Pay no mind," he said. "The sea makes men dream strange dreams, and not all are true."

"But some are," Jurian murmured. Menas said nothing, and Jurian sighed in frustration. "I wish Kat were here. She would know what to make of all of this."

It wasn't the first time since his exile that he'd wished for his friends. His longing for Sabra's quiet steadiness was a constant hum, but there were times when he missed Kat's fiery brilliance too. Needed it like the ship around him needed the wind in its sails. He rose from the bunk and motioned for Menas to lead the way to the deck. Menas turned and left without a word, but Jurian hesitated, his eyes on the sword once more. Then he turned abruptly on his heel and strode out of the cabin, leaving Excalibur behind.

The sails were swollen with a stiff breeze and the late autumn sun shone like shattered glass on the water. The captain and his men were in high spirits, and Jurian caught snatches of a rowdy Celtic sailing song as he made his way aft, where Agapius leaned on the rail staring back at the empty sea behind them. Menas, he noticed, had gone to stand with the two *gladiatrices*, the twin Celtic huntresses they had rescued from the gladiatorial games in Rome. Jurian guessed that Menas had somehow found a way to communicate with them, for they were all laughing.

Jurian clapped Agapius on the shoulder and his friend started, but his surprise faded to an easy grin when he saw Jurian. "About time you got up," he said. "Military discipline didn't last very long with you, eh?"

Jurian snorted. "Yes, and I suppose you were up with the dawn, practicing with your *spatha* here on the deck?"

"Not likely," Agapius laughed. "But he was." Agapius jerked his thumb over his shoulder. Jurian followed the gesture and saw Constantinus amidships, talking with Ivor, the stern sailor who had helped to rescue Sabra and Hanno. "That man," Agapius said, "is dedicated to the arts of war on a frightening level."

"He didn't get to where he is without it," Jurian said.

"Really? Then how'd you get his job?" Agapius asked, jostling him with a good-natured grin. "It obviously wasn't your stunning good looks. With your…barbarian beard and your head on fire."

Jurian speared him with a mock glare, then laughed quietly under his breath. "I honestly wish I knew," he said. "The whim of an emperor, I guess."

"What was the whim of an emperor?" Constantinus asked, joining them without warning.

Jurian nodded in greeting, his fingers restless on the rough wood of the rail. "How I became a *tribunus* of the Jovians."

"Ah," Constantinus said, and didn't contradict him, which both amused and infuriated Jurian.

Constantinus leaned on the rail beside him and they all watched the waves for a few moments in silence.

"I can't stop worrying about everyone we've left behind," Jurian said after a while.

"One in particular, I'm sure," Constantinus said, and Jurian felt a heat prickle up his neck.

"One in particular," he affirmed.

There was a long pause, then Constantinus said softly, "Casca won't stop, you know."

"I know." Jurian gripped the smooth wood of the rail in both hands, then shifted his gaze from Constantinus to Agapius. "But surely, if I'm not there, they will be safe? I'm the one who put them all in danger. Now that I'm gone, he won't have reason to target them…will he?"

Agapius's jaw tightened and he said nothing. Constantinus only looked grim.

Jurian slapped the rail. "I can't be here," he said. "I can't. I will go mad."

Agapius started to mutter something, but Constantinus cut over him, "Unfortunately you have no choice. If you go back, your life is forfeit. And there will be nothing I or anyone else can do to save you."

"Then maybe my life should be forfeit!" Jurian shouted, surprising himself with his vehemence.

There was a momentary hush on the deck, then a purposeful low hum of chatter swelled to fill the silence.

Constantinus caught his arm. "*Don't* do anything stupid."

"Like what? Like what I've already done, you mean?" When Constantinus said nothing, Jurian pulled his arm away and said, "I don't leave my friends behind."

"What would you have me do?" Constantinus said sharply. "Tell the captain to take us back to Portus?"

Jurian turned to look at Bleddyn, who stood smiling at the helm with Daffyd by his side. The two Celtic girls stood alone at the rail now, their long blond hair whipping in the sea breeze, and Jurian wondered where Menas had gone. One of them, the bolder of the two girls who always reminded Jurian of a lioness, glanced over her shoulder in their direction, and after a moment Jurian realized she was looking at Constantinus. Her sudden smile was like the sun on the water, and then she turned briskly around again.

Agapius muttered a curse under his breath, and Jurian sighed.

"So," Constantinus said. "Let go of this foolish notion that we are going back. That it would in any way be *possible* for us to go back. We have a course laid in, and we will hold fast. Your friends will be safe. Or, don't you trust that god of yours to look after his own?"

Jurian glanced up swiftly. *That's not how it works,* he wanted to say, thinking of Varro, of his mother, of Mari. *That's not how He works.* But he didn't know how to explain that to Constantinus, and so he swallowed the words.

"It isn't that I don't have my own fears for the people I've left," Constantinus said, quietly. "Aikaterina, in particular. She is the daughter of the *Praefectus Augustalis* of Egypt, and she will be married off into the Tetrarchy as soon as a match can be made. And there is *nothing* I can do about it, however much I would wish to preserve her from that nest of vipers."

"What?" Jurian said, the word escaping in a gasp. The Tribune's face was hard as carved marble. "You *wouldn't—*"

"I?" Constantinus said. "What did I just tell you? I have no say in the matter. Her father has no love for the notion, but he is a practical man and an efficient ruler. He understands the necessity, however little he values it."

"That..." Agapius said. "That is almost worse than anything Casca could contrive."

Constantinus shrugged. "It is what happens," he said. "And it is assuredly worse. But make no mistake. My own mother was put aside for political advantage. They will have allegiance at all costs, and the more ties they can use to bind themselves together, the better. They entangle themselves in a web of their own making, and cannot see the risks. Egypt is too valuable to Rome to allow her to remain long unfettered to the Tetrarchy."

Jurian ground his teeth, wishing in vain that he could persuade Bleddyn to turn the ship around. Everything he cared for, everything he had ever wanted, was fading fast in the ship's wake. But his path lay forward, and much as he tried to push the feeling aside, he was drawn north with a pull as strong as magnetism.

He would fulfill the mission laid on him by *Pappas* Marcellinus. But then, as soon as he was able, he would return to the court of Emperors, and there he would do everything in his power to put things right.

2

Tingi, Hispania — October, A.D. 300

Almost two weeks to the day since they had set out from Portus, Bleddyn put in at the port of Tingi. The journey so far had been in protected seas, with land within easy reach. But as Jurian stared out at the wide expanse of ocean to the west, he felt suddenly small and vulnerable. The roll of the swells seemed to come right out of the setting sun, to stretch forever and beyond, until they lapped the shores of some harbor he could not see.

Jurian wanted to ask Bleddyn how far out into that vast emptiness they would have to sail to get to Britannia, but the last thing he wanted was to sound like a frightened little boy. These were hard men, and they seemed almost invigorated by the promise of the untamed salt and wind that lay beyond the reach of the provinces. Jurian's whole life had been bounded by the Empire—even when he lived in Satala, skirting the very edge of the Empire like sunlight on a knife blade. The realization that he would soon leave its *limes*, perhaps forever, hit him in the gut like a heavy punch.

The men shuffled down the ramp to the dock below, their muscled backs bowed under the weight of *amphorae* and bundles of trade goods. By habit Jurian made to follow them, but Constantinus stepped in front of him and planted a hand on his chest. Agapius, who was a few paces ahead of Jurian, turned to watch.

"*Mane*, Jurian. This is Roman soil." He lowered his gaze fractionally and said, softer, "I'm sorry."

Jurian met Agapius's eye, and by the stricken look on his friend's face, it seemed that the reality of Jurian's exile had suddenly dawned on him as well. Jurian jerked his gaze away, seeking a glimpse of the bustling wharf behind his friend. The stench of raw and salted fish mingled with the rich savory smells of roasting spiced meats, and the hushing breeze carried the noise of barter and trade from the brightly-canopied stands. Jurian gripped the ship's rail as if to steady himself, his heart burning.

This might be the last chance he ever had to touch Roman soil. In Rome, on the docks of Portus, everything had happened too fast. He hadn't realized—but if he had, would he have dragged his feet on his way to the ship? Lingered as long as possible, letting his feet cling to the chalky stone, savoring the feel of Roman air on his face?

"Please," he said simply.

Constantinus said nothing more, but turned away and strode past Agapius, who barely managed to dart out of his way. Jurian hesitated, not sure what had just happened, but Agapius beckoned for him to follow.

"Come on! He's not looking…and deliberately not looking, see? He wasn't really stopping you…just the appearance of the thing." Jurian edged down the ramp until Agapius caught his arm and hauled him forward. "We'll be quick," he said. "Just a skewer of that roasted meat and a bit of beer, if they even know what beer is out here. Then right back to the ship with you."

"Beer?" Jurian echoed, wrinkling his nose. "Isn't that a barbarian drink?"

Agapius made a noise of profound displeasure. "Barbarian! Not in Egypt. And besides. *Jurian*."

He left it at that, but looked pointedly at Jurian's hair.

Jurian stifled a laugh and let himself be pulled toward the nearest market stand, shouldering up to the high city wall of white-washed stone. Warm morning sunlight filtered through a pair of towering palms, dappling the booth's flax canopy of red and tawny gold that fluttered restlessly in the rising breeze. Under its shadow stood a strikingly beautiful woman with dark, clear skin and the most brilliant blue eyes Jurian had seen since Kat had left for Alexandria. The woman's head was wrapped in a bright yellow scarf, and it reminded him of the day, all those months ago, that Kat had followed him to the harbor of Alexandria, when he'd tried to slip away from her father's court without anyone knowing. The memory made him smile.

The woman said something in a language he didn't recognize, and Jurian realized that she was staring—and trying not to—at his hair. He rubbed a hand through it until it stood on end and shook his head. She laughed, a bright, rich sound, and Jurian glanced around to make sure she wasn't drawing too much attention.

"Meat?" she said in Latin, offering him a thin wooden stick on which she had impaled folds of roasted meat.

The spicy, savory aroma set his mouth watering and his stomach grumbling fitfully. He nodded his thanks and she handed it to him, then turned expectantly to Agapius.

"I think she wants you to pay," Jurian said.

"Well, I want one too!" Agapius retorted. Then, to the woman, "Me too. Meat." He made a shooing motion for her to fetch him some.

The woman shrugged and disappeared into the enclosed portion of the stand. She returned a moment later with a trussed raw goat leg and dropped it on the counter in front of Agapius. Flies buzzed lazily around it and she waved them away with placid indifference. Agapius glared at the meat, then looked at Jurian, who looked intently at his skewer.

"What am I supposed to do with that?" Agapius asked the woman in Latin.

She smiled broadly and gestured the length of the leg. She

flipped it over and gestured again, as if it were some costly stuff she was showing off. "Meat," she repeated.

"Maybe she thinks you sound like a goat," Jurian offered, trying not to laugh.

Just then, Daffyd arrived behind them. He took one look at the leg and clapped Agapius on the shoulder. "That's good work!" he said. "Bring that aboard, would you?" He dropped three coins on the counter and grinned his thanks at the woman.

"We're not taking that on board, are we?" Agapius asked. "Won't it stink?"

"You want to eat on this voyage?" Daffyd asked. Agapius and Jurian exchanged a look, and Daffyd laughed. "Goat beats salted fish every day of the week. *Especially* in smell."

Daffyd leaned over the counter to see what else she had. He spotted a stack of flatbread, its skin a crisp golden brown and still steaming. "That too."

He pointed at the bread and said something that the woman seemed to understand. Her smile widening, she wrapped several loaves in a linen cloth and handed them to Agapius. Daffyd dropped another coin on the counter.

"Let's go," he said. "Take the leg, would you?"

Agapius made a face and Jurian hid his wicked grin in a bite of spiced meat. To his surprise, it was juicy and delicious, the richness of its flavors reminding him of the meat served in Constus's court in Alexandria.

As they followed Daffyd down the wharf, Jurian held the skewer out to Agapius. "It's delicious," he said. "Want a bite?"

"Oh, I wouldn't dream of it," Agapius said. "How did I end up being the pack mule? You're the one who's—" He stopped. A small troop of Roman soldiers passed them with only a cursory glance at Agapius's goat leg and Jurian's red hair. "Never mind."

Daffyd stopped at another stand and ordered several jugs of beer, while Agapius eyed the sign that read "Traditional Egyptian brew" with a suspicious scowl that made Jurian laugh. The merchant accepted Daffyd's coins and then roughly ordered several young Berber children to carry the jugs to the ship. They seemed to be hanging around for just this purpose, and they were quick. Almost before Jurian and the others had reached the next stall, Jurian saw them come racing back, hands open to receive the piece of hot flatbread offered them as payment.

They passed a man squatting between the market stands, shaded only by the inconstant palm trees, surrounded by intricately carved wooden boxes and musical instruments arrayed on a woven rug. His hands deftly chiseled a pattern into a shallow bowl, but his eyes were closed behind his shaggy mane of hair. Jurian, curious, paused to watch, and the man stopped his work abruptly and raised a clouded gaze in Jurian's direction. His hand drifted over his wares, then settled on a carved box of fragrant cedar and lifted it toward him.

"You may need this," he said in broken Latin, his voice low and rough.

"For what?" Jurian asked.

The man only smiled, showing a mouth with half its teeth missing.

"How much?"

"What can you offer me?"

Jurian patted his tunic and belt, but apart from a few coins he carried nothing except Mari's *ichthus* token and the tribute coin Diocletian had given him so long ago.

"I have nothing left to me in the world but grief and shame," he said softly.

The man tipped his head, considering. "But I see your grief turned to joy," he said, "and your shame to honor." He stood, carefully, and Jurian realized one of his legs was lame, and the hand that held the carved box to him was mutilated and deformed. "This is not for you," he said, and pushed the box toward Jurian's chest.

Jurian took it, marveling at its flawless workmanship. "How—" he started, but couldn't think how to proceed without offending the artisan.

The man lifted his thin shoulders and eased himself back onto his rug. "I use the gifts I was given," he said, "and don't lament the ones I was not." As he picked up his bowl to resume his work, he added, almost too quietly for Jurian to hear, "Do not be afraid."

Agapius, who had moved ahead of Jurian, came back and grabbed his shoulder, dragging him away from the woodworker.

"Please tell me you didn't spend money on that," he said, eyeing the box in Jurian's hand. "Everybody and their son makes those things in this region, because they know gullible travelers will spend exorbitant sums of money on them, when they're actually as common as sand."

"Not this one," Jurian said. "This one is different."

He paused there on the street and opened the box, startling when he saw an intricate mother-of-pearl inlay of a fish inside the lid. He showed it to Agapius without comment. Agapius studied it with a curious look on his face.

"Well, that is somewhat interesting," he admitted.

"Agapius, the man was blind."

"I suppose that makes it *very* interesting then."

"And he gave it to me."

Agapius eyed him sidelong. "The strangest things happen to you."

Jurian smiled crookedly and followed him down the street to join Daffyd. He had stopped to wait for them next to a stall where an old woman was folding finely woven fabrics in careful squares. Some were dyed deep purple, some a bright yellow like the meat-seller's scarf, and then there were reds and blues and shades of green that mirrored the sea in sunlight. Some were tied to the cedar poles that held the canopy, and they fluttered and snapped in the breeze. Jurian caught a deep red one in his hand and rubbed his fingers over it. The color of it reminded him of imperial copper and sunsets over the desert…of Sabra's fire-gold eyes more than anything. Musing, he unknotted the scarf and wound it around his hand.

Agapius noticed and grinned. "For that special lady of

yours?" he asked.

"What special lady?" Daffyd asked in his loud sailor's voice. Then he caught sight of the scarf and nodded knowingly. "Ah, of course. Yes, that would be a good color for her."

"Thank you for your approval," Jurian said stiffly.

As Daffyd laughed and moved on to the next stall to barter for some aged cheese, Jurian approached the old woman to pay for the scarf. She glanced up and sucked in a breath through her teeth, looking like she'd seen a spirit from beyond the grave.

Jurian glanced over his shoulder, thinking that perhaps someone she feared was standing behind him, but there was no one there. He turned back to her with a frown.

"You," she said, pointing at him with a crooked and wrinkled finger.

Jurian's heart lurched, hammering strangely against his ribs. "Do I…know you?"

"I know you." She caught in another breath, and her eyes welled with tears. "He said you would come."

Jurian's frown deepened, and he felt a surge of panic. Could Casca have discovered their route? Would he be here, in Tingi, waiting with a troop of soldiers to arrest him? Watching for him to break his exile, knowing the temptation would be too great for him?

He forced his thoughts to settle on a single question. "Who said that?"

"My son."

The relief that washed through Jurian almost made him laugh aloud. Agapius, who had noticed the strange interview, came to stand at Jurian's shoulder. "What's she talking about?" he asked.

Jurian shrugged and set a coin on the counter. She promptly picked it up and returned it to him. "How could I take silver from you?" she said. "My son said you would come. The Dragon-slayer."

Jurian gaped at her, and Agapius, immediately on alert, took over the questions. "Who said that? Who is your son?"

"Marcellus." She said it as though they should have known.

"And does he want to see me?" asked Jurian, finally finding his voice. "Where is he?"

The old woman smiled sadly. "I am sure he does. But you will not find him here. He has gone already to the Kingdom."

"Rome?" Agapius asked.

The woman shook her head and lifted her eyes wordlessly to the canopy.

"Heaven," Jurian said, his voice hardly more than a whisper. He suddenly reached across the counter to grip the woman's wrist, tracing the *signum* in her palm with his thumb. "What happened to him?"

"He shares a birthday now with Maximianus *Augustus*," she said, and returned the *signum*. "If you wish to partake in the breaking of bread, the one who can tell the story better than I will be there tonight."

"We do not know the way," Jurian said, releasing her.

"Come back at sunset and I will lead you."

Jurian and Agapius lingered for a moment longer, but the woman turned away from them and would say nothing more.

Agapius muttered, "The *strangest* things."

Daffyd circled back to collect them, and they made their way to the ship burdened by their wares. As they approached, Jurian saw Constantinus standing at the top of the ramp with his arms folded. The Tribune met his gaze, just for a moment, then he turned and strode out of view. Jurian shot a guilt-stricken look at Agapius.

"I'm not sure he's going to let me off the ship again," he said. "If I can't go tonight, you must."

"But Jurian," Agapius objected, "we're probably putting out to sea tonight. I don't think anyone will be going anywhere."

Jurian didn't respond. Agapius was right, of course. Frustration surged inside him, followed quickly by the certainty that he needed to know what this Marcellus had wanted to say to him. Agapius left to deposit the goat leg in the hold, and Jurian wandered toward the helm, where Bleddyn stood with

Menas. The captain was explaining the working of the sail, and by the eager expression on his face, Jurian realized that Bleddyn was overjoyed to have another hand—and such a hand—before the mast.

"These seas can be tricky this time of year," Bleddyn was saying. "I may need your help."

Menas inclined his shaggy head, and Jurian clapped him on the shoulder. "I'm sure he's delighted to help," Jurian said, "with his great love of seafaring."

Bleddyn gave Menas a great wide smile. "Ah!" he exclaimed. "I knew so mighty a man must have a love of the sea."

When Jurian chuckled, Menas gave him a look out of his one eye. "I do love the sea," the giant said, and then added in a voice so low that only Jurian heard it, "when I don't have to be on it, stuck in a boat."

"Bleddyn," Jurian said, "is there any chance we are staying the night in port?"

"Stay? In Tingi? Why ever for? We have Britannia to reach, man!" Bleddyn cried, and swung his gaze and his hand to the west as if to indicate their route. Then he caught himself and frowned, muttering, "Now, where'd that come from?"

Jurian followed his gaze, taking a step back in surprise when he saw the sky darkening under a lowering rack of clouds. Almost as if on command, the wind shifted around and gusted fitfully in their faces, heavy with the threat of rain. Jurian drew a shallow breath and reached up to clasp the pyx he wore always around his neck.

"So that would be a yes, then?" he said to Bleddyn, and the captain raised his burly shoulders.

"I can't say I like the looks of that," he said. "And these seas can be capricious enough without the weather."

He eyed Jurian curiously, and his gaze snagged on the scarf around his hand. Even as the surprise registered in his face, Jurian guessed the direction of his thoughts.

"No!" he said with a laugh. "No, no. But Agapius and Menas and I have business tonight in the town."

"I see," Bleddyn said, but there was still a ghost of suspicion in his eyes. "And who's that pretty thing for, then?"

"This?" Jurian held up the scarf and Menas nodded approvingly. "I thought I might send this to someone. As a gift."

Bleddyn opened his mouth in a silent *ah*, and then he smacked Jurian on the back so hard that he stumbled forward. "Well, find yourself a courier to Cyrene, then!" he roared. "Get off the boat and see to it!"

"And what if I won't let him off the boat?" came Constantinus's stern voice from behind them. "What's this about going back into the town tonight?"

Bleddyn seemed to fold into himself, and he excused himself with an incomprehensible mumble and a feeble attempt at a salute to the Tribune. He dragged Menas away on the pretext of showing him the rigging, leaving Jurian to face Constantinus alone.

"A woman at one of the stalls," Jurian said. "She said that her son knew me…that he knew I would come here. I have to find out what message he had for me."

"So you are going to meet him tonight?"

"Not…exactly. He's dead."

Constantinus's gaze was scalpel-sharp. "Dead."

"Yes. But there's something about his story… I need to know, Constantinus."

"I don't see what he could possibly have to do with you. You know that the longer we delay here, the greater the chances that your friend Casca will show up…or worse. You put us both in jeopardy if you step foot off this ship again. You have risked enough already."

Jurian sighed and watched the clouds building to the west. "I know that. But I have to go."

Constantinus shifted in surprise. "You mistake my meaning," he said. "You do not have the privilege of choosing your risks any longer. That is my duty now."

"Is it?" Jurian asked, folding his arms.

Constantinus held his gaze, and neither of them flinched.

"That's settled, then," Jurian said. "We'll be back before midnight."

THE RAIN CAME BEFORE sunset, and Jurian, Agapius, and Menas slopped wretchedly through the muddy streets behind the old woman. She led them through a labyrinthine network of back alleys, where no lamplight escaped the window shutters and no sound but the mewling of cats interrupted the patter of rain. Finally she stopped outside a small hovel near the outskirts of town and rapped three times on the wooden door. It creaked open a few scant inches and the woman murmured a few words in Berber to someone within, at which the door opened wide to admit them.

Jurian followed the others into the shadowy building, catching a deep breath of incense. They took places near the back of the makeshift *ekklesia*, and Jurian knelt down and closed his eyes as the hum of a chanted Psalm wove around them. And there, farther from Satala than he had ever been, he was filled with the strangest sensation that he was home. It was the feeling that he always got when he had attended the *eucharistia*—the feeling of being embraced by something familiar and constant no matter where in the Empire he found it.

The peace of the ritual drifted through him, and as the others joined their voices to the presbyter's prayers, he bowed his head and offered thanksgiving for the peculiar shift in the weather that allowed them to be here.

After all, he thought, *this may be the last time I can partake in the eucharistia.*

The thought overwhelmed him with sadness, but by the conclusion of the rites a fragile confidence had taken root in his heart, displacing the sadness just a little.

All things will be provided, he told himself, *just as they have been tonight.*

As the little congregation shuffled out of the hovel, Jurian held his friends back. An elder man remained behind on the front bench, and the woman who had guided them pointed her finger at him and nodded at Jurian. Then she turned and disappeared into the sodden night.

Jurian took a deep breath and motioned for Agapius and Menas to wait for him. He approached the man slowly, but when he saw that the man was deep in prayer he hesitated, not wanting to interrupt.

"Sit," the man said so suddenly that Jurian startled.

He obeyed, but for a long time the man remained in silence, eyes closed, lips moving silently in prayer.

He had a wise face, Jurian thought as he studied him, well-worn and with the same dark coloring as the woman in the market stall. In the light of the oil lamps, Jurian could just see the glitter of tears beneath his lashes. Finally, the man took a deep breath and turned to face Jurian.

"Tidir was right," he said. "When she told me she had seen you on the wharf today, I hardly dared believe it. We have waited two long years for your arrival." He placed a hand over his breast and inclined his head. "I am Ameqran, the memory-keeper."

"I don't understand," Jurian said. "She said that her son—Marcellus?—that he said I would come. But I never knew him. How could he possibly know me? Especially two years ago..."

When I was nothing, he finished in his thoughts, unable to say it aloud. *Before I lost everything.*

The old man only watched him steadily.

"Will you at least tell me who he was?" Jurian asked at last, helpless.

"Marcellus was a *centurio* with the *Legio Septima Gemina*. He rose to command, and he had the respect of the men. He was a good man, and steady. He spoke ill of no one, and kept himself in cleanness. When it came time to celebrate the birthday of Maximianus *Augustus*, just before the feast of the *Nativitas* two years ago, the Legion was called on to participate fully in the ceremonies." He tilted his head and regarded Jurian. "You understand my meaning?"

Jurian answered, his voice unsteady, "I expect there were to be sacrifices in honor of the Emperor."

"Just so. And Marcellus...he threw down his *vitis* and refused."

Jurian swallowed hard. Ameqran didn't have to speak further for Jurian to know how this story would end. It ended just like his father's story...and like Varro's.

"Tidir visited him in prison before his trial," the old man continued. "And I was there when he traded his vitis for the palm branch, and when Cassian, the scribe of the *Praefectus Praetorio*, cast off his office to follow him. Just before the sword fell, he spoke the words that we have been waiting ever since to see fulfilled."

"What did he say?"

Ameqran closed his eyes and took a deep breath. When he spoke again, it was in a low sing-song. "The slayer of the Dragon will come, touched by fire, and he will bring with him the sword of divine right. A great storm follows in his wake. He will cast away the sword, and he will take it up again, and the line of kings will be unbroken."

Jurian bowed his head as the man's voice died in the silence. *Tolle me, emitte me.* And the storm. *A storm of fire and blood.* Everything was coming together, converging on this moment—all the prophecies that had followed him since his flight from Satala.

A shiver ran through him, and the lamps around the altar seemed to gutter. Ameqran's eyes brightened, and he clasped Jurian's arm. "You must not fear what is to come," he said earnestly. "Do right by God, and He will do right by you, Dragon-slayer."

Jurian didn't know what to say, so he laid his hand over the old man's and gripped it tight.

After a moment Ameqran withdrew his hand and laid it on Jurian's head. "Go," he said. "And may God be with you."

Jurian rose and slipped back to his friends. Their solemn expressions betrayed them, and Jurian realized that they had heard every word the old man had said. Somehow the thought almost relieved him.

"Are you ready?" Menas asked, and his deep voice seemed too large for that small space.

Jurian glanced back at the lamps and the still form of the old man keeping his vigil.

"No," he said. "But I will follow."

3

CYRENE, LIBYA — OCTOBER, A.D. 300

IN THE *PERISTYLUM* OF THE GOVERNOR'S HOUSE IN CYRENE, IN THE LATE evening shadows and a wind heavy with the threat of rain, the messenger from Tingi stood facing Sabra like a man might face his executioner. She studied the man quietly, wondering if it was fear of her or fear of his message that made him pale and uncertain. Perhaps it was both.

Some days she wondered if she would ever be free of her past. If she would ever have the chance to be simply Sabra of Cyrene, and not Sabra, priestess of the dragon, voice of the old god. She shuddered and forced the thought away.

"I was told you had a message for me," she said softly.

The man nodded and opened the heavy leather bag he carried slung over one shoulder. Sabra frowned—most messages she had received came in the form of words, not objects. The man drew something into the guttering firelight and held it out to her, and she caught her breath. It was a beautiful carved box, made of the wood their western neighbors called *arar*. Every caravan of tinkers and merchants from Mauritania brought dozens of them to sell in the markets of Cyrene, but this one... this one felt special.

She lifted the lid carefully and found a beautiful red scarf nestled inside, not a Roman *palla*, but something of a more ancient fashion—something like her mother used to wear. The fabric was feather soft and glistened faintly in the firelight, and somehow Sabra almost thought it carried a scent of incense.

"Who is it from?" she managed.

"He gave no name," the courier said, frowning. "When I asked who I should say sent me, he said, *a farmer.*"

Sabra stifled a sudden smile. The courier used the Latin word, *agricola*, but in her mind she translated it to the Greek, *georgios*.

"How long ago did you see him?" she asked.

"Three weeks."

Sabra glanced up at him and he flushed, as if something in her face had chastised him. "And he had no...no message for me? Nothing but this?"

She tipped the box as she said it, and caught a glimpse of the mother-of-pearl inlay of the *ichthus* inside the lid. Hastily she closed the box again and hugged both it and the blood-red scarf close to her heart.

The messenger nodded once. "He gave me a message for you. He said to tell you: *I will hold you in my heart until such time as we meet again...whether here or in the terra nova that awaits me.* And he said..." The man faltered suddenly and stopped.

Sabra frowned. Messengers of the Roman Empire were not supposed to fumble in their delivery. "And what?" When the man didn't answer, Sabra took a step closer to him, regarding him in surprise as he recoiled from her. "What's wrong? I am no serpent."

But you used to serve one, a sinister thought whispered in her mind, and her blood turned cold. She drew a thin, steadying breath and focused intently on the courier.

"I don't know why he had to choose me," the man muttered. "This is a gods-forsaken place."

"Speak your message, and speak plainly," she said, voice low. "There will be no harm done to you for carrying out your duty."

The man stared fixedly at the pillar behind her left shoulder for a long moment, then cleared his throat and met her gaze. "Mistress, he said to tell you this: *Watch the weather on the seas. A storm is coming from the north.*" He eyed her expectantly, as if her reaction would explain its meaning.

Sabra kept her face very still but closed her fingers tightly around the scarf. *A storm, and from the north?* She knew when he said *terra nova* that Jurian wasn't speaking of Britannia.

"Three weeks," she murmured. "He is already so far away from me."

"That is all my message," the courier said with a small bow, after the silence had carried on almost unbearably.

Sabra shifted to look out over the peristyle, and heard his audible sigh of relief. "Go to my father the governor," she said. "I am sure he will want to hear any news you may have from your travels. We don't often hear tidings from the west."

The man bowed low and hurried away. His hasty retreat made her smile a little, but her heart was heavy with a weight she had not felt in many months. She paced the length of the peristyle, once, then again, twisting and untwisting the scarf in her hands as she tried to make sense of Jurian's message. It was a warning, obviously, but if he meant for her to do something, she had no clarity.

"Aikaterina would know," she said, aloud, then darted a glance over her shoulder to make sure no one had heard her talking to herself.

To her dismay she found Hanno coming toward her, but his expression was as calm and inscrutable as ever, betraying nothing.

"Mistress," he said as he joined her. Sabra held up the scarf and he took it from her hands. "Where did this come from? It is not one of yours."

"A courier brought it, just now," she said. "Jurian sent word from Tingi."

She shivered, the heaviness turning into a chill that wove its fingers around her, and crept deep inside her heart. Hanno peered into her face, keenly attuned to her moods as always.

"And what does he say, mistress?"

Sabra sighed. "He says a storm is coming."

Hanno straightened and handed the scarf back to her. "That is nothing we did not already suspect," he said quietly. "Lightning flashes long before the rains arrive."

"That is the truth." She resumed her pacing, but halfway down the length of the peristyle she paused and turned back to him. "Did you want something from me?"

"It is time for the evensong," he said. "Did you wish to go tonight?"

Sabra hesitated. Since returning to Cyrene a few months ago, she had watched the Christian community begin to flourish, like a new seedling in a once-barren land. The *episcopus* Theodorus and his flock welcomed her warmly enough in their gatherings, but Sabra could never quite shake the feeling that the people saw her as something of an outsider. She never went among them without pain. Of all of them, only Theodorus seemed to have entirely forgotten the darkness of her past.

After a moment she realized Hanno was still watching her closely, waiting for her answer, so she nodded and let him lead the way out of the palace. They tracked down the broad street and past the Greek *agora*, past the Roman *forum* and the little building where Sabra had once taught the city's children of the glory that awaited them if they were chosen by the god for the sacrifice. She shuddered, a cold numbness seizing her heart, and Hanno instinctively quickened his steps to keep pace with her as they passed by.

You served me faithfully, the voice whispered in the back corners of her thoughts.

She gasped and stumbled, and Hanno's hand was instantly on her elbow. "Mistress? You're shaking. What's wrong?"

Pursing her lips, she just shook her head fiercely and gestured to the street. Hanno released her and they continued on, but she could feel his worried gaze still fixed on her. Presently they arrived at Theodorus's *domus*, and Sabra could just hear a few voices raised in song from somewhere within. She lifted a hand, but before she could knock on the seashell-carved door, it swung open in front of her and a tall young man stepped out, almost barreling into her.

"Watch where—" he started, then stopped and frowned at her.

Sabra's stomach knotted, even when she recognized the young man as Theodorus's own son, Leontius. Everyone knew he had no love for the Faith, but Theodorus never permitted anyone to speak against him. Sabra had seen him before, but they had never spoken. She had never looked at him without pity.

"I beg your pardon, priestess," he said, giving her a slight bow.

She drew a thin breath. "I am not a priestess any longer," she said.

"A shame."

"How can you say that?" she murmured. "Did you approve of the slaughter of our children at the old god's command? The pain and the suffering and the death?"

His lips lifted in a faint smile. "I just enjoy the irony," he said. He took a step closer to her, and behind her, she could sense Hanno tensing. "What does this new god of my father's bring to anyone but pain and suffering and death?"

"You're wrong," Sabra said, but the words sent a chill through her.

"Unbelievable," he said, regarding her with astonishment. "You've seen it. You've seen what he does to his followers. What difference is there between the arena and that cave on the hill?"

He was pointing at the accursed place, but Sabra couldn't bring herself to look. She was trembling all over, fury and grief blurring over each other.

"You can't see the difference?" she said. "The difference is Love."

"Love," he echoed. His voice was cold. She would have preferred his mockery.

"He is Love," she whispered. "But Molech...we suffered, and died, for his hate. It was empty. It was an abomination. It meant nothing."

"How can death mean anything?" Leontius asked, then shoved past her and into the night-dark shadows of the streets.

Sabra covered her mouth with her hand, struggling to control her breathing.

You served me faithfully, whispered the sinuous voice again. *Why did you leave my service? You were honored, once. Now you are only feared, and hated.*

"Oh, God, help me," she murmured, and pushed her way into the little *domus.*

A few of the people who had gathered in the inner peristyle for the evensong saw her enter and gave her guarded smiles. Some of them watched her somberly, as if waiting for her to denounce them.

Why should they forgive you?

Sabra dropped onto one of the benches under the portico, burying her face in her hands. Presently she quieted her thoughts enough to try to listen to the words the others were chanting. The lines of a Psalm wreathed around her.

"See how they surround me, Lord, my adversaries, how many rise up in arms against me; everywhere voices taunting me: His God cannot save him now."

She shuddered and got to her feet, shaking her head violently.

A storm will come from the north...

The voice in her mind whispered, *Impostor.*

She pushed herself unsteadily to her feet, then turned and fled from the peristyle. Hanno caught her as she swept out onto the street, taking her elbow as she stumbled on the stone lip of the threshold.

"Mistress!" he cried. "What's wrong?"

"I am," she said. "Those words...did you hear those words? I'm beyond saving, Hanno."

And he laughed.

She stared at him, taken aback, but he couldn't banish the smile from his face. "Oh, mistress, you didn't stay to hear what follows."

"How do you know—" she started, but caught herself. Hanno had been applying himself devotedly to his studies of the Scriptures, even more than she had, with all her other concerns weighing on her mind. She lowered her gaze and asked, meekly, "What follows?"

He tipped his head back and closed his eyes, and said in his broken Greek, "*Yet, Lord, you are my champion, you are the pride that keeps my head high. I have only to cry out to the Lord, and my voice reaches his mountain sanctuary, and there finds hearing. Safe in God's hand I lay down, and slept, and have awoken; and now, though thousands of the people set upon me from every side, I will not be afraid of them.*"

Sabra's lips parted, and for several breathless moments she just regarded him in silent wonder.

You think your voice will reach God in His high mountain? Yours? He will never be pleased with your voice.

And the tiny flicker of hope that the Psalmist's words had woken in her shattered.

4

Alexandria, Aegyptus — October, A.D. 300

Aikaterina sat at the table in her great *Bibliotheka*, trying with valiant effort to pay attention to Diodoros, the tutor who had first opened her eyes to the mysteries of the Scriptures. But her gaze kept drifting to the high clerestory windows, and she finally sighed in irritation.

"You seem distracted," Diodoros said, closing the *codex*. "Perhaps a walk might do you good."

Aikaterina eyed him sidelong, then nodded. "And you are eager to work on your transcriptions," she said.

Diodoros ducked his dark head, looking a bit sheepish, like a schoolboy who had been caught doing something forbidden. "Yes, I would."

"Go to it, then," she said, waving a hand to dismiss him. "I need to think."

Diodoros rose from his bench but hesitated there a moment, his gaze thoughtful and intent upon her. She glanced up at him expectantly and folded her hands in her deep blue *palla*. When Diodoros said nothing, she shook her head at him.

"What is it?" she asked. "I said I needed to think—and I can't think properly with you staring at me."

"I just wondered…" he began, and then stopped. "You

seem troubled, *kyria*, and I wondered if there was something... if there was anything I could do to help."

Aikaterina didn't answer immediately. She *was* troubled. She'd had no word from Jurian, her uncle Constantinus, or even Agapius since they had left Rome, though she continually reminded herself that she shouldn't expect any word from them at all.

But the greater weight on her mind was the matter of her father. She had been shocked upon her return home to discover his condition—how rapidly, how unexpectedly he had deteriorated after leaving Nicomedia. His conflict with Diocletian seemed to have taken an incredible toll on him, and the robust man she had known all her life seemed to have shriveled like a grape left too long in the sun.

And then there was her mother. Her slave Nenet had said something, just yesterday...

"It's...nothing," she said, shivering, making a brave attempt at a smile.

"You have changed, you know," Diodoros said, almost wistfully. "You haven't spoken much of your travels with the imperial court. Did something happen while you were away?"

Aikaterina stared at the whorls and lines in the grain of the table, trying not to think of Varro, of the amphitheater, of Maximianus and Galerius and the mercurial Emperor Diocletian, whose face, lately, had dominated her nightmares.

"Many things," she said softly. "But those things, too, are my burden to bear."

Diodoros frowned. "Surely you must understand by now," he said, "that we don't have to carry our burdens alone. Not even you, *kyria*."

Aikaterina looked up in surprise, but Diodoros was already walking away. She pressed her lips together and rose. Diodoros was right, as usual. Sometimes she wished she could just vanish away into the desert like his sister—to spend her life in contemplation of the Highest Good, undisturbed by the whirlwinds of the world and its cares.

But that life, it seemed, was not for her. She left the *Bibliotheka* and stood for a moment outside its great doors, drinking in the sunshine. Perhaps Diodoros was right, and a walk would do her good. She took two steps toward the gardens and then heard the sound of running footsteps behind her.

"What is it, Nenet?" she asked, turning.

But it wasn't Nenet. It was an ashen-faced guard, who stopped before her and gave her a sharp salute. "*Kyria*," he said, bowing low.

But she knew. He didn't need to say a word, but she knew. She ran for the palace.

AIKATERINA BURST INTO HER father's *cubiculum*, where she found him lying in his bed with the covers pulled tight beneath his arms. His hands rested on top of the purple linen coverlet, and in the low lamplight his skin was almost translucent. For a moment Aikaterina stood frozen, racked with fear, and stared at his peaceful still face until finally she saw the shallow breaths that barely moved his chest.

Then she became aware of other people in the room—the *medicus* standing near her father's bed, mixing something in a flask, the servants gathered in a tight knot around him. When he saw her, the physician left his flask with the chief steward and stepped between Aikaterina and her father.

"You must not disturb him," he said in a low voice. "Come, we will speak in the corridor."

He led her from the room, one hand on her elbow. As the door closed on her father's still form, Aikaterina turned anguished eyes on the physician.

"What happened?" she asked, fighting to keep her voice steady. "This morning he was fine! He was fine. He ate his breakfast with me…"

The physician nodded gravely. "It happens this way sometimes. He has not been well for some time, *kyria*."

"I know that!" she snapped, but then checked herself. "I'm

sorry...I shouldn't..."

The physician smiled. "It is perfectly all right," he said. "Grief makes us angry, makes us say things we would not."

The mention of grief made her tremble with new fear. She gripped the physician's arm. "He's not—" she began, but couldn't bring herself to finish the thought.

"No, no," he said. "He is in a deep sleep."

"Will he wake?" she asked, searching his face.

The physician sighed and lifted his shoulders. "Who can say with these things?" he said. "He may indeed wake, but I cannot tell you when. We must work to keep him comfortable and see that he takes—"

Aikaterina caught herself before the sharp words that sprang into her mind could tumble out of her mouth. Instead, she closed her eyes and tried to think clearly. "Has my mother been told?" she asked.

"She knows, *kyria*. She was in the room when he collapsed."

Aikaterina's eyes snapped open. "Did she say something to provoke him?" she asked. "What were they doing? What was she saying to him?"

The physician seemed surprised by her tone. "That I could not say, *kyria*. I wasn't there when it happened."

"Then I will ask her myself," Aikaterina said. "Thank you."

The physician bowed and went back inside her father's chamber, where the servants still stood huddled together near the wall, frozen and silent. He closed the door gently behind him, and Aikaterina backed against the wall of the corridor.

She clenched her hands to try to stop them from shaking. They were ice cold, so she wrapped her *palla* more closely around herself. She felt like she was fragmenting in a hundred different directions all at once, even as she felt the weight of Alexandria fall on her shoulders.

No one needed to tell her that she would have to take up her father's rule, at least until he was strong enough to shoulder its duties again. She could not trust anyone Diocletian might send. Alexandria was a place rich in cultural and religious diversity, not to mention its energy for advances in philosophy, the sciences, and poetry. Her father's rule had been one of tolerance, and under his generous and kindly governance, the city had flourished.

But Diocletian was more and more under the sway of his *Caesar* Galerius—the man whose veins seemed filled not with blood but venom. She shivered violently and held herself more tightly. If Diocletian were to send someone to replace her father, Galerius would have a hand in it…and that would be the end of peace in Alexandria. Especially now, when the peace was already so fragile.

In the months since her return from Rome, she had felt the city suffering. There were rumors of grain shortages, and there were the barbarian tribes in the south of Egypt that had lately been consuming so much of her father's frail energy. If the city heard that their *Praefectus* was ill, that he was not at the city's helm…she could only imagine the anarchy.

And her mother? Her mother was not suited for governing a city.

Aikaterina pushed away from the wall and went to find her mother. Something had caused her father to fall ill so suddenly, and she had a strong suspicion she knew what it was. She just needed to find out for certain.

But even if it turned out that she was right, she had no notion what she would do, or what she could do. She pushed the thought away. For now, she needed to take one step at a time. That was as far ahead of her as she could see.

As she rounded the corner and headed down the corridor that led to her mother's chambers, she caught sight of Nenet hurrying toward her. Aikaterina ran to meet her and Nenet wrapped her tightly in her arms.

"Nenet," Aikaterina murmured. "What am I going to do?"

Nenet said nothing, but her arms tightened protectively around her. Aikaterina let Nenet hold her a moment longer, then she stepped back and took a deep breath.

"Where is my mother?" Aikaterina asked.

Nenet pointed at the door. "Hurry," she said, and her lips closed in a tight line.

Fear shivered through Aikaterina again, and she squeezed Nenet's hand. Then she threw back her shoulders, lifted her chin, and opened the door.

Her mother stood in the center of the room, her dark *palla* edged with gold thrown around her shoulders. Her dark hair, tinged with strands of silver, was piled high on her head. She looked like the statue of the goddess in the Temple of Isis—beautiful and proud, and remote.

A scribe sat cross-legged on the floor in the corner, a papyrus scroll in his hands.

"…and tell him that he may send his son—" her mother was saying as Aikaterina entered, but as soon as she saw her daughter, she paused and folded her hands in front of her. "Well?"

Aikaterina speared the scribe with such a look that he scrambled to his feet, bowed hastily to her mother, and scurried past Aikaterina into the corridor. Aikaterina shut the door and leaned against it.

"That is not Father's wish," Aikaterina said, with a force in her voice that seemed to surprise her mother.

"Your father, sadly, can no longer make these decisions," she said, so smoothly that Aikaterina wondered what her mother felt. She had always been something of an enigma to Aikaterina. "It falls to me now to see that your future is settled."

Aikaterina swallowed and took a small step forward. "And if I do not wish such arrangements to be made for me?"

"What other choice is there? Your father is ill, Aikaterina, and yet the city of Alexandria must carry on. It must know that the government that at the city's helm is stable and certain. Are you prepared to do whatever is necessary for Alexandria?"

"Of course," Aikaterina said, ashamed to hear herself whisper.

"And if Alexandria should need to see the visible hand of the Empire here within the palace?"

Aikaterina winced. "Is that what made Father ill this morning? Did you tell him you meant to write to the Emperor again about me, about me marrying into the Tetrarchy, against his express command?"

Her mother stood very still, her face pale behind the artificial color she used to heighten her cheekbones. Aikaterina needed no more proof than that.

"Alexandria does not need the Tetrarchy in the city to know that it is safe. I am assuming control of Alexandria," she said. "Until Father recovers, I will manage his affairs."

Her mother stared at her, stunned. "Do you think the *Imperator* will let you assume governorship here?"

"No," Aikaterina said. "Nor do I wish it. But until Father is recovered, I will work as his regent."

"And if he does not recover?" her mother said, very quietly. "What then? Will you ask Diocletian to instate you as *Praefecta Augustalis* of Egypt?"

Aikaterina lifted her chin and met her mother's gaze evenly. "I will always do what is best for Alexandria," she said. "But I will never compromise my integrity to do it. I will not marry, Mother. Not unless you can find someone who is at least my equal in all things."

To her surprise, she saw her mother's lips press in a stifled smile, a riddle Aikaterina couldn't solve. She said nothing, and after a moment Aikaterina turned and left the room. She almost couldn't make it down the hallway, her legs were shaking so badly.

Hot tears burned behind her eyes. Nenet was nowhere to be seen, and she suddenly felt very small and very alone. She tried to reach for words to speak in prayer, but nothing would come to her. Never had she been without words, and that filled her with more fear than any message her mother might send to the Emperors in their gilded palaces.

She had taken the next step, but it had brought her to the edge of a precipice.

5

Antiochia ad Orontes, Syria — October, A.D. 300

Casca shifted on his saddle as he navigated the busy streets of Antioch, guiding his weary horse toward the Emperor's palace. He was much less familiar with this city than Nicomedia, but Diocletian had gotten it into his mind that he wished to spend some time away from his central palace, and no one could persuade him otherwise.

Antioch was not an unpleasant city, as far as cities went, but Casca couldn't repress a faint displeasure at being there. And if Diocletian had left for Nicomedia after all, without telling him... He sucked his bottom lip between his teeth. Nothing would be as irritating as traveling all the way from Didyma only to be delayed in delivering his message because the Emperor wasn't where he was supposed to be.

He'd puzzled over the meaning of the Oracle's words all the way to the city. Who—or what—was the red dragon?

He shivered, remembering the legend that had sprung up so quickly after Jurian's travels in Cyrene. The ignorant peasants in every town from Cyrene to Nicomedia spun stories of his quest, and named him *Drakonotomachos*. Some were so bold as to call him a Dragon-Slayer.

But I heard he told the Emperor he'd killed a god, Casca thought, snorting softly. *If he killed it, how could it come back to life? What, is it Bacchus, that it can resurrect itself?*

He couldn't figure that part out at all, but there was something menacing about it, and he didn't care for it in the least.

The part he had figured out was the reference to the sword and the sea. Constantinus had taken that sword—Excalibur, wasn't it?—out of the *carcer* before boarding the ship with Jurian, and it had never been seen since. Everyone assumed he had given it back to Jurian, and Diocletian had never quite forgiven him for that. That, and so much else.

At last he arrived at the island in the Orontes, where Diocletian's palace brooded like a stone monstrosity, its face gleaming in the late afternoon sun. As he passed within the broad walls and entered the main palace courtyard, a slave immediately rushed from the stable to take his horse's reins. Casca dismounted, dusty and road-weary, and headed up the steps to the portico without a word or a glance at the slave. First, he would bathe, then eat a luxurious meal…something, he hoped, that didn't taste of fish.

But his hopes were quickly dashed. He was greeted in the *vestibulum* by Diocletian's massive guard Gorgonius, who always seemed to be scowling—whether he was looking at horse dung or the Emperor himself.

"Ah," Gorgonius said. "You've been expected."

Casca took a quick breath and followed him into the palace. It was like a small city, even larger than the palace at Nicomedia, and Casca grimaced in distaste at the sheer number of slaves, administrators, and petty court officials who hurried through the corridors. It was an almost ten-minute walk from the portico to the *Imperator*'s private *tablinum*, and by the time they reached it, Casca's forehead and neck were damp with sweat.

Gorgonius announced him, then stepped aside to let Casca enter the room alone. It was dark inside—the one narrow window had a screen covering it, warding away the last remnants of the day. A few lamps flickered around the room, but not nearly enough to banish the heavy shadows. Casca hesitated just a moment before stepping into the silent space, feeling like he ought to tiptoe, and speak in whispers.

"You were gone a long while," Diocletian said, from somewhere in the darkness.

Casca's hand tremored and he twisted his cloak around it, wishing in vain that Gorgonius had given him time to freshen up from the road before facing his Emperor.

"*Sacratissime Imperator*," he whispered. "I bring word from the Oracle."

"I should hope so," Diocletian said, stepping into a faint ring of lamplight. He regarded Casca a moment with a satirical stare, then added, "Since that is why I sent you there."

Casca swallowed hard.

"So, tell me." Diocletian lifted one brow in an elegant arch. "Did the god speak?"

Casca couldn't clear the knot from his throat. Had Apollo spoken? How was he to know? The Oracle had made no claim either way... She had been, in fact, infuriatingly ambiguous on the matter. Casca considered, briefly, weighing the value of the truth against the value of a lie.

Taking a deep breath, he bowed slightly and said, "The god spoke."

The very corner of Diocletian's mouth lifted. "Tell me." He paused a moment, then added, "And do so carefully. To muddle the words of the gods is a profanation worthy of death."

Casca nodded, but didn't speak immediately. He'd been practicing the words since Didyma, but they kept catching, refusing to come out. He cleared his throat twice. Diocletian's bearing changed fractionally, just a slight twitch of his fingers, but Casca had been observing him long enough to know that he was growing impatient.

"The god said he cannot speak while the just are on the earth," he said, all in a rush.

Diocletian's eyes narrowed. "Who are *the just?*" he asked.

"He...didn't specify."

For a long moment Diocletian just measured him in silence, as if trying to decide whether or not to cut out his tongue. Casca grimaced at the mental image, and scraped his tongue over his teeth.

"Go on," Diocletian said at last. "I presume that was not all of what you have to say. Although, if the god is silent, as you claim, one wonders what other message you could have to deliver."

"She spoke," Casca said. "After…after I heard those words. She said, *The way lies over the sea.*" There. That was the first part, anyway. And then, as if beyond his control, he heard his voice carry on in the Oracle's own sing-song tone, "*The standing stones watch the stars and wait for the coming of the king, whose hand will draw the sword. He will take it up and lay it down again, and the stone shall become the king stone. The blood of the stone shall adorn the banner of the king. Unleash the storm of fire and blood, and the red dragon will rise.*" He came back to himself with a sharp gasp and recovered with a slight bow to his *Imperator*. "So it was spoken."

Diocletian's hand rested, lightly, on the edge of his table, his gaze fixed on Casca's face, but he never moved. For a moment Casca wondered if he was even breathing.

Then he said simply, "Very well."

Casca faltered. Had his Emperor dismissed him? Was he pleased? Was he a feather's breadth from striking Casca down as an unworthy messenger? It was impossible to tell.

Diocletian's gaze suddenly sharpened on Casca's face, as if he had been looking at something else the whole while. Then, without a word, he glanced pointedly at the door behind Casca and shifted around to lean his hands on the desk. Casca fumbled over a low bow and took two steps back toward the door before his curiosity got the better of him.

"Divine *Imperator*," he whispered, and immediately rebuked himself for his boldness. "May I ask a question?"

"You may," Diocletian said. Without any humor, he added, "Though I may not choose to answer it."

"The red dragon? Do you know what it means?"

The tiniest smile played on Diocletian's lips. "Of course," he said. He turned to Casca, his blue eyes cold and fathomless and paralyzing. "I am this dragon," he said. "And I will rise, as she said."

Fettered under that stare, Casca could not imagine denying the truth of his Divine *Imperator*'s words.

Diocletian flicked a finger at Casca. "Now go. You have your duties, *Tribunus*. See to them."

"*Imperator*, I beg you to reconsider my request," Casca blurted all at once. "Please, let me stay by your side as your personal attendant, your counselor, your confidante. I would serve you faithfully."

"Do you not already?" Diocletian asked, his stare sharp as broken glass.

Casca bowed, trembling all over. "Of course, *Imperator*. I do. But—"

"But? But why should I indulge your wish?"

A prickle of indignation needled in Casca's heart, shifting almost imperceptibly to anger. "Because," he said. He almost shouted it—almost shouted at his Divine Emperor. "Because the god spoke to *me*, to Marcus Valerius Flaccus Casca, when he would speak to no one else!"

Diocletian's face was etched in marble. "Don't be a fool, Casca," he said, smoothly. "The god was speaking to me."

6

Portus Adurni, Britannia — November, A.D. 300

Over a month had passed since the Celtic merchant ship had left Tingi, with rough seas and late autumn storms slowing their voyage interminably. Jurian had almost given up watching for sight of land. There was little point to his ceaseless vigil anyway, he thought, as the seas this far north were often blanketed with heavy fog, and some days he could scarcely see from one side of the ship to the other—let alone catch a glimpse of land some miles distant.

He wasn't sure what to expect, either. With all the lands he had seen in the southern parts of the Empire, he had only ever heard rumors of the wild country of Britannia, and its wild people. He had imagined all sorts of possibilities, and finally settled on a barren landscape like the region around Cyrene, with tents instead of houses. He was going into exile; he had no hope of Roman comforts and civilized dwellings. Constantinus would leave him somewhere outside the protection of the Legions, and the Empire would soon forget about Lucius Aurelius Georgius.

"Land!" Glyn shouted from somewhere behind him. "Vectis!"

Jurian glanced over his shoulder and saw the boy up on top

of the mast, perching on it like a stool with his legs wrapped around the thick beam and one hand holding onto the flax of the sail. His other hand was shielding his eyes from the early sunlight that angled down through a break in the clouds.

A few moments later, Constantinus joined Jurian at the rail.

"What is Vectis?" Jurian asked, peering in vain through the patchy fog. Every now and then he caught a glimpse of what looked like jagged crops of rock, but it was all grey, and it all blurred together.

"It's an island off the coast of Britannia," Constantinus said. "We aren't going there. We'll head into the strait."

The ship skimmed the waves, the sails billowing out in the stiff breeze, and soon Jurian could see the island clearly, though it was large enough he might have mistaken it for the mainland if Constantinus hadn't told him otherwise. They sailed past it on the north, and gradually Jurian distinguished the land on the opposite side of the strait—stretches of sweeping chalky cliffs and high ground that looked, for the late month, far too green. And then, rising up at the head of a harbor, half-cloaked in fog, was one of the most impressive Roman forts he had ever seen.

"Constantinus," he said.

"Yes?"

"What is that?"

"Portus Adurni," he said, simply.

"*Portus*," Jurian echoed. He pointed at the fort. "That is a *castra*."

"Yes."

Jurian turned away from the ship's rail to face him. "I'm under *interdictio*."

"So you are."

"So am I going to be stuck on the ship for ten days again like when we were moored at Portus Blendium?"

Constantinus flashed him a rare grin and clapped him on the shoulder. "This is Britannia, Jurian." Then his smile faded and he added, with a strange wistful note in his voice, "Home."

"Then what will you do with me once we land?"

Constantinus glanced at him sidelong. "What *should* I do with you?"

The question surprised Jurian, but only for a moment. He knew Constantinus well enough by now to know that nothing should surprise him—just when he thought he'd figured the man out, he shifted.

"Help me, maybe?" Jurian said, half joking.

Constantinus nodded slowly. "Of course. And then you'll help me."

This time Jurian couldn't help gaping, and Constantinus's mouth inched up in a smile.

"Help you what?" Jurian asked.

"You're in the deep dark places of the Empire now," Constantinus said. "Out here, it doesn't matter so much what a man has done as how he wields a sword." He eyed Jurian for a moment, then added softly, "Brave service covers a multitude of evils, Jurian."

He slapped the rail and then disappeared again into the mists. Jurian stared after him, not sure what to feel or think. How could he serve the Empire, after everything that had happened?

But the chance to redeem himself—to regain his honor? And the chance to return, once that was done, to Cyrene?

He leaned against the rail and hung his head, shutting his eyes and closing out the confusing swirl and eddy of the grey mist.

"You are troubled," said a deep voice.

Jurian smiled faintly when he saw Menas beside him, watching him out of his one good eye. He opened his mouth to speak, but then hesitated. How could he tell Menas the truth of what gnawed at him? Menas knew what it was to serve the Empire, and he knew what it was to reject it fully, even to the point of death.

"It's...nothing," Jurian said, but his voice broke.

Menas just studied him in silence, and Jurian felt uncomfortably certain that even with only one eye, Menas could see straight into his heart.

But if he could, there was no judgment in that gaze, only a steady peace. After a long silence, he laid a hand on Jurian's shoulder.

"Do not fear, Jurian," he said.

"Everyone keeps telling me that," Jurian said softly. "But I'm not sure I know what it means."

Menas smiled and leaned heavily on the ship's rail. "Just know that this burden you carry, you do not carry alone."

They stood side by side as the ship sailed into the harbor and came to rest at a long pier among a handful of naval *triremes*. The sailors made the ship fast and helped to gather the travelers' few belongings, and finally Jurian pushed away from the rail to face Britannia.

At the top of the ramp, he stopped beside Menas, considering the stone pier below. "When we left Tingi, I thought I had stood on Roman soil for the last time. I never thought..."

"This is Britannic soil," Constantinus said, striding past him. "Rome has only built on it."

Menas and Jurian exchanged a glance, then made their way down the ramp on his heels. Agapius had already disembarked and was walking, a little awkwardly, in wide circles. Menas groaned as they stepped onto the solid stone of the pier, and leaned over his knees.

"This is the part I hate the most," he muttered. "Why does the ground feel like it's still moving?"

The two *gladiatrices* raced down the ramp behind them, grabbing Menas's arms and pulling him forward so fast he almost fell to his knees. They laughed when they saw how unsteady he was, and the bolder of the two girls threw open her arms and tossed her head back to the sky. The fitful sunlight caught in their golden hair, and Jurian thought both of them looked like wild horses penned too long in a dark stable, taking their first steps in the spring sun.

Bleddyn and Daffyd stepped off the ship and clasped Constantinus's arm in farewell, then turned to Jurian.

"Wherever that sword takes you," Bleddyn said, "I hope it's somewhere good."

"We're indebted to you all," Jurian said, and Bleddyn waved him away.

"It's a story," he said simply, and sauntered back onto the deck before Jurian could ask him what he meant.

"Godspeed, Jurian," Daffyd said, and staggered in surprise when the two *gladiatrices* both threw their arms around his neck at the same time.

Jurian couldn't understand the Celtic they spoke, but he knew just from the looks on the girls' faces what they were saying. Those sailors had brought them home. There were no words in any language that could hold enough gratitude for that.

"Come on then," Constantinus said. He jerked his head toward the end of the pier, where a lone Roman soldier stood, wearing plaid *bracchae* and a fur cloak against the biting wind. "I believe we have some introductions to make."

"What are we doing here, Constantinus?" Jurian asked, hesitating. "Where are we going?"

"We are going to get food and hot baths, and beds that don't feel like wood," he said. "And then we are going to Londinium, to see my father."

He turned without another word and went to meet the Legionary. Even trailing behind at a distance, Jurian could see the soldier start, fumble into a sharp salute, and then throw his arms around Constantinus. As Jurian and the others joined them, Constantinus and the soldier were both laughing.

"Georgius," Constantinus said, reminding Jurian of how long it had been since the Tribune had called him by his Latin name. "Allow me to introduce you to my half-brother, Flavius Dalmatius. This is Lucius Aurelius Georgius."

The soldier gripped Jurian's arm fiercely, then dragged him into a hearty embrace. "Any friend of Constantinus's is mine as well, and more than welcome!"

After they were all introduced, Dalmatius swung away

and waved a hand at them. "I got the message you sent from Portus Blendium," he said, as they headed toward the *castra*. "I couldn't believe that you were finally coming to Britannia! Did you know your message would get here faster than you would?"

"Yes," Constantinus said, indifferent. "We were obliged to go by sea."

Dalmatius stopped at that, turning to level his half-brother with a curious look. "Obliged?" But Constantinus just gave him a look weighted with meaning, and Dalmatius shrugged. "You always were in love with the sea," he said, and left it at that, as if that explained everything perfectly.

Jurian shook his head. Dalmatius looked a little bit like Constantinus, he thought, though he was younger by seven or eight years and had a slightly darker complexion. But his bearing was completely unlike Constantinus's, who, without the least effort, commanded any room he walked into. Dalmatius reminded Jurian of a gregarious *psittacus*, where Constantinus had all the aloof ferocity of an eagle.

"Well, so, hurry up," Dalmatius said, as they reached the gate of the *castra*. "We'll see you well rested, then I'll make sure you have horses to ride. I take it you're going to see the *Caesar*?"

"As soon as possible. He is still in Britannia, isn't he?"

"For now," Dalmatius said. "You've come at a perfect time. You get to see Father and your favorite brother in the same trip."

Constantinus gave him a fond smile that Jurian had rarely seen, and led the way into the fort.

CONSTANTINUS HADN'T LIED. THE Roman fort was massive, and the accommodations he and his companions were given rivaled, or surpassed, any Jurian had experienced in the south. The *castra* was equipped with every comfort—even the floor in Jurian's *cubiculum* was heated by an ingenious engineering feat his servant had called a *hypocaustum*.

Jurian lacked for nothing, and the chamberlain had seen to it that he had a hot bath and a change of clean clothes suited to the sharp Britannic climate—thick *bracchae* and a fine, heavy wool tunic crisscrossed with leather straps, which made him feel rather like meat trussed for the roasting.

But if Jurian had thought the garments looked strange on him, Agapius seemed even more out of place dressed like a half-Romanized Celt. When Jurian met him outside the *triclinium*, Agapius was fiddling with the straps over his tunic, looking remarkably self-conscious.

"Fine pair we are," Agapius remarked. "Give me back my plain traveling clothes and let's be off."

Jurian grinned. "Come on," he said. "I see Menas."

He pointed across the *triclinium*, where Menas stood among a crowd of young *milites*, who were gawking at his size and the number of scars he bore. They were obviously peppering him with questions, too, which Menas answered in his slow, patient way, though the look he gave Jurian over their heads was a long-suffering plea for deliverance.

Jurian stepped up to try to extract his friend from the crowd, and the Legionaries all fell abruptly silent. It took Jurian a moment too long to notice their stares were now directed at him.

"You're him, aren't you," one of the *milites* said.

He was staring at Jurian's head, of course, but his gaze kept drifting to the hilt of the sword he wore across his back.

"Dragon-slayer," one of the others murmured, while the first added, "*Cyrenicus.*"

"You were in the arena," another said, then jerked his gaze away from Jurian to stare at Menas. "You were both in the arena." His eyes drifted toward the entrance of the *triclinium*, where Jurian had a feeling he would see the *gladiatrices* if he turned around. "You were all in the arena," he breathed.

"I wasn't," Agapius said cheerfully. "I was handling the logistics of Menas's very cunning escape."

"It's true, then?"

Jurian said nothing. He watched the soldier closely, waiting for the moment that he would make all the connections. Then it came, and the soldier's mouth opened in an O of shock.

Jurian gave a little sigh and said, "Yes."

The soldier tried three times to speak, but each time seemed to think better of what he meant to say. Finally he settled for, "Wish I'd been there to see it."

He said it without any inflection at all, which left Jurian to wonder just what he meant. The others shuffled their feet and echoed his words, and a few of them looked at Jurian with what he could only perceive as awe. It made him strangely uncomfortable.

He gave them a brief nod and clapped a hand on Menas's shoulder, leading him away from the group. Agapius stayed to talk to the men, occupying their attention to give Menas and Jurian a chance to get away. When they were far enough apart, Jurian stopped and folded his arms.

"What was that supposed to mean? Do they know I'm under interdict here? That I'm…violating my interdict here?"

"That is safe to assume, I think," Menas said mildly.

"Then…should I expect to wake up to a sword at my throat tonight?"

"I believe," Menas said, "that they showed you as much admiration as they dared, given the insignia they wear."

Jurian frowned up at him. "Admiration?" he echoed. "They admire me for defying the Emperor? But…"

"This is Britannia," Menas said.

Jurian thought that over for a long time, turning the notion around in his mind. Finally he nodded and said, "I think, perhaps, I'm beginning to understand what that means."

7

LONDINIUM, BRITANNIA — NOVEMBER, A.D. 300

CONSTANTINUS WAS PACING IN THE VESTIBULE OF THE *PRAETORIUM* when Jurian left his chamber early the next morning—too early, by Jurian's reckoning, but Constantinus had insisted they set off at daybreak for the two-day ride to Londinium. As Jurian joined him, the Tribune paused and gave him only a faint nod of acknowledgment.

"Something troubling you?" Jurian asked.

Constantinus let out a breath and waved a hand. "They don't have enough horses that they can spare for us in the *castra*. Dalmatius and a few other *milites* left this morning to find more, but they haven't returned. Which means you are free to rest and get some food, and wait for further instructions."

Jurian stifled a noise of frustration and nodded, trying not to resent the loss of a few hours of extra sleep in the comfortable bed he'd been given.

Constantinus must have sensed his thoughts, because he turned to Jurian with an apologetic smile. "I'm sorry you woke so early. I only hope this delay doesn't mean I miss my father."

"Is he likely to move that quickly?" Jurian asked.

"The *Caesar* does everything quickly, when he sets his mind to it."

That must be where Constantinus gets it from, Jurian thought wryly, watching the Tribune swing away and resume his restless pacing, one hand worrying his jaw.

Jurian left him to his thoughts and went in search of Agapius and Menas. They ate a breakfast of hot porridge and oatcakes outside in the crisp morning air, and then Agapius and Menas promptly fell asleep leaning against a stone pillar in the feeble sunshine, while Jurian watched the activity at the heart of the *castra*. It must have been a few hours later that Constantinus found them, and Jurian startled out of a faint doze at the Tribune's hand on his shoulder.

"They're back," Constantinus said. "Get your things and meet me in the courtyard when you're ready."

Menas woke immediately at the Tribune's voice, but Jurian had to nudge Agapius a few times to rouse him. They gathered their few belongings from their chambers while Menas tracked down the *gladiatrices*, then they all congregated in the courtyard where Dalmatius and a few other soldiers held the reins of half a dozen horses.

Jurian took the reins Dalmatius offered him and considered the small bay horse, his heart twinging with regret at his loss of Aster, the white horse Sabra's father had given him, who had shared so many journeys with him. Then, with a sigh, he swung into the saddle.

"Come, Menas," Constantinus said, as his brother handed him the reins of a grey horse. "The sun won't wait for us."

Jurian turned his horse and found Menas standing nearby with arms folded, staring uneasily at a massive horse that the soldiers had somehow managed to find in one of the neighboring villages. Its hooves were easily as large as Jurian's head, and they were covered in the most peculiar way with long feathered hair. Its whole body was blanketed in thicker, shaggier fur than Jurian had ever seen on a horse, and it wore no saddle but a curious rigged harness that had been padded generously with leather and wool.

"I have never seen a horse that size," Jurian remarked. "It's like it was designed just for the likes of you."

Menas snorted. "I'm still afraid I might break its spine. The likes of me weren't meant to ride but to carry."

"Well, there you have it," Agapius said, nodding at the horse. "A *Christophoros-phoros.*"

Jurian laughed. Dalmatius looked faintly puzzled, but said nothing, and Agapius, as if afraid that he'd misspoken, refused to translate his pun into Latin. They knew nothing of Dalmatius's sympathies, and Jurian just prayed that his Greek was as bad as his brother's.

Constantinus clasped Dalmatius's arm and then pulled him into a brief embrace.

"I will not forget your hospitality, *frater*. You're certain you can't spare a week to travel to Londinium with us?"

"Certain," Dalmatius said. "Unfortunately." He clapped Constantinus on the shoulder. "Give my regards to the *Caesar*."

Constantinus nodded and swung onto his horse's back. The *gladiatrices* had already mounted their horses—matching white mares, which Jurian was certain the *milites* had arranged on purpose. Their infectious joy from the day before had subdued, fading into cautious alertness. Jurian wondered if they knew where they were going, and, if they knew they were heading for the palace of the western *Caesar*, did it trouble them? Menas had been talking to them quietly when they all arrived in the courtyard, but Jurian still wasn't sure just how much of the Celtic language the giant could actually speak.

They bade their farewells to Dalmatius and the other *milites*, then Constantinus led them through the gate and onto the wide paved road that wound northeast from the coast through a forsaken countryside. Only a few flocks of sheep and a scattering of massive, rangy trees broke the endless sweep of frost-shrouded grass. There were no *vici* to be seen.

At midday they stopped under a coppice of hazel trees to rest the horses, and Jurian grinned as he dismounted, stooping immediately to scoop up a handful of fallen nuts.

"*Nux sylvestris,*" he said, holding them out to Agapius.

Agapius gave him a strange look. "How do you know?"

"Because I've gathered these nuts for as long as I can remember, back in Anatolia."

He almost said, back home, but the word caught in his throat, and he shook his head briefly to banish the thought. The bolder of the two girls snatched a nut from his open hand, flashing him a taunting grin. Then, to his surprise, she turned and held it out to Constantinus. The Tribune caught Jurian's eye briefly before accepting the nut with a silent nod of thanks. The girl laughed, and wandered away to join her sister as she gleaned nuts from under the rangy branches.

"I wish I could speak their language," Jurian said. "We've known those girls since Nicomedia, and traveled the ocean with them, and none of us know their names."

"I do," Menas said suddenly, gruff. "The taller one is Eilwen, and her sister is Brigit."

"One of them is taller?" Agapius whispered.

At the sound of their names, the girls turned, flashing Menas bright smiles. Jurian narrowed his eyes as he watched them standing side by side, trying to figure out which one was which. They looked identical in every way—it was only by the way one of them always carried herself, with a fierce lift of her chin, that he had ever been able to distinguish them.

"The bold one," he said. "Eilwen or Brigit?"

Menas chuckled, watching the girls fondly. "Brigit."

Eilwen returned a moment later, the fold of her cloak filled with ripe hazelnuts. The others settled down on the frosty ground and set to cracking open the nuts for a meager meal, but Constantinus stood a little apart from them, leaning on a tree trunk and watching the empty road. But he was toying with something in his hand, and after a moment Jurian realized it was the hazelnut Brigit had given him. He turned to see if Agapius had seen it, too, but Agapius had promptly fallen asleep after finishing his share of the nuts.

Constantinus tipped his head back to study the sky, then swung around to face them. "If you're finished, pack up."

They rode on as the wind picked up and a few light flurries began to fall. Agapius looked miserable, huddled in his fur wrappings, but Constantinus rode with his red cloak tossed back over his shoulders, facing the cold with the same stoic indifference he faced a battlefield. Or perhaps, Jurian thought, he didn't notice the cold at all.

"How long has it been since you were in Britannia?" he asked after a while.

"Many years," Constantinus said, the words heavy with regret. "I was sent to Diocletian's court when I was still quite young, and it's been some time since I ventured back." He glanced at Jurian. "You'll find things are very different here."

Jurian shrugged his cloak more tightly around his shoulders, while the snow began to gather on its fringe of fur. "I'm finding that already," he said, then added, "And you'll find I'm used to border country."

At that, Constantinus grinned, and his reaction took Jurian by surprise again. Maybe the crisp air, scoured of the cloying scents of the Roman court, was actually refreshing to the Tribune.

"I honestly didn't think I'd ever see this place again," Constantinus admitted. "Galerius thinks I'm subversive. The man doesn't like to let me out of easy arm's reach of the imperial court."

Jurian laughed aloud. "Subversive?" he said. "You? You're not one of those hangers-on who obeys everything without question, but—"

"Like Casca, you mean?"

"Why do you have to bring him up again?" Jurian muttered. "He's on the other side of the world from us. Let him stay there and rot. I hope he discovers just how little it serves in the end, to try to satisfy such masters."

Constantinus said nothing, but his silence felt more like an argument than an agreement. Jurian blew out his breath and watched the steam hang in the air. He pulled in another breath, feeling the cold seep through his lungs.

It's good to be here, he thought. *Casca will have grown bold indeed if he dares follow me this far from the heart of the Empire.*

As the early evening drew on toward night, a few hovels of a small *vicus* appeared ahead of them, marked by the glimmer of bright torches. The houses were all made of mud and thatch and wood, unlike any building Jurian had ever seen before. Here there were no bright stone facades, or red tile roofs and colorful awnings, with houses built around open gardens to let in the warm sun and breeze. These houses seemed drawn up from the very earth, almost living things themselves, and the people who moved through the streets were as unRoman as any Jurian could imagine. He had been from one end of the southern Roman Empire to the other, but the people he had met had always been *Roman*. These people, though…these people wore their native culture like a shield.

As they neared the farthest outlying hovels, they saw one lone man standing motionless in the middle of the road, looking like a ghost under the halo of misting torchlight as he watched their arrival. His shaggy head reminded Jurian of a bear's, and his thick beard was braided in a dozen places, but there seemed to be more hair left wild than tamed. He wore a leather jerkin and leggings bound with thick leather straps, but his burly arms were bare and laced with a gleam of scars.

Agapius let out a breath. "Are all the men they breed here like that?" he asked, gesturing to the man. "Because if so, I can see why Rome is as skittish as a new colt up here."

Constantinus slowed his horse as they approached the man.

"*Salve*," he called, holding up a hand.

The man settled one massive fist against his belt and lifted his chin, eyes narrowed with mistrust. Jurian almost didn't notice that his fingers were playing over the haft of a heavy axe that hung from a ring on his belt.

Suddenly there was a commotion behind him, and before he could call out a warning, Brigit spurred her horse forward and cantered the rest of the distance toward the man. As soon as she reached him she swung down from the saddle and strode straight up to face him, chin lifted in defiance. Constantinus let out his breath in a quiet hiss.

For a few moments Brigit spoke to the man—it sounded like an argument, but then the man's hand dropped away from the weapon and his face, improbably, lit up with joy. Then Brigit turned away, tossing her head and giving a sharp flick of her hand. When none of them moved, she rolled her eyes and waved her hand again.

"It's fine," Menas said, nudging his horse forward. "We're welcome."

"Welcome," Constantinus echoed, skeptical.

Menas gestured to Brigit, fixing Constantinus with a severe look. "Obviously."

Constantinus and Jurian exchanged a glance, but they followed Menas and the other man into the town without a word of complaint. The man led them to a hostel, a building of two stories that towered over the other hovels, where two bare-armed boys raced out of the shadows to take their horses. As soon as Menas dismounted and stepped into the ring of torchlight, one of the boys stumbled backwards and fell onto the street, holding his hands in front of him as if to ward off an attack.

The other boy just stood paralyzed, mouth open in a silent O, one hand stretched out and pointing at Menas. Jurian could barely hear the whispered word he said.

"*Woden!*"

Brigit just laughed. She stooped to pull the fallen boy to his feet, but he shook his head fiercely and scrambled a few feet further back. Eilwen grabbed Menas's hand and pulled him forward, wrapping both her arms around his upper arm and trying desperately to explain something to the terrified boys. Brigit even pointed at Menas's bare feet with their six toes, but that only seemed to make the situation worse.

"What is going on?" Agapius asked out of the side of his mouth.

Constantinus, Jurian realized suddenly, was shaking with

suppressed laughter.

"What's so funny?"

"They think Menas is the god Woden," Constantinus said. "It's the missing eye, I think. And his—" he measured a mark in the air with his hand, high above his head.

"Oh," Jurian said, and couldn't think of anything else to say.

Somehow Eilwen and Brigit managed to persuade the boys that they were not in the presence of a deity, but even when they collected themselves enough to take the horses, they never stopped staring at Menas. Nor, for that matter, did anyone within the hostel, from the innkeeper who brought them bowls of thick stew to the other guests who shuffled back from the fire to give Menas room. Menas ate his stew with a scowl fixed on his brow, then retreated to the upstairs common room without a word to anyone.

Jurian didn't blame him—as soon as the giant had disappeared, all eyes in the hostel fixed on him instead. Feeling just as cross as Menas had looked, Jurian choked down the rest of his food and pushed his stool back from the table.

"I'm going to bed," he said, and left the rest of the group staring after him in surprise.

THEY RODE HARD THE next day, stopping only for a brief repast at noon, until finally, as the evening shadows were growing long, Jurian caught sight of a broad river twisting through the snow-crusted fields, an ink stain in the twilight. At the river their road became a massive bridge that cut across the water, leading up to the walls of the largest city Jurian had seen since they'd left Rome.

As they clattered across the bridge, Jurian heard a shout go up from the guard towers on either side of the gate, and the *portcullis* lifted on heavy ropes. Constantinus passed through the archway at a canter, never stopping until they reached the palace, which sprawled close to the city wall above the river. He led the way to the inner courtyard, where they finally reined in their sweat-flecked horses. Several slaves scurried out of the shadows to take the horses as soon as their riders dismounted.

"Follow me," Constantinus said, tossing his cloak over his shoulders as he strode toward the palace.

"That's what we've been doing," muttered Agapius.

Jurian followed wordlessly, taking in the impressive design of the palace. It was richly adorned with mosaic tile and florid frescoes of animals that Jurian had never seen before. There was something stark and remote about its beauty, as harsh and wild as the land it occupied, yet Jurian thought its grandeur could easily rival that of Diocletian's palace in Nicomedia.

As they stepped inside the grand *atrium*, a servant came forward and bowed low.

"We saw the signal fire yesterday, *Tribunus*," he said. "Your father is expecting you."

Constantinus waved in acquiescence, and the servant led them through the winding corridors and into a spacious *tablinum*. Several men stood around a long wooden table, and a robust man, ruddy-cheeked and almost completely bald, sprawled in a chair at its head.

"By Mithras!" he roared as Constantinus stepped into the room. His fist came down on the table so hard that everything—parchments, inkwells, and all the men surrounding him—jumped. Then he sprang to his feet, arms open. "Boy, I've missed you! So, that lynx Diocletian finally let you go?"

Constantinus's face broke into a wide smile and he stepped into the embrace. Jurian was sure he heard something crack as the man's massive arms squeezed Constantinus tightly.

"*Caesar*," Constantinus said, stepping back and turning a little to gesture to Jurian and the others. "Allow me to introduce my friends."

Jurian and Agapius each bowed in a military salute, and Menas simply stood there quietly, watching everything out of his one good eye while the *gladiatrices* hovered, wary and watchful, on either side of him.

"Friends, eh?" the *Caesar* said, appraising them. "They rather look like you dragged them out of a rat's hole."

"Isn't that what you always call Rome?" Constantinus asked drily.

Constantius Chlorus let out a roar of laughter. "So it is! By the gods! And that one there—what, did you summon Woden to walk among us?"

"Who is this Woden?" Menas asked, surprising Jurian with the plain frustration in his voice. "Why does everyone call me that?"

Constantius Chlorus waved a hand. "Some god of the *pagani*," he said. "One eye."

"Why does he only have one eye?" Menas asked, sounding aggrieved.

The *Caesar* shrugged his massive shoulders. "As I heard it, he sacrificed it to gain wisdom, insight into invisible realities, or some such. Is that what happened to you?"

"You'd think so," Jurian said, grinning at Menas. "He sees more than anyone I've ever known."

Menas ducked his head and Constantius Chlorus laughed out loud.

"I heard Woden has an eight-legged horse, too. You have one of those? Is that how you managed to get here so fast?"

"We met Dalmatius in Portus Adurni," Constantinus said. "He sends his love. And I need to send back his horses."

Constantius Chlorus nodded, a fond smile on his face. "He couldn't come with you, though?" he asked, and Constantinus shook his head. "Ah, well. A pity. You look like you got dragged through Hades and back—twice. Take some food, get some rest. You can tell me everything in the morning."

He shouted for a servant, and instantly a bandy-legged man trotted in, his neck thrust out in front of him like a rooster. He swept a low bow and then clasped his hands, waiting for his orders.

"Take them to their chambers, Aldred," the *Caesar* said. "See to it they have everything they need to be comfortable."

The man bowed low and led them out of the room. Constantinus glanced at Jurian as they headed through the smoky corridors on the servant's heels.

"So, that is my father," he said, and Jurian got the strange sense that he was waiting for Jurian's judgment.

"You are…very different sorts of men, aren't you?" Jurian said carefully.

Menas laughed aloud at that, surprising the servant who led the way. Even Constantinus chuckled, and gave no argument.

"Your room, *Tribunus*," Aldred said suddenly, stopping before a closed door.

As Constantinus stepped through the doorway, Jurian said, "Constantinus." The Tribune paused and glanced at him over his shoulder. "Does your father know who I am?"

Constantinus shrugged, indifferent. "Of course he does." Then, as he stepped inside the shadowy room he said, "Don't anyone dare wake me up in the morning."

Aldred bowed low, and Constantinus shut the door behind him without another word.

8

Cyrene, Libya — November, A.D. 300

The late autumn wind was heavy with the threat of rain as Sabra paced the shadows of the peristyle, twisting the length of Jurian's scarf between her hands. It was late, perhaps close to the *tertia vigilia*, but the nightmares had driven her from her bed. Even the peristyle offered none of its usual peace and comfort, and her thoughts would not be quiet. There was something in her mind now, the ghost of a whisper twisting in her thoughts like a living thing. For all that she prayed, and for all she tried to drive it back by sheer force of will, it lingered.

Her chest felt suddenly tight, like something poison in the air that made it hard to breathe.

Leave me alone, she whispered in her mind. *Please. Leave me in peace.*

Peace, came the sinuous reply, mocking her.

You've been banished. You can't hurt me now. You're just a figment of my memory, no more.

Banished, am I? That boy with his sword has no such power.

Sabra stumbled and fell, cutting her knees on the rough stone.

Hands lighted on her shoulders, and she almost screamed in terror before she realized they belonged to Hanno.

"Mistress!" he cried. "Are you ill? What are you doing up at this hour?"

Sabra stared up at him, dazed, but accepted the hand he offered to help her to her feet. "I was dreaming," she murmured. Pressing her palm to her forehead, she swallowed and said, "No, I...I don't know. I can't sleep. Hanno, what are *you* doing here?"

Hanno withdrew his hand gently from hers. "I thought I heard something, but then I woke, and I was cold."

Sabra tilted her head to study him. The words seemed so harmless, the way she first heard them, but then a chill prickled over her skin and her heart began to pound, hectic against her ribs.

"It's coming back," she said. "You can feel it, can't you? The terror. The plague of death. Oh, God, mercy." She pressed her knuckles against her lips, then reached out and shook his arm. "Go fetch Theodorus, quickly. I'll be back...I'll be back soon."

She turned and headed for the *atrium*.

"Wait—"

The sound of his sandals flapping against stone hounded her steps, but she didn't slow down to wait for him. She could hear the bewilderment in his voice, but she couldn't explain anything to him—at least, not in any way that he would understand. She barely understood it herself.

Something was stirring in the hills of Cyrene. Something as familiar to her as the feel of her own skin.

Hanno caught up to her on the portico, snatching at the scarf she had twisted around her right hand until she turned back to look at him. His face was etched with concern and deep horror, and everything inside him seemed to recoil from what he read in her face.

"Mistress, where are you going?"

"There is something I have to see," she said. "I'll be all right. Please go."

"Don't go alone," he said, the words almost a moan of terror. "I know where you mean to go. Please, *please* don't go to that place."

She looked at him for a long moment, then shook her head and said, "I must." Her fingers stirred over the soft fibers of the scarf, and she gave him a faint smile. "And I don't go alone," she said.

He clasped both his hands around his head, muttering a blessing in Punic that Theodorus had taught him. If Sabra stayed, if she listened to his words, if she let herself be moved by his fear, she would never do what she knew she must. So, without giving him a chance to stop her, she hurried down the hill from the palace, her steps almost stumbling with her speed. She crossed the *agora* and took the *cardo* to the north gate of the city, which opened onto the path into the hills.

In memory she heard the din of the musicians, the wailing of the people. She could smell the flowers wreathed in the children's hair. Her breath choked and she staggered, hating every step of that accursed hill. But still she went up, because she had to.

She had to see for herself what was stirring in the cave of the dragon.

At the top of the hill she paused, staring at the black scar etched in the mountainside. A cool, damp air breathed from it, and a shiver laced through her, fingers to toes. It was now or never. If she waited, she would lose all her courage.

Courage? You think it is courage that drives you back to this place? You know you have never escaped my service. It still calls to you.

Your name was chosen, Sabra of Cyrene.

I will have your blood.

Sabra closed her eyes, snatching vainly in her thoughts for the words of the Psalmist to strengthen her, but she could find none. With a single deep breath, she stepped into the cave.

She stood in the pitch darkness, her eyes open wide. There was no sound except her own breathing. But she could feel it. It was close—not close enough to touch her, but close enough to raise the hairs on the back of her neck and gloss her skin with a clammy, clinging damp. In all her life, she had never felt quite so afraid. It was even worse than when she had stood chained to the pillar, waiting to be devoured.

This darkness she did not know.

This darkness she had never seen. In all the years of her slavery, of her priesthood, she had never once stepped foot inside that cave.

How had Jurian entered so boldly?

"You were banished from this place," she said aloud. Her voice was steady, even though her heart was hammering in her chest. "Why have you returned?"

You should know, the voice came within her, just as it had then, in the dark days. *How long do marvels last? The shattered sinews of a dragon on the hill of bones, and how soon do the hearts of men forget? You should know. Evil things will always grow in the dark places of the earth and the deep places of the heart.*

"Not if good things can be planted there first," she said.

Something like laughter seemed to wind around her, like the breath of fume from some foul vent in the stone. *And what good things have you planted? How have they born fruit? You are alone, as you have always been alone, and will always be alone.*

Sabra winced. Clenched in her palm, the fabric of Jurian's scarf felt damp and cold. She had tried to push that feeling down as deep as it could go—that wretched sense that she should have gone with Jurian in his exile. He had promised he would never forget her, but the sea was wide, and time moved slow.

You know it in your heart, the voice continued. *He will abandon you. You will be left behind. You will always be left behind.*

"No," Sabra whispered, and her voice sounded thin and weak. She had to get out. She had to escape, now, before it broke her. When she drew a breath to steady herself, the darkness seemed to choke it out of her. "There is a love that does not fail," she said. "And it can reach even the darkest places."

You should know. The blood of children stains the hem of your garment. Suffering, and pain, and death. These are your workings.

These are your legacy, and your heritage. And you dare to call on love? You should know. You put love in the tomb.

Sabra bowed her head, hot tears scoring guilt upon her cheeks. She did know. She knew it all.

There were no words. Her mind churned, empty, tattered, and nothing she told herself could drive out the hateful voice. Finally, breathless and racked with horror, she spun away and felt her way back out to the clear night air and the stars that glittered so high above her.

For just a moment, she thought she saw the shadows around her feet slip and slither, fading into the cave behind her.

Legs trembling traitorously, she forced herself to move as far as she could from the white pillar and its unfading stain of blood before her strength gave way. She sank down on a stone and dragged in deep breaths, trying to clear the cobwebs of fear and confusion from her mind and heart.

The evil had returned to Cyrene, and Jurian was a world away.

She made her way slowly back to her father's palace, bits and fragments of prayers tumbling through her mind. From somewhere deep in her heart emerged the memory of Aelia Capitolina—the ancient city of Jerusalem, where Love had poured itself out for the sins of men. Her heart whispered that this love was strong enough, and more than strong enough, for what lay ahead, but her hands still shook with fear, and the words of accusation never faded from her thoughts.

Then, abruptly, she stopped in the middle of the street, not far from the Greek *agora*. As priestess of the darkness, she had taught the children the nobility of sacrifice. That it was an honor to be chosen to give one's life to the god.

She squeezed her eyes shut, remembering Ayzebel's brave sacrifice—her courage in the face of ruthless hate. She remembered Varro and his men, who had willingly given their lives in the arena. And now, she would tell Theodorus that the storm was coming…and she would have to tell the children who flocked to hear his stories that it was a high and noble thing to be called to give their lives for their faith.

Yes. The mercurial whisper in her mind curled itself around her grief. *You see, you can never truly leave the service of death. You have so much blood on your hands already. Have you not had enough of death? Have you not had enough? You can save them...all of them. When the time comes, you will understand.*

The voice released her and Sabra gasped, pressing her palms violently against her eyes.

"God," she mumbled, her voice thick with the heaviness of fear and grief, "please, give me the strength."

She bowed her head, then finally lowered her hands and staggered forward once again. Theodorus would know what to do. It wasn't her place to guide them. It was his. He was the shepherd—she was but a lamb in the flock.

The tree branches overhead shook in the windless night, leaves hissing against each other like a serpent's scales...or laughter.

You, a lamb? You delivered the lambs to the slaughter.

She shook her head violently and forced her steps onward. When she staggered into the peristyle of her father's house, Hanno was there waiting for her, hands in tight knots at his sides. But one look at her face and his worry shifted to fear, to dismay.

"Oh mistress," he said. "What happened?"

She waved him off. "Where is Theodorus?"

Hanno motioned for her to follow him, and they made their way quickly to the small *tablinum* in the palace where Theodorus waited for her. As soon as she entered the room, he rose from the low couch and came forward to take her hands.

"*Kyria,*" he said gently. "What has happened?"

Sabra opened her mouth, but nothing would come out. And the tears, which she had fought so hard to control, finally spilled over her cheeks in silent weeping. Theodorus led her to the couch and helped her to sit, then turned to Hanno.

"Fetch her some wine and something to eat," he said briskly.

Hanno bowed and slipped out of the room. Once he had

gone, Theodorus sat down beside Sabra, hands folded on his lap, and waited for her to speak. There was no impatience in his face, and Sabra was grateful—as she had been so many times in the past few weeks—for his gentleness and his understanding. It wasn't until Hanno returned and Sabra had taken a few sips of the diluted wine that she was able to find her voice.

But when she spoke, all she managed was, "It has returned."

Theodorus straightened, almost imperceptibly, and the glance he cast at Hanno was troubled. And Hanno—she could tell just from the way he stood there that he was reeling with fear, just as she was.

"You are sure?" Theodorus asked.

Sabra nodded. "I had a message from Jurian, some weeks ago now. He sent a warning. A storm is coming from the north, he said. And I...I can feel it, Theodorus." She shuddered and gripped the goblet of wine tightly in both her hands. "It spoke to me in the darkness. Terrible things. Things I..." She stopped and clamped her lips shut.

"Do not listen to lies, child," he cautioned.

"But that is the difficulty," she murmured, lifting her gaze to his face. "They were all true."

Theodorus sighed. "Many things seem true in the darkness that are false in the light," he said.

"Do you know what it is to be accused?" Sabra asked, her voice so low that Theodorus had to lean forward to hear her. "Do you know what it is to stand confronted with every evil thing you have ever done?" She choked on her tears, and her gaze wavered from his. "And I have done so much evil, Theodorus. So much."

Hanno moved suddenly from his post at the door to kneel in front of her. "You have done so much good, mistress," he said. "And you have turned from that evil!"

"Have I?" she whispered. "Why then does it still haunt me? Why am I still tormented by that voice?" She looked at Theodorus, wild grief in her heart. "I came back to Cyrene because I wanted to help my people. I wanted them to find peace. But how can I help them find peace when my heart is at war?"

Theodorus took her hand gently. "That is wisdom, Sabra. Tend first to your inner palace, and only then will you be in a place where you can do good for others."

She held his gaze for a long moment, a sudden weight of certainty falling over her. "I cannot stay here," she said, so quietly she almost couldn't hear her own words.

"No," Theodorus said. "Cyrene is the battlefield. First, you must train for war."

9

LONDINIUM, BRITANNIA — NOVEMBER, A.D. 300

Jurian saw very little of Constantinus in the days that followed their arrival. The Tribune stayed locked away with his father in the *Caesar's* private *tablinum*, and on the rare instance Jurian did catch sight of him, he thought the man looked like a trammeled maelstrom—all restless energy, and no way to use it. It wasn't until Constantius Chlorus held a feast almost a week later that Jurian was finally able to pin Constantinus down.

He found the Tribune standing near the side of the grand *triclinium*, cloaked in scarlet, watching the banquet's guests like a commander surveying a battlefield. Constantinus barely moved as Jurian joined him, and didn't say a word.

After a few moments of tense silence had passed, Jurian remarked, "You've been busy."

"Yes."

"Is something wrong?"

Constantinus shifted his weight, folding his arms. "Possibly," he said. "My father received a message, the same day we arrived in Britannia." He measured Jurian in silence, then glanced back over the feast hall. "It came from Nicomedia."

"Nicomedia?" Jurian echoed, trying to keep the alarm from

his voice.

"Not to worry. It was from my keeper," he said. The word was laced with bitterness. "*Caesar* Galerius requests my immediate return to the south. He apparently cannot manage his campaign along the Danuvius without my presence."

Jurian wanted to breathe a sigh of relief but couldn't, not with Constantinus standing beside him, looking like a volcano on the brink of eruption.

"I thought you were part of Diocletian's court," he said. The words sounded feeble, and they only earned him a dark glare from the Tribune.

"Oh, they both like to keep me as their private pet, depending on what use they have for me at the time," he said. "But by whatever gods there are, I am heartily sick of being passed between them like a tool or a bauble."

Jurian nodded. He felt a little sick, and the noise of the room swarmed around him, almost unbearably loud. "Does that mean you'll be leaving?"

"Do I have a choice?" Constantinus asked, blandly.

"When?"

Constantinus gave an indifferent gesture. "In a few weeks. I have some preparations to make, and Galerius has no way of knowing how quickly I would receive his summons. These things are always fluid." He finally turned to face Jurian, catching hold of his elbow. "Don't worry, Jurian. I won't leave you to the wolves. I will make sure you are safe before I go."

"Safely out of sight?"

His lips pressed in a thin line. "That too. Half of my father's court is still in Eboracum right now, but they will be coming to join him here in Londinium within the month. And the *Caesar* does not trust all of them. Nor, for that matter, do I."

"Where can I go?" Jurian asked. "Are you going to send me past the *limes* of Britannia after all?"

Constantinus opened his mouth to reply, but a sudden commotion in the *triclinium* interrupted him—a flurry of shouts and an inexplicable frenzy of excitement. Constantinus's hand went instantly to the hilt of his *pugio*. Then a great bear of a man in splendid robes strode into the *triclinium*, scattering guests and servants around him like autumn leaves, and Constantinus released his knife with a faint grin that caught Jurian by surprise.

Below, Constantius Chlorus pushed through the crowd to greet the older man, who folded him into a hearty embrace.

"Do you...know him?" Jurian murmured.

"What!" the man shouted suddenly, his huge hand on the *Caesar*'s shoulder. "He's here? Where is he?"

He scanned the crowd and his gaze lit on Constantinus. With a booming laugh, he parted the crowd like sheep and caught Constantinus in a bone-cracking embrace.

"As fine a man as could be hoped!" he cried. "By the divine, it's been too long! Let me look at you. I'm heartily glad to see you haven't been spoiled by life in the serpent's den!"

Constantinus looked almost embarrassed as the man held him at arm's length and appraised him, as if the Tribune were a growing boy yearning for a grandfather's approbation. Constantius Chlorus came to his son's rescue and laid a hand on the older man's shoulder.

"Come to table," he said. "Eat, and tell me what news from Camulodunum."

He led the man away, and Constantinus let out all his breath in a barely audible sigh.

"Who was that?" Jurian asked.

"That is Coel, my mother's father," Constantinus said, sounding a little rueful. He slanted Jurian a sidelong glance, one brow lifted, and nodded toward the two men. "Those two are cut from the same cloth, if you couldn't tell."

Jurian stifled a laugh. Constantinus—reserved, stern, self-possessed—could not possibly have been more different than either man. The Tribune was Helena's son, through and through.

"As far as I have ever heard, he doesn't often come to Londinium, or within half a league of my father's court. But perhaps he heard the brood of vipers is still absent." He pushed away from the pillar he had been leaning against, and touched Jurian's elbow. "Come. They're bringing out the food."

They went down and joined Constantius Chlorus and Coel at the high table. Coel insisted that Constantinus sit at his left hand, and Jurian took his place across the table from them both, with Agapius and Menas on either side of him.

Coel gave a low whistle, measuring Menas as the giant sat awkwardly at the table. "And here I thought I was the largest man in Britannia! What, did you dig up the very giants of legend to oust me from my place of glory?" he asked Constantinus. Then, to Menas, "Honor to you, friend. You look like you have a story to tell. Or many stories."

Menas inclined his head. "As we all do," he said.

"Yours I would like to hear."

"I would be glad," Menas said. "Another time, perhaps."

Coel studied him a moment longer, more sober than he had looked since he arrived, then grinned broadly and turned to say something to Constantius Chlorus.

A strange sadness swept over Jurian as he watched Menas, remembering suddenly the exaggerated stories the giant had once told to him and Mari in the mountain cave in Anatolia, not so very long ago. He'd made them both laugh until their sides ached, helping to pass the miserable hours as they waited out an endless blizzard. This Menas was not the same man. He had never lost his joy, but it was stiller now, and deeper. It was a broad and gentle river, not the quick bubbling of a mountain creek.

Jurian's thoughts were interrupted as the servants brought out roast boar and duck, and a myriad of other dishes Jurian had never seen or tasted before. The rich spices of the southern Empire were absent here, but there was something wholesome and hearty about the food that filled every empty corner of his stomach.

"Your father tells me you come recently from Rome," Coel said to Constantinus, hoisting a massive leg of roast fowl in one hand and a goblet of wine in the other. "What new plots are hatching in the court, eh? I tell you, my merchants here don't trust imperial silver. I hope your father's mint in Augusta Treverorum starts minting coin we can put our faith in! I've sent messengers...I've sent letters...but does Maximianus listen to my complaints? And how is my wool supposed to compete with linen from Egypt, I should like to know?"

Constantinus glanced at Jurian, a faint look of despair on his face, and Jurian hid a smile in his goblet. He couldn't blame Constantinus's discomfort—the economic workings of the Empire were never something Jurian had troubled himself about, but he'd seen enough of trade by now to know that prices were climbing, and that merchants were growing desperate.

"I—couldn't say," Constantinus said carefully.

"The boy is *Tribunus Angusticlavius* of the Jovians, Coel," Constantius Chlorus said. "Not some *denarius*-hoarding merchant from Carthage!"

"Was," Constantinus said, as if without thinking, then pursed his lips and held his peace.

But he had said enough to attract his father's attention. Constantius Chlorus snapped his gaze to his son's face, and all his good humor faded.

"What's that? What do you mean, was? Did that rat Galerius sabotage—?"

"No," Constantinus interrupted, lifting a hand. "Nothing like that. Diocletian named me *Tribunus et Comes Ordinis Primi*."

For a moment there was absolute silence, then the scowl vanished from Constantius Chlorus's face and he clapped Coel on the back with a great laugh. "You see?" he said. "That's a son fit to take his father's place in the Empire."

"A grandson fit to take his grandfather's place," Coel agreed. "I always said so." His gaze drifted over the row of faces across from him, settling at last on Jurian. "What's your story, then, you with the uncanny red hair?" he asked. "You are friend to my grandson? Legionary friend?"

"Yes," Jurian said. "I served under his command in Nicomedia and Rome."

"And what brings you to Britannia, then?" he asked. And then, with a brusque laugh, "Rome not to your taste, eh? Nasty climate. Attracts blood-sucking insects."

Jurian started to reply that Anatolia had more than enough pests of its own, then realized Coel wasn't talking about insects at all. For a split second he hesitated over his response, and he didn't dare look at Constantinus for help.

"I had an opportunity to come north with Constantinus, and I took it," he said at length. "In truth, I had my own reasons for coming."

Coel raised his heavy white brows with a bark of laughter. "A man with secrets," he said. "I can respect that. Tell me, boy. You've come from the south. You've seen things, I wager. You have a look in your eye of a seasoned soldier, but you can't be more than what, eighteen, twenty? So, what's your opinion on the state of the Empire? Where do Rome's enemies lie, outside the *limes*, or within her own chambers?"

Jurian held Coel's gaze for a moment, but he felt everyone's eyes on him—the *Caesar*, his attendants, Constantinus.

"Any governing body will have more than enough of both, I imagine," he said. Coel's eyes narrowed slightly, and Jurian added before he could stop himself, "And the enemies within aren't always the ones they say."

A slow smile inched across Coel's face. "Indeed," he said. "And is it true? Do men, women and even the little children find themselves condemned to death as entertainment for the mob? Have you seen what goes on in the arena? My daughter says it grows worse by the day."

Jurian wondered suddenly if Coel himself were a Christian— if that was, perhaps, where Helena had learned her faith.

"I have had no recent news from the south," he said. "But I do know your daughter a little, so if she says the violence is growing worse, I am sure it is so."

Coel's eyes sharpened suddenly, and he set the gnawed bone on his plate with a heavy thunk. "You've met her? My daughter?"

"In Nicomedia, yes." Jurian smiled. "I was with her great niece, Aikaterina of Alexandria."

"I know of this girl!" Coel exclaimed. "My daughter writes that she has a brilliant mind and a brave spirit. Much like my Helena. Dangerous traits, in times like these."

"You would like her, *avus*," Constantinus said suddenly.

"Well, but Alexandria!" Coel said, turning back to Jurian. "You have traveled far, then."

"Yes, I suppose I have," Jurian said. "But there is further to go still, I think."

"Oh? You have plans that will lead you further abroad? You have already come to the utmost reaches of the Empire. There is no further to go, unless you plan to come and stay with me in Camulodunum?" Coel asked, his eyes twinkling at Constantinus. "I could use a man like you in my court."

Jurian caught himself smiling. Somehow he could imagine making a place for himself in Coel's court, making a life there.

It could be a good life, he thought. *One where at least we would be free.*

We.

His heart warmed suddenly, because he wasn't thinking of Agapius or Menas, or even Constantinus, at all.

With his thoughts turned to Sabra, he almost didn't hear Constantinus say, "There is something he must do first. Once he has, I may have use for him for a while longer, then he is free to go and do what he will."

"And those other two?" Coel asked. "Are they under your command as well?"

"We are bound to no one," Menas said quietly.

"Ha! I like this man!" Coel cried, tipping his goblet toward Menas. "If you won't let me have that one, send this one instead! He's a mighty man. I like his steadiness."

Constantinus laughed. "*Avus*," he said, "you just heard the man. He is not mine to command."

Jurian glanced at Menas. His head was down, his one good eye fixed on his plate. But that expression on his face... Jurian's heart surged with dismay within him. Would Menas actually consider such a proposition?

And then, as his feeling of shock gave way, Jurian hoped that he would.

WHEN THE FEAST HAD ended, and the guests had faded away like sparks in the night, Jurian found Constantinus in one of the inner palace courtyards, standing next to a bronze brazier in a light flurry of snow. The Tribune startled a little when Jurian stopped beside him, then welcomed him with a faint smile.

"Your grandfather," Jurian said. "He's...not exactly Roman, is he?"

Constantinus laughed softly. "Not exactly," he said. "He will always be more Britannic than Roman, till the day he dies. He's a good man. Even if he stands apart, he has been a great ally to my father in these lands."

"Did he mind that his daughter married a Roman *praefectus*?"

"At first he did," Constantinus said. "For years he circulated a rumor that my father hadn't married his daughter at all, but some stable-maid from Bithynia, or some gods-forsaken place near there. He didn't want anyone to know that his family was allied through marriage with the Empire." He shrugged, contemplating the burning embers in the brazier. "Well, he eventually accepted the fact, but by then, his daughter was living in effective exile in Anatolia, far from the embrace of the man she loved. And all for political advantage."

He spoke bitterly, and Jurian regarded him in silence for a few moments. Constantinus was a man of many secrets, and Jurian couldn't help wondering if he was speaking of more than just his mother Helena. But he didn't feel he had any right to inquire too closely, so he just nodded and kept his questions to himself.

"Well, Jurian," Constantinus said abruptly. "I think I have the solution to the problem we were discussing earlier. I must go south, but you...how would you like to stay in Camulodunum until my return? Coel would let no harm come to you. Nor, for that matter, would my father."

Jurian's mouth dropped open in surprise. He hadn't even dared to imagine the possibility of taking up Coel's invitation.

"I can't think of a better place for us," he said. He waved a hand toward his shoulder—Excalibur was in his *cubiculum*, but the gesture was still as natural as breathing. "But what about my task?"

"Are you in that much of a hurry to get rid of your sword?" Constantinus asked.

There was a more subtle question implied behind the words, but Jurian wasn't quite sure what to make of it. He chose to ignore it instead. "It weighs on my mind," he admitted. "I won't be able to rest, or move forward with my life, until I've unraveled that mystery."

"And you're certain you were meant to leave that sword here?" he asked. "This prophecy you speak of—how do you know it was not simply meant to bring you to Britannia?"

Jurian shook his head. There was a darkness in his thoughts that haunted his waking moments, a shadow that he had been trying for weeks to drive away. He hadn't spoken of it to anyone, not even Menas, but somehow he heard himself telling Constantinus, "The sword belongs in Britannia. It belongs *to* Britannia. And as for myself, I could see myself making a life here. Finding a home here. But, I honestly don't know that I will ever belong here. There's something about this place that I love more than any other place I have been, but…I don't know. I'm being foolish, perhaps."

"Britannia needs you, Georgius," Constantinus said softly, then turned to head back into the palace. "Leave these worries for tomorrow, or tomorrow's tomorrow. There will be time enough for that in the months to come. When I come back from the South, if you haven't figured out where you are meant to take that sword, I promise you I will do my best to help you."

And with that he was gone, before Jurian even had a chance to thank him.

10

Cyrene, Libya — December, a.d. 300

It was a clear day in early winter, the cold sun shining crisply on the streets of Cyrene and the wind brisk and clean from the north, but Sabra was closeted in her inner chamber with her head in her arms. She had been trying desperately to figure out where she ought to go—where she could go—but the torment in her mind gave her no clarity to think. Her traveling trunk lay open against the wall, empty.

Sitting beside her was Hanno, patient as the hills, his hands clasped loosely on his knees. He hadn't said anything for at least an hour, but he hadn't moved, either.

"I need to talk to Theodorus," Sabra said at last, lifting her face. Hanno simply nodded and stood, but panic rushed over Sabra and she scrambled to her feet after him. "No, don't leave me alone. I'll go with you."

He gave her a small, anxious smile and nodded again, and together they left the governor's palace and followed the familiar path down to Theodorus's home. They found the *episcopus* within his *tablinum*, carefully copying out a text that someone had brought him from Alexandria. As they were admitted into the room he favored them both with a kind smile, but he didn't stop his work until he had reached the end of the passage.

Then he sat back, regarding his handiwork with satisfaction, and pushed both *codices* to the side of his desk.

"Sabra, *kyria*, what can I do for you?" he asked, gesturing for them to sit. "Were you not planning to leave, to find refuge somewhere away from this troubled place?"

"I was," she said. "But I can't seem to think...I don't know where to go."

He tipped his head, stroking his beard thoughtfully. "Why not go to Alexandria? I have a daughter in the faith, Synkletika, who governs a community of women consecrated to God just outside the city. They live their days in prayer and work, and might help you in your struggle."

Sabra bowed her head. "I've already been consecrated once," she said, hollowly. "If they've found peace in that life, I envy them that, but I can't go back to it."

He regarded her a moment, a thoughtful light in his eyes, then he nodded. "I understand that. And you can not learn to face the world by withdrawing from it, and I think that you, daughter, are meant to be a light for the world, not a fire hidden underground."

Sabra shivered, remembering the temple of the old god where she had spent so many years of her life, hidden at the heart of a labyrinth, with only a single fire to chase away the shadows.

"Could your friend Aikaterina give you solace?"

Sabra shook her head. "She has more than enough on her mind, without me burdening her."

"Ah, yes. Her father's illness." Theodorus got to his feet, pacing back and forth as he thought. "What of Rome? You made a few acquaintances there, didn't you?"

Sabra shook her head. She would have gladly renewed her acquaintance with the healer Anastasia, but the thought of Rome tormented her almost as much as the shadow in the hills of Cyrene.

Finally she sighed and said, "I keep thinking of a man I met once…or, twice, perhaps. He was dear to Jurian. Only, I don't know where to find him. He has always found me, before."

"What was his name?" Theodorus asked.

"Nikolaos."

"Nikolaos!" Theodorus exclaimed, and his sudden laugh startled Sabra into a hesitant smile. "That rascal. I wish I knew how he could get from one place to another as fast as he does. He always seems to know precisely where he's needed."

"You know him?" Sabra asked, astonished.

"Honestly, I'm not sure if there's anyone in the faith who *doesn't* know Nikolaos." Theodorus stopped beside her, patting her arm. "He lives in Myra, in Anatolia. And if anyone can guide you in the arts of spiritual warfare, it is he."

"Myra," Hanno said. "That is not very far from here."

Sabra sank down on Theodorus's low bench and covered her face with her hands, her mind, for once, at perfect peace. "I'll leave before the week is out," she said. She glanced up at Hanno. "And…"

"I'm going with you, mistress," Hanno said. "Do you even have to ask?"

11

CAMULODUNUM, BRITANNIA — DECEMBER, A.D. 300

CONSTANTINUS STAYED THREE WEEKS IN HIS FATHER'S COURT BEFORE he finally declared he was ready to leave. Jurian and the others stood in the palace courtyard, cold and miserable in a mix of sleet and snow, watching the servants lead out Constantinus's horse. The Tribune stood a little apart from them in a fur-lined scarlet cloak, twining leather wraps around his hands against the bitter chill. His face was set, expressionless, but Jurian could sense the frustration and anger roiling inside him. Finally he finished with the wraps and dusted his hands off on his wool tunic, and turned to face Jurian and his friends.

"You all look like you're at a funeral," he said, sweeping an inscrutable gaze over them. "I won't be gone forever." He clasped Jurian's arm, then pulled him into an embrace. "Take care of your friends while I'm gone," he said. "And take care of yourself. If you can help it, stay clear of Londinium and Eboracum, and my father's court."

Jurian nodded. "Stay safe."

Constantinus snorted softly, giving him a look that was almost reproachful. "Safety is an illusion," he said.

"What will you tell Galerius, if he asks about me?"

"I'll tell him I left you in barbarian hands," he said.

Jurian laughed and nodded, and Constantinus turned to bid farewell to Agapius and Menas.

Menas planted a large hand on his shoulder. "We will miss you, Tribune," he rumbled. His gaze drifted over to rest on Eilwen and Brigit who stood close by, holding hands, and he added placidly, "Some of us perhaps more than others."

Jurian stared, because—he was sure he didn't imagine it—a faint blush crept over Constantinus's face at Menas's words. His curiosity piqued, Jurian watched hawkishly as Constantinus turned to say goodbye to the two girls. Eilwen threw her arms around his neck and hugged him briefly, but Brigit just stared icily at him, arms folded, until Constantinus held his hand out toward her. She finally gave in, but glanced away as she held out her own. Constantinus took it and kissed it, which brought her gaze flashing, startled, back to his.

But he didn't say a word, only took his horse from the waiting servant and swung into the saddle, and cantered through the gate without a backwards glance.

Brigit turned and saw them all staring at her, and she flung a hand toward them in exasperation. "*Eu, apage,*" she grumbled.

Agapius burst out laughing.

"You taught her to say *go away?*" Jurian asked Menas, stifling a grin as Brigit glared at Agapius.

Menas shrugged his broad shoulders. "I thought it would be a useful thing for her to know," he said.

THEY LEFT LONDINIUM SHORTLY after Constantinus's departure. Jurian and Menas had agreed it would be best for them to leave the city the same day as Constantinus—while the Tribune was in the *Caesar*'s court, Jurian and his friends were under his protection, but when he left, Jurian knew they would be open to all the suspicion and questions that Constantinus had shielded them from. And Jurian was still unsure how far the *Caesar*'s favor would extend without his son there to intercede on their behalf.

It was a day and a half journey to the court of Coel in

Camulodunum, and the snow fell steadily the entire time. Agapius grumbled constantly—he had never seen snow before Britannia, and he was not in any way enjoying the experience. Every time they stopped to rest the horses, he tried to warm himself by blowing into his hands and stamping his feet, muttering under his breath about civilized regions of the world with civilized climates.

Jurian couldn't blame him. Satala had seen hard enough winters, but there was something about Britannia's gnawing damp that had wormed its way into his bones. He was just grateful that the land was gentle, not the rugged mountains of Anatolia. Menas endured the cold with the steady patience of an ox, and only Brigit and Eilwen seemed at all happy about the snowfall. They cantered their horses in circles around the others, chasing each other over the hills and back again, until Agapius groaned and leaned over his horse's neck.

"I'm exhausted just watching them. Can't you make them stop?" he muttered.

"I'm certain Constantinus could make them stop," Menas said, without the least inflection.

Agapius stared at Jurian, and they both burst into laughter. At just that moment the girls rode up to join them, and Brigit glared at each of them in turn.

"What you laughing, foolish boys?" she asked in extremely broken Latin, which only made Agapius laugh harder.

Brigit turned without ceremony and slapped his horse hard on the haunches, and sat back with a smirk as it bolted away. Eilwen spurred her horse after him, laughing merrily.

"They are insane," Jurian said.

Menas chuckled. "They are Britannic. They are never quite so happy as when they're at war."

They arrived at Camulodunum late in the afternoon, and skirted around the city walls to the southern gate because the western gate of the city had been barricaded against the threat of Saxon raiders. The town was a bustle of activity, and no one paid much attention to the odd collection of riders passing down the broad paved streets. Without Constantinus to lead them, Jurian found himself reluctantly riding at the head of the group, directing them toward a massive stone *castra* that looked like it had been rebuilt one too many times over one too many centuries.

Coel himself came out to greet them as they rode up to the fortress, dressed in flagrantly imperial purple as if he were trying to give offense to Diocletian from over three thousand miles away.

"Welcome, friends!" he shouted, his voice echoing off the stone walls of the fortress.

Jurian's horse tossed his head at the noise, but Jurian only jumped down and accepted Coel's hearty embrace. As soon as two stablehands had scurried into the courtyard to take their horses, Coel led them up into the old fortress. If it had been Roman at one point, Jurian realized, it had shifted since that time, melding over the centuries into an almost barbarian style. There was more wood inside that fortress than Jurian had ever seen inside a building, from the floors to the rafters high above, and even, in some places, lining the walls. It made him feel a little like he was walking within a forest, barely cultivated by human hands. And, Jurian decided, it was now far more of a palace than a utilitarian military garrison.

A servant showed Jurian to a *cubiculum* that had the same foreign feel as the rest of the palace. The bed was covered with furs and the floor scattered with thick pelts. There were heavy iron brackets fixed to the dark wood walls, holding flaming torches that couldn't quite chase the shadows from the room. The wood and firelight wrapped around him like a warm blanket, and after settling Excalibur against the wall, Jurian threw himself unceremoniously on the bed with its nest of coarse furs. He couldn't remember falling asleep, but the next thing he knew, someone was hammering on his door—and sounded like he had been for some time.

When Jurian reoriented himself enough to make it to the door, he found a servant waiting in the corridor to take him to the *triclinium*. All of his friends were already there, and they were watching the doorway as if they, too, had been waiting too long for him.

"Finally," Agapius said, waving him toward the table. "Come have something to eat."

"Benches," Jurian said, eyeing the long boards surrounding the table with a skeptical look. "Benches inside. For dining on."

"Barbarian," Agapius whispered.

Brigit and Eilwen just rolled their eyes at him and turned back to Menas, whom they were trying, unsuccessfully, to coax down onto the bench beside them. He shook his head, staring at the bench just as warily as Jurian.

"I'm afraid it will tip over if I sit on it," he said. "But they won't listen."

Coel entered the hall at that minute, and laughed aloud when he saw Menas's face. "I don't blame you. Sit in my chair, man, and be welcome to it!" he said, waving Menas toward a massive, rough-carved wooden chair at one end of the table. As Menas went obediently to sit down, Coel chuckled and shook his head. "What will my people think if they see this? They'll believe Woden *Jolfaedr* has come to preside over our *Jol* in person, and will I be able to persuade them otherwise?"

"What is the *Jol*?" Menas asked, a faint look of horror on his face.

"Ah, it's a tradition in many parts of the world up here," Coel said, waving a hand. "Burning a large clog of wood, celebrating the night when Woden rides free through the sky on his wild hunt. But I think, if I am not mistaken, that you will all have another reason to celebrate tonight?"

"What day is it?" Jurian asked.

"What month is it?" Agapius asked, at almost the same moment.

Coel's laughter boomed through the hall. "Tomorrow marks the eighth day from the *kalends* of Januarius."

Jurian jolted and looked at Menas, whose look of horror faded instantly into joy. Jurian wanted to share his happiness, but a shard of grief twisted in his heart—the year before, when they had celebrated the Nativity with Nikolaos, Mari had been with them. Had a year truly passed since that day? It seemed to have escaped in the blink of an eye, and he could still remember every moment of that night as if it had just happened.

"You know what we celebrate?" Agapius asked Coel, cautiously.

Coel regarded him with suppressed amusement. "If you celebrate the same feast that I am celebrating, then, yes. Sadly not all of my people share our beliefs, but they know enough not to interfere with my feasting. Woe to the man that gets in the way of that!" He sat down, gingerly, on the bench beside Jurian and plucked a chunk of ham from the slab in the center of the table. "Maybe if Woden-among-us teaches them the meaning of the *Nativitas*, they will give up their misguided ways."

"Do you think they would?" Menas asked, his one eye widening.

"Perhaps." Coel polished off the slice of ham in a single bite, slapped a hand on the table, and got back to his feet. "Come find me after you've supped. I have an idea."

THEY FOUND COEL OUT in front of the fortress as the day stretched into evening. The town was ablaze with light. Some of the homes were adorned with holly berries and sprigs of other plants that Jurian had never seen before, while others were lit more somberly with tallow candles or oil lamps in a quieter sort of expectation. A number of people had gathered out on the street leading up to the fortress, and all eyes were watching Coel and his guests. A handful of soldiers—Coel's personal garrison, who did not march under the sign of the eagle—milled about behind them.

"I've never given up the *jol-clog*," Coel told his guests. "I like the fire. I like the feasting! Good idea, that, spreading the feast out over days. And maybe part of me always hoped my people would see it as a bridge to the stable in Bethlehem. But I can't see how to persuade them of it."

"Where is this log?" Menas asked.

"My men have brought it to the end of the street there. I told them to leave it there until I could decide what to do with it."

Menas's face broke out in a sudden smile, and he rested his hand on Coel's shoulder. "Leave it to me," he said.

Jurian went with him, partly out of curiosity, partly to offer his help if Menas needed it. As they walked down the street, the people parted around them, some falling to their knees, invoking Woden with reverent whispers. Menas walked stiffly through their midst, keeping his gaze fixed on the massive log settled in the snow at the end of the road. Four men stood around it—the four men who had dragged the thing this far into the town—and now waited patiently to be told what to do.

"Stand back," Menas said, and they obediently moved away from the log.

Without another word, the giant crouched down and wrapped his arms around the width of the log, then, with one powerful motion, lifted the whole thing onto his back and stood upright. Jurian stepped back, staring at his friend in astonishment, while the four men looked like they truly had seen a deity in the flesh. Menas met Jurian's gaze and nodded once, then turned to carry the log down the street toward the fortress.

"Woden," someone called out. "Woden bears the *jol-clog!*"

All the people followed him down the road, echoing the words, until a massive crowd had gathered around the fortress courtyard. When he reached Coel, Menas stopped and turned to face the people.

"I am not Woden," he said, his voice booming out, silencing the crowd. "I am only a humble servant of the one God, the true God, the Christ, whom I once carried across a river as I now carry this wood. The Christ, who carried the Tree of the Cross as I now carry this wood, and who gave His life upon it for your salvation. He burned away the guilt of your transgressions as the wood of this log will now be burned. The light of His divinity banishes all shadows of death and sin as the light of this fire will now banish the winter darkness. I preach the Christ, whose birth we celebrate tonight, the Tree of Life, the Light of the World."

With that, he turned and carried the log into the fortress. The people stared after him, silent, wondering.

Agapius, standing close to some of the onlookers, said in Latin just loud enough for them to hear, "The *Christophorus*."

The title was echoed, wonderingly, by someone near him, then another. Little by little a swell of murmured conversation rose up, and Jurian watched as the crowd slowly dispersed.

"They don't know what to think," he said to Coel.

"The seed has been planted," Coel said, clapping him on the shoulder. "Give it time. Now come, and join my feast! I daresay you've never seen a banquet like the one we'll share tonight!"

12

Myra, Anatolia — December, A.D. 300

The bow of the ship plunged into the winter gray waves, spraying Sabra with the sharp tang of salt water. The sky had been lowering all day, threatening rain or snow, but Sabra hoped it would hold off until they put into port. She thought she would go mad if she were confined below decks—it was only the open sky and the open sea, and the noisy rush of the waves against the ship's hull, that had kept the voice in her mind at bay since she had left Cyrene.

The Andriake port was just visible now, half-shrouded in damp cloud. All around her the sailors scrambled, making their final preparations to navigate the passage into the harbor. Sabra took a deep breath and retreated as far from the hectic bustle as she could, perching on a coil of rope in the stern of the boat, where, on a vessel not unlike this one, she had once sat and talked to Jurian. It felt like a lifetime ago, and yet she remembered every moment of it like it had been yesterday.

That was the voyage when she had first seen Nikolaos, sitting along the quay in Carthago, giving them a distraction so she, Jurian and Menas could get safely back to their ship. He had known precisely what they had needed, without them even having to ask.

Perhaps he will know what I need. And maybe he will have guidance for me as he once did for Jurian, she thought. *God knows I need it.*

The ship made its way into the harbor and soon nosed up alongside the quay. The sailors heaved the lead and wooden anchor over the bulwark, and it dropped into the choppy water below with a loud splash. As soon as the vessel was secure, the sailors ran out the ramp and began unloading their cargo.

Hanno emerged from below decks, already laden with their luggage, and Sabra gave him a faint smile.

"I'm only sorry I won't be announcing the arrival of the *filia regis*," he told her with a taunting grin.

She laughed as she followed him down the ramp, and the sound surprised her—she hadn't realized how long it had been since she had truly laughed.

Almost as soon as she had stepped off the ship, the clean, sharp tang of the sea was replaced by the stench of days' old seafood and unwashed bodies, and the acrid smoke from burning damp wood. And somewhere behind it all was a putrid stench unlike anything Sabra had ever smelled. She stopped and pressed the back of her hand against her mouth and nose, wondering how the people on the docks could stand the smell, day after day. Even Hanno wrinkled his nose.

"The *purpura* dye," he said after a moment. "I believe they make it here."

"It smells like rotting fish," Sabra said, and shuddered. "How can something so beautiful smell so foul?"

That brought a grin to Hanno's face, and Sabra followed close behind him as he carried their belongings toward a ramshackle *taberna* that stood near the quay.

Though it didn't look like much on the outside, inside it was clean enough, and the floors were well scoured. A bright fire burned on the hearth, and the few sailors gathered around the tables seemed more like merchants than the rougher sort of deck hands who spent their shore leave drowning in *posca*.

Hanno led the way to a small alcove near the fire and then

went to secure her a room for the night. When she tried to protest that she hadn't come to Myra to stay in an inn, he merely looked at her and went anyway.

He's probably right, Sabra thought, stretching her chilled fingers toward the fire. *I don't even know where to begin looking for Nikolaos. It would be just my luck if he's not here any longer.*

"And why should he not still be here?" said a cheerful voice beside her.

Sabra startled in alarm, only to find a small, bald-headed man at her elbow, watching her through dark, twinkling eyes. He gestured to the seat across from her with a questioning glance, and she nodded mutely.

"Well," he said, taking a seat and planting his hands on his knees. "Now that we've established that I'm here, tell me why you are."

Sabra frowned at him, a nagging sensation tugging at the back of her mind. There was something *very* familiar about his face, but she wasn't sure...

He broke into a merry chuckle. "That bad, eh?" he said. "It's not every day I get to rescue princesses."

"You!" she gasped, lifting a finger to point at him. "It *is* you! I've come looking for you...but how did you know I was here?"

"How did I? I know many things, and I couldn't say how." He stared up at the ceiling and lifted his shoulders. "I just see what I see and know what I know." After a moment he sat forward, his gaze on her once more, its keenness tempered with pity. "It is an unfortunate necessity that has driven you across the sea to my door," he said.

"You see that too?" Sabra murmured.

Nikolaos smiled gently. "It doesn't take a mystic to see your torment," he said. "But come. You can tell me everything once you are safely home."

Sabra flinched. "I have no home," she murmured. "Ever since I returned from Rome, I've felt...adrift. My childhood home feels foreign to me now, and there is nowhere I feel welcome..."

"You are welcome in Myra," Nikolaos said, looking her intently in the eye. "Here you have a home."

He rose as Hanno returned, still laden with all their luggage, face fixed in a faint scowl.

"What's the matter?" Sabra asked.

"The keeper said there is no room," Hanno said. "I even offered him twice his stated price, and he would have nothing of it." He looked down at his feet. "I even told him I was escorting a princess, and that didn't work either."

Sabra wanted to laugh, but Hanno looked so distraught at his failure that she couldn't.

Nikolaos rocked on his heels. "No room in the inn, eh?" he said, his dark eyes twinkling at Sabra. "Then it seems you must take me up on my offer of hospitality," he said.

Sabra stared at him in astonishment. "How did you understand that? He was speaking to me in Punic!" she cried. "You spoke to me in Greek, but…"

Nikolaos just gave her a subtle wink and folded his hands, regarding Hanno patiently. Hanno looked him up and down, twice, then turned to Sabra.

"Who is this?" he asked.

"Who do you think?" Sabra asked, smiling in earnest. "This is Nikolaos."

Hanno, his face shifting from surprise to embarrassment, adjusted his grip on the luggage, but couldn't free a hand to clasp Nikolaos's. Nikolaos only laughed and put a hand on his shoulder.

"Hanno, I am pleased to meet you," he said.

"Did you—" Hanno started, flashing a glance at Sabra, who shook her head with a bemused grin.

Nikolaos turned to leave, but said over his shoulder, "Come along, *falakros!*"

Hanno's brows flew up in surprise, but Nikolaos just winked at Sabra and led the way out of the *taberna*. They followed him through a small market, and soon they had left the town behind. The paved road gave way to a simple dirt track. Up ahead, at the very end of the lane, Sabra saw a small house in the Greek style, with a carved fish at the doorway.

"Here we are!" Nikolaos said, unlatching the door and showing them inside.

The inner courtyard was sparse in the winter chill, but in the bright glow of a fire and a dozen candles it somehow felt inviting, as if cold stone could somehow carry its own warmth. Sabra sat down on a bronze bench at the table and Hanno set down their bags in the corner, near a flight of wooden steps which led, Sabra supposed, to the sleeping quarters. Nikolaos vanished through a narrow doorway into the kitchen, and soon the rich smell of roasting meat and bread wafted through the courtyard.

Hanno settled on the bench across from Sabra and folded his hands. "Well," he said. "That's that."

Sabra said nothing. She rubbed her finger along the grain of the table, shivering a little as she thought that maybe Jurian had once sat in this very place, not so very long ago. It was such a strange feeling—finding these places where the memories of the past and the life of the present seemed to weave together. She had felt it most strongly in Aelia Capitolina, at the place where Christ had embraced the Cross, but even here there was the sense that the world and time were much…smaller.

Nikolaos soon bustled out with thick slices of roasted ham and hot, fresh flatbread dusted with herbs and salt. There was a jar of fresh honey and some aged cheese, and olive oil that was far finer than any Sabra had ever tasted. Nikolaos brought wine too, which he mixed for Hanno, but Sabra shook her head and poured herself water.

"Jurian would have appreciated this," Sabra said as Nikolaos took his place next to Hanno.

"It was exactly a year ago that I first broke bread with Jurian," Nikolaos said with a delighted smile, tearing the bread in chunks and handing a piece to her. "To celebrate his birthday, and the birth of Him who is the Firstborn of all creation."

"Wait," Sabra said, startled. "Today?"

She glanced at Hanno, who sat frozen with the bread halfway to his mouth.

Nikolaos laughed and shook his head. "Nothing is a coincidence, daughter," he said. "Today is the eve of the Nativity. Did you know that Jurian shares a birthday with our Lord?"

"I didn't," she said, and couldn't keep the smile from her face.

Nikolaos closed his eyes for a moment, then nodded his head slowly. "Ah, Jurian. And my dear friend Menas. All is well."

Sabra looked at him sharply. "What do you mean, all is well? How can you possibly know that?" Her voice caught in her throat. "Can you…can you see them?"

"In a way, I suppose I can."

He dipped his bread in some olive oil, eating it contentedly as if he hadn't just said something completely unbelievable. Sabra shivered again. Maybe that was what gave this place that feeling that it didn't quite belong to this world. Maybe it wasn't the place. Maybe it was the man himself.

"And now," Nikolaos said, drizzling some honey over his crumbled cheese and sopping it with the rest of his bread. "You were going to tell me why you have come."

"If you have the sight," Sabra said quietly, "I should think you would already know."

"Perhaps I do."

"Then why will you make me speak of such things?"

Nikolaos set down his spear of bread and regarded her with sudden sharpness. "There is a shadow clinging to you," he said. "Blurring the edges of the light."

Hanno closed his eyes, lips moving in a silent prayer, but Nikolaos ignored him and watched Sabra steadily. She was shivering uncontrollably now.

"The sins of my past will not let me go," she said.

"I loosed those chains, and you chose to let them go, on the hill of bones not so long ago," Nikolaos said. "Why are you choosing to take them up again?"

Sabra's eyes filled with tears. "You think this is my choice?" she said. "I didn't ask for this...for any of this." She bowed her head. "All I ever wanted...the only thing I ever wanted in my whole life...was peace. Peace for my father, peace for my people, peace within me, and peace with God." She lifted her eyes to Nikolaos's face, feeling the burn of fear and frustration tighten her throat. "And yet, here I am. An exile, hunted and haunted by the sins of my past."

The sharpness had gone from Nikolaos's face, replaced with only gentle pity and love. "To long for peace is to desire God," he said. "But some of us must wait longer than others to find Him."

Sabra glanced away. "I don't know what that means," she muttered.

"Will you let me teach you?"

"I was hoping you would," she said, holding his gaze briefly. "I'm at war in my own mind, and I have no weapons to fight."

"Then put on the armor of God," Nikolaos said, "and take up the sword of the Spirit." He reached across the table suddenly to clasp her hand, his eyes intent on her face. "You are in a dark night, daughter—the tenth region of the night—but not alone."

She nodded. She felt suddenly, inexplicably weary, in every last bone and sinew, as if she had been staggering under a heavy weight for far too long. The voice in her mind was silent, at least, but she felt no peace, only a faint stirring of hope.

"I'm tired," she said. "Please, is there somewhere I might sleep for the night?"

Nikolaos pointed to the stairs. "I took the liberty of preparing a place for you," he said, and when she frowned at him, bewildered, he only grinned.

With a murmured goodnight, Sabra left him and Hanno to finish their meal and pulled herself slowly up the stairs. The upper *cubiculum* had indeed been readied as if for a guest. A cot with a mattress freshly stuffed with fragrant grasses sat against the wall, and a wooden table held a small amber vase with a bright sprig of lavender—lavender, too fresh and too bright for the winter month. Sabra touched it briefly, then bent to smell it. It was spicy, and somehow the scent of it tugged at her heart like a voice calling her name.

She lay down on the cot and pulled the woolen blankets up to her chin. Through the narrow window she could hear the gentle rush of the ocean, mingling with Nikolaos's soft, mellow voice as he sang a hymn for the Nativity until it sounded like his voice was part of the sea, and part of the night. It soothed the tangle of worry from her mind, and coaxed her gently to sleep.

13

Myra, Anatolia — December, A.D. 300

The next morning, Sabra stood alone in the cold wind and the early grey light, watching the waves crash against the sea wall. She had hoped the noise of the sea would drown out the torment in her mind, but the voice only grew louder, more insistent, as the words it had spoken in the cave wreathed through her memory.

You are alone, as you have always been alone, and will always be alone. You will be left behind. You will always be left behind.

Do not dare to call on love, with your garment stained in the blood of children.

Sabra shuddered and tried to cover her ears with her coarse traveling *palla*, but as she stared at the wet sand where the waves receded, all she could see was blood. The waves were red, and the sand was red.

No, she whispered to herself. *Not here. Not here too.*

No matter where she went, death followed. Horror and pain and confusion.

She crouched down, burying her head in her arms.

You think you know now what it means to be alone, but only wait. The time will come—

"Be still," someone said, and there was a hand on her head,

calm and steady.

And the voice fell silent.

Sabra lifted her face and found Nikolaos standing just behind her, watching her gravely. He sat down after a moment, cross-legged in the sand, and Sabra shifted her weight to sit beside him. Feeling suddenly self-conscious, she stared at the foam on the sand, and refused to look at him again. But she could feel his gaze steady on her face for a long while, then he turned and faced the sea.

"Hanno was worried about you," he said. "I told him I would find you."

Sabra nodded.

"I want to tell you a story," he said, "and when I am through, you can tell me what troubles you."

She lifted a hand in acquiescence. After all, she had come to Myra to learn from Nikolaos. How could she blame anyone but herself if she refused the lessons he had to teach her?

"Now," Nikolaos said. "Perhaps you have heard that Our Lord the Christ, when He walked among us on this earth, had dear friends who followed Him throughout his earthly mission. Among those friends was a young woman named Mariam, called the Magdalene. She had done much wrong in her life. The stories say that the Savior banished seven demons from her soul."

Sabra shuddered. "Seven?" she murmured. "So many!" Shame and guilt and a deep, endless horror wove through her heart, and she kept her gaze lowered, as if Nikolaos would see it if she glanced his way. "You know where I have been. What darkness I have seen…and served."

Nikolaos did not answer immediately, and Sabra, staring at her fingers twisted in her lap, felt the heaviness of the silence settle on her. Even through the endless rush of the waves on the sand, she could hear the thin whisper of the voice again, quiet in the back of her mind, accusing her, mortifying her. She wondered if Nikolaos could hear it too. She wished in vain that he would lay his hand on her head again, and bid the voice be silent.

"You think that because you have served the darkness that you can never be free," Nikolaos said. "That you can never walk in the light."

Sabra glanced up. It wasn't a question, nor was it completely a statement of fact. Nikolaos had his head tilted just to the side, as if he were listening. Then he drew himself upright with a sharp glance at her face.

"You should not listen to that voice," he said. "Listen instead to the voice of the Magdalene."

"But you have no idea..." Sabra stopped, but her throat tightened, trapping the words inside her. *No idea what I've done.*

"No, I don't. And you have no idea what I have done," Nikolaos said. He lifted his shoulders and dropped them again. "Do you think it matters, if I know? If anyone knows? The God who sees all things knows. He knows, and He loves." Sabra said nothing, and Nikolaos laid a hand gently on her shoulder. "It frightens you to hear that, to think that God knows every worst moment of your life. But even the hearts most darkened can be brought to life again," he said. "Just as eyes that are darkened can be made once more to see."

He withdrew his hand and Sabra caught in a shaking breath. "What happened to her, after that? The Magdalene?"

"After that? She followed the Savior. Love draws all after itself and to itself. She followed its call even to the foot of the Cross. She was there with His own Mother, and then after three days, it was she who discovered the empty tomb. She was the first to witness the glory of the Resurrection. Such was the reward of love that Love gave her."

"But how?" she said, a little hoarse. "How could she...have just stood there, at the foot of the Cross? And watched..."

"I should think you know something of that strength—to bear love all the way to the uttermost."

"Why do you say things like that? How could you know about that?" Sabra cried, surprising herself with the vehemence in her voice.

"I think we hear the pieces of stories that strike something in our own experience—that give us food for our present journey. I told the story of the Magdalene once to Jurian's sister, before they left Myra. She heard the Magdalene's part in the Resurrection—a witness to the truth, a believer in the face of unbelief. But you heard her part at the foot of the Cross. And so that makes me think that you have seen something of that in your life."

Sabra shuddered, remembering Varro's face, and the quiet acceptance of his soldiers in the face of death. Being unable to do anything but sit, and watch.

"Yes," she whispered. "And I do not think I can endure it."

"Love endures all things," he said. "And hopes all things. There may be darkness around you and even within you, but only remember that the light is stronger than the darkness, especially when the darkness seems to overwhelm it." He leaned back on his hands and tipped his head to study her. "Now, would you like to tell me what troubles you?"

"I don't want to be tormented," Sabra said after a long silence. She wasn't sure how to capture everything she felt in sensible words, but she determined to try. "Jurian's faith is so strong, like a beacon, guiding and undergirding everything he does. I wish I had a faith like his, but every time I think I am certain, I'm haunted by my past. And I doubt…I doubt that I could ever be loved."

"Jurian's faith was not always so strong," Nikolaos said. "And he has been sorely tried, and will be sorely tried again. You say you are haunted by your past? You are not alone in that."

You are always alone…

"See," Sabra cried, frustration surging within her. "When you say that, I hear this voice in my head contradicting you. When I listen to the words of the Psalms, the voice is there to steal the joy of them from my heart. I've prayed, and I've prayed, and it never changes. Why? Isn't that just proof that God doesn't love me? If He won't even give me peace?"

Nikolaos smiled, but it was a sad sort of thing. "If you are tested, it is because your Father in Heaven knows that you can endure it. And not only endure it, but come out stronger in the end."

"Why would He do that?" Sabra said. "It seems...it seems almost cruel."

He canted his head, running his fingers through the sand. "Imagine an officer in a Legion, Sabra, who has a young man newly recruited into his cohort. This young man has been pampered and coddled all his life, and has never had to do anything for himself. But the officer is an excellent judge of men, and he sees the potential of that young man to become a great soldier, a leader, a man he could trust with every task. But right now, the young man thinks he deserves to continue his easy way of life, and never be asked to change. Would it do that young man any good for the officer to indulge his weakness? To give him comforts and withhold duties and privations?"

"No," she whispered.

"No. And not only will the officer expect him to perform all the duties that his other soldiers do, but mightn't he also lead him more firmly, inflicting tougher punishments, and making more difficult demands of him, all to draw out that strength that is hidden within? Might that soldier think that he is being unfairly tested, and burdened with trials and discomforts far beyond what the other soldiers endure?"

She couldn't answer, but none was needed.

"I know that we often can't understand why we are asked to suffer the things we do. Why do some people seem to sail through life on calm waters, given every joy and every blessing, and no hardships to speak of, while others, who genuinely love God and wish to serve Him, struggle and fight and suffer in a bitter and stormy sea? It doesn't seem fair. It doesn't seem just. But can we see all ends?"

He leaned his chin on his hand, and Sabra stayed quiet, knowing he had more to say.

"A child doesn't understand why her mother gives her

foul medicine when she is sick. All she knows is that it tastes bitter, and it feels like the greatest betrayal of her mother's love. Does it give the mother joy to watch the baby weep over the medicine? Of course not. But she administers the bitter dose anyway, because she knows that only with the medicine will her beloved child get well. In a way it doesn't make any difference if the child understands the mother's reasons. If the child trusts her mother, and loves her, she will believe that her mother is doing what is best for her even when—and *especially* when—she doesn't understand."

For a long time they sat side by side in silence, Nikolaos lost in contemplation, Sabra turning over his words in her heart. They carried such a promise of such joy and peace, but she was afraid to reach out for it. If she reached out, surely it would be snatched away.

"You know how hard it is to concentrate on a task when a gadfly is nagging you?" she asked quietly. He nodded. "That is what this voice in my head is like. I try to do good works. I try to pray, and I try to trust and be at peace. But every time I think I have found peace, that voice comes and torments me."

He eyed her, his gaze bright and sharp. "And do you look for peace for your own contentment, or God's?"

"What...do you mean?"

"You pray, and that is well. You do good works, and that is to be praised. You seek peace, as all men do. But do you seek these things for your consolation, or because it pleases God?"

"I don't know," she stammered.

He smiled gently. "If you do them for love of God, what difference does it make if the gadfly bothers you?" He patted her arm. "There is nothing wrong with wanting peace, Sabra, but don't expect it as if it were a payment for a service rendered. Hope for it, as you might hope for a gift, but don't pursue your good works in expectation of being rewarded for them. You may find that the gadfly has much less power over you when it has nothing to steal away."

Sabra stared at him a long while, bewildered, as if she had

been led through a dense forest only to realize she stood at the peak of a high mountain she didn't even know existed. She seized his hand suddenly and kissed it.

"Thank you," she whispered.

He withdrew his hand gently from her grasp. "You have seen that there is hope," he said. "But there is still much you need to learn. And learning alone doesn't make you a soldier of the Faith, but practice and daily effort." He got to his feet, dusting the sand off his robes. "I've taken the liberty of asking a family that is dear to me if you might live with them for a while—a woman with two daughters, who I think would be good company for you. They work very hard, and would be glad of your help, I think, when we aren't training you up for war."

14

CAMULODUNUM, BRITANNIA — MARCH, A.D. 301

THE AIR WAS HEAVY WITH THE SCENT OF APPLE AND CHERRY blossoms, and on the southern shore of Meresig, the wind was mild and just touched by a late spring chill. Jurian sat on a low dune near the water's edge among a few tufts of beachgrass, watching Agapius, Eilwen, and Brigit chasing the waves. Menas sat beside him, quiet as ever, knowing as he always did when Jurian had something on his mind.

"Menas," Jurian said finally. "What am I doing here?"

Menas regarded him in surprise. "On the island?" he asked, and Jurian gave him a peeved look and said nothing. Menas chuckled, then said, as if it were obvious, "You're living. You are doing what people do. Well, you are doing what nobles do, when they don't have other work to fill their time."

Jurian grumbled, pulling up a handful of grass and watching it scatter in the breeze. "I've been sitting in Camulodunum for three months. I've done *nothing*. I haven't even managed to find anyone who will take this sword from me, and part of me is starting to fear that it's cursed and I won't be able to get rid of it at all."

"You've only searched a very small part of Britannia," Menas said mildly. "Have you asked Coel?"

"Coel, why?" Jurian asked, and shrugged. "He's got more than enough on his hands without me troubling him about some old sword."

"*He's* old, and he knows many things," Menas said. "Ask him. See what he says."

Jurian nodded, and for a few moments, held his peace. Then he sighed and plucked another bunch of grass. "Let's go now and ask him. I am sick to death of doing nothing. How can people stand to live like this?"

"What would you be doing if you could?"

Jurian hesitated. What *would* he be doing? It seemed like he had always had a direction—some task, some goal to pursue, some mission to fulfill. Now, with nothing but the sword weighing on his back, he felt aimless, adrift. If only Sabra were there...

"I wrote to Sabra," he said abruptly. Menas glanced at him in surprise, which Jurian expected—he hadn't told anyone about the letter, not even Agapius. "I sent it two months ago. Why hasn't she responded?"

"You don't really want me to list all the possible explanations, do you," Menas said, and Jurian laughed and shook his head. He knew them well enough—he reminded himself of them every time he began to worry. Menas reached over and squeezed his shoulder briefly. "You will hear from her soon."

"I want her to come to Britannia," he said. "Is that wrong of me? How can I ask her to come here to be with me? Me, an exile, spurned by the Empire?" He shook his head. "I can't do that to her. But I want nothing more."

"Do you think she cares overly much about your interdiction?"

"No, but..." Jurian started, and faltered. "I do."

"There is nothing you can do about it."

"There may be," he said, and pushed himself to his feet.

He walked a while along the beach, his bare feet sinking into the cold, damp sand. When the winter had faded into spring, Meresig had become one of their favorite haunts, and Coel rode out with them more often than not to stay a few days in one of the old Roman villas that occupied the island. There was a gentleness to the sea that always seemed to soothe the worry from Jurian's mind, but today, even the whisper of the waves on the sand couldn't bring him peace.

After a while he wandered over to join Brigit as she stood ankle-deep in the water, staring out to sea. Eilwen and Agapius were hunting for oysters in the shallow tidal pools nearby, and the sound of their laughter carried over the chortling of the waves. But Brigit was quiet, arms folded, her face still and remote as a carved statue of Minerva.

"You look sad," Jurian said, standing beside her, facing the sea.

At Menas's encouragement they had been trying to teach the girls Latin ever since they had reached Camulodunum, and by now they could carry on simple—if short—conversations together, which made everyone a little happier.

Brigit sighed and tossed her head back, hooking her thumbs through the heavy leather belt that held up the hem of her long tunic. "Long time we heard nothing," she said.

Jurian didn't have to ask her what she meant—he had been thinking the same thing only moments before. A few weeks after Constantinus had left Britannia, he had sent a message from Augusta Treverorum. It was short and rather impersonal, only telling them he was well and describing the harsh comforts of the camps he had stayed in during his travels. Since then, they had heard nothing.

At first Eilwen had been distraught, but gradually she adjusted to his absence, and Agapius managed to keep her in high spirits. It was Brigit who puzzled Jurian. She was just as fierce and stubborn as she had ever been, but Jurian thought her fire had subdued a little as the weeks turned into months. She didn't smile often these days. She didn't even glare at him as much as she once had.

"We will hear from him again soon," he said, and hoped it was true. "He's gone far south by now, and messages will take longer to reach us."

She pursed her lips and didn't reply.

"What else is troubling you?"

She took a moment, forehead knotted as she parsed the question, then she lifted her shoulders in a defeated sort of shrug. "We come home so close," she said. "But not home."

Jurian turned to her in surprise. The idea that the girls were homesick had never even occurred to him, and the realization shamed him. They had reached Britannia, but here they were, still far from their homes. And, Jurian thought with another flush of shame, he didn't even know where *home* was for them.

"You could go, any time you want," he said, feebly.

Her gaze darted toward him, but she didn't turn to look at him. It was a peevish look, almost a glare, which made Jurian stifle a smile.

"You save us," she said, flinging one hand toward the sea, toward the south. "We go with you."

"You don't *have* to."

She drew up a little, but kept staring at the sea.

"Where are you from?" he asked.

Her lips parted, trembling, and Jurian stared at her in shock when he realized her eyes were full of tears.

"Britannia," she whispered, and covered her mouth. After a moment she lowered her hand and said, "Far from here. Here—" She turned, gesturing to the beach where it swept away to the east. "Here the sea greets the morning. Home…the sea says goodnight."

"You're from the west coast," Jurian said, and thought, *That is no small distance.* He reached out impulsively and clasped her hand. "We will get you home, I promise."

The corner of her mouth lifted in a grin, then she pulled her hand free and punched him in the arm. "Wait first."

"For what?"

She tossed her head and glared at him, then went back to watching the waves. Jurian chuckled and nodded.

"Don't worry," he said. "We won't go anywhere without Constantinus."

When they arrived back at the island villa later that afternoon, Jurian went immediately to find Coel. He was sitting out on a white stone balcony that overlooked the sea, drinking diluted wine and eating oysters raw from their shells. Jurian grimaced as he joined him, but didn't turn down the cup of wine Coel offered him.

"Something on your mind, Jurian?" he asked.

Jurian sat down on the marble bench and gestured toward the hilt of his sword. "Do you know what this is?"

"No, but I've been wanting to ask you about it since I first saw it. Does it have a story? Is it a good one?"

"It's a good one," Jurian said. "Its name is Excalibur, and it was forged for Caratacus some two and a half centuries ago by a man named Merlinus."

"Caratacus!" Coel exclaimed, leaning to get a better look at the sword. "That blade doesn't look anywhere near that old."

"I know," Jurian said. "But it is. I was given it in Rome, along with a prophecy, that I was meant to bring the sword back to Britannia. Only I can't seem to find where I'm supposed to take it. I don't imagine I was meant to just land on the coast and plant the sword in the sand."

Coel considered that a long while, sipping idly at his wine. "Man named Merlinus made it, you say?"

"That's right. Or, in the native dialect they called him Myrddin."

"Myrddin." He shook a finger in Jurian's direction. "You might want to try out toward Maridunum. Seems I've heard rumor of a name like that, out around Nidum, Isca Silorum, that region. If you've had no luck here in the east, go west! The island is not *that* large."

Jurian grinned. "I promised a friend we would go west anyway," he said, getting to his feet. "Now we just have to wait for Constantinus."

15

Antiochia ad Orontes, Syria — April, A.D. 301

In the heart of Antioch, under a blaze of late spring sunshine, Aikaterina found herself standing before the palace of the *Imperator* Diocletian on the Orontes river. She took a deep breath and, steeling her nerves, stepped through the doors into the spacious marble-clad vestibule. Nenet and Diodoros followed closely on her heels, and Theokritos, whom Aikaterina had forced to accompany her, staggered up the steps behind them. He had been seasick the entire voyage, and Aikaterina didn't imagine he would ever forgive her.

As soon as the slaves had escorted her to a spacious *cubiculum* and left her in peace, Aikaterina sat down on the bed. Nenet immediately busied herself with organizing their things, but Aikaterina could hardly force her thoughts to line up in an orderly fashion.

"I never expected to be called to Diocletian's court again," Aikaterina said, twisting her fingers in her lap. "And me personally, not my father."

Nenet glanced at her over the top of the chest that held Aikaterina's clothes. "And why shouldn't you be invited? Six months now you have held the reins of Alexandria, in fact if not in name. If Diocletian has business with Egypt, who else would he invite?"

"It wasn't an invitation," Aikaterina said sourly. "It was an imperial summons."

"Isn't that an invitation?" Nenet asked.

"No. It's an order. Do you think I had any choice to refuse?"

Nenet shrugged and closed the lid of the chest. "Why not? What would he have done, come and taken you by force?"

"Perhaps," Aikaterina said. "I don't know what to expect from anyone. As far as I am concerned, people are capable of almost anything."

"I will not argue with that," Nenet said. "But it may be nothing. Perhaps Diocletian only thought you might be fit companion for his wife."

"Prisca Alexandra?" Aikaterina said with a smile. "She is lovely. I do hope to see her again. I always regretted not having the chance to speak to her more the last time I was here."

"Well then," Nenet said. "Something to look forward to." She skirted the chest and cupped Aikaterina's chin in her strong hand. "Not everything has to be sinister, *kyria*," she said gently.

Aikaterina sighed. "Can you blame me for thinking so? When I feel myself hemmed in by plots and schemes, and my father..." She stopped, wrestling with the lump in her throat. "That's the worst part about this entire arrangement," she said softly. "What if...Nenet, what if I return home, and he's gone?"

Nenet pulled her into a close embrace. "Keep faith," she said. "And see where the road leads you. He was doing better when we left, so, maybe you will return home and find him in full health. Do not borrow trouble, *kyria*. You don't know all things."

Aikaterina had to be satisfied with that, but she couldn't banish all the worry from her mind.

"What if..." she started, and faltered. "Nenet, you know how my mother sent a letter to Diocletian about me. About finding me a suitable match." She almost spat that word, and drew her knees up to her chest. "What if Diocletian summoned me here because he's found someone to marry me off to?"

"It's a possibility," Nenet said, with an indifference that infuriated Aikaterina.

"I won't do it. I'd sooner throw myself into the sea."

"You wouldn't!"

"No," she said, softly. "I wouldn't. But I might disguise myself as a slave like Sabra did once, and sneak away."

Nenet clucked her tongue but made no answer. After sifting through Aikaterina's belongings, she selected a deep blue *chiton* and a white *palla* for her to wear to the evening's banquet, and Aikaterina left her to choose what bangles she thought would be best. She needed to get out of the palace. Even here in Antioch, in a city and a palace where she had never been before, she found herself choked by memories, and she needed fresh air to clear her thoughts before she faced the Emperor.

She made her way out to the gardens and found a solitary stone bench, secluded from the path by a cluster of low-growing shrubs and shaded from the sun by towering date palms. In the mild breeze and dappled shadows, Aikaterina breathed a long sigh of relief. Perhaps she could finally have some time, and some space, to think. She drew Diodoros's *codex* out from the folds of her *palla* and opened it to her favorite passage. But although her eyes traced the letters, the words seemed to stay on the page. Frustrated, Aikaterina set the book aside and closed her eyes.

The fresh smell of budding lilies and crocuses wafted over her in the gentle wind, a welcome change from the abrasive salt of the sea air. But still calm and clarity eluded her, and the longer she sat, the more unsettled she felt.

"Aikaterina?" said a soft voice.

She glanced up, startled, only to see Diocletian's wife, Alexandra *Augusta* herself, standing nearby. Aikaterina rose quickly to greet her.

"No, no," Alexandra said, holding up a hand. "Please, I didn't mean to disturb you."

"You aren't disturbing me at all," Aikaterina said.

Alexandra smiled and embraced Aikaterina warmly. "I was

so pleased to hear that you would be joining us," she said.

"I honestly can't say I was pleased to come," Aikaterina said, then rebuked herself and added, "But I *am* very happy to see you again, *Augusta*."

Alexandra laughed quietly and gestured to the bench, and Aikaterina resumed her seat on its corner. Alexandra perched on the other end, hands twisting in her lap.

"I thought being alone would help me collect myself, but it isn't working as I had hoped," Aikaterina said. Alexandra nodded, but her gaze was fixed on the path, or something, unseen, at the end of it. Aikaterina leaned forward and touched her arm. "Is there something wrong?"

Alexandra gave her an unsteady sort of smile, which seemed entirely out of character for the Empress, who always seemed so regal, so self-possessed.

"I heard that your father has been ill," she said, which Aikaterina somehow felt was not what she truly wanted to talk about. "And that you have been doing your best to govern during his remission. I'm so sorry. I can only imagine the burden you carry."

Aikaterina winced and turned away. "Thank you," she said. "You are very kind."

"I'm not," Alexandra said, so forcefully that Aikaterina glanced at her in surprise. "You are too clever for platitudes."

"I'm...not sure what you mean, *Augusta*," Aikaterina said slowly. "Have I given offense?"

Alexandra made an impatient gesture with her hand. "There you are again. We have no need for such superficialities, do we?"

"What would you have me say?" Aikaterina asked. "That it grieves me more than I can say to be separated from my father in his illness, from my city in its time of need? That I don't understand why I have been summoned here? That I am lost, and can't seem to find my way?"

Alexandra laid one of her slender hands over Aikaterina's. "There," she said. "Was that so hard?"

Aikaterina stiffened suddenly. Was she a spy, sent here by Diocletian to wring complaints out of her so that he could have her arrested on some spurious charge? Something of her alarm must have been visible on her face, because Alexandra's expression softened and she laughed.

"I know what you're thinking," she said. "But my husband the *Imperator* doesn't know I'm here. And he certainly wouldn't send me to speak with you. Of that I'm almost entirely certain."

"Why?"

Alexandra pulled her hand back and toyed with the hem of her richly embroidered *palla*. "I'm not sure. But there is something about you, which I think either draws in or convicts those around you. A light, maybe, inside you. And this has become a very dark place of late." She glanced back down the path again, then said, more quietly still, "You come at an evil hour."

"Is there any other sort these days?" Aikaterina asked.

"But it is worse than when I last saw you," Alexandra said. "Since you left Rome…you have no idea the things that are being discussed. What Galerius is advocating, and that snake of a tribune who is always hanging about in his shadow."

"I have a fair notion," Aikaterina said wryly. "I know Casca well."

"You'll be glad to hear that Galerius is not currently in Anatolia. But Casca, unfortunately, is."

Aikaterina shuddered. "I wish with all my heart that I could just go home," she said. "I could be packed and off at a moment's notice. Perhaps the *Imperator* wouldn't even realize that I'd come at all!"

Alexandra caught her arm, as if Aikaterina were about to take flight like a bird. "Could I give you leave to go?" she asked, and Aikaterina couldn't tell if it was regret or amusement in her voice. "No, you must stay. For now, there is nothing settled, no plan in motion. As far as I know, he only summoned you here to talk, to discuss the benefits of a marriage alliance."

Aikaterina gritted her teeth. "I have no intention of

marrying," she said softly. "Not now. Not ever. But no one seems to understand that."

"I understand," Alexandra said. "Stay close to me tonight. I will do what I can to shield you from the court serpents."

THE *TRICLINIUM* GLITTERED WITH all the splendor she remembered from Diocletian's palace in Nicomedia. There was the *Imperator* himself, sitting aloof on his *sella* on the raised dais, watching the guests mingling below him like an indulgent, if bored, deity. The sparkle of gems, the warmth of gold on slender arms and necks, the brittle laughter—the falseness of it all made the whole affair feel like some sort of scene from a comic play.

Aikaterina followed Alexandra through the crowds, holding her head high and trying to calm her nerves. The last time she had been in an assembly like this, she had made a fool of herself. She prayed she would have better sense this time.

And then they were kneeling on the steps before Diocletian. Alexandra kissed the hem of his robe, but Aikaterina only inclined her head. Diocletian sat forward and took her chin in his hand.

"So, Aikaterina of Alexandria," he said. "We meet again."

Aikaterina said nothing and kept her eyes lowered. After another moment, Diocletian released her, and Aikaterina barely heard the faint breath that escaped his lips.

Disappointed? she wondered. *Annoyed?*

Then Alexandra got to her feet, a subtle cue to Aikaterina. As Aikaterina rose, Alexandra took her hand, and together they backed down the steps. It wasn't until they were once more in the swirl and noise of the crowd that Aikaterina could breathe properly again.

As she struggled to regain her bearings, she noticed a man watching her steadily from across the room. Their eyes met, and Aikaterina drew a sharp little gasp as if she had been punched in the stomach. The young man might have been a few years older than Jurian, not quite as tall, with his dark curls worn just longer than the common fashion. If not for the sharp, shrewd look in his eyes, Aikaterina thought, he might have been strikingly handsome.

The man suddenly stepped forward into the crowd. The people parted like oil to make way for him, then closed in behind him with hidden whispers. Some of them even glanced in Aikaterina's direction, making her skin crawl with nerves.

Alexandra's hand suddenly snaked out and gripped Aikaterina's wrist. "Smile," she said, modeling the expression and speaking through her teeth, "but don't say a word."

As soon as the young man reached them, he bowed low to Alexandra, saying in a languid voice, "*Augusta.*"

The Empress inclined her head, and then said, still through that frozen smile, "Maxentius, allow me to present Aikaterina, daughter of the *Praefectus Augustalis* of Alexandria. Aikaterina, this is Maxentius, son of *Imperator* Maximianus."

Maxentius bowed again and lifted Aikaterina's hand to his lips. "A pleasure," he said. He angled back and studied her as if she were a statue on display. "It is rare to find such gems here in the East."

"You are too kind," Aikaterina said with frigid politeness, silently willing him to go away.

"Not at all," he said. "Only honest. I was very sorry to hear of your father's illness."

"Thank you," Aikaterina said.

Maxentius slipped his hand beneath her elbow and guided her gently but firmly through the crowds to an open space. Aikaterina glanced over her shoulder and saw Alexandra staring after them, her face set in tight lines of worry. That look set Aikaterina's heart pounding. If Alexandra was worried...

"You must tell me more," Maxentius said. He stopped near an alcove draped with purple, where a bust of the Emperor stared at her with cold, marble eyes. "Are you managing? Is there any assistance I can provide?"

"There is nothing to tell," Aikaterina said.

She couldn't run, so she might as well make a stand. She threw back her shoulders and lifted her chin. *If I could manage*

Casca, I can manage this man, she thought.

Maxentius smiled and leaned a bit closer to her. "Now, we both know that isn't exactly true. So young, and yet, if the rumors are true, you have taken the reins from your ailing father and managed your city so adeptly, most of your citizens don't even realize the change."

"I think you overestimate my abilities," Aikaterina said, hoping he couldn't see the rush of blood in her cheeks.

"May I not even pay you a compliment?" he asked. "But if you believe I am overstating your abilities, does that mean you are finding the challenge of rule to be too great for you?"

Aikaterina snapped a sharp glance to his face, alarm prickling through her. Was this Maxentius's play? To trick her into some admission of her own inadequacy, and use that as proof that her city needed someone else in charge?

"Not at all," she said smoothly, with a slight lift of her chin. "I only mean that I've enjoyed excellent support from the government in Alexandria." She gave him a demure smile and added, "They do so much prefer to have an Alexandrian at the helm, as you can imagine."

He chuckled at that. "I find you to be…intriguing, Aikaterina of Alexandria. Sit by me at dinner."

At that moment, a plump young woman fluttered up to them. Her soft peach *palla*, the color of the inside of a sea shell, was slipping off her round shoulders, and her face was mottled red, as if the heat in the *triclinium* were too much for her.

"There you are at last, Maxentius! I've been looking everywhere for you!" she said, her breathy voice carrying the hint of a lisp. "*Domina* Alexandra said you were over here."

Maxentius stiffened. "Valeria," he said.

The girl turned to eye Aikaterina with suspicion. "Who's this, Maxentius?" she asked. "What's she doing here?"

"She is here by invitation of the Divine *Imperator*, and she is the daughter of the *Praefectus Augustalis* of Alexandria," Maxentius said.

Valeria planted her hands on her waist. "That's not what I

meant."

Aikaterina smiled warmly at Valeria. "I can see you have much to discuss," she said. "Please excuse me."

As she turned to go, she heard Maxentius call after her, but she refused to turn back. She wove her way through the crowds, desperate to find Alexandra, the one friendly face in this sea of serpents. The Empress was waiting for her near the place Aikaterina had left her, leaning elegantly against a carved golden pillar.

"Did she find you?" she asked, straightening up as Aikaterina joined her.

"Valeria? Yes, she did." Aikaterina glanced back at the alcove where Valeria was chattering at Maxentius, like a little bird driving a hawk away from its nest. "Who is she?"

"The daughter of *Caesar* Galerius, my daughter's stepdaughter," Alexandra said, "and she is intended for Maxentius."

Aikaterina's eyes widened and she laughed. "Oh, no wonder she was so upset to find him with me!" she said. Then, considering what Alexandra had said, she asked, "Did you say Galerius's wife is your daughter?"

Alexandra arched her brows elegantly. "Does it surprise you? You of all people should understand how these things work."

Aikaterina grumbled a response, then said, "I only thought you didn't look old enough to be her mother."

The Empress laughed, but before she could reply, they were called to take their seats for the banquet. Aikaterina took a seat as near to Alexandra as she could, and Maxentius, trailing Valeria in his wake, angled for the seat across from her. Valeria plopped down beside him, squeezing out the elderly wife of a Senator.

"Now," said Maxentius, lifting his goblet in Aikaterina's direction, "tell me your whole life's story."

16

Antiochia ad Orontes, Syria — April, A.D. 301

Aikaterina of Alexandria was in Antioch. Casca fumed to himself as he rode through the streets of the city, trying to make his way back to the island on the Orontes where Diocletian was overseeing the construction of some new building for his elaborate palace—as if the place were not already fitting for the gods. He crossed the bridge onto the island and followed the colonnaded *stoa* to the *hippodromos*, and the whole way there he tried to conjure an explanation for why he needed to be in the *Imperator*'s presence.

At last he arrived at the building site. He left his horse in the care of one of the *agasones* lingering near the wall, who glowered at Casca as if he had been interrupted from some more important task. Inside the hippodrome, in what would eventually be the imperial box, Casca found Diocletian. Some other man was with him—not Galerius. A younger man. And just beside him stood the figure he'd expected, the figure he would recognize anywhere—dark curls clinging to her straight shoulders. Regal in white and dark blue, arms folded as though she were a goddess of judgment.

His insides quavered like jelly. He'd come all this way to see her, but he wished inanely that she weren't there. Why would

Diocletian include her in his daily affairs? Didn't he know what she was?

It didn't matter. She had information he needed, and he was determined to get it from her one way or another.

He climbed the stone stairs to the box and was puffing gently when he finally reached it, much to his shame. Diocletian and the younger man turned as he approached, but Aikaterina, he noticed, chose to ignore him.

"Ah, Casca," Diocletian said. "What a surprise."

Casca swallowed. He knew Diocletian had told him to take care of his duties, but couldn't the *Imperator* see that that was exactly what he was doing? If only he knew in what ways Casca was currently serving him...

The man standing with Diocletian was stifling a smile, and Casca rounded on him, eyes narrowed.

"Do I know you?"

"This is Marcus Aurelius Valerius Maxentius," Diocletian said, "son of Maximianus *Augustus*."

"I see," Casca said.

He didn't much like the look of the man, even if they did share two names, and he wondered what he was doing there. Of course he'd seen Maxentius in Rome, and had heard much of him besides. But most of what he'd heard had come from Galerius, who seemed to positively despise him. Casca also didn't care for the attentive way Maxentius was watching Aikaterina.

"Did you have something to tell me?" Diocletian asked.

Aikaterina, Casca noticed, had finally turned to look at him, and he faltered for words under the piercing blue of her gaze.

He cleared his throat, twisting his tremoring hand in the folds of his tunic. "*Imperator*, with your indulgence, I actually had a question for your lovely Alexandrian guest."

Maxentius looked at him sharply, which gave Casca a moment of bitter triumph, but Diocletian's mouth lifted in a strange smile that turned Casca's blood cold.

Aikaterina took a few steps away from the two other men

and their escort, going to stand at the outer edge of the imperial box, which Casca was half-afraid would collapse beneath them. At Diocletian's permissive wave, Casca followed her. She lifted her gaze as he approached, and her eyes—almost violet in the shadows under the awning—met his. He stopped, too abruptly, feeling as though a knife had pierced straight through him with that single look.

"What do you want with me, Casca?" she asked.

"I heard you were in Antioch," he said, feebly. "I came to see if you were well."

"Since when did you care if I was well?" she retorted.

Casca stiffened. "That's hardly fair."

"I wouldn't speak of fairness, if I were you," she said, and there was a deep note of warning in the softness of her voice. "I wouldn't dare."

"I meant only that—that—" He stopped. It was pointless to argue with the girl. He should get straight to the point and leave her alone. The less he had to do with her, the better.

Dangerous, Casca, he reminded himself. *Tread carefully.*

"I have come to ask for a favor."

Her laugh was like the rill of clear water over stone. "And you think I want to do anything for you?" She speared him with those eyes again. "After what you have done to me, and to those dear to me?"

"I think you will want to help me once you hear what I have to say," Casca said.

She straightened up. "Is that a threat?"

"More like a promise."

"What do you want, Casca?"

Casca took a breath. "Georgius took the sword Excalibur to Britannia. What was he going to do with it?"

For a moment, Aikaterina stared at him, and then slowly she shook her head. "No," she said. "I can see the workings of your mind. I won't help you."

Casca took a step closer to her, but she edged away from him. "Do you know how long I have sought that sword for my

Divine *Imperator*?" he asked. "How many miles I have traveled, how many trials I endured, and then, when I thought it was finally within my reach, to have it stolen away again?"

"I am very sorry for your troubles," she said, and didn't sound the least bit sorry.

"I have been to the Oracle at Didyma," he said, blurting it out, though he didn't know why. What business was it of Aikaterina's that he had heard the voice of the god in the darkness?

"False promises for false hearts?" she said.

His breath escaped in a faint hiss. "She spoke of this sword. It's...been on my mind. I can guarantee you it has been on the *Imperator*'s as well."

She cocked her head at that. "What did she say?"

"Ah," he said, with a faint laugh, and wagged his finger at her. "Now you're curious. But those words were for the Emperor, not for you."

She lifted her chin. "Well, this is all the more reason for me to tell you nothing, then, wouldn't you say?"

"I wouldn't say that at all," he said, "since I'm certain you are as eager as I am to serve the *Imperator*."

She said nothing but inclined her head, which infuriated Casca inordinately.

"What was Georgius going to do with the sword?" he repeated, emphatic now.

"You speak of prophecies? He had his own to fulfill."

Casca took half a step back, stunned. He had no idea what to make of her words. Surely, Jurian hadn't consulted the Oracle of Didyma or Delphi...not if Jurian was what Casca believed he was. And it had never even entered Casca's imaginings that Constantinus and Jurian might have *intended* to go to Britannia, rather than just been forced there by necessity.

The thought was absolutely infuriating.

"Aikaterina," he said, patiently, as if talking to a small child. "I need a little more information than that. We've known each other for quite a while now, and you understand, probably better than anyone else here, that I control all the moving pieces in your life. I have the power to make your life an absolute hell."

Aikaterina leaned toward him, surprising him with a smile. "Only if I choose to let you," she whispered.

Casca scowled, more at himself, finding himself breathless, than at her, impudent and reckless as she was. "What?"

"I will not help you find Excalibur," Aikaterina said, lifting her chin. "So do whatever you will."

"You may regret that you ever said that to me," Casca said.

"I am not the one who walks the way of blood."

He started and seized her by the forearm. "What? Why did you say that?"

"Let me go. You're hurting me."

He tightened his grip until she gave a little cry of pain. The sound twisted the knife blade in his heart, but he forced the sensation away, away behind a sharp wave of alarm. "Why did you say that?"

"Aikaterina?" came a deep voice behind them.

"Maxentius!" Aikaterina gasped.

Casca dropped her arm as if it burned his hand and she slipped past him, retreating, of all things, toward the *Imperator*. Casca turned slowly to find Maxentius standing mere inches behind him, his face like a thundercloud. Maxentius took another step closer, until Casca, angling away from him, felt himself on the very edge of the unfinished platform, with nothing to catch him if he stumbled.

"If you ever—and I mean ever—hurt her again," Maxentius said, "I will snap your neck. Do you understand?"

Casca nodded, lips flapping noiselessly, and Maxentius whirled away, taking Aikaterina's arm and leading her away from the imperial box. At the threshold she paused, and glanced over her shoulder at him, then vanished into the long corridor.

The smoldering fire in his veins blazed suddenly white-hot with hatred. She would regret challenging him. He would make sure of it.

He didn't realize he was still staring after her until Diocletian cleared his throat.

Feeling his face grow foolishly hot, he swiveled away from the corridor. His Divine *Imperator* almost smiled, and that only made the situation worse. Casca straightened his tunic, and Diocletian shifted his gaze to watch the stonemasons drag a massive block across the floor of the hippodrome, once more implacable, inscrutable.

"I can't quite figure her out myself," Diocletian said. "She is a fascinating creature."

"Dangerous, you mean," Casca muttered.

Diocletian turned to him, one eyebrow arched. "Do you think so?"

Casca shrugged, and then realized he shouldn't respond that way to the Emperor. But Diocletian at least did not seem to notice his impertinence, for he had turned his gaze back to the builders.

"What question did you ask of her?" Diocletian glanced at him, fractionally, a smile in his eyes that Casca could only describe as taunting. "Was the outcome not to your satisfaction?"

Casca wanted to glare at something, so he glared at the slaves, because he couldn't very well glare at Diocletian. "I asked her about Georgius's sword."

"Ah," Diocletian said. "Not a day passes that I don't regret the loss of that weapon."

He turned abruptly away, leaving Casca staring after him and wondering, irrationally, what weapon he meant.

17

Camulodunum, Britannia — May, A.D. 301

As spring drifted into summer, Jurian spent his days training with Coel's private garrison, embracing the chance to learn their unfamiliar—and highly unRoman—battle tactics, as well as the use of their favored weapon, the axe. With something to occupy his mind and body, the days slipped by quickly, and Jurian found he was almost happy in Coel's court. Only the long silence from Sabra troubled him, and none of the messengers who came to Camulodunum had anything to report of events in Cyrene. As far as he had heard, the region was at peace. It was the only thing that brought him any consolation.

It was midmorning in early summer and Jurian had just finished a training exercise with Coel's men, when a courier came into the courtyard calling his name. Jurian immediately went to meet the messenger, heart hammering, and hope against hope stirring in the back of his mind.

"Lucius Aurelius Georgius?" the messenger said, bowing low before him.

"*Adsum*," he said. "Do you have a letter for me?"

"No letter," the messenger said. "I've come from Flavius Aurelius Valerius Constantinus, in Augusta Treverorum."

Jurian stifled a surge of disappointment, nodding at the

courier to bid him continue.

"He sends just one message to all of you here," the courier said. Jurian couldn't quite tell, but he thought the man was smiling. "He says, *I'm coming home.*"

Jurian nodded again, then the words registered all at once. "He's...oh! He's coming...excellent! Thank you," he said, the words tumbling over themselves.

The man grinned and bowed, and disappeared back into the fortress. Jurian watched him go, and then, shaking himself out of his stupor, ran to find his friends. Menas was in an inner *hortus* where he liked to pass the time, sitting on a bench shaded by carefully cultivated fruit trees. Agapius, to Jurian's surprise, was with him.

As soon as he saw him, Agapius jumped to his feet. "What's wrong?" he cried. "Did someone die?"

Jurian glared at him, then gestured emphatically at his own face. "Do I look like someone died?"

"Well, maybe if it was Casca," Agapius said, which only put Jurian in a sour mood.

"No one died. Constantinus is on his way back to Britannia."

Agapius dropped back onto the bench with dramatic defeat. "It's about time."

"He sent the messenger from Augusta Treverorum," Jurian said. "That's a journey that takes, what, ten days, twelve?"

"He was likely not far behind the courier. We should expect him any day," Menas said. "I'll go tell the girls."

"Better you than us," Agapius muttered under his breath as Menas turned away, which made Jurian laugh.

He dropped onto the bench beside his friend. "Finally," he said. "This sword has been a splinter in my thoughts for months."

"I thought you liked it," Agapius said.

Jurian scowled. "Only when I thought I was going to get rid of it."

CONSTANTINUS ARRIVED SIX DAYS later, right in the middle of one of Coel's renowned feasts. They were dining in the fortress's lone open-air *triclinium* in the mild summer evening when the fortress doors swung open, and Constantinus strode in like a general taking a battlefield. Everyone fell silent at the sight of him, and even Jurian couldn't restrain a slight gasp of surprise—the Tribune looked half-barbarian himself, with his hair shaggy and his jaw shadowed by a rough beard. His cheek was raked by a long laceration, and he carried one arm bound lightly in a sling.

He stopped in the entry when the guests all turned to look at him, and lifted his other hand in dismissal.

"Don't let me interrupt," he said, in the way that only Constantinus could—everyone turned immediately back to their meal, and their former conversations, and no one so much as glanced at the Tribune except Coel and Jurian, and his friends.

Jurian moved over on the long bench as Constantinus approached their table, giving room for the Tribune to sit between him and Menas. As Constantinus took his seat, smiling guardedly at Jurian and the others, Coel sat back and laughed.

"By all that's holy, boy, you smell like horse."

"My apologies," Constantinus said. "I would have stopped at Londinium, but my road was faster coming straight to Camulodunum. I heard there was food."

Coel shoved a slab of meat toward Constantinus, and Jurian caught the Tribune casting a brief glance toward Brigit and Eilwen. But he said nothing to them, only applied himself to the food and wine that Coel served him as if he hadn't eaten in months.

"I see you still have that cursed sword, Jurian," he said, as he finished the last of his meat. "No luck?"

"We were waiting for you," Jurian said. "We want to take it west, to Maridunum."

"Maridunum!" Constantinus echoed, catching Coel's eye. "By the gods, man, what good could you expect from that forsaken region?"

Jurian shrugged smoothly. "An answer, maybe. And

besides, we may finally be able to get Brigit and Eilwen home."

Constantinus regarded him in surprise, and he glanced from Brigit to Jurian and back again. "Home," he said. "In Maridunum?"

"In that region, possibly. They're from the west."

Constantinus nodded, then shifted his left arm in its sling with a faint grimace.

"Are you all right?" Agapius asked.

"Fine," he said. "Only tired."

"Go get yourself a bath," Coel said, "and get some sleep. You look like a *draugr*, boy."

Constantinus nodded, but hesitated as he moved to stand up. "How soon did you want to leave?" he asked Jurian.

"Soon," Jurian said. "But only when you're ready."

"Next month then," Constantinus said, and laughed quietly when he saw the horror on Jurian's face. "Give me ten days. I have business in Londinium, then we can leave. We'll go by boat. I'm sick to death of horses."

Two weeks later, Jurian stood at the prow of a small merchant ship as it drifted toward a lone pier jutting into the waves. The twilight was heavy, thick with a cool mist that cloaked the shore and muffled the calls of the sailors and the creaking of the ropes like a heavy blanket. When the clouds swirled and parted under the stiff breeze, Jurian could just glimpse the coastline, but all its details were blurred under the swirling fog. All he could see was a sweep of dusk-purple hills, strangely barren after the tree-shrouded hills that surrounded Camulodunum. Even in that summer month, the wind bit like needles through his cloak.

"Are you sure this is where you want to be?" Constantinus asked, appearing at the rail beside him.

"I'm honestly not sure," Jurian said. "What is this place?"

"It has no name," Constantinus said, "but here we are in the westernmost reaches of Britannia."

The ship's captain called out a hail in Celtic, and a voice

from the fog shouted back a moment later. Ahead, Jurian could just make out a few ramshackle buildings huddled just inland from the waterline. Bright lanterns burned in the windows, but all Jurian could think of was that magnificent Pharos lighthouse in Alexandria. There was no such clear light—a marvel for all mankind—guiding him to his destination this time. This was no safe harbor. The inlet was large enough, but there was no bustling port, no docks leashing a score of merchant ships.

As they drew up to the pier, Jurian could make out a solitary figure standing in a ring of lamplight, watching the vessel approach. He had that faintly barbarian look that Jurian was slowly growing accustomed to—hair shaggy and unkempt, beard long and twined with braids. His arms were bare, wrapped only with a few leather straps, and he seemed as indifferent to the chill sea wind as Constantinus.

No sooner had the ship been made fast than Brigit and Eilwen raced down the ramp, quick and lithe as cats, and threw their arms around the waiting man. He roared with surprise and exclaimed over them in a stream of incomprehensible Celtic that might have sounded angry if not for the overwhelmed joy in his eyes.

"What's he saying?" Agapius asked no one in particular as he and Menas followed the girls.

"Welcoming them home," Menas said.

As Constantinus stepped off the boat, the man sobered immediately, pushing the girls back gently. Jurian thought, as he always did, that there was something about Constantinus that made people stand a little straighter and keep their eyes down, even when they had no notion who he was.

The man said nothing to him, but only bowed and gestured for them to follow him. He led them around behind the dilapidated huts, where a well-worn and muddy track wove down to the waterway that emptied into the bay. A long, flat barge was tethered to a wooden dock, the waves slapping thickly against its hull. The girls leapt onto the barge with enviable ease, then Brigit took Menas's arm and pulled him gently aboard, planting him in the exact center of the vessel on a sturdy barrel. Agapius perched up on a barrel across from them, but Jurian couldn't sit. He leaned against a barrel that stank soundly of fish, and managed a faint smile at Menas.

A moment later Constantinus appeared out of the mist, accompanied by another burly man with an even longer beard than the man they had met on the quay.

"More braids," remarked Agapius in a low voice. "Must be the man in charge."

Jurian stifled a laugh.

As the driver got the vessel underway, poling the barge slowly up the river, Constantinus moved to stand beside Jurian. He looked pensive, Jurian thought—or, more than usual, and didn't seem particularly in the mood for conversation. Jurian turned to Brigit instead.

"You knew that man?" Jurian asked her.

Eilwen's face broke out in a radiant smile. "Father brother," she said, clasping her hands under her chin. "Many years we see him."

Constantinus turned to look at her, surprised. "You're learning Latin," he said.

Brigit made a noise of indifference and turned away, bracing her hands behind her on the barrel, but Eilwen nodded enthusiastically.

"I'm glad of it," the Tribune said softly.

No one else said anything.

DAWN WAS JUST BREAKING through the mist when they reached the Roman fort and town of Maridunum. As the barge butted gently against the dock, the bargeman jumped ashore to tie the vessel off. Eilwen and Brigit helped Menas onto solid ground, then caught him by the hands and pulled him toward the stone steps that led up to the town. Agapius, grumbling, followed them ashore, but Jurian waited as Constantinus dropped coins into the bargeman's open palm. They disembarked together.

The *vicus* of Maridunum was not unlike the small villages

Jurian had seen on the eastern coast of Britannia, with its rough wood and thatch huts and the predictable layout of a Roman settlement. But Maridunum was surrounded by hills and old forests, and they gave the whole place an ancient feel that unsettled Jurian strangely.

They soon came into the residential streets of the town. Jurian caught sight of an old woman wrapped in a patchwork cloak standing outside the nearest hut, her rough twig broom scratching relentlessly at the dirt threshold and a handful of persistent hens clucking around the hem of her tunic, hunting for insects. As Jurian's unlikely procession drew closer, she stopped her sweeping abruptly and squinted at the travelers with a pinched and suspicious expression.

All at once the two *gladiatrices* squealed with joy and ran forward, dragging Menas between them. The chickens clucked and scattered like leaves as the broom fell from the woman's hands, and she pulled the girls close in her thin and pale arms. Tears of joy trickled down her worn cheeks.

Menas stood back a few paces, head bowed in polite silence. As Jurian and the others joined him, the girls turned and gestured at Menas, babbling something to the woman in their incomprehensible language.

The woman took one look at Menas and immediately dropped to her knees, joining her hands above her head and whispering, "Woden!"

Menas heaved a long-suffering sigh, his one eye raised to the heavy clouds above. "Not again," he grumbled.

The girls were obviously trying to convince the woman that she was mistaken about Menas's identity, and finally Brigit tapped the woman on the shoulder and pointed emphatically at Constantinus. The old woman glanced in their direction, and her awe of divine visitation was suddenly replaced by a studied wariness. Lifting her chin, she regarded Constantinus with more boldness than an empress.

The tension in the air grew with each heartbeat. Agapius cleared his throat softly. Constantinus seemed to be waiting for the woman's gesture of respect, but she showed no willingness to give it.

Just as the silence became unbearable, an elderly man stepped out of the hut and smiled amiably at them.

"Greetings, *amici*," he said in perfect, if heavily accented, Latin, and immediately the tension evaporated like mist. "You have made a long journey by the looks of it. Please, come in and share our fire and what we have for table."

He bowed his head to Constantinus and winked at the two girls.

They wasted no time in hustling Menas inside, though the giant barely managed to squeeze through the diminutive doorway, and the rest of the party followed the old woman. The hut was a single room, and the wood walls were daubed with clay. A simple wooden table with two stools sat in one corner, beneath the hut's only window. A heavy animal skin had once been tacked up around the opening, but the corner of it had been released to let in the cool, fresh air, which made a relentless little war on the warmth from the fire. In the back of the hut, a ladder climbed to a narrow loft, and the disgruntled hens from the front stoop had taken up roosts on its rungs, clucking indignantly at the intruders.

Eilwen made Menas sit on one of the stools, which he did as gingerly as possible, then she respectfully gestured for Constantinus to take the other. Jurian and Agapius leaned against the wall.

"I'm just glad the man speaks Latin," Agapius murmured. "That old woman was about to beat Constantinus about the ears with her broom."

Jurian snorted with laughter as he imagined that scene playing out. The old man approached them, rubbing his well-worn hands together. His pale blue eyes twinkled at them as he *tsk*ed softly.

"Not about the ears, lad," he said to Agapius. "She's been waiting for a chance to use that broom on a Roman since they took our girls."

He glanced with fondness at the *gladiatrices*, who were busy helping the woman fry oatcakes over the fire as if they had always been there.

"*Your* girls?" Agapius asked in surprise. "Are they your daughters?"

The old man smiled wistfully. "Not by nature, but by blood. They are my sister's daughters. She died when they were very small, when her son was born, and as we had no children of our own, we took them in." He placed a hand on his breast and inclined his head. "My name is Idris. My wife there is Blodwen. Brigantia and Eilwen you know, of course."

"Brigantia?" Jurian echoed. "We've always called her Brigit."

Idris waved a hand. "Brigit, yes. That's her pet name. Her mother named her for the goddess of wisdom and war." He jerked his chin at them. "I imagine she is rather like your goddess Minerva."

Agapius cleared his throat quietly and Jurian shifted his weight, wondering what to say. He had never quite figured out if Brigit and Eilwen were Christian, but if they were, he guessed it had happened recently. Idris studied them a long moment, then he gave a subtle nod.

"So, perhaps not *your* goddess," he said, and that was all.

"You never taught your daughters Latin?" Agapius said, to change the subject. Brigit turned to him at that, staring a challenge at him through those clear, fierce eyes. "We've been trying to teach them what we can, but…"

Eilwen brought a trencher laden with food from the stew pot and placed it before Menas, whom Blodwen still seemed to regard as some sort of deity. Brigit, her head tossed back, silently offered a dish to Constantinus, who took it without comment.

"There was no need for it," Idris said, answering Agapius, as he watched the girls with a wistful smile. "Though I suppose it might have served them in their captivity." His eyes shadowed, and he lowered them abruptly. "They were…not harmed? Please. Tell me they were not harmed."

Jurian glanced at Agapius. "They were highly valued by the Emperor," he said carefully. "And he is jealous of the things he values."

The man nodded. "I suppose I shall have to be satisfied with that," he said, then fixed a fierce gaze on Jurian. "But they were brave? They fought well?"

It was a curious question, Jurian thought. He could hardly imagine a Roman father asking such a thing about a daughter, or a niece.

"Among the bravest I have seen in the arena," he said.

The man cocked his head. "You yourself have been in the games?"

Jurian grinned at Menas and Constantinus dropped his head in his hand.

"Yes, actually," Jurian said, ignoring him. "My friend there, whom your wife seems to think is Woden, was also captured by the Romans and put in the arena. To get him free, yes—I fought. We both fought. That's how he lost his eye."

And how I lost my citizenship, he wanted to add, but kept it to himself.

The man looked impressed. "There are not many, they say, who enter the arena willingly, nor many of those who survive." A shadow passed across his face, but he hid it as soon as his girls approached with their food. "Even here," he said, taking a trencher from Brigit's hands, "we have heard tell of the games... and the sport they provide. So you will forgive Blodwen if she does not think much of your red-cloaked companion."

Agapius opened his mouth and Jurian speared him in the side with his elbow. Idris seemed not to notice, and he inclined his head to them and moved to the table to greet Menas and Constantinus.

"Wouldn't it make a difference if he knew who he was?" Agapius asked, nodding at Constantinus.

"That is not our truth to tell," Jurian said. "He knows more about this region of Britannia than we do. Who knows how highly his father is regarded in this part of the country?"

He bit into the oatcake and closed his eyes, relishing the taste. The bread was lightly sweet and toothsome, with just enough richness from the fat it was fried in to make it sustaining.

The door opened suddenly behind them with a swirl of chilly air, and a young man burst into the room. His hair was wild, as if he'd been running in a stiff breeze, and behind the patchy scruff of a youth's beard, he had a bright and easy smile. As soon as he saw Brigit and Eilwen, he threw his arms in the air with a whoop of joy. He caught them both and danced them around the tiny room, kicking over a bucket of water that stood near the fireplace.

Blodwen erupted in a string of abuses belied by the warmth in her eyes, but Idris just laughed and clapped his hands. Then the young man stopped abruptly in front of Jurian, one arm around each girl's waist, and he shook back his hair.

"Who are you?" he asked in brusque and heavily accented Latin. "With your…head on fire."

Jurian bristled faintly. "We were about to ask you the same thing."

"Maybe, but I asked first." He released the girls and they slipped away to help Blodwen clean up the mess he'd made. As soon as they'd gone he folded his arms and tossed his head, reminding Jurian of a wild horse. "So speak."

"My name is Jurian."

The young man snorted. "What kind of a name is that?"

"You can call him Georgius, if you like Latin better," Agapius offered.

The young man wrinkled his nose and shook his head. "No, thank you." He narrowed his eyes at Agapius. "And you, who look like a piece of cherry wood left too long in the sun?"

"I beg your pardon?" Jurian said, surging with indignation, but Agapius only waved him off with a faint roll of his eyes.

"It's not the first time I've been stared at, Jurian," he said softly, then, with his widest smile at the young man he said, "I'm Agapius."

"Romans," he said.

"In a way," Jurian said. "Aren't we all?"

"Depends on who you ask."

"I'm asking you."

The young man lifted his chin, looking so much like Brigit that Jurian stifled a smile. But he just measured Jurian for a long moment, calculating.

"Is that what this is?" he asked, finally. There was no hint of his easy manner now. "You bring my sisters back so that you can torment us and put us to the test? What happens if I don't give you the answer you want to hear? You'll drag me off next and put me in the arena? Or my ancient father?"

Agapius glanced at Jurian, forehead creased, obviously surprised by the young man's vehemence—and even more obviously choosing to let Jurian handle it.

"I only just left the arena. I'd really rather not go back just now," Jurian said evenly.

"What?" the young man said, stepping back a pace, head tipped to one side. And then that wide, warm grin flashed across his face again and he seized Jurian's hand, shaking it until Jurian thought his shoulder would come out of its socket. "I'm Alban," he said, and tossed his head at Agapius. "Or Albanus, if you like Latin better. These are my sisters. My parents. My house. My town. I'll show you everything. Let's go."

"I haven't finished eating," Agapius said, brandishing his oatcake like a weapon.

Albanus stared at him like he was a talking fish. "What do you need to eat for?" he said. "We have things to do!"

"We do?" Jurian said.

But Albanus had already flung open the door and waved to Blodwen. She called after him and started forward, unleashing another tide of words in his direction, but he just grinned at her and ducked out the door. Jurian and Agapius hesitated, staring at each other in bewilderment, until Albanus poked his head inside again.

"Come on! We'll miss him if you don't hurry up!"

18

Camulodunum, Britannia — May, A.D. 301

Albanus led them down the street, his huge strides eating up the distance and his words flowing nonstop, until Jurian decided that Agapius was positively laconic by comparison. He took them along the Roman wall to the fort, which seemed no longer garrisoned except by a colony of bats. Jurian opened his mouth to ask how long the Romans had been absent from Maridunum, but Albanus had already whisked them away again.

"There's no trouble this side of Britannia," he said as they hurried along behind him. Albanus seemed to have one speed, whether in motion or in speech. "Constantius Chlorus—he's our *Caesar*, you know, but I don't know why they call him *Chlorus*, since he's as red in the face as your hair—he's having more trouble in Germania. Pulled the garrison as reinforcements. Oh, don't worry. There's another garrison over Leucarum way, should we get too itchy—"

"Do you ever breathe?" Agapius asked.

Albanus gave him that look again, like he was some kind of mythic creature, and then continued, "Leucarum—that's the fortress Carausius used it for a time when he styled himself ruler, before the *Caesar* overthrew him. I think it's a point of pride for Constantius Chlorus to keep it garrisoned with proper Romans now."

"What are you even talking about?" Jurian burst out.

Albanus just laughed. They left the Roman road and the town behind as they struck out on a stony path that wound into the hills. A few huts lay along the path, set well back and almost invisible in the bracken and the trees that seemed to scrape the sky.

As Jurian stared up at their crowns, he suddenly remembered a dream he'd had what felt like a lifetime ago, when he had first felt the call in his heart to travel to Britannia—long before he had gone to Rome and received Excalibur from *Pappas* Marcellinus. He remembered dreaming of ancient and towering trees. The man who looked both young and old, who looked half-barbarian but spoke perfect Latin. The pool of water where he'd seen his own reflection, dressed in Legion armor.

Well, that part at least wasn't true, he thought bitterly. *And I've not met anyone like that man here, either.*

"Here we are!" Albanus said, plunging into the undergrowth beneath a grove of alder and poplar trees. There was barely a path now—just flattened places where footsteps had tracked in and out of the clearing.

As they neared the hut, Jurian saw a wiry man in a simple brown tunic and *bracchae* bent over a raised garden bed near the wall of the hut. He was carefully weeding his crops with a curious spade, but as he heard them approaching he straightened, and then planted one dirty hand on his hip.

"You!" he said. "I just got rid of you!"

Albanus grinned. "I brought some friends!" he said. "They may have news."

"Friends," the man snorted with mock gruffness. "You mean you found someone else who could tolerate your babbling for more than five minutes?"

He leaned the spade against the rough wall of the house and wiped his hands on his tunic. As Jurian and Agapius got closer to him, he looked them up and down and nodded once.

"There's a chill in the air this morning," he said. "Come inside and share a bit of breakfast with me."

"See?" Agapius said to Albanus. "*He* eats."

The man led them inside and busied himself at the fire. Instead of oaten cakes, he ladled some hot mush into a few rough wooden bowls and then drizzled honey on it from a small clay pot.

"You promised I could help with the honey this year," Albanus remarked as the man handed him a bowl and a wooden spoon.

"Can't come too soon," the man said. "I'm nearly out. They're still gathering the nectar flow, though, so we'll give them a few more weeks before we harvest."

As soon as they were all seated and with food in hand, the man settled into his chair—the kind of strange, backed seat that seemed so common in Britannia.

"So, tell me who your friends are, Albanus," he said, stretching his feet to the fire and folding his hands across his stomach.

"That's Jurian," Albanus said. "And he's…" He looked at Agapius and frowned, as if he couldn't remember.

"I'm Agapius."

"That's right! I thought it was something to do with *gapa*," he said, then added with a wicked look at Agapius, "*Hias*. Gape, gape, gape."

Jurian almost choked on his porridge, and the man seemed faintly amused at the look on Agapius's face—mouth hanging open in indignation.

"Names don't tell much," Jurian said, recovering. "I come from Satala, near the border of Anatolia and Persia—"

"That's the other side of the world!" Albanus exclaimed suddenly, his eyes as round as his porridge bowl.

"Agapius is from Alexandria."

"The Library!" gasped Albanus. His expression was such a transport of joy that Jurian thought he would float to the rafters. "Did you see the Great Library?"

Agapius stared at him. "Of course. Every day, it seemed."

"Every day! But...wasn't it destroyed?"

Agapius shrugged. "Some parts of it were burned, years ago. We lost many manuscripts. But they're restoring it, and I've never seen anyone work as hard as *domina* Aikaterina to replace the texts we lost." He shook his head, scowling at Albanus. "How do you know so much about this?"

The old man rose and went to a narrow shelf above his bed, where several small scrolls sat side by side. "I am teaching him to read," the man said, drawing one down and bringing it to the table. He unrolled it and Jurian saw that it was written in Greek.

"You're teaching him Greek?" exclaimed Agapius. "This gets stranger by the minute!"

"Wait—" Jurian said slowly. As he scanned the words, he realized he recognized the passage. "These are the Scriptures!"

"And should I teach him Hebrew instead?" the old man asked Agapius at the same time, a twinkle in his eye. "It was many years ago, but my travels took me to your fair city, and I was able to copy just a fraction in the time I had. These are now my most priceless possessions."

"These are our Scriptures," Jurian repeated.

"Yes."

"Then you are—"

"Amphibolos."

Jurian looked at Agapius and frowned. "You are?"

"I'm what?"

"Ambiguous."

The old man chuckled. "Well, that may be, but that is my name. Amphibolos. And to answer the rest of your question, yes. I am a follower of *Christus*, and His presbyter here in these parts."

Jurian gripped Amphibolos's hand tight. "It is a blessing to meet you," he murmured.

Amphibolos gently drew back his hand and traced the *signum* on Jurian's forehead, then sat down again in his chair. "Now, Albanus seems to think you have news."

"About what?" Agapius asked. His fingers lingered over the scroll, tracing the Greek letters, but from the wistfulness in his gaze, Jurian wondered if he were seeing the text at all.

"Everything!" Albanus exclaimed. "Tell us all your story!"

Jurian smiled. "That would take too much time."

"You said you escaped the arena," Albanus said. "Tell us that part."

Amphibolos drew his feet away from the fire and straightened up. "The arena? You mean the gladiatorial games?" He gripped the arms of his chair. "And did you see any of our brethren?"

Jurian hesitated, a weight tugging at his heart. "Too many," he said, and squeezed his eyes shut, as if that could somehow block the memory of Varro's brutal execution.

"They brought my sisters home," Albanus said after a short silence.

"Did you?" Amphibolos asked. "That, at least, is good news."

"That may be all the good news there is to share," Jurian murmured. "There is a storm coming…fire, and blood."

Amphibolos nodded slowly. "I have feared as much. I have a friend in the court of Diocletian. She sends news as she is able."

"Nicomedia to Maridunum!" Agapius said. "Has Helena's arm stretched so far?"

"*Helena!*" Albanus cried. "You know of her?"

"We know her. She is my lady's aunt."

"Oh? And who is your lady?" Albanus asked, a wicked smile flashing across his face.

"The daughter of the *Praefectus Augustalis* of Alexandria," Agapius said, somewhat flatly. He moved his hand away from the scroll and pressed it against the table. "And I only meant that I serve her. I didn't mean…" His voice trailed off and he shook his head in irritation.

Albanus chuckled, disbelief mixed with delight. "How impossible," he said, "that you should come to our corner of the world!"

"Well," Jurian said. "I was given a choice, and I chose this."

"What do you mean, you were given a choice?" Albanus asked.

Amphibolos nodded again, thoughtful. "He has been exiled," he told Albanus. "There are not many corners of the world any more that are outside the boundaries of the Empire."

"But we're not outside the Empire," Albanus argued. "Why is he here if he's supposed to be outside the borders? He should go across to Hibernia. *That's* barbarian country."

Amphibolos considered Jurian and Agapius for a moment, then said, "I think it may have to do with the company they keep," he said. "I do not take it that they came to Carmarthen alone."

"Company," Albanus repeated, and Jurian smiled as he watched the young man put the pieces together. "Wait. They did have company. Another man—a Roman…oh!" The gasp came all of a sudden, and it pulled him upright. "No."

"Yes, actually," Jurian said.

"No," Albanus said again. "Her son. Helena's. Isn't it? That Roman commander sitting at the table. That is the *Caesar*'s son. In my house. In my—" Albanus's face shifted from flushed to very pale. "My mother meant no disrespect."

Agapius laughed out loud. "You weren't there! How do you know what happened?"

"I know my mother," Albanus said with all seriousness. "And I know how she despises all Romans."

"All's well," Jurian said. "Your father smoothed things between them, I think."

Albanus blew out his breath in relief and then pushed his hands through his hair until it stood up even more rakishly than before. "But what can it mean, you coming here?" he said. "From the very corners of the world…to Carmarthen?"

"I've been in Britannia for half a year," Jurian muttered, reluctantly. "It doesn't mean anything. Anyway, as Amphibolos said, there are not many places outside the boundaries of the

Empire," Jurian said. "But I chose Britannia for another reason. I came to return this."

He unbuckled Excalibur and laid it on the table beside the scroll. It settled with a heavy *gong* that sounded too loud for the small space. Albanus's eyes grew even wider at the sight of the massive sword. His hand drifted forward, tentative, and touched its hilt, and he gave a low whistle.

"The trouble is," Jurian admitted, "I don't know where to take it. I was advised to bring it here, to Maridunum, but I don't know what I expect to find here. I have only a message, which was given to me with the sword, and it was signed one Merlinus Ambrosius."

Albanus's head snapped up. "You're sure that was the name? Myrddin Emrys?"

"Merlinus Ambrosius," Jurian repeated, more slowly this time.

"That's what I *said*," Albanus retorted. He glanced at Amphibolos, as if asking permission. The presbyter opened his hands, and Albanus took a breath.

"If you are looking for the Myrddin," he said slowly, "he lives up on the hill, not far from here. I can take you to him."

"What?" Jurian asked, recoiling. "That's not possible. How can he be alive? The prophecy he wrote—he wrote it over two hundred years ago."

Albanus just grinned. "Come and see."

They left the hut of Amphibolos with a basket laden with what provisions the generous presbyter had to spare. As they tracked back through the grove of alders to the path, Albanus kept looking at the hilt of the sword above Jurian's shoulder.

"Stranger and stranger," he mumbled, but that was all he could say. He seemed, for the first time since they had met him, at a loss for words.

19

Antiochia ad Orontes, Syria — May, A.D. 301

Three weeks had passed since Aikaterina's arrival in Antioch, and every day that passed, she grew more and more anxious to return home. She began to suspect that the Emperor was detaining her on purpose, and she was sick with worry for her father and her city. She sent message after message home, but she never received anything in reply.

And then there was Maxentius. The presence of his soon-to-be wife seemed to have no effect on the man, and he haunted her steps at every available opportunity. The one place he would not go, she discovered, was the library, and so she had taken to hiding there for several hours every morning. Diodoros and Theokritos seemed thankful for the chance to return to some semblance of the life of peace they had known before Jurian had come into their lives, trailing a storm in his wake.

But somehow it all felt hollow, and she found it hard to concentrate on anything other than her fears.

"Do you still read your *codex?*" Diodoros asked as she fidgeted on the bench in the dim library. "It might help to reassure your mind."

"Yes, but I struggle to find comfort there," she admitted. "Ever since Rome, and my father's illness, I feel…strangely shaken. Everything I thought I knew, all the things I was sure I believed, they all seem so…distant to me. Like the stars. They shine, but they are cold and out of my reach." She bowed her head. "I have never felt so alone."

Diodoros leaned forward and peered into her face. "You are not alone," he said. "I am with you, and Theokritos." He hesitated, and then added, "And…Nenet."

Aikaterina looked up with a smile. Nenet never ceased hounding Diodoros at every opportunity, and Aikaterina knew by that alone that she loved him like a son.

"But it is an aloneness inside," she said. "I can't explain it. It's like I have a hole here—" she laid a hand over her heart— "and it aches, Diodoros. There is a yawning abyss at my feet and I must descend into it, for my people, for my family, but I am all alone."

"I understand the feeling," Diodoros said softly. "Not a day goes by that I do not feel it myself."

"You?" Aikaterina said in surprise. "But I thought—"

"Thought what?"

"You seem like a man in love to me," she said. "Joyful, and content."

Diodoros cleared his throat and shifted on the bench. "Joyful, yes," he said. "But joy is a choice, not a feeling, *kyria*. I choose joy, even though my beloved is so very far away from me."

Aikaterina tilted her head and studied him as if she had never seen him before. He was flushed and refused to look at her, and she wondered suddenly whom he meant. *Was* Diodoros in love, and she had never known it?

"Diodoros," she said. "Are you saying—"

"I am saying, *kyria*," he said, clearing his throat again and taking a deep breath, "that you can choose to embrace the emptiness, or you can choose to embrace the promise. The former will lead to grief. The latter, to hope."

Aikaterina drew in her breath sharply. She felt as though he had just unlocked a secret, and everything came clear. "But nature proves that very thing!" she breathed. "Diodoros! It's marvelous!" She leaned forward. "The bud is not the flower, but only the promise of one. To love the bud for what it is and what it will become—instead of grieving that it is not yet the flower—to feel that wonder as it grows every day, until one morning…there it is!"

Diodoros gazed at her silently for a long moment, and then murmured, "I wish I could see what you see. It is like someone lit a fire in your soul."

Aikaterina pressed both hands over her heart. "But that is exactly what it feels like…like a fire." She stood suddenly. The walls of the library felt like they were closing around her, and she needed to get out—to be in the open, where the breeze and the sunshine could take the song in her heart. "I have to go," she said. "Tell Theokritos we can read Aristotle tomorrow."

Diodoros smiled up at her and nodded, and Aikaterina fled the confines of the library. She made her way to the lush gardens near the palace and wandered the paths, smelling all the early summer flowers that were in full bloom. The sun was warm on her head, and somewhere nearby, a bird warbled in the palm trees. She tilted her face into the sun and opened her arms, feeling as though she could be swept up and fly away.

"I hoped I would find you here," said a voice behind her.

That warm and wonderful world burst around Aikaterina like a bubble, and she whirled to find Maxentius standing a few paces behind her.

"I was just going in," she said. "If you will excuse me."

She tried to edge past him, but he stepped into her path and offered her his arm. "Allow me to escort you."

Aikaterina barely restrained a shudder. She remembered a moment much like this one not so very long ago, when Casca had offered to escort her to the games, and had sat there gloating over her as she watched Varro die.

"What is it?" Maxentius asked, his voice warm with concern.

She shook herself out of the memory and tried to smile. "Nothing. It's…nothing."

He didn't seem content with her answer, but she didn't elaborate, and he didn't press her. She took his arm and he led her slowly along the path back to the palace.

"What good fortune that I happened to be here when Diocletian decided to summon you to Antioch," he said. "Otherwise I might never have met you."

Aikaterina wanted to say that she thought that might have been better, but she was wise enough now to know that sometimes the best thing to do was to smile and say nothing at all.

But she couldn't resist asking, "How is Valeria?"

"How should I know?" he asked, eyes narrowing in annoyance.

"I thought—"

"I don't want to speak of her. She irritates me."

Aikaterina nodded, and thought, *I wonder how he can stand the thought of marrying the woman.*

The idea that anyone would bind themselves to another person solely for the sake of political ambition revolted her. But perhaps he had no choice—no more than she would if a marriage were arranged for her political advantage.

A servant met them as they entered the palace, bowing low to each of them in turn. "The *Imperator* has asked for you, *domine*," he said to Maxentius, then, to Aikaterina, "And you also, *domina*."

Aikaterina swallowed hard and lifted her chin, willing herself not to let Maxentius see her fear. What if the *Imperator* had decided that she was a better match for Maxentius than Galerius's daughter? What would she do? She struggled to breathe as the servant led them down the corridor, while the walls of the palace seemed to fold in around her.

The servant opened the door to Diocletian's *tablinum*, then bowed and left them. Diocletian and Galerius were both within, and Aikaterina fought down the almost overpowering desire to bolt out the door. As far as she had known, Galerius had been in the north, fighting the barbarians along the Danuvius.

She couldn't bear to imagine what might have brought him to Antioch.

"Ah, Maxentius," said Diocletian. "Thank you for collecting our little Alexandrian butterfly for us."

Aikaterina released Maxentius's arm and stepped away from him. "I did not know you were looking for me, *Imperator*," she said, "or I would have come immediately myself."

Diocletian turned to Galerius, gesturing at her as he did so. "You see?"

Aikaterina glanced at Galerius. He was eyeing Maxentius with ill-concealed suspicion, ignoring Aikaterina entirely, as if he didn't even realize she was in the room.

"Now, Aikaterina," said Diocletian. "Come, and let us speak together on a matter that concerns us both dearly. I am troubled by the state of things in Egypt. We must look to the stability of Alexandria."

"I could not agree more, *Imperator Augustus*," Aikaterina said. "And that is why I have come to ask you for your leave to return home."

Maxentius snapped his gaze to her. "What?" he said. "You said nothing to me about this plan."

Aikaterina regarded him, chin lifted. "I was not aware that I needed your permission or your advice on the matter."

Out of the corner of her eye, she saw Diocletian smile, but Galerius only looked more sour than he had a moment ago.

"What concern is it of yours what she does?" Galerius snapped. "Look to your own affairs."

Maxentius turned to him and said smoothly, "I have them well in hand, I assure you."

"Peace," Diocletian said, and then, to Aikaterina, "I will consider your request."

"Thank you," she breathed.

"I received word this morning that your father is somewhat better of late. He has been attending the Alexandrian Senate."

Aikaterina caught a sharp breath, willing away the burn of tears in her throat. "You heard!" she murmured, torn between relief and indignation. "I've had no word…"

Diocletian waved a hand, brushing away her dismay. "I also heard your merchants and farmers are having difficulties with the currency. I'm preparing to issue an edict on prices, which ought to ease their burden." He turned away, sifting over some parchments on his table and added, without preamble or explanation, "I've also issued a grain tax on Alexandria."

"A grain tax!" Aikaterina echoed. "But *Imperator*, as you know, my farmers have been enduring a drought all this spring. If we don't see rain soon, we will have a poor harvest come autumn. How can you burden them with a tax as well?"

"Your understanding of the matter is, of course, highly limited, circumscribed by the borders of your region," Diocletian said, unmoved by her protest. "I do not undertake such things lightly. I trust you will understand that I've weighed the matter carefully, and made the best decision I could for the Empire as a whole." He turned to face her, eyes cold and fathomless, and utterly inscrutable. "On another subject," he said, "there is someone I would like you to meet—a distinguished guest who will be joining us at the feast tonight. The *Caesar's* nephew, Maximinus Daia."

Maxentius stiffened, and a glimmer of triumph flashed in Galerius's eyes. And suddenly, she understood. It was not Maxentius that they planned for her, but this other man.

She inclined her head to Diocletian. *So this is the game they are going to play*, she thought. *I will make them regret it.*

But at the feast that night, Aikaterina did not have the opportunity to meet the *Imperator's* distinguished guest. Maximinus Daia had been recalled to his Legion on the Danuvian *limes*, and had left without delay. The more tolerant members of Diocletian's court praised Daia's valor and dedication to the army. Others whispered that the dignity and expectations of the court hobbled his licentious ways, and he had been only too eager to leave it behind. Aikaterina didn't care either way—she was, at least for another day, free.

20

Maridunum, Britannia — May, A.D. 301

Albanus led Jurian and Agapius along a narrow path as it wound its way up the hill. Ravens perched on rocky outcroppings, rebuking the sky with raucous cries. As the sun climbed higher, the chill morning fog faded, leaving just its ghostly vestiges clinging to the tops of the trees and shrouding the crown of the hill. The air was heavy with the scent of damp earth and leaves.

A faint trickle of water muttering over rock broke the peaceful quiet of the hillside, and Jurian glanced around to find its source. A tiny stream flowed out of a crack in the rock to his left, running off a small outcrop to cascade onto a moss-covered stone. Beside it was a tiny cairn etched with strange symbols.

"What is that?" he asked Albanus.

"A shrine."

"A shrine to whom?" asked Agapius.

"The god of this place." Albanus shrugged and made a sign with his fingers that Jurian recognized as a sign against evil. "The Myrddin," he said, "you should know...he's not—he—well, you'll see."

Jurian stared at the shrine a moment longer, thinking of another spring in another hillside, far from the mist-shrouded hills of Britannia. But Albanus had already pressed on, so Jurian, shuddering with a sudden chill, left the spring of the old god behind and hurried after him.

Just around the next bend in the path, they came out on a wide crop of stone. Moss grew like a thick cushion between the end of the path and the gaping mouth of a cave. The sunlight filtered down through the bright green leaves of the aspen trees to dance with the shadows, and everything felt still. Not even the cawing of the ravens reached them here.

But at the sight of that dark mouth in the hill, Jurian stopped abruptly and backed a step. His breath caught in his chest, his fingers drifting instinctively to the hilt of his *seax* knife. If he went inside, who knew what he would find?

"Are you all right?" Agapius asked as Albanus set his basket down on a flat stone near the entrance.

"I'm...not sure," Jurian said, still hanging back, fighting every impulse in his body to turn and walk back down the path. "What is this place, Agapius?"

"I guess we're about to find out," he said.

From somewhere inside the cave, they heard the sound of singing, faint at first, growing steadily louder. Jurian couldn't understand the words, but the voice that sang them was deep and strong, and the melody was bright like the joy of spring and starlight. Listening to it, Jurian felt the cold fear around his heart slowly begin to loosen.

"Lailoken!" Albanus shouted, and the song stopped abruptly.

Just as Albanus turned to Jurian and Agapius with an expectant smile, the man himself appeared at the mouth of the cave. He was completely bald, but his face was young, and his arms, which he held crossed over his chest, were as burly as a blacksmith's.

Jurian started back so violently that Agapius caught his arm to steady him.

That's him, he thought, with a rush of certainty that was half fear, and half excitement. *That's the man I saw in the dream.*

"Who summons?" the man said.

"Lailoken, it's me," Albanus said, stepping forward. "I brought you some things. A bit of honey."

Lailoken uncrossed his arms and moved to the basket. He walked like a wild thing, or as if the ground couldn't hold him down. For a few moments he pawed through the offerings, and then stuck his finger in the honey pot and planted it in his mouth.

"That is fine," he said, smacking his lips. "Fine indeed." He cocked a bright eye at Albanus and said in elegant Latin, "Honey drips from the mouths of liars, and the bees become as maggots in the deep places of their hearts."

Agapius visibly started, and Jurian caught his arm just above the elbow, whispering, "He's mad."

"You think?" Agapius said.

Lailoken laughed aloud and turned to them, but when he saw Jurian, he froze. He eased forward a step, sideways, head tipped like a wild animal testing the air for danger. Jurian stiffened and waited, hardly daring to breathe.

"Pendragon," Lailoken said.

A chill raised every hair on Jurian's arms. "I'm not—"

"Pendragon."

"You have me confused with someone else," Jurian said. "I'm looking for Merlinus Ambrosius."

"Emrys." Lailoken edged forward another step, then sat down on another wide, flat stone soaked in sunshine. "I am Myrddin Willt. This Myrddin you speak of, Myrddin Emrys—he has gone beyond. But he will return when the bear takes up the sword from its case of stone."

Jurian swallowed hard, the inscription on the sword's hilt weaving through his thoughts: *Ex calce liberandus urso*. "I have a message from him. I have journeyed far…" He drew the sword and held it out, naked in the morning sunshine, across his palms. "I have come to return this to him."

Lailoken dragged his breath in through his teeth at the sight of the sword. "Dragon-slayer," he said.

"Yes, it is."

Lailoken speared him with his bright, tawny eyes. "You are." He lifted a finger and pointed up at the sky. "The banner of the king will bear the sign, and under that sign, he will conquer."

"What sign?" Jurian asked. "What king?"

Lailoken was staring at him now, or through him, at something unseen. "The rolling dark is coming, blotting out the stars by half and half again. Lands under the darkness will be lit by hellfire, and the rivers will flow with blood."

Jurian shuddered, as if his soul were a lyre and Lailoken had set all the strings humming at once. "The storm of fire and blood," he murmured.

"Honey drips from the mouths of liars, and the gall of anger swarms like smoke in the heart," Lailoken said. "From the cave it will come forth, and to the cave it will return. The end of exile is the city of fair love, shining bright beneath the banners of the sun. The gates are open wide, but the path is perilous."

Lailoken slumped forward, his ponderous arms draped across his knees.

Jurian drew in a broken breath, as if he had been held under deep water until that moment. Somewhere nearby, a bird warbled out in the branches, a clear, high song.

Albanus inched forward and touched Lailoken's shoulder. The man stirred and then sprang to his feet. "Oat and honey cakes," he said. "You always bring the best, my young friend." He glanced at Jurian and Agapius, who hadn't moved from the end of the path. "Come, let us sit down a while and enjoy the sunshine!" he said, beckoning them forward. "Presently I will pull out my harp and this one will play for us, eh?"

Agapius turned to Jurian. "So he's not crazy anymore?" he asked. "Is he just sometimes crazy, or how does that work?"

Jurian opened his mouth but nothing would come out. The hermit's words tumbled through his mind, but their meaning eluded him, like trying to catch smoke in a fishing net. The only thing he knew clearly was that the darkness was coming—and when Lailoken had said that it would come forth from the cave, he knew, as if a shaft of light had pierced straight through him, that it would begin in Cyrene. And there was nothing he could do to stop it. Not this time.

Sabra, he thought, but no other words would come. He could only exhale and hope that it was prayer enough for God to understand.

After Lailoken had devoured a few of the honey cakes Albanus had brought, he retreated into the cave and brought out a curiously carved stringed instrument that reminded Jurian of a lyre. He seated himself on his stone in the sun and carefully tuned the strings. As soon as he had it pitched to his satisfaction, he beckoned for Jurian and Agapius to come forward onto the mossy sward.

"Sit!" he said. "You stand there like the stones of fallen gods. This is for life and for light. Come!"

Jurian and Agapius drew closer and settled on a large boulder. Jurian leaned Excalibur against the stone, and it seemed strangely at home there, its point resting in the moss, its hilt shining in the sunlight. Albanus sat cross-legged on the moss near Lailoken's feet, grinning in anticipation.

"Now you will hear something," he said to Jurian and Agapius. "Listen and watch!"

Lailoken began to play, and the music was like nothing Jurian had ever heard in his life. There was a wildness to this music that made it seem somehow closer to the truth of things. It wove in and around the stones, the sunlight, the rippling of the water, the tall trees and the bright, clear sky, and Jurian thought suddenly, absurdly, that maybe this was an echo of the music God had used to call all things into being.

He closed his eyes, letting the music weave through him too. It filled him with a peace he had not felt in months. Caught up in the rapture of that wild joy, he could almost forget Lailoken's warnings of hellfire and blood.

"Hello there, friends!" Lailoken's cheerful voice called out over the music.

Jurian opened his eyes and turned in surprise to see

Constantinus and Menas standing at the head of the path. Menas's foot was tapping on the mossy stone, but Constantinus looked more than mildly annoyed.

"What is this place?" he asked brusquely.

Jurian stifled a smile when he saw Albanus staring at the Tribune like he'd seen an avenging angel of God descending from the clouds. But when Constantinus's gaze drifted in his direction, Albanus jerked away, the color high in his pale cheeks.

"I am the Myrddin," Lailoken said. He eyed Constantinus with a sudden keenness, and a shadow passed across his face. His fingers on the strings never faltered, but the music suddenly changed—like a ship's sails in the shifting wind that heralds a storm. "You are just in time," he said.

"In time for what?" Constantinus said.

"The eagle nests in the alder tree, but soon he will fall. The snake will devour the eggs in the eyrie, and his offspring will grow wings. Under the sign of the dragon the bear will rise and take up the sword of kingship."

Lailoken stopped, and his fingers fell from the strings. His head drooped, as if he had fallen asleep. For a moment longer, the air hummed with music, and then the only sound was the faint burbling of the stream down the hill.

"What is the meaning of this?" Constantinus asked, his voice low. "Who says the eagle will fall?"

"I'm sure he didn't mean anything by it," Agapius said briskly. "He's crazy. We think."

"He is not," Albanus said, indignant. He rose and planted his fists on his hips. "He speaks riddles, that's all. Not many know how to understand him."

"At least he doesn't write them on leaves," Constantinus muttered.

"What?" Jurian said.

"I want to know what he means by the eagle and the snake and the bear," Constantinus said to Albanus, ignoring Jurian's question. "Wake him."

Albanus, still skittish under the intensity of Constantinus's attention, shrugged a little and laid a hand on Lailoken's shoulder. "He has questions, Myrddin," he whispered loudly. "Wake up!"

Lailoken stirred and raised his head. "I speak what is spoken," he said. "Answers he must find elsewhere."

Constantinus snorted. "What, do you style yourself like the oracle at Delphi, prattling empty prophecies for fools and emperors?"

Lailoken cocked his head and studied Constantinus again. "And which of those are you?"

Agapius stifled a laugh and Jurian elbowed him in the ribs.

"I speak what is spoken," Lailoken said again. "But whether you hear or not, that is not for me."

"What am I supposed to hear?" Constantinus said. "Are you saying that Rome will not last in Britannia? Speak!" He took a step forward, his voice ringing out like thunder.

Jurian had seen greater men than Lailoken quail at the sound of that voice, but the Myrddin seemed completely unperturbed. "What I have spoken, I have spoken," he said placidly. "It is for you to hear."

Constantinus bristled, but he subsided.

"Perhaps," Menas said, "he knows where to take the sword."

He nodded at Excalibur, and for just that instant, everyone seemed to be caught in a moment of time, staring at the sword.

"Yes," Jurian agreed finally, turning to Lailoken. "You said you are not Merlinus Ambrosius, whose sword this is."

"It is not his," Lailoken corrected. "He was its maker, but it has passed out of his hands and into yours."

"It's not mine either," Jurian said. "I was told to bring it—"

"It is yours to lay down for another to take up," Lailoken interrupted. "It must go to the isle of the apple tree and sleep. A little while, and then a little while again."

"Ynys Afallon?" Albanus said, his eyes widening. "Is that the place you mean?"

"That place is cursed," Constantinus said suddenly. "None go there if they wish to remain whole." He gestured at Lailoken.

"They go mad, like him. It's the mist. People say they can see things."

"They see women," Albanus said. "Isn't that right, *domine*?"

Constantinus's jaw tightened. "Yes."

Lailoken sniffed and nibbled on another oatcake. "It is not always evil that comes of the sight," he said. "Your father did not think so, when he saw your mother."

Constantinus crossed the mossy space in two furious strides and seized Lailoken by the shoulders, setting the harp strings jangling in discord.

"What do you mean by that? My father is not mad!"

Albanus stared at Constantinus, his mouth a perfect O. Jurian and Agapius jumped to their feet. Menas alone did not move, but watched Constantinus placidly with his one good eye.

"He is not mad," Constantinus repeated, releasing Lailoken.

Lailoken brushed his robe off and set the harp aside with a gentle pat. "Nor said I that he was," he observed. "You were the one who said that all who go to Ynys Afallon go mad. Your father went, yes. And he had a dream there, it is said—a dream of a magnificent lady. The daughter of Coel, the fairest maiden in all the land. And it has served Rome well for him to have dreamed it. This Rome and the one to come after."

"Has it?" Constantinus said. "When she is treated as an outcast, and her son as a political prisoner?"

Lailoken merely looked at him, and Constantinus spun away with a noise of exasperation.

"Well," Jurian said, "I suppose I must take the hazard, and go to this place."

"You're already half-mad anyway," Agapius said, just loud enough for Jurian to hear.

Jurian rolled his eyes and ignored him, instead asking Lailoken, "Do you know the way?"

Lailoken pointed at Constantinus and called after him, "You know the way. It is written in your heart."

Constantinus didn't turn, only brushed past Menas and

headed back down the path without a word of farewell. Jurian stared after him for a moment, then took up the sword and slipped it into the sheath.

"Thank you," he said. "For giving us directions."

Lailoken grinned at him, but then sobered just as suddenly. "The path is being laid before you," he said. "May you have the courage to walk it."

He lifted his hand as if in benediction, and Jurian turned away and followed Constantinus down the hill.

21

Maridunum, Britannia — May, A.D. 301

Jurian jogged down the path from Lailoken's cave, leaving Agapius to help Menas with the rough places, and caught up with Constantinus at the bottom of the hill.

"Wait," he called. "Constantinus, wait."

Constantinus stopped and turned as Jurian drew up beside him. "What?"

"I need you to take me there," Jurian said. "To Ynys Afallon."

"And what if I say no?"

Jurian studied him, wondering at the glint in his eyes that looked so much like anger. "Why would you say no? You'd come all this way on the promise that you would help me, and now you will say no?"

Constantinus laughed, but it was a hard laugh, and without mirth. "No one goes to that accursed place," he said. "No one, do you understand?"

"Your father—"

"If my father went there, then he was a fool!" Constantinus snapped, and his eyes darkened with bitter grief. "What good has come from a marriage that could never be sanctioned by Rome?"

"Well," Jurian said mildly, "you're standing here, aren't you?"

He snorted and shifted away, murmuring, "And sometimes I wonder why that is."

"We all do, I think," Jurian said. "But if you are standing there, it is for a reason. I don't think there is anything that happens by accident or without purpose."

Constantinus swung around to fix him with his sharp gaze. "Not even your own sister's murder?"

Jurian swallowed hard and lowered his eyes. Mari's death was still, in so many ways, a fresh wound that never quite seemed to heal, and Constantinus's words brought pain welling like blood to the surface.

"Not even that," he said. After a long silence, he continued, "You know the way. You are probably the only one here who does…or the only one bold enough to actually take the path."

Constantinus stared a long while at the hills around them, eyes distant, then he heaved a sigh and nodded once. "Very well," he said. "But that had better be the end of this business with the sword."

Jurian couldn't keep a sudden grin off his face. "I can't promise that," he said, "but I'll have done my part."

They set out for Ynys Afallon three days later. They gathered in the yard outside Idris's hut, the stocky island horses pawing at the chalky gravel of the road. Eilwen and Brigit, their blond hair twined in long braids down their backs, clung to Menas's hands, speaking rapidly over each other, half in their native dialect, half in broken Latin.

Jurian could just make out a few of Brigit's words. She said, "Come back that you can. Soon."

"I'll come back if I can," Menas agreed, embracing them both in his gruff way. It was only by the glint of his eye that could Jurian tell how deeply their affection moved him.

Jurian clasped Albanus's hand at the wrist. "Take care of Amphibolos," he said. "And thank him for me."

"I will." Albanus smiled. "I wish I could go with you."

"You'll get your chance at adventure someday, I'm sure,"

Jurian said. "Though sometimes I wonder if it's not a better life, living in peace."

Albanus looked skeptical, but he only nodded and stepped away from the horses.

Constantinus stood a little apart with his horse, watching the others give their farewells. After a moment Idris approached him, laying a hand over his breast and inclining his head.

"You do our house honor, *domine*," he said. "Our door is always open to you, should you find yourself in Maridunum again."

Constantinus nodded and swung onto the saddle, turning his horse's head a little too quickly away from the group gathered to see them off. Jurian noticed, and wondered, but he couldn't understand the stillness of Constantinus's face, or the resigned light in his eyes.

"The day is wasting," he said abruptly, meeting Jurian's gaze and lifting a hand.

As Jurian rode up beside him, the Tribune turned slightly in his saddle. Jurian didn't shift around to look, but he had a feeling he knew what—or who—Constantinus was looking at. Only he didn't say anything, and didn't wave in farewell, but set his heels to his horse's flanks.

As it leapt forward, Jurian heard him mutter, "What is the use of it all?"

The weather remained cool, and the mist lifted only a little as they turned their horses onto the *Via Julia Maritima* that would take them most of the way to the *colonia* of Glevum. Constantinus told them that the road had been constructed under the direction of Julius Frontinus, who had subdued this area for Rome some two centuries prior. It would take them through the garrison town of Isca Silurum, where the *Legio II Augusta* had been based in Frontinus's time, and from there they would continue on to Glevum.

Once they had left Maridunum behind, Constantinus slowed the pace until their horses were fairly plodding along the road. The Tribune obviously was in no hurry, but Jurian was hesitant to press him. The fact that Constantinus was leading them to Ynys Afallon at all was a remarkable favor. Jurian decided it was best to let him do it in his own time.

They stopped around noon in a mossy hollow just off the road. When Agapius moved to gather wood for a fire, Constantinus stopped him with a shake of his head. They ate cold lamb and drank some wine, and then mounted again and rode on. Jurian was thankful for it—the longer they sat, the more the damp seeped into his bones, and he doubted even the warmth of a campfire would banish it.

The road climbed steadily now into hills littered with tumbled stone and tall pines, their peaks stretching higher into the sky than Jurian had ever imagined. The mist wreathed their crowns, giving them the appearance of ghostly sentinels. Not since his encounter with the dragon in the cave of Cyrene had Jurian so strongly felt the presence of powers more ancient than the gods of Rome. Under the thin drizzle he pulled up the hood of his *birrus* and clasped his pyx, which hung around his neck beneath his tunic. This wasn't an evil place—not like the cave. But it was a place of mystery and of watchful waiting, as if the trees and the very ground were holding their breath.

Menas nudged his massive horse alongside Jurian's and they rode together a while in silence.

"There is something about this place," Menas said, his deep voice rolling through the mist.

"Yes," Jurian said.

They said nothing more, and Jurian watched Constantinus thoughtfully as he rode at the head of their little party. He sat straight in his saddle, head bare in spite of the cool rain. The further up into the hills they rode, the more regal he seemed, as if lordship in these lands were his and his alone.

He belongs here, Jurian realized suddenly. *No wonder they wanted to keep him in the south, safely away from this place.*

They rode until the daylight faded and they could no longer see clearly to pick their way along the track. The heavy fog hid the moon, and as darkness settled around them, the drizzle strengthened into a chill rain.

"This is miserable," Agapius muttered as they tethered their horses in a grove just off the road. The branches of the trees afforded some shelter from the rain, but not much. "Please tell me we can light a fire this time."

Constantinus said nothing, but wrapped himself in his cloak and settled against the bole of a tree. Agapius took his silence as consent and stumbled about in the underbrush gathering twigs and sticks. Every now and again, the deep stillness was punctuated by a sharp *ow* and mumbled bits of what sounded like curses.

Jurian let Menas and Agapius see to the fire and took a spot on the damp ground near Constantinus.

"How far is the journey?" he asked.

"To Glevum? About another two days. We'll stop tomorrow in Isca." Jurian couldn't see his face clearly in the dark, but he could hear the smile in his voice as he added, "It should provide more comfortable quarters."

"And will the garrison in Glevum welcome us? If they learn that I am violating the terms of my exile…"

Constantinus stirred, resting one arm easily on his knee. "I wouldn't worry. Do you want to go to Ynys Afallon with that sword or don't you?"

"I think I must."

"Then don't speak of your terms of exile. You violated those the moment we landed in Portus Adurni, after all, and no one has threatened your life yet with retribution for the insulted honor of Rome, as far as I'm aware. Or should we go back further, to Tingi? The only people in Britannia who will care about your interdiction are somewhere far away from us, and I could honestly not care less what information they pass along to the *Augusti* in the south. Let them whine and moan, for all it matters."

Jurian couldn't help a laugh of surprise to hear Constantinus speak like that—Constantinus, who was so passionately *in love* with Rome, who had never spoken against the Empire or its rulers except in subtleties and implications. Jurian doubted he had ever heard him speak so bluntly about anything.

"I didn't know you had such strong feelings on the matter," he said, as lightly as possible.

Constantinus took a deep breath and sighed it out. "Maybe it's just being here again...out from under the cloying, rotting corpse of imperial court life, or the frontier camps with *Caesar* Galerius. Say the right things, do the wrong things, all in the name of an emperor whose only concern is keeping and maintaining power."

Jurian said nothing.

"Varro understood," Constantinus said suddenly.

Jurian peered at him through the gloom, but Constantinus had turned his head, and Jurian felt keenly that the conversation was over. Nearby, Agapius was striking flint, trying to get the damp wood to light.

"Let me do it," Jurian said after watching him a few moments, and made his way over to join his friend. "You city folk. No notion of lighting fires in the wild."

"I am not city folk!" Agapius protested. Then, when Menas snorted with laughter, he laughed too. "Well, maybe I am. Where is Eleutherius when you need him?"

Jurian grinned, remembering the soldier in Nicomedia with his inexplicable fondness for fire. Taking the firesteel from Agapius's hand, he struck it again and again against the flint, trying to get the kindling to catch. A few sparks drifted from the flint, and did nothing.

Jurian's face burned, but at least Constantinus didn't seem to notice his failure. He was preoccupied, working at something in his hands with his *pugio*, but Jurian couldn't see what.

"Hah," Agapius said. "It's your fault we can't start a fire."

"My fault!"

"Well, you're the one under interdict of fire and water," Agapius muttered, and gestured with a flourish to the smoking pile of twigs. "Behold, the consequences."

Jurian glared at him and Menas chuckled. Then, to Jurian's

surprise, Constantinus took the flint and firesteel from his hands, mounded a small pile of fungus he had scraped from the tree, and with just a few sharp strikes of the firesteel against the flint, got the tinder to smolder. Agapius looked suitably impressed, but Constantinus returned to his place under the tree without so much as a word, leaving Agapius to coax the smoking tinder into flame.

Jurian, chagrined, wandered back to join him.

"Tell me something," Constantinus said, his face eerie in the dancing shadows. "I have always wondered, what would you have done if I hadn't stopped you, at Varro's trial?"

Jurian, startled by the unexpected question, stared down at his hands. What would he have done? He hardly knew. He didn't have the gift of argument like Aikaterina, who could stand against emperors and not shrink.

"You would have joined him, wouldn't you?"

"Yes, I suppose I would have," Jurian answered. "Your niece would have seen to his defense."

Constantinus laughed softly. "Aikaterina knows her own mind," he said. "And woe to any who think they can persuade her to change it."

"But she will be persuaded against her will," Jurian said. "To marry into the Tetrarchy."

Constantinus leaned his head back against the tree and closed his eyes. "Yes. I suppose she will."

"Well," Jurian said with a smile. "Maybe she will find a way to argue her way out of that too, in the end."

Constantinus said nothing, and Jurian could see that he was troubled. Deciding it was best to leave him with his own thoughts, he got up and joined Agapius nearer to the fire. As the warmth of the blaze filled the little glade, everyone's spirits seemed to lift, and Jurian felt the clouds of doubt and worry begin to shift to the corners of his mind.

"Did I hear Constantinus say that we would be somewhere civilized soon?" Agapius said. "Like somewhere with hot food and an actual bed?"

"I never thought you were one for such comforts," Jurian said. "Where is your sense of adventure?"

"Well, I miss Camulodunum. Maybe I'm just getting old."

Menas laughed, a great rolling laugh that made the glade echo. It was contagious, and soon even Constantinus was chuckling.

"I'm glad we brought you," Jurian said, catching his breath.

"It's the least I can do," Agapius answered mildly. "Since apparently I'm useless at starting fires."

22

Glevum, Britannia — May, A.D. 301

Two nights later, in a haze of fine rain that clung to everything from their eyelashes to their short cloaks, Jurian's little party rode through the gates into the town of Glevum. After the wide open and seemingly deserted hill country they had traveled through since Maridunum, Jurian was almost shocked by the bustling of the city—even at this late hour. Unlike the half-abandoned settlement of Isca Silurum, the main street of Glevum was broad and well paved, and grey-stoned shops crowded each other on either side. Up ahead, Jurian could see the impressive outline of the Roman fort, which sat on a low hill just above the level of the town. Its walls blazed with torchlight, interrupted only by the silhouettes of several guards on duty in the towers.

Jurian and the others passed single-file through the busy *forum* and trotted up the hill toward the *porta principalis* of the fort. As soon as the soldiers on duty saw Constantinus in his red tribune's cloak, they opened the gates, and one of them staggered off to alert the *praetor*. The other soldiers tried desperately to straighten their tunics and stand at attention as Constantinus led their company in. The unfortunate *miles* at the end of the row kept slumping over on his neighbor's shoulder, only to be shrugged violently off.

"This should be interesting," Constantinus muttered under his breath as they dismounted in the courtyard. Two slaves, who at least were sharp and alert, sprang forward from the shadows to take their horses, while another came to lead them into the *praetorium*. They passed several large courtyards intended for military drills, and then came into a long, narrow *triclinium*.

Huge braziers burned in the corners of the chamber and the firelight danced on the tessellated floors, which were adorned with the intricate pattern work of geometric shapes, animals, and leaves that Jurian had come to associate with Britannic design—whimsical and a little grotesque, straddling the line between the real and the supernatural.

His thoughts were interrupted by the appearance of the *praetor* himself, who hurried forward to greet Constantinus with a low bow and attempt at a military salute.

"It is an honor, *Tribunus* Constan...tantinus," he said, his voice slurring. "We did not expect you."

"No, I can see that," Constantinus said. He studied the man a moment longer, then turned to Jurian abruptly and said, "Deal with this."

He strode to the back of their group and folded his arms, leaving Jurian, alone and stunned, in front of the *praetor*.

The *praetor* swallowed hard, obviously trying to figure out how to make his tongue form words properly. It required intense focus, and he shifted unsteadily, unwittingly almost stepping on Jurian's feet.

"Would you...like to inspect the fort?" he asked. "Shall I call the soldiers to assemble in the—"

"No need for that," Jurian said, drawing himself a little straighter and leaning slightly away from the *praetor*. "And stand back, man. You're breathing on me."

He heard an indecorous snort from Agapius's direction. The *praetor* wobbled back a few steps and straightened his toga. Clearly, he'd not taken time to allow the servants to dress him properly—even his sandals were on the wrong feet. Suddenly

Jurian couldn't blame Constantinus for walking away. The Tribune had just spent months in rigid military discipline, campaigning along the *limes*, risking life and limb for the Empire. The *praetor*'s drunken, slovenly idiocy had to be like a slap in the face.

He met Agapius's gaze, silently pleading for help. Agapius's mouth lifted in a sudden grin.

"Are you celebrating a feast of Mithras tonight, or did I forget the *Caesar's* birthday?" Agapius asked, with feigned innocence.

The *praetor* laughed, but it came out as a kind of hiccuping. Menas's mouth was beginning to twitch.

"What, *Trib*...no, *miles*...no...*domine*?" the praetor asked, blanching. "Did I miss a feast? Was it his noble father's birthday?"

Agapius said, very seriously, "Yes. It was our dear *Caesar's* birthday."

"And I missed it!" he wailed, his eyes filled with drunken tears.

"You missed it? But I thought surely that is why you had drunk so much wine."

The *praetor* frowned and scratched his head. "Was that why?"

Constantinus, having collected himself, came forward to stand beside Jurian again. "Glevum is where all the retired Legionaries come to stay once their service is concluded," he said. "Obviously, they don't feel the need to stay vigilant about the barbarian threat!" His voice rose, dark and menacing, as he said this, and he turned on the praetor. "What is the meaning of this?"

The *praetor* seemed to shrink into himself. "Your father's birthday?"

"No. It is not my father's birthday. Get out of my sight. Find me Agricola. Marcus Aesibuas."

"Marcus...Marcus...Marcus," mumbled the praetor, then shook his head. "Agricola? He's not here. He left for his villa two…two days ago? Two days ago. I think."

"Then I require food, rooms for the night, and our horses first thing in the morning," Constantinus said. When the *praetor* hesitated, Constantinus took a step forward. The man turned and scuttled away, hollering for the servants at the top of his lungs.

As soon as he was gone, Agapius burst out laughing, but Constantinus almost looked embarrassed.

"He will be reprimanded for this," he said.

"Surely there's no cause for anything quite so official?" Jurian said.

Constantinus shook his head. "Glevum might be a bustling commercial town and a center of trade, not to mention a place of rest and relaxation for soldiers who have done their labor for the Empire, but its strategic position cannot be overstated. The Severn River connects Glevum with Virconium, and from there, our Roman roads can take you anywhere in Britannia—Londinium, Eboracum in the north…"

"Is Britannia so precarious, then?" Agapius asked, sobering.

"For many reasons, yes. But its resources are of great importance to the Empire." Constantinus laced his fingers behind his back and paced to one of the glowing braziers. "We will find out more tomorrow. Marcus Aesibuas Agricola is an old friend of my father's. He was the former *praetor* here, but Maximianus *Augustus* didn't like his politics."

"How unsurprising," Agapius said.

"His villa is on the way to Ynys Afallon, and I would not mind taking some rest there," Constantinus said. "And since I doubt my father has been out this way recently, it would be useful to have some intelligence to bring him of the state of affairs here."

Several servants bustled into the *triclinium* with trays of cold venison and fowl, flatbread, and wine that had been warmed and spiced. They arranged the food on the table and then bowed and left again. Menas sat down at once and helped himself to a heaping portion of venison.

"We haven't had a decent meal in days," he said.

"What, you don't like Constantinus's camp cooking?" Agapius said, taking the seat beside him.

"You were in charge of the rations," Menas observed. "That stew last night was...indescribable."

As Menas and Agapius settled in for their meal, Jurian joined Constantinus at the brazier. "You said before that you would have use for me here," he said quietly. "What do you have in mind, exactly?"

Constantinus rolled his broad shoulders. "I'm not sure yet," he said. "I suppose it partly depends on what happens to you at Ynys Afallon."

"What do you mean by that?" Jurian asked.

Constantinus flashed him a startlingly broad grin. "Well, if you come back from that place and you're completely insane, I suppose I'll just have to send you back here to keep the *praetor* company."

THE NEXT MORNING DAWNED clear and warm, with bright sunlight in a vivid blue sky. After a cold breakfast in the *triclinium*, Constantinus ordered their horses to be made ready, and they left the fort without even taking their leave of the *praetor*.

They headed due east from the town, cutting across wide rolling fields sparkling with dew. Under that glittering shawl the fields seemed to stretch all the way to the horizon in swells of endless grey-green, reminding Jurian of a vast and briny sea.

The words of his mother's prophecy wove into his thoughts, and he suppressed a smile.

All this time, he thought, *I assumed that the sea the sword must pass over was the ocean. Maybe it always meant Britannia itself.*

As they rode, he could see short, straight stones standing upright in the fields, which seemed to mark off boundaries. Some were carved with strange-looking graffiti, and Jurian wondered idly what they meant. They passed several fields that were better fenced with wood pilings, with herds of shaggy sheep scattered over the distant hillsides.

By midday, the sun had warmed the land enough to dry the morning dew, and they could see the rich earth where a field of spring crops had been harvested and plowed under for a summer planting. A line of trees cut northeast across the landscape a short distance ahead, and as they approached, Jurian realized that they marked the path of a wide Roman road. They stopped for a quick meal once they reached the trees, and then Constantinus turned north along the road.

The sun had slipped low in the sky, casting long shadows across the road, when they saw the huge hulking shape of a villa just to the east. A gravel path led away from the road and up a gentle slope, and then finally through a gateway in the low wall. As they cantered through it, wide fields opened out on either side of the path, with the dark ribbon of a river running nearby. Agapius let out a low whistle as they passed a garden with an elaborate labyrinth of low hedges.

As they reached the villa, servants filed out of the house to take their horses as if they had been expecting them, and then the master of the house himself came out to meet them. Marcus Aesibuas Agricola was a portly man, and his hair, though still thick and curly, was completely white. He laughed aloud as Constantinus came forward, and he threw open his arms as if he were welcoming home a long-absent son.

Constantinus embraced him, then the older man turned to Jurian and the others with a broad smile.

"Welcome, friends!" he said. "If he hasn't told you, I'm Marcus Aesibuas Agricola, but please, show an old barbarian the kindness of calling him Aesibuas."

Jurian grinned, a little bemused, and followed the man into the vestibule. The villa, which seemed to have been the work of centuries of labor, was almost as impressive to Jurian as the Emperor's *Villa Hadriana* outside of Rome. Intricate mosaics patterned the floor, and each room was richly decorated with its own unique design. The ceilings were lined with wood, but compared to the fortress of Camulodunum, they arched so high overhead that they gave the whole place a feeling of openness, as if they were standing within a grove of towering pines.

Aesibuas led them into a bright *tablinum*, which offered comfortable low couches and a view of the river from the narrow windows. Agapius immediately settled onto one of the couches and stretched out his legs, but Menas stood at the window, pensive, watching the river. After calling for some wine, Aesibuas gestured for Constantinus and Jurian to sit.

"Now, what brings you out this way, Constantinus?" he asked. His Latin carried a curious accent, Jurian thought, not quite southern, but not as clipped and harsh as the Britannic accent. "I never expected to see you, not this time of year. Last I heard, you were off campaigning with Galerius. Made quite a name for yourself down there, eh?" He cocked an eyebrow at Constantinus and then chuckled. "By Martius Lenus, it's good to see you."

"When did you get back from Augusta Treverorum?" Constantinus asked, accepting a cup of wine from a servant.

"Five, six months ago? About the same time you headed out that direction, I suppose. I came west as soon as the *Caesar* would let me."

Something in his tone drew Jurian's attention, and from the sharp light in Constantinus's eyes he could tell the Tribune had noticed it as well.

"Why do you say that?" Constantinus asked.

Aesibuas twirled his goblet between his hands and sighed. "I thought once we'd dispatched Allectus for his treason that we'd have some unity in Britannia. You know…real *peace*. But there are elements around your father who seem determined to stir trouble up whenever and however they can."

"What elements?"

"See, when you look like that, I'm never sure how much I should say," Aesibuas laughed. "My boy, you were born with a spear in your hand."

"I've known that he doesn't trust all the members of his court, but they were, luckily for us, absent when we stopped in Londinium. Are you saying they're back now?"

"Back, and pulling at their traces, too," Aesibuas said.

"Whatever information you have, tell me. I mean to return to Londinium after we're done here. Give me names, and give me offices, and tell me just how dangerous you think they are. I need to know what I'm going to walk into."

"And bringing strangers too," Aesibuas observed. He looked hard at Jurian, and then suddenly tilted his head and narrowed his eyes. "You look familiar to me," he said. "Do I know you?"

"We have never met that I remember," Jurian said. "But if you served in Germania, it might be that you knew my father, Lucius Aurelius Gerontios?"

The man sprang to his feet, his empty goblet falling to the floor with a ringing clang. "Gerontios!" he cried. "No, it can't be...not after all these years! But yes, now that you say it...you are the very image of him when I knew him! Is he well? He must be proud to have a son such as you to carry on his name!"

Jurian said nothing, and Aesibuas's smile froze on his face. He turned to Constantinus for some explanation, but the Tribune only met his gaze in silence.

"My father is dead," Jurian said at last. He closed his mouth on the rest of the story, deciding that there was no need to share too much detail of the *hows* and *whys* of his father's murder at the hands of his own men.

Aesibuas sank down again on the low couch and collected his goblet. "You know," he said slowly, "I always wondered how he would turn out, whether life would treat him nobly, whether he would live to dare great deeds, after I found him near the Danuvius that day."

Jurian started forward on the couch, breathless. "What?"

"Did he ever tell you the story? There was a battle near my home," Aesibuas said. "Afterwards, we went to see if we could help the wounded. I found him face down on the riverbank, half-drowned, with a knife—"

"Knife wound in the back," Jurian said. "But he said...he always said a farmer saved his life. Called himself Jurian."

Aesibuas chuckled. "So I did." He spread his hands on his knees. "I suppose that's why I wanted this place. Farming is in my blood, thicker than Rome is. Anyway, he stayed with me for a few days. We didn't have much to say—I had no notion of Latin back then, and he didn't know anything of my own tongue beyond the choice words he'd heard used in battle." He chuckled. "Can't have much conversation using those."

An old barbarian...

Jurian laughed in disbelief and shook his head. "But this is amazing," he said. "Ever since I can remember, my father called me Jurian, in honor of the man who saved his life that day." He couldn't stop grinning as he held out his hand to Aesibuas. "It's not every day you get the chance to meet your namesake...and to thank him."

Aesibuas took his hand and squeezed it firmly, then slapped Constantinus's knee. "See?" he said. "Good things always happen when you come to see me."

"So how did you end up in the Legion?" Agapius asked.

"Simple, I suppose," Aesibuas said. "After Gerontios left to rejoin his men, I went up to Augusta Treverorum and offered my services. They made me a proper Roman, three names and all. Called me *Agricola* as a sort of joke, I think, because I was so keen for them to know I was a farmer. Well, I was a quick study in Latin—always had an ear for language, I suppose—but since I spoke the native language, I was employed as a scout. Then when Constantius Chlorus came as the new *Caesar*, he kept me and a few others as senior advisors. This villa was his gift to me, for my long service. When he goes back to Germania, I often go with him, even though, officially, I've retired from service."

"Which brings me back to my question," Constantinus said. "What elements in my father's inner circle are causing trouble?"

"Julius Asclepiodotus," said Aesibuas, haltingly, as if the name had to be wrung out of him. "He is the worst of the lot. I think his loyalties are out of priority."

"Then we'll just have to set him straight," said Constantinus.

23

Myra, Anatolia — May, a.d. 301

Sabra opened her eyes to a shaft of bright sunshine spreading across the floor of her little *cubiculum*, and for the first time in weeks, the ache in her heart was only the breath of a memory. She lay quietly for a little while, listening contentedly to the hush of the waves against the shore, and from somewhere downstairs, the soft chatter of the two girls who had become almost sisters to her during her stay in Myra.

Once she had dressed and had a bit to eat for breakfast, she made her way to Nikolaos's home, where the presbyter sat in his courtyard with Hanno. Nikolaos was reading aloud from a scroll—a scroll in Hebrew, she realized as she drew closer, which he was translating effortlessly into Greek for Hanno's understanding. Hanno had been dutifully studying Greek ever since they had returned from their first trip to Rome. Sabra had been a little envious of how quickly he had picked it up, but, for all his efforts, he still struggled with Latin.

They both favored her with a smile as she entered the small courtyard, and Hanno passed her a dish of honey-drenched cheese.

"You look well this morning," Nikolaos said, allowing the scroll to roll closed. "Sleeping better?"

"Much," Sabra said.

Even with her newfound resolve and the lessons she had learned from Nikolaos, she still suffered from nightmares—her unconscious mind still straying far beyond her control. But the nightmares were slowly losing their force as well, and sometimes Sabra went for nights at a time without suffering one. After years of torment, she was finally beginning to learn what it was to feel truly rested.

"Nikolaos," she said after a while. "I was thinking I would like to send word to Britannia."

"To Jurian?" he asked, and she gave him a look.

"No, to the *Caesar*," she said, which made Hanno laugh. She sighed and folded her hands in her lap. "But I don't know where to send it. I can't send it *to* Britannia exactly, because Britannia is Roman, and Jurian is in exile. How could a messenger ever find him beyond the borders?"

"You may choose to wait, instead, for word from him," Nikolaos said.

Sabra studied him curiously, thinking of how he had so miraculously appeared on the hillside in Cyrene, and, before that, on the docks of Carthago. He had some sort of power that she wasn't sure she understood, but maybe he could use it once more.

"Can you see him? Do you know where he is? Could you… take a message to him for me?"

He tossed his head back and laughed, the sound so merry and gentle that she couldn't feel embarrassed. "Oh, Sabra," he said. "I am not an angelic courier, that I can flit here and there whenever I choose! It would, of course, be marvelous if I could."

"But you know things, don't you? You can read souls and see people's pasts, and…"

He patted her hand and stole back the dish of cheese. "I know what I know," he said, echoing what he'd told her months ago, "and I see what I see. Can I make demands of God?"

Sabra scowled.

He leaned forward to catch her eye, his dark eyes smiling.

"But I see enough. I see no details, but I have a sense. Jurian is well. Our friends are well."

"Thank you," she murmured, and the words sounded pale in comparison to the relief she felt.

He grinned and slapped his hands on his thighs, then jumped to his feet. "Enough of lonely thoughts! I have an enterprise for you."

"For me? What is it?"

"But if I told you, it would ruin the surprise," Nikolaos said.

Skeptical, she watched him slip into his small *cubiculum*, wondering what schemes he was up to. He always seemed to be popping in and out in the most unexpected ways. Most of the time, he came laden with foodstuffs, or with other trinkets that were of varying preciousness. She never knew where he got any of it, and while she had entertained the notion for a few weeks that he was the jolliest thief she had ever met, that suspicion was gone now. Instead, she preferred to think that he had commerce with the angels.

"Do you know what this is all about?" she asked Hanno, accepting a cup of water from him.

"I never know what that man is all about."

She laughed and sipped her water, waiting until Nikolaos reappeared. He had a small leather sack in his hand, and he chuckled all the way across the *atrium*.

"What mischief are you planning?" Sabra asked, feeling laughter bubble up inside her too.

He was like a child, delighting in surprises, and she could hardly wait for him to tell her what he had for her to do.

"This, daughter, is just the thing for your precious heart," he said, sliding onto the bench across from her. He placed the bag down in the middle of the table and leaned over it, lowering his voice like a conspirator. "You've lived some time now with Melitta and Chloe," he said. "As you know, their mother is a widow, and all the money her husband had left her has been spent, because the man who owns their home is a ruthless mercenary." His usually kind eyes darkened, and he added,

"I've had business with him before."

Sabra watched him with wonder. "I'm sure you have," she said, unable to keep herself from smiling.

"And so," he said, "this dear widow is quite desperate for her daughters to marry so that they can have homes and be provided for. One more month, and the landlord will scoop them all up and sell them into slavery to pay their debts."

"Oh!" Sabra exclaimed, as if all the breath had been punched out of her. "I had no idea!"

"No, she keeps this very close. At any rate, it will never happen," Nikolaos said, "because you are going to help me."

"How?"

Nikolaos indicated the sack, and Sabra lifted it. It was heavier than she expected, and she heard the rich clink of coins inside.

"It's a little venture I began over a year ago, when Jurian was with me. The eldest of the daughters had just come of age, so, I made them a little present of some money. Just enough for a dowry for the girl, so that she could be free to marry."

"You!" Sabra gasped. "Melitta told me about the miraculous gift they'd gotten, which let their sister Korinna get married! It seems like every week they come up with a new guess for who gave them the money, and they argue over it for hours!"

Nikolaos laughed at that, looking more delighted than anyone she had ever seen.

"Excellent!" he said. "Well, what do you think this is for?"

"Chloe," Sabra said promptly. The girl was recently of age, and Sabra had comforted her on more than one occasion as she had wept over her uncertain future.

"Yes. For Chloe." His eyes twinkled at her. "You are perfectly accepted in the house now, so you are exactly the right person for this task. You're going to drop this bag in Chloe's shoes, after everyone has gone to bed. Do you see?"

Sabra grinned and shook her head. "They know well enough that I have no money of my own," she said. "They'll never suspect me."

"Perfect!"

"But Nikolaos," Sabra said. "Why don't you just give them the money yourself? Surely they would be delighted to know who it came from, so they could thank you properly."

"But I want none of the thanks," Nikolaos said. "All I have, I am given, and what I am given, I provide where it is needed. It is not me who sees, but the Father of all." He smiled at her. "And I know you know what it is to be in chains…so this gift of freedom means most coming from you."

Sabra's eyes filled with tears, and she reached suddenly across the table and seized his brown hand in hers. "Thank you," she whispered.

"Your tears are all the thanks I could ever need," he said.

Sabra squeezed his hand again and he got to his feet.

"Now, I have business in the city to attend to," he said. "Stay as you like, or not."

He waved a hand over his shoulder as he left the house, and Sabra and Hanno watched him go in bemused silence.

For a while they sat in peace in the courtyard, soaking up the warmth of the early summer sun and listening to the warbling of the birds in the fruit trees that surrounded the house. Hanno had his legs stretched out and his head tipped back, and for a while Sabra thought he might have drifted off to sleep.

Then, without moving, he said, "How long will we stay in Myra, mistress?"

"Are you unhappy here?" she asked, alarmed. She had been so contented with her little family and studying with Nikolaos, she had simply assumed that Hanno was too.

"No!" he said, sitting up. "Rather…I will be sad when it comes time to leave."

She let out her breath in a quick sigh of relief. "I know," she said. "I think this is the first time in my life I have felt at peace. I do miss Cyrene…or at least, I miss my father."

"I miss not smelling *purpura* mollusks," Hanno said under his breath, which made her laugh.

"I think…I think I need to stay at least until I know I am

strong enough to stand on my own."

"You never have to stand on your own, mistress."

She scowled at him, but he had his eyes closed again and didn't see it. "You know what I mean, Hanno. There are some battles we all must fight alone. But…I am no longer afraid to face them."

She saw him smile, but he didn't say anything else. A few minutes later, she heard him snoring softly, and she left him there in peace.

24

Glevum, Britannia — June, A.D. 301

Jurian and his companions rested for a week at Aesibuas's villa, and the night before they planned to leave, Aesibuas feasted them like royalty. In the time they had been there, word had gotten out that the *Caesar's* son had returned from the Danuvius, and the villa was soon filled with wealthy retired Legion commanders, their wives, and, notably, their many unmarried daughters. Jurian had to smother a laugh as he watched Constantinus wade through the swarms of young ladies who giggled and flirted and followed him about with unflagging enthusiasm—and all to no avail.

"Does he have his heart already set on someone, I wonder?" Agapius asked Jurian as they took their places at the table of honor.

"Who can say? He keeps his personal business very... personal." He paused. "Do you think Brigit..."

Menas chuckled. "I'm sure she has her affections set on him, but I could not say what is in his heart. As you say, he keeps these things very close." They observed the scene a few minutes longer, then Menas nodded and said, "Well, these parents will be very disappointed."

"Parents?" said Agapius, taking the seat on Menas's left.

"Those girls will all be crying in their pillows tonight."

The *triclinium* slowly filled, and Jurian couldn't help wondering how many of the older Legionaries had known his father. Some of them studied him with furrowed brows, as if his face tugged at a thread in their memories. Either that, or they simply found his red hair surprising, just like everyone else.

Constantinus took his place between Jurian and Aesibuas, his mouth set in a terrifying scowl.

"That bad?" Jurian asked with a grin, understanding Constantinus's expression perfectly.

"You have no idea." Constantinus took a slow sip of wine. "Count yourself fortunate that you were not born into high position, Jurian," he said. "Fraud and flattery plague us wherever we go. Everyone wants something."

"Are these fresh fighters for your father's wars against the barbarians?" one of the Legion commanders asked Constantinus, nodding at Jurian and his friends. "If he takes that giant with him, they will all fall down in fear, thinking the *Caesar* has summoned Woden himself to visit his wrath upon them!"

"I like the look of them," another man said from the other end of the table. "Mettlesome. They would be a fine asset to the Legions. Where did you find them, Constantinus?"

Jurian kept his gaze on his plate, suddenly uneasy, wondering how Constantinus would answer the question.

"This man," Constantinus said, gesturing at Jurian, "saved my life in battle."

A murmur of approval rippled around the table, and several soldiers lifted their goblets in a silent pledge.

"And this man," Constantinus said, indicating Agapius, "distinguished himself in service to the *Praefectus Augustalis* of Alexandria. And the giant, as you call him, was the Emperor Maximianus's champion in the arena."

"And Maximianus just let you take him?" the first Legionary asked. "How did you manage that?"

"I fought," Menas said, his deep voice rolling across the

table, "and I was given my freedom. And I chose to come to Britannia."

This drew a round of cheers from the men, and Aesibuas rose and lifted his goblet. "That is something we can all drink to!" he said. "Britannia!"

Cries of *"Britannia! Britannia!"* echoed around the table, and Jurian glanced sidelong at Constantinus. He seemed satisfied enough, but Jurian wondered if he could sense the shift in the men's mood that he himself felt keenly. Britannia was dearer to these men's hearts than Rome, clearly, and Jurian wondered what would happen if Rome ever made the mistake of crossing *Caesar* Constantius Chlorus, or his son.

The talk revolved away from the newcomers to local politics—mostly in mockery of the new Legion commander in Glevum, who, apparently, had quite the reputation as a drunkard. A few seasoned soldiers farther down the table were enthusiastically debating the finer points of battle tactics against the Alemanni. Jurian listened with idle interest, while in a corner of his thoughts he wondered if service in the border wars with the barbarians in Germania was the use Constantinus intended for him.

As the meal concluded and the guests once more rose to mingle in the *triclinium* and the grand *atrium,* Jurian slipped out into the gardens of the massive peristyle. He needed fresh air, and he needed space to think. The moon ghosted behind a mosaic of swift-scudding clouds, and the cool air that breathed through the towering northern trees carried a heavy scent of rain. The wind was fitful, and everything around him, and within him, felt restless.

He followed a stone path that led roughly northwest and presently arrived at a small pool, the surface of the water speckled with long-fallen leaves. The shifting moonlight and the guttering light of a lone torch danced off the water and cast lithe and twisting patterns of radiance on the gently curving wall that embraced the pool. Jurian guessed that the space was intended as a *nymphaeum,* a shrine to the nymphs of the spring that fed the pool, but it felt nothing like the pagan shrines he had encountered in the southern reaches of the Empire. This place felt not only quiet but full of peace, and Jurian breathed a long sigh as he sat down cross-legged at the edge of the pool. He leaned his head in his hands as if somehow that could force his thoughts into clarity.

The prospect of military service for the Empire—if, indeed, that was what Constantinus had planned for him—unsettled him strangely. On the one hand, hardly a day passed that he didn't recall how he had felt after the campaign in Anatolia, when he had saved Constantinus's life and earned his place as *tribunus angusticlavius* of the Jovians—that bittersweet glory, that pride marred by torment. Taking the life of another man, even in battle, was never something he could accept lightly, and he knew that if he were to enter service with *Caesar* Constantius Chlorus, he would have to do so with a clear conscience.

On the other hand, this could be an opportunity like no other for the life he so dearly wanted to build for himself. He had set out from Satala with the desire to serve the Empire as his father had done, to distinguish himself and bring honor to his family's name. Even though he now understood that his father had not died in disgrace, but, like Varro's men, had preferred to die than compromise his Faith, Jurian still longed to absolve his father's reputation. And then, too, if he could distinguish himself in battle, defending the Empire against the encroaching barbarian hordes, perhaps he might earn remission of his own sentence of exile. Once freed from his interdict, he knew exactly what he would do.

The thought made him smile. After so much struggle and toil and suffering, the hope of settling in some quiet corner of the Empire—a place like this, perhaps—and living out the rest of his days with Sabra by his side made his heart ache with longing, and he determined to broach the subject with Constantinus if Constantinus didn't bring it up himself.

But not my will, he found himself saying. *Not my will, but Thine be done.*

The pines behind the *nymphaeum* sighed in the restless breeze, the rustle of their long needles recalling the endless whisper of waves on a shore. Jurian found a small white rock near his hand, and almost without thinking, he took it and etched the *chi-rho* on the stone lip of the pool.

The sword had brought him to Britannia—and it would be by the sword that he would return.

He got to his feet to return to the villa, but suddenly froze, and glanced back at the pool. He saw nothing but his own reflection now, but for just one moment, from the corner of his eye, he could have sworn he'd seen the flash of Legion armor reflected in the moonlit water.

THEY TOOK THEIR LEAVE of Aesibuas late the next morning, even though the weather had turned during the night and the gray dawn welcomed them with a soaking downpour. Aesibuas followed them out under the front portico, wrapped in a fur-lined cloak that Jurian thought looked more barbarian than Roman.

"Why not stay a little longer?" he asked, scowling at the sky. "At least until this storm breaks. You soft southerners will surely catch your death in this accursed weather."

Constantinus snorted. "Not as soft as you think us." He clapped Aesibuas on the shoulder, then slung on his own red wool cloak and eyed Jurian thoughtfully. "This errand doesn't suit me," he said, "but I've put if off as long as I can. The sooner it is over and behind us, the better I will sleep at night. And besides, I fear I need to see the state of things at Aquae Sulis for myself, and I want to reach Londinium before my father leaves again for Augusta Treverorum in Germania."

"What?" Aesibuas said. "Again? You had word from him."

The last statement had nothing of a question in it, but Constantinus still nodded. "And I don't want to miss him. Not now."

"Well," Aesibuas sighed with a shrug. "If you must go, then go. Give my regards to your father. You can tell him we have an eye on things here."

Constantinus clasped his hand at the wrist. "Thank you," he said. "I will."

"And as for you, Jurian," Aesibuas said with a broad smile. "I am sure your father would have been proud to see the man you have become."

Jurian bowed his head. "That means a very great deal to me," he said. "More than you can know."

Aesibuas laid a hand on his shoulder and gripped it tight. "I do not know the path that the gods have laid for you," he said. "But if you are anything like your father, then I know that, whatever the trials that lay ahead of you, you will face them with courage, and with honor."

Jurian seized his hand. "Thank you."

They mounted their horses and cantered down the path back to the main road.

In spite of the rain, Constantinus kept them moving at a steady pace. The ancient Roman road was wide enough to march a Legion force, and Constantinus explained, in clipped phrases as they rode, that it ran all the way from Isca Dumnoniorum in the far southwest to Lindum in the northwest, designed for the efficient movement of troops throughout the region. The names and geography meant little to Jurian, but he appreciated—as he had so often since he had first left Satala—the genius of Rome when it came to roads.

They stopped around noon, or as near as they could guess with the dense cloud cover, to rest their horses and take a cold meal, and then, without any time spared for leisure, they continued on.

"We will stay in Aquae Sulis tonight," Constantinus said as they remounted their horses. "Ynys Afallon is not a place to attempt at night." Jurian thought he heard him say, under his breath as he spurred his horse forward, "Nor at all by those who are sane."

The rain slackened as the afternoon wore on into evening, and they pushed their horses hard the final leg of the journey.

Menas's massive horse had just begun to lag behind the others when they finally reached the town of Aquae Sulis. It was fully dark, and the rain had subsided into a thick mist that hung ghostly between the low stone buildings, dampening the sounds of the horses' hooves on the road.

They found a *taberna* close by the baths and soon had their cloaks and boots steaming by a bright fire. The innkeeper brought them wooden bowls filled with hot lamb stew and some hard chunks of bread, and Jurian thought he had never tasted anything so delicious.

"It's amazing," he said as he sopped the last of the sauce with his bread, "how much better food tastes when you've had to battle bad weather all day."

"I just think it's amazing how good food tastes," Agapius said. He breathed deeply. "Have you ever noticed, even their fires smell different up here."

Jurian sniffed the smoky air experimentally. Whatever wood was burning in the massive hearth had a sharp, clean fragrance that reminded him a little of cedar, but yet…older. Somehow it seemed to fit with the whole feel of the town, as if it had existed long before Rome had even dared to look so far to the north.

Thinking of that, he turned to Constantinus and said, "This doesn't seem a Legion fortification."

"Not like Glevum, no. Aquae Sulis attracts pilgrims to the shrine here, and my father has kept a light military presence in a castra a little to the northeast, just to keep an eye on things and make sure the place stays peaceful and orderly. But, I suppose, as one of the chief waypoints along the road from Isca Dumnoniorum, it is a place of some importance."

"Why didn't we stop at the *castra*, then?" Agapius asked.

"I thought we would get better food here," Constantinus said.

Jurian and Agapius both laughed aloud at that, and Agapius finished his stew with gusto. "You weren't wrong about that," he said. "I wonder if there's more of this."

"You said pilgrims?" Menas said. "What shrine?"

"Sulis is a goddess of the native Britons," Constantinus answered. "She bears a great resemblance to Rome's Minerva, and so, along with the baths, there is a temple in her honor here. Many travel for the baths and leave requests for blessings, or curses, from the goddess."

"Brigantia is supposedly like Minerva too, isn't she?" Agapius said, flashing a half-hidden, wicked grin at Jurian.

Constantinus didn't rise to his bait, only set his bowl aside and sipped his wine. "You find that often here," he said. "Local deities absorbed into the Roman pantheon, just as we have absorbed their people." He stopped abruptly and stood, turning a little aside. "We start early tomorrow. Good night."

He took his wine and headed up the creaking stairs to the common loft that would serve as their quarters for the night. Jurian glanced at Menas and Agapius.

"What was that about?" he asked.

Menas stared after Constantinus, a curious light in his one eye. "His heart is restless," he said softly. "And he fears, I think, the choices that will lie before him."

"What choices?" Jurian asked with a frown.

Menas sighed deeply and shook his head. "That is not for me to know."

"Well," Jurian said after a long silence. "When we get to Ynys Afallon tomorrow, maybe we will all of us find the answers we seek."

Menas gazed steadily into the fire. "Perhaps. But they may not be the answers we wish to hear."

25

Ynys Afallon, Britannia — June, A.D. 301

The morning dawned fair. Not a cloud marred the deep blue of the sky, and the mist had pooled in the hollows and low places of the landscape as if it had been poured there from a pitcher. Jurian's heart lifted as he drew the tanned leather skin away from the loft window and saw the glorious morning that awaited them, but somewhere behind the anticipation he felt a little thrum of nervousness, and even deeper, a twinge of sadness that he hadn't expected.

Today was the day he would finally fulfill the mission that *Pappas* Marcellinus had entrusted to him.

The sword had finally come home to stay.

As Jurian made his way down the stairs, Menas's great laugh rolled through the common room of the inn, and Agapius was doubled over on his bench, shoulders shaking. Even Constantinus was smiling, and his dark mood of the night before seemed to have departed with the rain.

"Did I miss something?" he asked, sliding onto the bench next to Agapius as his friend shoved him a bowl of thick gruel.

"Breakfast," Menas said.

Agapius snorted and waved a hand. "It was just—it was…"

He couldn't find the words to finish, and Constantinus

diverted the conversation, asking, "Sleep well, Jurian? They were about to take wagers on how long you would be abed."

Jurian shot him a mock glare and Agapius cackled, then stole back the bowl of gruel that Jurian had barely tasted and polished it off in a few bites.

"That was—" Jurian started to protest.

"Cold," Agapius finished. "Let's go."

Jurian rolled his eyes and claimed the last piece of oatcake for himself as he followed the others out of the *taberna*.

Their horses seemed to share their high spirits, and they stomped their feet and jangled their harnesses as the stablehands held them in the inn yard. The air was cooler than Jurian expected, but the brilliant sunshine promised a warmer afternoon.

"Don't trust it," Constantinus said, eyeing the sky, as if he had guessed Jurian's thoughts. "The weather is fickler in Britannia than even the will of the gods."

They left Aquae Sulis and continued southwest along the *Via Fossa*. The breeze carried the faint scent of the sea, and before the sun reached its height, Constantinus stopped his horse. The others drew rein beside him.

"It's that way," he said, pointing to their right.

Jurian shifted in the saddle for a better look. The mist lay heavier here, shroud-like, and even the bright noon sun hadn't been able to dispel it fully. Vaguely he glimpsed the top of a hill rising abruptly out of the fog, like a bit of broken earth the winds of time had failed to smooth.

"Is that it?" he asked. "Ynys Afallon?"

"That is the Tor," Constantinus answered crisply. "We go to the lake." He turned his horse off the road, and then reined in once more. "Stay close," he said over his shoulder, "and follow my lead. These lands are always flooded, and the marshes are perilous to those who do not know the safe paths."

They guided their horses behind his and plunged into the mist. Time seemed to slow as they lost sight of the sun, and soon Jurian had lost all sense of how long they had been plodding along, following the droveways used by local farmers. The rich smell of moist peat hung in the air, and Jurian saw the spectral shapes of willow trees lamenting over the still waters of the marsh pools.

Finally, he heard the gentle lapping of water, and then, almost too soon, a lake of dark water appeared out of the mist. Constantinus dismounted and led his horse along the shoreline, and Jurian followed closely, the hairs on his arms prickling with cold or something like fear. A short distance away slouched a wooden dock, and a small boat, just big enough for four, was tied off there. A fisherman's hut stood back from the water, raised on stilts to keep it from flooding. It had obviously been abandoned long ago, with its peat roof crumbling in places and the log walls rotting. One of the stilts had buckled, and the hut leaned crazily to one side.

"What is this place?" Jurian asked, keeping his voice low.

"They call it the Seeker's Hut," Constantinus said. "Long before my time or my father's time, it has stood here. No one lives here, but someone tends the boat. It is always waiting for those who would make the crossing."

Agapius, without a moment's hesitation, looped his horse's reins over the low branches of a nearby shrub and made his way toward the boat. His boots splashed in the shallow water and he seized the side, pulling it close.

"Seems like it'll float with us in it," he said, his voice loud in the stillness.

"I will stay with the horses," Menas said.

Jurian turned to him in surprise. "But you have to come!" he said. "This is the end of the journey."

"The end of one and the beginning of another, I think," he said with a small smile. "Go on. This has always been your task, never mine. I was not with you when it began in the catacombs, and I cannot be with you when it ends on that island. Besides," he added with a chuckle, "that boat may hold four of you, but I fear I would send it to the depths, and I do not think that is the way your journey is meant to end."

"Come on, Jurian," Agapius called, vaulting himself into the boat and taking up the oars. "Let's see what this mystical island is all about."

"You're coming, aren't you?" Jurian asked Constantinus.

The Tribune regarded him in silence for too long, then handed his horse over to Menas. Jurian blew out a breath he didn't realize he had been holding and followed Constantinus to the boat. Once they were all settled on the narrow benches, Agapius pulled on the oars and they drifted away from the shore. Slowly the shapes of the horses and Menas's giant form vanished into the mist.

It was like passing into another world. The sun filtered through the shifting mist, spearing down into the water around them in ripples of bright green that vanished as quickly as they appeared. And as the mist closed in their wake, it seemed to part to allow their passage, and slowly, the dark hulking shape of an island emerged.

Jurian could hear Constantinus's breathing change—not the steady inhale-exhale of the experienced warrior, but uneven, shallow, as if he were afraid. And the thought of Constantinus afraid—of anything—set Jurian's own heart jarring against his ribs. Only Agapius seemed indifferent to the eerie sight. He gave one final mighty pull on the oars and the hull scraped on the shore.

They clambered into the shallows and hauled the boat up onto the pebbled beach. There was no dock on this side, Jurian noticed, nor anything that seemed like human habitation. The air was almost too still, as if time hung frozen over the island. The shore sloped gently uphill, and Constantinus, without a word, led them forward.

As they gained higher ground, the mist thinned, becoming almost blindingly bright as the sunlight was refracted and reflected through it. A vague, sweet smell wafted toward them.

"What is that smell?" Agapius whispered.

"Apple blossoms," Jurian answered without thinking. And then it occurred to him that there should be no blossoms, not this late in the summer.

Constantinus stopped so suddenly that both Jurian and Agapius plowed into him. As they recovered, Jurian lifted his head and saw that they stood at the edge of a wide ring of standing stones, rising up into the white curls of mist.

"Oh," Agapius breathed.

They were like sentries, those ancient stones—guardians of a sacred place that felt more ancient than any temple to the gods of the Romans, the Greeks, or even the ancient power in Cyrene.

Jurian hardly dared to breathe. It did not seem like a place for the living, nor did it feel like the catacombs built for the dead. He had no cold, creeping sense of evil as he had when he had entered the cave in Cyrene, but nothing inside him felt comfortable, either.

"If this is where you were meant to come," Constantinus said, "then step inside the stones."

Jurian glanced at him. Everything about him was tense, like a bow drawn to its limit, and his gaze was sharp and heavy as he stared at Jurian. Jurian found he couldn't hold that gaze, so he turned to Agapius.

"Go on, Jurian," he said, his voice barely more than a whisper. He was as wide-eyed as a boy, though not with fear.

Jurian nodded once and unsheathed the sword. Carrying it naked in his right hand, he stepped through the boundary stones.

26

Ynys Afallon, Britannia — June, A.D. 301

The ground within the standing stones was cushioned with moss, and Jurian's feet made no sound as he moved toward the center of the ring. The mist seemed almost to form a dome above him, and when he glanced back, he couldn't see his friends.

He stopped, the hilt of the sword strangely cold in his hand. What if this place did drive him mad? What if he wasn't supposed to be here at all? What if this was nothing but a fool's mistake?

He clasped the pyx beneath his tunic and closed his eyes.

I followed all the signs, he prayed. *Every direction You sent, I have followed. Do not abandon me here...not when all I have wanted is to do Your Will.*

Jurian opened his eyes again and took a few steps forward. A massive table of gray stone stood in the center of the ring. Its four legs were half Jurian's height but as thick as his waist. The slab that lay across them seemed impossible for any human hands to have lifted.

Again he hesitated. The slab bore no carvings, and there were no markings on the stones that surrounded him—nothing that might indicate the purpose of this strange place.

Jurian's heart hammered in his chest, and he felt the cloying damp of fear creep over his skin.

"Step forward, Jurian Pendraig," said a voice from the other side of the stone. It was a woman's voice, low and sweet, with a cadence like falling water.

If fear had not already frozen him to the spot, Jurian would have bolted for the edge of the stone circle. But he recognized the voice, and when he glimpsed the woman, half-ghosted in the mist, he thought somehow that he recognized *her*.

She was all in white, save for a deep red cloak that pooled around her feet. Her hair hung in dark ringlets around her pale face, which was neither terrifying nor kind.

"Who are you?" Jurian breathed.

The lady stretched out a slender hand and pointed at the slab. "Bring here the Sword of the King," she said.

Jurian laid the sword across his palms and carried it forward, his gaze riveted on the woman's face. As he drew closer, he could see that her eyes were a deep blue, deep as the fathomless sea. Her nails were like pearl.

"Who are you?" he asked again.

The lady looked at him, and Jurian felt a shock like lightning shiver his entire body.

"I am the Lady of Ynys Afallon," she said. "Place the sword upon the stone."

Jurian gently placed the sword in the center of the slab, but still, the weight of the blade touching the stone made a low gong that rippled endlessly between the pillars. And there it lay, glinting softly, a dull ribbon of silver against the damp stone. As soon as it left his hands, Jurian felt a weight lift from his heart, and he risked a faint smile at the Lady. She merely looked at him.

Jurian stepped back and waited to see what she would do or say, but she only folded her hands beneath her cloak and watched him in silence that seemed to stretch time. There was nothing awkward in her manner, and somehow, under the intensity of her gaze, Jurian felt strangely at peace. But finally, when it seemed that she had no intention of saying anything, he drew breath to ask the question that was now burning in his mind.

"What am I to do now?"

"Rise, Pendraig. You have cast down this steel, but take up the steel in your heart that will speak truth to kings."

Jurian's brows drew together. "I don't understand."

The Lady's gaze shifted to glance past Jurian's shoulder. "Constantinus *Augustus*," she said. "Step forward."

And then she leveled her eyes at Jurian once more and lifted her hand in valediction. Jurian bowed his head and backed slowly away, then turned and hurried to rejoin his friends. Constantinus met him within the mists, and somehow Jurian thought he almost looked angry.

"Is it done?" he asked.

Jurian nodded. "She called you."

"I wouldn't be standing in the circle if she hadn't."

Jurian gripped his arm and then stepped outside the circle, leaving Constantinus to speak with the Lady alone. As soon as he was outside the stones, all his strength left him, and he dropped into a crouch. Agapius took a knee on the ground beside him.

"What happened?" he asked. "What did you see?"

"It's done," Jurian said, his voice weaker than he expected. How to explain to Agapius what he had seen, what had happened? "I saw…a lady."

"A lady! You saw a lady, just like they said…" He faltered, then, suspicious, "What lady?"

Jurian didn't answer. He felt strange, almost lonely, without the familiar weight of the sword across his shoulders, and his thoughts were troubled as he struggled to make sense of the Lady's words. He had expected to leave Ynys Afallon with peace and clarity, but he felt more restless than ever. For the first time in his life, he had no clear direction to guide him. For the first time, he felt like a bit of driftwood, tossed aimlessly on the waves.

He bowed his head and closed his eyes. A moment later, Constantinus strode out of the mists. Jurian jerked his head up as soon as he heard the Tribune's footsteps, but Constantinus had already passed them by.

He didn't stop, but called over his shoulder, "Come. We have lingered here too long."

"Don't I get to see this lady?" Agapius said, face etched with disappointment. "That's hardly fair!"

He helped Jurian to his feet, but just as they were about to follow Constantinus back down to the boat, the Lady's voice rippled toward them from within the stones.

"Gallio Vergilius Agapius," she called. "Step forward."

Agapius froze mid-step, then gripped Jurian's arm and grinned. Jurian managed a smile and nodded.

"I'll wait for you here," he said, glad of the chance to sit down once more.

Agapius vanished into the ring and Jurian settled cross-legged on the mossy ground. His throat felt suddenly parched, and he wished idly that they hadn't left their water skins with Menas and the horses. He wondered what the Lady had said to Constantinus that had put him in such a state—and if the Tribune would even tell him if he asked. Agapius, he was sure, would tell him everything.

He picked aimlessly at the moss, turning the Lady's words over in his mind once more. And then, suddenly, his head snapped up. He had seen her before. She was the lady from the dream he'd had on the voyage to Tingi. Her words all tumbled together now in his mind.

The stone shall become the king stone. The blood of the stone shall adorn the banner of the king. Rise, the red dragon.

Rise, Pendraig. You have cast down this steel, but take up the steel in your heart that will speak truth to kings.

He shook his head. Kings. Stones. Blood. Truth. And...the dragon. He felt like the meaning of it all was just outside his grasp, and his head ached with a dull pain that made his eyes burn.

Then another thought occurred to him. Maybe he didn't need to understand any of this. He'd returned the sword and fulfilled his commission. His part in the sword's story was over now. So maybe none of those words were meant for him, but rather for one who was to come after him.

That has to be it, he thought. *It's all for someone else.*

He almost smiled in relief. Then he saw Agapius emerge from the mist, which was once more descending in a thick curtain around them, and he got slowly to his feet. Agapius seemed unusually somber, Jurian thought, and there was a strange, almost wild, look in his eyes. He didn't stop beside Jurian, but started down the hill without even a glance in his direction.

"Let's go," he said over his shoulder.

"Wait!" Jurian called, hurrying to catch up to him. "What did she tell you?"

Agapius didn't answer until they reached the shore of the lake and heard the gentle lapping of the waves against the stones. Then he turned, and Jurian saw with surprise that he was smiling.

"She said, *The joy that belongs to the sea sings in your heart, and the sea will call it home.*" He shook his head. "I don't know—but I can't help feeling like she was trying to tell me about my death."

"How can you be so happy, hearing a prophecy about your death?" Jurian murmured, but Agapius only smiled more broadly.

"All her words speak death," Constantinus said from behind them. Jurian glanced at him, curious, but he only motioned for them to get into the boat. His face was grave, and his eyes, usually so bright and sharp, were filled with shadows. "That is why men go mad…trying to sort the words. But they are nothing more than ciphers on dry leaves, scattered in the slightest breeze."

"Why?" Agapius said, eyes dancing with his usual impish good humor. "Don't you like the message she gave you? Want to go back up the hill and ask for another?"

"Shut up and get in the boat," Constantinus said.

Agapius laughed as he took his place on the bench, oars in hand, and Jurian climbed in and settled on the seat beside him. Constantinus shoved the boat out into the water and then vaulted aboard.

"She said nothing to me," Constantinus said.

"Nothing?" Jurian asked in surprise. "But—"

"Nothing that made any sense."

"Tell us what she said!" Agapius encouraged. "Maybe we can help you sort it out."

Constantinus regarded him with a long-suffering look and then shrugged. "She said, *The bridge you must cross will bring four into one, and the bridge-builder will mark the sign in the sky.*"

Jurian frowned and glanced at Agapius, who rowed thoughtfully for a few strokes.

Constantinus finally grew impatient. "Well? What did she mean? You claim to have some insight into her madness, so, do explain."

"I'm guessing you will have a bridge to cross someday," Agapius said. "So I hope you like bridges."

Constantinus gave him a shove and Agapius nearly dropped an oar into the lake. "*Ohe!*" he cried. "If I lose an oar, we'll be going around in circles in this mist forever."

"I can't think of a worse fate," Constantinus muttered.

"But some journeys are meant to end where they began, don't you think?" Jurian asked. "Speaking of circles."

"No journey ever ends where it began," Constantinus said. "There is no going back. Something has always changed when you return." He heaved a sigh and stared out over the water. "Always."

None of them spoke again, and the silence of the lake settled around them. But when they reached the opposite shore, and Agapius abandoned the boat to find Menas, Jurian stayed behind to help Constantinus to moor the boat. Something had been gnawing at his mind since he had left the ring of stone, and finally he remembered what it was.

"Constantinus," he said softly, winding the mooring line around the post. "She called you *Augustus*."

Constantinus turned away. "I know."

27

Antiochia ad Orontes, Syria — June, A.D. 301

Casca was in a foul mood. If he hadn't known better, he might have thought his Divine *Imperator* was purposefully thwarting him at every turn, sending him on foolish missions, ordering him to train with common soldiers—as if swinging a sword like a barbarian were the pinnacle of Casca's talents. He had barely been in Diocletian's presence at all over the last month, and he was running out of pretenses for insinuating himself into the Emperor's notice. He needed something—he needed some task, some mission, that he could use to demonstrate his value to the imperial court once more. Anything would be better than being shuffled off like any ordinary *tribunus*.

He scowled to himself as he left the *triclinium* after the evening meal. It had been a simple affair, for once, but he'd been relegated to the lower tables like a commoner, far from the presence of Diocletian and his favored guests...like Aikaterina of Alexandria.

Casca's stomach knotted. He still couldn't understand how Diocletian could tolerate her brazen disregard for his dignity, instead keeping her close and showering her with attention like a favored granddaughter. How could she so easily win his tolerance, when Casca had fought so hard and for so long to edge into the *Imperator's* circle? Casca refused to acknowledge the voice whispering in his thoughts that Diocletian was capricious—still, the very thought of Aikaterina's favor made Casca ill.

He was halfway across the grand peristyle when he heard someone call his name from the shadows. His steps faltered, and a little prickle of alarm chased over his arms. Then he let out a breath in a sigh of relief, because it was *Caesar* Galerius coming across the courtyard to greet him, followed at a distance by two of his personal guards.

"Casca," he said. "Walk with me."

He waved a hand at the two guards, and Casca fell in step beside him. For a few moments the *Caesar* walked quietly, hands folded behind his back. Casca knew the man's temper well enough to keep his peace.

"I'm returning to the *limes* tomorrow," Galerius said at last. "What have you been occupying your time with?"

Casca's head snapped up, and he studied Galerius in surprise. "If I may speak candidly," he said, "nothing of any importance at all. I feel as if I have done something to offend the *Sacratissime Imperator*, only I have no idea what."

Galerius snorted softly. "It may be he doesn't appreciate your many talents."

"That is exactly what I was thinking, *Caesar*. I don't suppose…I don't suppose you have any use for me?"

Galerius glanced at him sidelong, one brow lifted. "I may. My son-in-law Maxentius and I have both become greatly concerned about the Libyan provinces. Notably, Cyrene."

Casca stopped short at that, which made Galerius laugh knowingly.

"Yes, I thought that might interest you. It's where your old friend Georgius made his name, isn't it?"

Casca swallowed. "What troubles you about Cyrene?"

"It is, by all reports, a veritable hotbed of that repulsive cult of Christians," Galerius said. "And yet…they escape this without punishment, and that concerns Maxentius greatly."

Casca heard the unspoken rebuke in Galerius's words—a rebuke that would verge too close to treason, to blasphemy: *Diocletian will not raise a hand against them.*

"And it concerns you as well," he said, carefully.

Galerius smiled. "Indeed. You know, I find myself growing more and more fond of Maxentius. He is truly a man after our own hearts."

Our hearts, Casca thought, a little prickle of pride chasing through him. Then, with a sinuous darkness, his heart murmured, *Men of blood.*

"Maxentius believes," Galerius went on, "that if no action is taken there, the entire city might eventually lose its faith in our Roman gods. We are already chastised by the gods, Casca. We cannot lose Cyrene."

"And what use," Casca said, carefully, "does my *Caesar* have for me?"

Galerius smiled. "You're clever, Casca. Figure it out." He turned to go, but paused and said over his shoulder, "You may want to start at the top. And don't leave any loose ends."

Casca watched him go until he had disappeared back into the palace, his heart hammering, his mouth dry. *Caesar* Galerius was trusting him with this task? He truly believed that *he*, Marcus Valerius Flaccus Casca, was the answer to the crisis in Cyrene?

A slow smile tugged across his face. Cyrene was the home of Jurian's beloved, Sabra.

He would make them pay. He would make them repent. And above all, he would make absolutely certain that Jurian heard about it.

Patience, Casca, he told himself. *These things take time.*

JUST OVER TWO WEEKS later, Casca stood on the pier at the port city of Apollonia, on the coast near Cyrene. He was dressed in the simple clothes of a servant, and idly he wondered what Sabra would say if she could see him in that disguise. After all, he thought, if the stories were true, then she had once slipped out of Rome dressed as a slave. Perhaps she wouldn't appreciate the irony as much as he did.

He hired a horse to travel the remaining distance to Cyrene and rode the beast hard, arriving just as the sun was lowering toward the horizon. The guards at the city gate paid him no notice as he rode in, and he sought out a *taberna* near the old Greek *agora* for his evening meal.

The innkeeper brought him stew and flatbread, and dilute wine of abysmal quality. Casca was tempted to send it back and demand something better, but forced the thought aside—he was dressed as a slave, after all. Slaves had no right to the fine things of life.

"What news of Cyrene?" he asked the innkeeper.

There were no other patrons in the *taberna*, and Casca imagined the man might be in want of a little conversation. As he expected, the man pulled up a stool to sit with him, helping himself to a bit of Casca's bread. Casca bristled, and commended himself for his ability to conceal his distaste.

"Not much news to tell, traveler," the innkeeper said. "The dark days are gone, and the city is slowly putting itself back together. Not that the past is easily forgotten, but, we're adapting."

"Dark days?" Casca echoed, innocently.

"Surely you've heard," he said, his face registering surprise. "Most every traveler who comes through here has heard the story of our dragon, and how Georgius, whom they call the *Cyrenicus*, came and defeated it."

"Ah, the *Cyrenicus*. I think I have heard the name. But I have so little time for stories—I thought surely all that talk about a dragon was simply fanciful tales."

The innkeeper shook his head. "Sounds fanciful, sure," he said. "But it's true as I'm sitting here. We've not had a single earthquake since the beast was defeated, and even Apollonia is thriving again. To think we lived in such abominable fear for so long, and for what? A false god with false promises."

"Surely not a false god?" Casca said. "How can we judge

the claims of the divine?"

The innkeeper smiled tolerantly at him, but didn't rise to his bait, much to Casca's frustration. "It's above me, I'm sure," he said. "I don't meddle in any affairs I can't control with a ledger or a dagger."

"Well said!" Casca slapped a hand on the table, and forced himself to swallow a bit of the bitter wine. "So business is good?"

"Well, as good as we can expect, I suppose," the innkeeper said. "We've fallen on hard times, lately. Not sure when that's apt to change."

"Surely the governor is doing all in his power to get the city back on its feet."

"He's doing his best," the man said, carefully. "But he won't listen to Dignianus. Some say that's because they disagree on... fundamental matters. But no one has proof of Lucius Titianus being a Christian."

"Would the people of Cyrene mind if he were?"

The innkeeper hesitated. Casca could tell the man was getting nervous—he fidgeted, and adjusted his seat on the stool like he meant to get up.

"I don't know about that," he said finally. "Some would, some wouldn't."

"So things aren't quite as stable here as you suggested," Casca observed.

That was too much. The innkeeper sat back, hands flat on the table, and eyed him intently. "You speak very well for a slave, stranger."

"I've had my privileges," Casca said with stiff formality.

"Well, it's been a pleasure to talk to you. You'll excuse me, though. I have my duties."

No, you don't, Casca thought, but only nodded agreeably. As the man got to his feet, Casca reached out and snatched at the sleeve of his tunic.

"I have a commission from my master for a woman named Sabra. Do you know anyone by that name?"

The innkeeper stared at him a long moment, mouth hanging a little open. "Sabra?" he said. "But that's the governor's daughter. And I'm sorry, but you've missed her. She isn't in Libya at the moment."

Casca waved him away and turned his attention back to his stew as if the news hadn't stunned him.

So, Sabra wasn't in Libya. Casca wondered where she had gone. To Alexandria, perhaps, to visit Aikaterina? It was impossible to know.

At least she wasn't around to recognize him. Casca could pursue his investigation in peace, without fear of discovery. And he knew exactly where he would start.

Lucius Titianus had presumably fallen in with the cult of that Galilean, and Dignianus, his second-in-command, was not pleased.

28

Londinium, Britannia — June, A.D. 301

Constantinus rode them hard over the four-day journey from Aquae Sulis to Londinium, only stopping when the horses needed rest, or to bed down for the night in the small *vici* that dotted the countryside. Toward evening on the fourth day, Jurian saw the city of Londinium rising up on the other side of the great river Tamesis, and he couldn't restrain a slight sigh of relief.

"Constantinus!" Agapius called a few hours later, as they rode onto the massive bridge that spanned the river. "Do you think this might be your bridge of destiny?"

Constantinus only glared at him.

They wound their way through rain-sodden streets to the palace, where they left their horses in the care of the *agasones*. A man came to meet them in the vestibule, his dress and bearing setting him somewhat above the common household servants, and he bowed low to Constantinus.

"Is he still here?" Constantinus asked.

"Yes, *domine*," the man said. "They've received conflicting reports from Augusta Treverorum, but you will want to discuss the matter with him yourself."

Constantinus waved a hand and the man led them to the

Caesar's private *tablinum*. Even though it was now late at night, Constantius Chlorus was still awake, surrounded by his advisors and a few Legion commanders, poring over a map on the broad table. Jurian recognized most of the men by sight at least, but standing a little behind the *Caesar* was a tall, thin man, with narrow features and a perpetually dour look pinching his face. As soon as they entered the room, he fixed his gaze hawklike on Jurian, which made Jurian's stomach knot uncomfortably.

"About time you came back!" the *Caesar* cried, as Constantinus led them into the chamber. He left the table and embraced his son. "You look like you rode hard."

"I did not want to miss you," Constantinus said. "I had word you would be returning to Germania."

Constantius Chlorus waved a hand in irritation. "It was my wish to leave last week, but would you believe, we had two couriers arriving on the same day, carrying the exact opposite information from my Legion commanders about the Alemanni's movements. We've been waiting on clarification."

"You know how these things go," the dour man said suddenly. "We must be so careful, how we proceed, lest we waste our resources and energies on idle ventures. But perhaps you are not accustomed to practicing prudence, Constantinus."

Constantinus's brows lifted.

"You may not have met my *praefectus praetorio*, Julius Asclepiodotus," Constantius Chlorus said, gesturing to the man. "Or, as I like to call him, my *perfectus praetumidus*."

Asclepiodotus pulled himself up and puffed out his cheeks in indignation, which made Constantius Chlorus point and let out another hearty laugh.

"*Tribunus*," Asclepiodotus said to Constantinus, with an apparent effort to recover his insulted dignity, "your father has spoken much of you. Especially lately."

Constantinus ignored the barb in the man's words. "And what is it you do, exactly?" he asked.

"I advise your father on matters of imperial policy," Asclepiodotus answered, that pinched vinegar look returning to his face. "And, as the representative of Maximianus, I send official reports to Rome on any happenings of note."

Jurian stiffened. Constantinus never looked at him, but he could imagine what the Tribune would have said if he could. This was the man Aesibuas had warned them about, and Jurian had no doubt he was also one of the brood of vipers in the *Caesar's* court that Constantinus had wanted to avoid. Jurian didn't blame him. The man made his skin crawl.

"What he means is that he's here to spy on me and tattle to Maximianus *Augustus* whenever I do something he doesn't like," Constantius Chlorus said. "That's what oversight means, isn't it? Spying and tattling?"

Asclepiodotus glowered and said nothing. The mood darkened suddenly, and for a moment, Jurian was afraid Constantinus would do something rash. But then the *Caesar* gave the table a smart smack, making Asclepiodotus jump.

"Forget all that nonsense! You're weary, you smell, and I'm sure you will want some food before you retire for the night. Aldred!"

The rooster-necked servant scurried into the chamber behind them, bowed low to the *Caesar*, and beckoned wordlessly to Constantinus and his companions.

"What was that about?" Jurian said to Constantinus as they followed Aldred out into the corridor. "Does Maximianus really need a spy to keep check of your father's activities?"

"I don't know, but the situation is worse than I feared." He rubbed his chin thoughtfully and said, "Don't worry...my father has been playing this game for a long time."

"I'm not worried about your father!" laughed Jurian. "He is fearless. But..." His voice trailed off and he met Constantinus's gaze. "If word gets back to Rome that I'm here, and here with you..."

Constantinus rolled his shoulders, a gesture of supreme indifference. "As I said, I wouldn't worry."

They arrived at his private *cubiculum*, and Constantinus nodded to the others, then ducked inside and closed the door behind him. Jurian sighed. He knew he should trust the Tribune, but Julius Asclepiodotus reminded him altogether too much of Casca. He didn't trust the man, and he couldn't think of a single reason why Constantius Chlorus would choose to keep him so close.

Jurian bade goodnight to Agapius and Menas when they reached their chambers, and followed Aldred in silence farther down the corridor.

I thought I'd left that all behind me, he mused. *But perhaps Constantinus is right. Perhaps no harm will come of it all.*

He startled in surprise when Aldred stopped abruptly in front of him, clucking in annoyance, and his stomach sank. Julius Asclepiodotus was lingering in the corridor just ahead of them, leaning against the wall and toying with something in his hands that might have been a knife, or a stylus. Jurian didn't care to find out which one.

Asclepiodotus took a step forward and Aldred straightened up, pulling his neck in and looking more like an indignant rooster than ever, but Asclepiodotus ignored him entirely.

"A moment of your time," he said to Jurian, touching him lightly on the elbow.

Aldred cast a nervous glance at Jurian, who only waved a hand to reassure him. To Asclepiodotus he said, "What can I do for you?"

Asclepiodotus said nothing, but stared for a long time into Jurian's face through squinted eyes, as if he were taking precise measurements. When several minutes had dripped past in that unsettling silence, Jurian moved to pass him by.

"If there's nothing you need from me," he said, "I'm going to bed."

"Oh, certainly, by all means, traveler." But as Jurian stepped past him, the man's gaunt hand shot out and gripped his arm. "You seem familiar to me," he said.

"We have never crossed paths before," Jurian said. "You must be mistaking me for someone else."

Asclepiodotus pursed his lips, unsatisfied. "I don't like

mysteries," he said. "And you have something of a mystery about you. Be sure I will find you out."

Jurian managed a smile that he hoped would hide his sudden surge of anxiety and pulled his arm free of the man's pinching grip. "I wish you luck," he said, and left him standing in the corridor, staring after him.

29

LONDINIUM, BRITANNIA — JUNE, A.D. 301

After the most restful sleep he had gotten in what felt like years, Jurian woke in his *cubiculum* in Constantinus Chlorus's palace with a renewed sense of hope. The clouds of foreboding that had seemed to trail him since he had left the sword in Ynys Afallon had finally lifted, and for the first time in months he felt like he knew exactly which path his steps should take. He rose and dressed, and by the time he had descended the stairs, he had decided to send another letter to Sabra.

Brave service covers a multitude of evils.

The plan he had concocted in Aesibuas's villa had finally come clear and settled firmly into intention. He knew exactly what he meant to do, and if things turned out as he hoped, he could be free of his interdict at last—perhaps not welcome as a member of the imperial court, but a Roman citizen nonetheless. And with that freedom, coupled with Coel's standing invitation to return to his court, he could see the months rolling into peaceful long years. There would be no need for them to hide, and nothing for them to fear.

He found Constantinus pacing the *atrium*, his hands laced behind his back, a troubled look warring across his face. Jurian hesitated, debating whether he should disturb him, but

Constantinus caught sight of him and immediately smoothed his frown away.

"You look in remarkably high spirits," he said, motioning for Jurian to join him. "I might have mistaken you for Agapius if it weren't for that red hair of yours."

"That's a fine way to speak to a friend!" Jurian said with a grin. "Speaking of high spirits, what's put you in such a good mood?"

Constantinus scowled fiercely at him. "Do you remember me telling you that things are always fluid here? My father told me this morning that we will be in Londinium for another two months."

"Are you that anxious for the frontier?" Jurian said. "Or are you just annoyed that we made such a hasty and miserable journey for nothing?"

Constantinus laughed softly. "No. But I am anxious to be out from under the sniffing nose of Julius Asclepiodotus."

Jurian's grin widened. "If I told you I might have an answer for that, would you listen?"

"You're not going to tell me we need to break someone out of the amphitheater here in Londinium, are you?" Constantinus asked.

"No, although you didn't get to participate much last time."

"I'd like to think I played a critical role." Constantinus regarded him for a moment, then made an impatient gesture. "Well? What's this grand plan that seems to have you treading air this morning?"

"Well, that's not..." he started, and waved a hand. "Anyway, I was thinking, why don't we all just return to your grandfather's court? He was sorry enough to see us leave, and I would be glad to continue training with his soldiers."

"You were training with Coel's garrison," Constantinus said flatly, and heaved a long sigh. "Of course you were."

"Well, I couldn't let *all* my skills go to waste," Jurian said. "So, what do you think? We can stay in Camulodunum until your father is ready for us to go to Germania."

"Us!" Constantinus echoed.

They exchanged a long look as Jurian tried to figure out if Constantinus was honestly surprised, or just dissembling with him.

"Wasn't that what you had in mind for me?" he asked finally, flustered. "You've always said you wanted to put me to use up here. Well? Let me help in the campaigns."

"You think that, by serving honorably in war on the *limes*, you will have your citizenship reinstated, your transgressions remitted? You who were so anxious about Julius Asclepiodotus sending word to Rome about your presence here...you want to go and make a name for yourself on the frontier, in war?"

"Well?"

Constantinus surprised him with one of his rare grins. "That is exactly what I hoped you would say. As for Camulodunum..."

He swung away from Jurian and paced around the *impluvium*, while Jurian watched him anxiously, feeling like a boy waiting for his father's permission.

"I suppose it has its advantages," Constantinus said at last. "It's not so far that I can't be back and forth as my father needs me. But it gets you out of sight of that court serpent. I'm sure he's in his *tablinum* right now, preparing a letter to Rome."

"I'm glad you mentioned that," Jurian said, and Constantinus turned to him in surprise. "Well, not that, exactly. I need to send a message."

Constantinus waved a hand at him. "So send it."

"Just like that?"

"What do I look like, an imperial courier? There are always messengers coming and going here, so find one and send him." Jurian nodded his thanks and turned to go, but Constantinus called after him. "As a point of interest, Jurian, would this message be heading to Cyrene?"

Jurian turned. "You think I shouldn't send for her?"

Constantinus clasped his hands behind his back and took a few steps closer to him, weighing his words carefully. "Jurian, I won't tell you what to do. But consider what you're asking.

You will be campaigning against the Alemanni in Germania. If you send for Sabra, where will you tell her to go? To Germania, where she will be far from civilized comforts at best, and in danger from barbarians at worst? Or to Britannia, where she knows no one, where she has no family, no home, nothing to sustain her? Do you have any idea how long you may be gone on this campaign? It may be mere months, but it may be years. I have no way of guaranteeing when your part in that mission will be over. Is it fair to her to ask her to leave all that she has ever known on the hopes that you may be reunited soon?"

Jurian listened quietly, feeling all his ecstatic hopes dwindle, and a heavy weight settle in his heart.

"I'm sorry, Jurian," Constantinus said. "Truly. Believe me, I know…" He glanced away. "I know how hard it is to be parted from the woman you love." When he turned back to Jurian, his expression had cleared, and his eyes were as inscrutable as ever. "As I said, I won't tell you what to do. Just consider carefully before you make promises or demands."

Jurian nodded in silence and left Constantinus to his pacing. The Tribune's words weighed heavily on his mind, and for a while he paced the length and breadth of his own *cubiculum*, considering what to do. Perhaps it would be best, as Constantinus said, not to send for Sabra…not when his own future was so unsettled. But that didn't mean he couldn't commission a courier to take a message to her. The least he could do was tell her what he intended. The least he could do was tell her she was always in his heart. And for that, he wanted to send her more than a simple letter.

He found his friends in the *triclinium*, clearing away the remnants of the breakfast under the waiting servants' impatient eyes.

"You missed breakfast," Agapius said. "Again."

"Sleep was better than food."

"Sleep is never better than food."

Jurian waved a hand dismissively and slid onto the bench beside Agapius, picking up a stray tidbit of dried fruit. "Are you planning to spend the whole day scrounging for scraps like hounds, or are you going to come with me into the city?"

Agapius elbowed him in the ribs. "Who's scrounging?"

"I was only keeping Agapius company," Menas rumbled with a faint wink at Jurian.

"Well, come and keep me company," Jurian said. "I'm going to the *forum*."

They were on their feet and following him before he'd taken two steps, and soon they had left the palace with a pouch of Britannic coins that Agapius had somehow procured from the palace *nummularius*.

The summer market in Londinium was one of the largest Jurian had ever seen. It reminded him of the hectic port of Alexandria, but while Alexandria's sun-drenched streets saw business conducted with a lazy sort of languor, everything in the grey, misty square of Londinium happened with a sharp sort of urgency, as if everyone had somewhere else they needed to be—even the merchants. Shops surrounded the *forum*, and merchants, haggling over goods and prices, shouted over each another in Latin and various Celtic dialects. A slave market occupied one corner of the square, and the whole place was bustling with people.

Jurian, Menas and Agapius stood a few moments on the periphery of the market, while Jurian scanned the stalls for one sort of merchant in particular. Finally his gaze snagged on a small tent, its dark blue banner blazoned with the symbol of tongs and hammer, and he waved his friends toward it. A young woman stood behind a table, smoothing a fine dark woolen cloth over its top. Beside her, a man with a wild mane of blond curls was setting out his wares: fine wound arm bands, rings set with rough-cut gems, and earrings and neck collars studded with precious stones. When Jurian and his friends stepped under the canopy, the man glanced up and favored them with a wide smile.

"Ah! New faces!" he said, his Latin thick with that strange Britannic accent. "Finest work in all Londinium. Indeed, in all of

Flavia Caesariensis!" He picked up an arm band and offered it to Jurian. "A gift for a lady? Might I suggest this piece? Straight from the mines at Vebriacum."

Jurian took the band and turned it over in his hands. It was certainly fine workmanship—set with tiny fine gems and smooth as new-stripped wood.

"It's beautiful," he said, handing it back to the jeweler, "but I need something smaller. Just a token."

The man lifted a finger as he set the cuff back in its place. "I have just the thing," he said.

He turned and opened a small chest and drew out a small silver ring. The band was plain, but it was set with a rich red stone that seemed almost the color of blood.

"Is this more what you require, *domine*?" he asked, dropping it into Jurian's palm.

Jurian ran his fingers over the smooth band, peering into the stone which seemed to carry an eternity in its heart. "Yes," he said. "This is exactly what I was looking for. How much?"

The man's grin broadened, showing a wide gap between his two front teeth. "For you?" he said. "I can make a special price just for you. I can see that you are nobility. Perhaps new to Londinium? Recently arrived from Rome?"

"Something like that."

"For this ring, just for you, I will take just fifty *nummi*."

Jurian set the ring down on the table. "No," he said. "I'm afraid not."

"Forty, just for you. I am making a special deal. For anyone else, it would be sixty."

"I'm sorry," Jurian said. He'd seen enough haggling in the markets the Empire over to know this game. "Thank you for your time." He turned away and grinned at his friends. "Let's go."

"Wait! I just remembered...I can offer something a bit better." Jurian turned expectantly, and the man said, "This ring—no one wants it. I carry it everywhere, and I'm tired of carrying it, so I have an idea. Twenty *nummi*, and that is my final offer."

"Done." Jurian paid the man and pocketed the ring. "Now we can go," he said to his friends.

Once they had arrived back at the palace, Jurian left his friends to seek out a courier. As Constantinus had suggested, it was a simple enough task—Jurian found two of them lingering just outside the *Caesar*'s *tablinum,* waiting to be dispatched.

"Do you have a commission?" Jurian asked one of them.

The man straightened up and gave him a slight bow. "Not unless you have one for me, *domine."*

Jurian smiled as he gave him the ring and a letter for Sabra, and his last handful of coins as payment.

30

Alexandria, Aegyptus — July, A.D. 301

Aikaterina stood in the sun-drenched expanse of her beloved gardens in the palace of Alexandria, her heart caught somewhere in her throat. On the bench in front of her sat her father, feeble and frail, but awake—incredibly, impossibly, awake. Even in the mid-summer heat he was warmly wrapped, his head covered in the folds of his toga to keep the sun from damaging his thin skin. He looked so weak, so fragile, but the eyes that smiled at her were the eyes she remembered.

Uprooting herself, she ran to the bench and dropped on her knees in front of him, gently clasping his trembling hands in both her own.

"Ah, Aikaterina," Constus murmured, withdrawing one of his hands to lay it on her head. "Welcome home, *cara*."

Aikaterina pressed her forehead to his other hand, swallowing back her tears. "I shouldn't have been gone so long, but Diocletian wouldn't give me leave to come any sooner. I'm sorry. I should have been here with you."

He patted the bench beside him and she sat down, still clinging to his hand. "Don't trouble yourself about the past, Aikaterina." His voice was unsteady, mumbling a little, so different from the stern, strong voice she knew so well. It made her heart ache almost more than the sight of his gaunt face and near-translucent skin. "But I am heartily glad to have you back. We have...trouble here."

"Surely not!" she said. "I knew we were struggling when I left, but I didn't think it was anything we couldn't weather. Has something new happened?"

"The *Imperator's* new grain tax is weighing heavily on our people. And there are barbarians in the south, pressing on our borders. I've asked our senate to dispatch the Legion, but they are stalling. They say we won't be able to sustain a conflict. Our people are hungry, and with the drought, will likely be hungrier still in the months to come. And how can we provision an army when the people call out for aid?"

He broke off coughing, and for a few minutes he sat quietly, shoulders slumped and head bowed, like a man defeated. Aikaterina bit her lip and held onto his hand.

"What can we do?" she asked.

"I don't know. Senate won't do its job. I can't...I can't attend their sessions regularly. If only I had my old strength, Aikaterina." He looked at her suddenly, his gaze fierce and almost desperate. "Don't let my sickness be the death of Alexandria," he said. "You must...you must govern her well, even if I cannot guide you. Be bold as a lioness, my daughter, and never stoop to let yourself be ruled by lesser men."

"Don't talk like that, Father! Look at you—you are so much better than when I left!"

"An illusion, no more," he said. "I can feel it inside me, this sickness. I've done my best, but I know I'm only pretending."

FOUR DAYS LATER, CONSTUS collapsed, without warning, on his way to the evening meal. Aikaterina hovered against the wall of his *cubiculum* as his servants carried him to his bed, watching numbly as one of them raced out to find the palace *medicus*. With all the frenzy of activity, her mind felt blank and shattered, and she drifted like a spirit without a body to hold her down. Moments after the *medicus* arrived, Aikaterina's mother stepped into the chamber, pale, her eyes red-rimmed and swollen.

"What's happened, Aikaterina?" she asked, stopping beside her daughter. "Why is this happening to us?"

Aikaterina shook her head. She didn't trust her voice. More than anything she wanted to escape into her beloved *Bibliotheka*, to take refuge in her scrolls and codices, but she couldn't. Not now. Alexandria needed her.

Her father needed her.

And, she realized with some surprise, her mother did too.

She pushed away from the wall and clasped her mother's hand. Her mother didn't react to the gesture, but Aikaterina didn't release her.

"We can't go on like this," her mother said, her gaze fixed on Constus's bed. "What is Alexandria to do?"

"We will endure," Aikaterina said, "as we always have."

"It's too much." Her mother passed a hand over her eyes, lifting her shoulders in a long sigh. "I know you think you can do it all on your own, Aikaterina, but Alexandria needs certainty. She needs to see that her ruler is strong and unwavering, and in absolute control of her fate. Can you give them that?"

Aikaterina swallowed and released her mother's hand. "I'll try," she murmured.

"That is exactly what I mean," her mother said.

Aikaterina left her then, wandering out of the palace and, finally, into the *Bibliotheka*. It was full night now, but a few scholars sat around the long tables, carrying on their work by lamplight. Diodoros was there, to Aikaterina's surprise—she had never seen him in the evenings, and she realized she had never once considered what he called home. Did he live in the palace, among the servants? Or was he a free man, with a house in the city? Somehow she had never imagined him outside the context of her own life. The realization shamed her.

He smiled at her as she approached, and pushed aside the *codex* of the Psalms he had been reading.

"It's late for you to be here," he said. He peered more closely at her through the heavy shadows. "Is everything all right?"

"My father has fallen ill again," she said, dropping onto the bench across from him. "He was doing so well...but now..."

Her lips trembled and she pressed them together. Diodoros reached across the table to touch her hand.

"I'm so sorry," he said.

"That isn't all though," she said, and told him all that had been weighing on her mind—the drought and the threat of famine, the grain tax, the barbarians in the south. "And Alexandria needs someone in control who can protect them from all this," she finished. "I just don't think it is me."

"Nonsense," he said. "Alexandria doesn't need someone to protect them. Does a ship's captain ward away the storms? Or does he guide the ship through to a safe harbor?"

"Well, he doesn't let his sailors all fall overboard either, or starve on the journey," Aikaterina said.

"Indeed," Diodoros said, blandly.

Aikaterina sighed and glanced away. "The trouble is, I know what I ought to do. I just...can't." When he only looked at her expectantly and didn't say a word, she drew her shoulders up and said, mumbling, "I ought to send word to Diocletian, and ask for his aid."

"And why can't you?"

"Because," Aikaterina said, and her cheeks warmed at the childish answer. "Because I am afraid of him. And I'm afraid he will take the governance of Alexandria away from me. Because I'm afraid he will marry me off to Maximinus Daia, and I would rather die than marry him." She bowed her head. "But I'm afraid of myself most of all, because if I thought Alexandria's survival depended on my marrying him, I would do it."

Diodoros said nothing for a long while. He sat with his hands clasped loosely on the table, dark head bowed, until Aikaterina was dying to know what he thought of her words. Finally he sighed and glanced up, a look of such pity in his eyes that Aikaterina caught her breath.

"I would give anything to take this burden from you," he said. "But if I were advising your father, I would tell him to send word to the Emperor. He may be able to help us. *Kyria*, what is your hesitation founded on? Personal, or political, interest?"

She bit her lip, staring up at the window. "Personal."

"And is that a good reason to jeopardize your city?"

"No."

He opened his hands. "Well then."

She nodded and got to her feet. "Well then. I suppose I don't have a choice after all."

As she walked away she heard him say softly, "I hope the outcome is better than you fear."

31

Camulodunum, Britannia — July, A.D. 301

Coel had received Jurian and his friends warmly back into his court, and they soon settled back into the easy rhythm of life they had enjoyed before—though they all thought the fortress felt a little too empty without Brigit and Eilwen there. As the days stretched into weeks, Jurian's spirits stayed high, even though he knew it would be another month or longer before he could even expect any sort of reply from Sabra. He tried not to let himself feel discouraged that she had sent no message to him yet, but worry still needled in the back of his mind, buried deep behind his jubilant hope.

Only Constantinus seemed restless—he was gone for days, sometimes weeks at a time, and rarely spoke of his travels to anyone. Jurian finally pinned him down one late afternoon toward the end of summer, when the Tribune had just returned from a week-long trip to Londinium. He waited for Constantinus to bathe and refresh himself from the road, then intercepted him on his way to the *triclinium* for the evening meal.

"How is your father?" he asked, hoping that was an innocuous way to open the conversation.

Constantinus lifted a hand in an ambiguous gesture. "Well enough, I suppose."

"Have you heard any word from the south?"

That brought a halt to Constantinus's purposeful stride; he turned and faced Jurian, eyes dark. "There's trouble in Egypt," he said. "My half-brother is ill, and Aikaterina is doing her best to act as his regent, but she must have her hands full. There's a food shortage, and Diocletian's grain tax is doing the region no favors. And barbarians are encroaching on their southern borders." He paused, measuring Jurian quietly, then finished, "Diocletian is massing his Legions."

"He is going to Egypt?"

Constantinus nodded. "Soon. Not yet. But I am worried about my niece. If Diocletian thinks the region is unstable, they will be pushing hard to arrange a marriage for her."

Jurian gritted his teeth. "Is there anything we can do?"

"From this far away? No. News and messages take so long to travel from one corner of the Empire to the other. For all we know, she may already be married off to some great-nephew or step-cousin of the Tetrarchy."

"Don't say that," Jurian said, feeling ill.

"It's the truth," Constantinus said. "And Galerius is not taking my absence well. I may have to go back sooner than I had planned, and reassure them that I have not turned Saxon raider during my stay in Britannia. Galerius is having trouble with the Carpi."

"But the Rhenus—"

"Nothing is going to change that campaign," Constantinus said, and swung away from him. "We are mustering our troops and supplies in Londinium. It'll be soon now."

But soon was still a long time in coming. It wasn't until summer had almost faded into the golden glow of autumn that Constantinus returned from Londinium with orders to stand by for departure. Coel found Jurian in his *cubiculum*, packing his belongings, and for a few moments he stood in the doorway, watching in uncharacteristic silence.

"Where is your weapon, Jurian?" he asked presently.

Jurian paused and glanced up in surprise. He hadn't thought about what he would do for a weapon on the battlefield—he had almost forgotten about his loss of Excalibur. Coel chuckled at the look of dismay on his face and gestured for him to get up.

"Come with me," he said.

Jurian followed him to an inner chamber in the fortress. It reminded him of a private *fabrica*, filled with a vast number of weapons on display the way some nobles might display pottery or statues. Coel gave him a brief history of the weapons in the room, most of which he had won in some campaign or other over his long military career. Massive swords, much like Excalibur in design, hung next to double-bladed battle axes, shapely bows, and ash spears with gleaming blades.

"This," Coel said, taking down an axe with a wound leather hilt and bold runes etched on the blades, "belonged to my grandfather. We were not always friends to the Romans." He handed the weapon to Jurian. "This has seen its day in battle."

Jurian twisted it in his grip, testing its heft under Coel's approving gaze. He had grown fond of fighting with the smaller axes Coel's soldiers trained with, but this weapon had a weight and balance that reminded him more of Excalibur.

"It's a mighty weapon," Jurian said, handing it back with a little hitch of reluctance. "Like nothing the Romans had ever seen, I'm sure."

"It is a good thing to be fearsome in battle," Coel said. "I'd noticed that you carry no weapon now save that knife, which is a *seax*, if I'm not mistaking my blades. Where'd you get a blade like that, I wonder?"

"From my father," Jurian said. "He served with the Legion in Germania."

Coel nodded and spun the axe once in his hands with enviable ease, and then offered it to Jurian. "I would be honored," he said, "if you would carry this into battle once more."

Jurian's mouth dropped open as he accepted the axe. "I...I don't know what to say."

Coel winked at him. "*Thank you* is usually appropriate, I think."

"Thank you."

Coel slapped him on the back and left him standing in the dim shadows. As soon as he had gone, Jurian tried an experimental swing. It seemed like a brutal weapon, even more than Excalibur, and certainly more than the lighter axes he was familiar with. He tried another swing, then strapped the axe's harness across his chest and left the armory in search of Agapius.

He found him in the *hortus*, sitting on a stone bench under a potted citrus tree. Agapius's gaze fixed instantly on Jurian's shoulder.

"What is that?"

"My new weapon," Jurian said, withdrawing it from its sling. "Like it?"

Agapius took it from him and tested the blades. "Impressive. I wouldn't want to meet these edges in battle." He glanced at Jurian. "Well, but you'll be the one wielding it, so."

Jurian punched him in the arm. "I just need practice," he said. He leaned the axe against the stone bench and sat down beside Agapius, eyeing his friend sidelong. "Agapius, are you reading?" he said, noticing for the first time a leather-bound *codex* on the bench beside him.

Agapius nudged the book aside and opened his mouth to protest, but just then, Menas appeared and planted himself in front of them.

"A moment, Agapius, if you would. I need to speak with Jurian."

Agapius nodded and left them with a wave of his hand, and Jurian indicated the empty place on the bench. Menas sat down and folded his hands.

"There is something that weighs heavy on my heart," he said. Jurian leaned on his knees and met his gaze, nodding for him to go on. "This next journey you will take. Going with the *Caesar* and Constantinus to Augusta Treverorum. Returning to service in the Legion."

"Yes?"

"You know that is something I cannot do. One journey that I cannot follow you," Menas said. "And after what happened in Nicomedia…and in Rome…"

Jurian laid a hand on his shoulder. "You don't have to explain anything to me," he said. "I understand. Tell me your wish, and I will see it done, if I can."

"I have grown fond of Coel, and this life in his court," Menas said. A glimmer of a smile flickered in his eye. "He is a man I could serve." Jurian grinned so broadly that Menas frowned at him. "You think this is funny? That I am making a joke?"

"Not at all," Jurian said. "It's only…I think this is exactly where you need to be."

"You do?"

"Yes. I do. I thought so as soon as Coel mentioned it that first night at the feast. This is a perfect place for you to be, and you could not ask for a better man to serve. And Constantius Chlorus is a fair and just man, too. I think that maybe, just maybe, we may have found our way home at last."

"We?" Menas asked, straightening a little.

"Of course, we." He smiled at Menas. "I mean to campaign with Constantinus in Germania, to serve with distinction. I mean to compel the Emperor to lift the exile and reinstate my citizenship. He may never value me as he did my father, but if I'm here, far away from Nicomedia, we may safely ignore each other. There will be nothing to stop me from making a life here. And as soon as I am free, as soon as I have won my honor back, I will send for Sabra, and she can join us here at last." He jostled Menas's arm. "Can you imagine it?" he asked. "After everything we have been through, after everything she has been through, to finally have peace."

Menas looked grave, but he nodded. "I can imagine it, though it is hard to believe that such a future could be ours."

Jurian rose and hefted the axe. "Then pray for me," he said, "that I may see this through, whatever it may take."

32

Augusta Treverorum, Germania — September, A.D. 301

A LITTLE OVER THREE WEEKS AFTER SETTING OUT FROM BRITANNIA, Jurian caught his first glimpse of the partly ravaged city walls of Augusta Treverorum, nestled among the rolling hills that nosed up to the banks of the Mosella river. In the late afternoon sun, the pale stone of the towers and battlements gleamed like it was on fire, reflecting in the calm waters of the broad river. The road had been following the sweeping curve of the Mosella for some time, and closer to the city walls Jurian could see a massive Roman bridge spanning the river's breadth, leading straight to the city's western gate.

"Eh, Constantinus," Agapius said, nudging his horse to ride alongside Jurian and the Tribune at the head of the imperial column. "Do you suppose *that* is your bridge of destiny? It must be, right?"

Constantinus didn't even favor him with a glare.

"Welcome to Augusta Treverorum, oldest city in Germania," he said as they cantered their horses through the Porta Media, and that was all.

They made their way to the barracks, where Constantius Chlorus left the main body of his troops, then the *Caesar's* smaller personal party moved on to the palace. After they had bathed and dressed, the party reassembled in the *Caesar's tablinum*.

When Jurian entered the room, Constantius Chlorus was seated in his *sella*, with Julius Asclepiodotus close by his right hand. The *Caesar's* counselor had traveled to the city ahead of them, and Jurian wondered what mischief he had been up to while they had lingered in Camulodunum.

Jurian had come to loathe the very sight of the man. Every time they were in the same room together, Asclepiodotus watched him with hawkish attention, as if by staring hard enough he could see straight into Jurian's soul. Jurian didn't know why the man had taken such an interest in him—but Jurian suspected it had something to do with Coel, whom everyone knew Asclepiodotus considered a personal enemy.

"This is more like it," Agapius said as he joined Jurian, surveying the utilitarian features of the *tablinum* with a nod of approbation. "Plain, military-style. I like it."

"It's only plain because the Alemanni came and sacked the city," Constantinus said wryly. "We're still rebuilding."

"Oh," Agapius said, and Constantinus exchanged a faint smile with Jurian.

They took seats near the dais, and slaves immediately appeared with stone pitchers of wine. It was almost clear, and heady and sweet, a far cry from the rich wines of Rome or the bitter mixed wines of Myra and Anatolia. Jurian found himself smiling as he sipped it.

"Asclepiodotus tells me that we may have another problem brewing with the Suevian tribes," Constantius Chlorus said. "Some of our soldiers stumbled on one of their barbarous rituals of human sacrifice in the woods near Ara Agrippinensium. They slaughtered every last barbarian and desecrated the grove. So the local tribe has been threatening retaliation, gathering their forces, shaking their shields. We must be prepared with a response, in case they decide to advance an attack."

"They will," Constantinus said without looking up from the map he was studying.

"I want you to take this command," the *Caesar* said. "It's

hardly necessary to mobilize the entire military force of Germania Secunda for one tribe. And from what I hear, your tactical modifications might offer just the solution we need."

"You know about that?" Constantinus said.

Jurian had rarely seen him look so surprised, but Constantius Chlorus only chuckled.

"I keep up with your comings and goings," he said. "I heard about your victory near Heraklea. Very impressive. And just the thing, I think, for this."

Asclepiodotus's face puckered with displeasure.

"Thank you, *Caesar*," Constantinus said, inclining his head. "But I'll need time to choose my cohort."

"Make it fast. I want you on the road in two days."

Constantinus rose and bowed. "We will see it done," he said. He paused when he saw Jurian and Agapius still seated with their wine, then gestured sharply for them to stand. "Well, come on," he said. "Finish your wine or give it back. We have work to do."

Two days stretched into two weeks as delays and changing intelligence worked their way through the Legion. Jurian was beginning to expect that nothing in the military was ever settled until it was in the past, and he took the changing situation with a stoic indifference that finally smoothed away Agapius's impatience.

They spent the time in preparation—refitting their supply wagons, repairing armor and equipment that had worn out on the march across Gaul. Constantinus seemed genuinely happy to be back with his soldiers and away from the endless courtesies of his father's court, and the troops seemed happier still to have him there. They tackled even the drudgery of campaign preparations with rare enthusiasm.

As Jurian had hoped, he and Agapius numbered among the soldiers Constantinus had selected for his cohort, but Jurian, much to his dismay, had not been given any special role.

"Don't worry," Agapius told him one day. "You just have to

prove you can actually use that in a fight."

Jurian was practicing with his battle axe in the sandy training yard near the barracks, while Agapius perched on the low stone wall, watching him.

"And I suppose you could do better?" Jurian grouched, leaning on the axe's haft and wiping the sweat from his forehead.

"We don't use uncivilized weapons like that in Alexandria," Agapius said loftily. "Or…anywhere else in the entire Empire, actually."

"Well, I like it." He hefted the weapon again and took a few practice swings.

"It's not subtle," Agapius said.

Jurian laughed. "No. It's not."

"Then again, neither are you, oh head of dragon-fire."

Jurian rolled his eyes and lunged forward, miming a thrust.

"Maybe you can help build a new fort while we wait for the barbarians to come out of their hovels," Agapius added. He watched Jurian for a few more moments, and then said, "Or maybe Constantinus will just put you on construction duty to start. I don't think that's how you're supposed to use that."

"Thanks for the confidence," Jurian said.

He tried a few more swings, but had lost interest in the exercise. Finally he hooked the axe into its sling across his back and wandered over to join Agapius.

"What do you suppose the Suevi are like?"

"Barbarians," Agapius said cheerfully. "I've heard they like bloody sacrifices."

"Animals?"

Agapius met his gaze, and a faintly ill look passed over his face before he glanced away. "No, human."

Jurian swallowed. "Is it wrong of me to say that I am glad?" When Agapius just looked at him in surprise, he shrugged and said, "That is *evil*, Agapius. What they do is a wretched, evil thing. So, we aren't just fighting for the glory of Rome. We're fighting for the law of God."

"It does make it easier," Agapius said. "No prick of the

conscience in a battle like this."

"If only we could expect all our battles to be so clear."

THE FOLLOWING DAY THEY finally left Augusta Treverorum to make the four-day journey to Ara Agrippinensium. The crisp autumn weather held, the horses were fresh, and they made excellent time through the thick, towering forests and rolling hills. As they drew close to the city at sundown on the fourth day, Jurian blew out his breath in appreciation.

"That is something to see," Agapius said from beside him, and Jurian nodded.

Ara Agrippinensium was a sprawling fortified city, the headquarters of Constantius Chlorus's forces in the region. It reminded Jurian, more than anywhere else he had been in his journeys, of Satala—the final stronghold of Rome on the outskirts of barbarian territory. Watch fires illuminated the massive walls, and fortified guard towers loomed above the parapets at regular intervals. When the guards posted above the *portcullis* spotted their party they raised a mighty shout, and the gate creaked up to grant them entry.

Constantinus led his cohort to the *castra*, where they relinquished their horses to the *agasones* and reformed in an inner courtyard to await orders. A scout had been waiting for them within the *praetorium* when they arrived, and Constantinus now stood with him a little aside, receiving the man's report as his troop waited in rigid formation for him to address them. Finally he dismissed the scout and returned to his men.

"Take your rest tonight," he said. "You have liberty to explore the city, but conduct yourselves in a manner befitting your rank and insignia. The Suevi have been seen massing north of the city, so do not under any circumstances venture outside the walls. If you are captured you will be killed, if not sacrificed to their gods in their gruesome rituals. Go nowhere alone. We will ride out at first light in two days. If you aren't sober enough to stand, you will be left behind, and when I return, you will be stripped of your rank and privilege. *Centuriones*, report to my *tablinum* at daybreak tomorrow. Dismissed."

He turned sharply and strode into the *praetorium*, leaving his men to situate their belongings in the barracks and spend the evening as they chose.

"Where should we go?" Agapius asked as the company broke up. "Should we just follow the others?"

"They're going to get drunk," Jurian said. "I have no interest in drowning my wits in the bottom of a wine cask."

"Constantinus said—"

"That won't stop them."

"Well? Then...where should we go?"

They hesitated in the guttering torchlight just outside the gate, frowning at the streets that opened before them. Before they could make up their minds, a shadow fell across theirs, and they glanced up to find, to their surprise, Constantinus standing beside them.

"If you want to...make things right by your God," he said softly, "take this road to the right and follow it all the way to the wall. Go left, and then stop at the third house on the right. Ask for Maternus."

He said nothing more, only nodded to them briefly and turned away, leaving them to stare after him in bewilderment.

"What was that?" Agapius said. "Did he just give us directions to—"

"Yes," Jurian said, gripping the pyx beneath his tunic. "Let's go."

They stole down the street, navigating their way through the crowds of soldiers, trying not to attract undue attention as they went. But as they passed a large building decorated with arches and blazing with torchlight, a soldier swayed across their path, gripping Jurian's arm for balance and pointing at the doorway.

"Are you going to see the play?" he asked, his voice slurred with drink. He waved a *libellus* in their faces.

"No," Jurian said, and the man shuffled off, despondent.

"A playhouse!" Agapius exclaimed, almost wistfully, as he

peered at the *libellus* in the torchlight. "I've never seen one...not even in Alexandria! And to see Plautus..."

"Who?"

Agapius favored him with a long-suffering look. "Plautus. The greatest writer of comedy ever known to this world...and this play is my favorite. *Miles Gloriosus*."

"That figures," Jurian said. Agapius elbowed him. "Ow! And how do you know about plays?"

"You're forgetting that in my former life—before I had the misfortune of falling in with you—I served the lady Aikaterina of Alexandria."

"True," Jurian said. "How could I have forgotten?"

A roar of laughter spilled into the street from the playhouse, and Agapius heaved a sigh.

"Come on," Jurian said. "We don't have time for the play tonight. Maybe another day."

"You're assuming we'll live another day," Agapius said morosely as they continued on their way. "What if we die in battle at the hands of the barbarians?"

Jurian grinned at him. "Then I will be very glad to have seen the presbyter, and I won't miss the play."

"Fine," Agapius said. "But you have to promise me something."

"What?"

"That if we don't get killed, we'll go to the play."

"I promise," Jurian said with a laugh.

They continued on down the street until they reached the wall. The noise of the central city faded, and all Jurian could hear now was the low murmur of the guards on the walls high above them. They turned down a narrow track, counting doors until they stood before the house Constantinus had indicated. It looked completely unremarkable, but Jurian put his hand suddenly on the lintel over the door.

"Look," he said softly. The *ichthus* was etched into the wood, and Jurian smiled at Agapius. "I guess this is the right place."

He rapped lightly on the door. For a long moment, nothing

happened, and they were about to retrace their steps back to the *castra* when the door opened, revealing a man who seemed not much older than Agapius, but whose eyes were wise and deep beyond the appearance of his age. He held a torch, which he lifted higher to peer at them.

"Yes?" he said.

"Are you Maternus?" Jurian asked.

The man tilted his head, squinted his eyes for a moment, and then stepped aside, opening the door wide for them to enter the house's narrow *fauces*. He closed the door behind them and led them through a tiny *atrium* and into a cramped room furnished only with a small table and a low bench. The man lit a lamp on the table and gestured for them to sit, then went to replace the torch in its holder on the wall in the *atrium*. When he returned, he remained standing across the table from them.

"Are you Maternus?" Jurian repeated.

"I am."

"Then you are the presbyter?" Agapius asked.

The man tilted his head again, his hand pausing in midair as he reached to adjust the lamp. "I am not familiar with you," he said. "I know all the soldiers here by sight, but I do not recognize you."

Jurian exchanged a surprised glance with Agapius. *There must be well over five thousand troops in Ara Agrippinensium, and this man knows them all?*

"We just arrived today. With Constantinus, the—"

"I know who he is," Maternus said with the barest hint of a smile. "All know him here. If he knew how many prayers were said daily on his behalf, he would throw the lot of us out."

"Why?" Jurian asked. "All men need prayers."

Maternus laughed. "Yes, they do...but some don't like to think that they do. So, you have arrived with Constantinus."

"He told us to seek you out," Agapius said.

"Ah. So I would assume you are not here to arrest me?"

Jurian made the *signum*. "We have come to confess and receive your blessing before we go into battle," he said. And then, because he couldn't silence the desperate hope that welled up within him, he added, "And to partake in the *eucharistia*, if it is possible."

Maternus's smile widened. "Come," he said. "Let us make all things new."

33

Myra, Anatolia — October, A.D. 301

In a patch of warm autumn sunshine, Sabra was helping Chloe and Melitta sort through the apples they had gleaned from the wild orchard on the outskirts of Myra. Melitta had already eaten more apples than she had put in her basket, and Chloe had finally given up rebuking her and was munching on her own wrinkled apple.

Sabra worked patiently, putting the wrinkliest fruit into a basket for Nikolaos and setting the smoother ones aside for the poor of Myra. The first time they had sorted fruit, earlier in the summer, she had tried to save the best for Nikolaos, but he had laughed and told her to switch the baskets.

"The poor are Heaven's royalty," he had told her. "We can make do with the seconds, but give the finest fruits to them, for they are other Christs among us."

She smiled as she recalled his words, and selected the most crinkled apple she could find and bit into it. An explosion of flavor filled her mouth—crisp, sweet, and tart all at once—and Chloe laughed aloud when she saw Sabra's expression.

"I told you they were delicious," Melitta said.

"All right, I believe you. Come on, girls. Let's take this down to the docks."

She got up and settled one of the baskets on her hip. With Chloe and Melitta close on her heels, she headed back through the winding streets of the town to the busy Andriake port, where some of Myra's poorest people lingered throughout the day, desperate for work or a bit of food. An older woman named Aspasia saw them coming and scrambled to her feet, her worn woolen cloak slipping down over her shoulders.

"Good morning, *kyria*," Sabra said, receiving the woman's embrace.

Aspasia always laughed when Sabra called her *kyria*, as if she were teasing her. She never wanted to believe that Sabra meant it sincerely.

"Here, take your pick."

She held her basket out, and soon five or six people had gathered around her, their faces tight with hunger, hands outstretched for her offerings.

"Disgusting," someone said behind her, in Latin, and the people scurried like mice back into the shadows of the port buildings.

Sabra turned and found a richly dressed man standing not two feet away, his face fixed in a sneer. If not for that look he might have been handsome, she thought, and if not for Nikolaos's instruction, she might have been angry at his comment.

"I would not call them that," she said, also in Latin, and he regarded her in some surprise.

"You'll never be rid of them if you keep feeding them," he said. "They're a plague on the Empire."

Sabra only smiled and held the basket of fruit toward him. His nose wrinkled and he took a step back.

"You must be new in Myra, *domine*," she said.

"I'm only passing through." He sniffed distastefully. "Gods, everything about this place stinks. How can you stand it?"

"I thought the same when I first came," she said, setting her basket against the wall of one of the port buildings.

Chloe and Melitta stood a little way away, she noticed, and

the poor had now gathered around them. They were watching her anxiously, but she only smiled and lifted her hand at her side in reassurance.

The sneer finally left the stranger's face, and he appraised her with blatant interest. "Are you repaying some favor of the gods?" he asked, and when she just stared at him in confusion, he pointed at her basket.

"Ah," she said. "Something like that, I suppose." She bowed her head a little. "If you'll excuse me, *domine*..."

"Where can I find the governor's house?" he asked suddenly, hand flashing out to catch her arm.

She pointed up the hill.

"Will you lead me there?"

"I'm sorry, *domine*, but I have my duties to attend. It is straight up the *cardo*. You can't miss it."

"I didn't think I would," he replied. "But I would be glad of your company, Sabra of Cyrene, *filia praefecti*."

She faltered and stared at him, all her blood running cold. "What?"

He knows the truth about you, whispered the voice in the back of her mind.

She ignored it. For months now the voice had been growing weaker, less insistent, and the more she ignored it, the less effect it had on her—just as Nikolaos had taught her.

"I thought my eyes were tricking me at first, but no, it really is you," the man said. Seeing her still skeptical, he gave her a small bow and added, "I'm from Cyrene, *domina*."

"You are?" she cried. "How is the city? My father? Is everything well?"

The man smiled faintly. "Well enough. Dignianus has been pressuring your father at every turn, as I'm sure you could imagine, and all of northern Africa has been under a drought this year. The harvest has been poor. Some people in the city are growing restless, and claiming that the drought is because we've offended the gods."

Sabra felt the blood drain from her cheeks, and she turned

away. "Droughts come and go," she said. "We've had them before and we will have them again."

"As you say."

He was still studying her with open curiosity, and Sabra suddenly felt cold, and self-conscious.

"You're from Cyrene, and you know who I am," she said softly. "It's a wonder that you're speaking to me at all."

"I have no concern for gods or sacrifices," he said with an indifferent shrug. "People do as they may. If it's any consolation to you, I know you better as the daughter of Lucius Titianus than anything else."

She regarded him curiously. "You lived in the shadow of the dragon's hill," she said. "It surprises me that you could still dismiss spiritual things."

He gave a wave of his hand. "There are many things I don't understand in the world. I don't attribute all of them to divine powers."

"Well," she said, bowing her head in courtesy. "I thank you for the news."

She turned to go, but he reached out and took her arm again. "Have you heard any news of Cyrene's famed dragon-slayer? What is that Greek name they gave him—*Drakonotomachos*? If the rumors are true, you were quite dear to him."

Her cheeks flushed hot, and she gently pulled her arm free of his grasp. "He is in exile," she said quietly. "I've had no word from him."

"You love him?" he asked, and backed a step away. "That is hard to believe."

"Why?"

"You didn't go with him." He gave her a slight bow. "*Domina.*"

And with that he turned and strode away, leaving her staring after him, her eyes blurred with tears.

SHE FOUND NIKOLAOS IN his courtyard that night, sorting vegetables from his autumn harvest with Hanno's help. They both glanced up in surprise when she burst through the gate, and Hanno was on his feet immediately.

"Mistress," he said, taking her hands. "Are you all right?"

"I have to leave," she said.

His face fell in a look of utter dismay; she ignored it.

"Where are you going in such a rush?" Nikolaos asked.

"Britannia," she said. The word caught in her throat, and she pressed a hand against her mouth. "He said I didn't really love Jurian. If I loved him, I would have gone with him."

"Who was this foolish person?" Hanno asked, his voice a growl.

"A man, from Cyrene. He saw me...he recognized me."

Nikolaos sighed and got to his feet, brushing dirt off the knees of his tunic. "Sabra, Jurian did not want to risk your life or your happiness by making you follow him into an unfamiliar land, where he knew he would be friendless and cut off from all Roman comforts. You know he wanted to settle himself there, and that he would send for you as soon as he could."

"Do you think so?" she whispered. She'd hoped it, every day since that night she and Jurian had said goodbye in Portus, but hearing Nikolaos say it made it suddenly seem real.

"I know so," he said, with a firmness that reassured her even more. He sighed and bowed his head. "Also, I think...Jurian is no longer in Britannia."

"What?" she and Hanno asked at the same time.

He held up a hand to forestall their questions. "I cannot say for certain. It's just a sense I have. If you go to Britannia now, daughter, you will not find him there." He reached out and took her hand, holding it with warm and steady strength. "Wait for him to send word to you. In the meantime, it is perhaps almost time for you to think about returning to Cyrene. You have learned all I can teach with words and exhortations. The rest must come with time."

"You're not sending me away?" she asked, feeling suddenly hollow.

She knew it was ridiculous—only moments before, she

had been intent on packing her things and leaving on the next ship bound for Britannia. But now the thought of leaving Myra gnawed at her heart.

Nikolaos laughed. "No such thing," he said. "You may stay as long as you wish. I think I will miss the company when you go." He nodded at Hanno. "And the help."

Sabra took a deep breath and smiled.

IN THE MORNING, SHE arrived at Nikolaos's house to find a man standing in the courtyard, and Nikolaos, beside him, looking ecstatically happy. As soon as he saw Sabra, Nikolaos clasped the man's shoulder and rushed toward her, grabbing her by the hand and drawing her forward.

"Who do you suppose this is?" he asked, gesturing dramatically to the stranger.

"I'm sure I can't guess," Sabra said. Then, since Nikolaos had spoken in Latin, she said to the man, "*Domine?*"

"I've just arrived from Cyrene," the man said, giving her a polite bow. She started forward a half step and he held up a hand, smiling. "And I arrived in Cyrene after being commissioned in Londinium, in Britannia."

Sabra's breath caught in her throat. "From Britannia?" she asked, the words escaping in a scant whisper, caught between hope and fear.

If he came from Londinium...then he couldn't possibly be sent by Jurian, could he?

"From one Lucius Aurelius Georgius."

Sabra covered her mouth with her hand and Nikolaos laughed.

"Don't keep her waiting, man!" he said.

"What does he say?" Sabra asked.

The man withdrew a small package from his bag and handed it to her. "Read it for yourself."

Sabra took it almost reverently, then, darting a glance from Nikolaos to the courier, she whispered, "Thank you," and bolted from the courtyard.

She took the little package down to her favorite spot along the shoreline, where the wind was mild and the waves were gentle. Perched up on a bit of crumbling wall, she carefully untied the twine and loosed the leather wrapping. Inside was a letter rolled into a narrow scroll, held shut by a silver ring set with a garnet stone. She slipped the ring off the letter and pressed it to her lips, then unrolled the letter.

Carissima, it has been too long since I saw you, though it was already too long the very first day we were apart. I have received an opportunity from our mutual friend C. to try to win back what I have lost. I will not be in this region long, and I do not know how long I will be gone. But when I have finished, I hope you will not have forgotten your promise to wait for me. As for myself, my heart is always and only yours. J.

That was all he had sent, and Sabra read the words over and over again until she could see them even when she closed her eyes. Jurian was safe. He had been—impossibly—in Britannia. And Constantinus, if she understood the letter correctly, was hoping to reinstate him as a Roman citizen.

She knew that Jurian prized his citizenship far more than she did. Though she would happily have lived as an exile with him, it was the one thing that stood between them. But if that obstacle could be dismantled…Sabra couldn't even imagine what happiness would be in store for her.

She twisted the signet ring in her fingers, her heart pattering with hope and joy. Was this ring Jurian's promise to her? Even if he hadn't meant it that way, she would wear it as her own pledge. Pressing it once more to her lips, she slipped it onto the fourth finger of her left hand, then bent her head and wept.

34

Ara Agrippinensium, Germania — October, A.D. 301

The morning of the battle dawned chill, and a heavy fog cloaked the autumn gold of the fields around Ara Agrippinensium. Constantinus's troop moved swiftly and silently through the long grasses like wraiths in the grey dawn, and even the birds were silent, as if they could sense the rising danger. Up ahead, a grove of tall, straight oak trees stretched as far as Jurian could see, their burnished leaves shaking like bits of tarnished copper in the wind. It almost seemed that the trees had marched to the field line to stand sentry there, silent watchers in the mist.

Jurian knew, as surely as if Constantinus had whispered it to him, that the Suevi would be waiting to ambush them in those trees. But the cohort did not slow its pace. Jurian, his heart hammering and his hands slick on the haft of his axe, knew that if the Suevi were watching, they would think that the Tribune had made a fatal mistake.

But then, as if by some secret signal, the cohort divided itself into three. Jurian, Agapius and the rest of his troop followed Constantinus straight toward the forest, but the other two sections slipped away to the left and right and were soon lost to sight.

Then, abruptly, their division came to a halt. From where he stood near the front of the cohort, Jurian could see movement in the trees, shadows slipping almost silently among the thick tree trunks. Then, before it seemed possible, a troop of wild men emerged from the cover.

Their leader was a giant of a man with a knot of long hair bound with leather cords on the top of his skull. It was ornamented with tiny bones of birds and crows' feathers, and it sat so high on his head that he seemed even taller than he actually was. At his side he swung a massive axe, not unlike the one Jurian carried, and a *seax* knife hung at his belt. He wore no tunic, and his bare chest was scrawled with intricate woven designs, as if he were a child of the forest itself.

"Roman," he shouted in Latin, his voice ringing clear in the still air. He shifted the axe so that he could be ready to swing at any moment. "You are trespassing. This is sacred ground."

Jurian held his breath. He hadn't anticipated this, but he couldn't tell from the way Constantinus carried himself if this were any surprise to him as well.

"Go back to your homes," Constantinus said. "You should know better by now than to test Rome's patience."

The Suevian chieftain threw back his head and laughed. "You think to frighten me, boy?" he scoffed. "If you want us, you will first have to find us."

Jurian heard the slither of steel on leather as Constantinus drew his sword, but the chieftain and his men had vanished as if into thin air.

A barely audible gasp of dismay rippled through the ranks. Agapius, who stood close to Jurian's left hand, murmured, "What are these people?"

Shouts rang out suddenly behind them, cut off almost as soon as they began. The cohort wheeled around, but they could see nothing through the swirling fog that seemed to drop like a curtain all around them.

"Defend the man next to you!" shouted Constantinus.

And then the man on Jurian's right fell suddenly to the

ground. "Help me!" he shrieked.

Before Jurian could react, the soldier was dragged into the mist, and his scream was drowned in the gurgle of blood.

"Jurian!" shouted Agapius.

Jurian swung around. Agapius stood facing him, frozen in fear, and then without a word, without warning, he was pulled off his feet. He crashed onto his stomach in the grass. Jurian sprang forward, swinging his axe down where he anticipated the Sueve would be. He felt the blade connect with something soft, and then there was a sickening crack and a cry of pain. Agapius scrambled to his feet, sword drawn and ready, and Jurian yanked the axe free. Its blade shone dully in the misty light, scarlet red with blood. Jurian looked from it to Agapius, who managed a shaky smile of thanks.

Then Agapius's expression shifted suddenly from relief to terror, and the hair prickled on the back of Jurian's neck. He heard the battle roar as if from a distance, and before he could react, something slammed into his back. He hit the ground hard and the axe spun from his grip. A Suevian warrior rolled Jurian onto his back and knelt over him, his *seax* knife raised to plunge into Jurian's chest. For one awful moment, Jurian's eyes locked with the warrior's, and he read death in his stare.

The Sueve's muscles tightened and he straightened up, grinning like a madman. Jurian's hand groped in vain for the haft of his weapon, but it was too far to reach. The barbarian's blade flashed in the cold light, then plunged toward his heart.

It never struck. There was a blur of motion and a confusion of noise, and suddenly the Sueve toppled sideways, tangled in Agapius's grip. But as soon as he hit the ground, he slithered free and rolled aside, twisting and thrusting with the knife at the same time. Agapius couldn't stop his momentum as he tumbled after the Sueve.

The blade sank deep into his right shoulder.

Agapius cried out and the Sueve planted a boot in his stomach, shoving him over. Agapius crashed to the ground, scrabbling desperately for his sword hilt with his good arm.

Jurian drew his own *seax* and planted himself between the Sueve and Agapius, and the warrior's mouth opened again in a manic grin. They circled each other slowly, the barbarian's lithe movements reminding Jurian of the tigers he had battled in the amphitheater in Rome.

Patience, he told himself.

The Sueve struck out with his knife and Jurian dodged aside. He switched the *seax* to his left hand and stabbed the blade into the warrior's forearm, jerking it free just as quickly. The warrior grinned all the more fiercely and switched his own knife to his left hand, his right arm hanging useless by his side. Blood ran down his arm and through his fingers, staining the bright grass.

"You don't have to die today," Jurian said.

The Sueve's face changed, the manic grin shifting to fury, and he sprang on Jurian with a ferocious roar. Jurian crouched and rolled to the side, then plunged the blade up into the man's chest. He jerked the knife free and the man crumpled to the ground.

For a moment Jurian stood over his lifeless body, breathing hard and shaking with adrenaline and triumph. Finally, becoming aware of the battle still raging around him, he left the corpse to recover his axe, then wiped the blade of his *seax* clean in the damp grass and slipped it into the sheath at his waist. Agapius was lying still a few feet away, the grass beneath him a startling shade of red.

Jurian dropped to a knee beside him. "Agapius! Can you move?"

Agapius tried to sit up, but fell back with a groan. "Not... really," he said.

Jurian moved his friend's hand away from the wound in his shoulder and winced. The cut was jagged and deep, and Agapius's face was ashen with pain and loss of blood.

"I'm going to get you out of this," Jurian said.

Agapius managed a laugh. "You might not be able to get yourself out of this."

Jurian didn't answer. He tore a strip of fabric from the

bottom of his tunic and wadded it up, pressing it against the weeping wound.

"Hold that there," he said, placing Agapius's good hand over the cloth, and got to his feet.

All around them the mist was thinning, torn to tatters by the sunlight gleaming through. A short distance away, Jurian glimpsed Constantinus grappling with the Suevian chieftain, the hewn and bloody bodies of Romans and Suevi littering the ground all around them. But Jurian could see Constantinus's second division coming at a run from the direction of the forest, where they had somehow managed to route the barbarians.

The Suevian chieftain twisted suddenly, unexpectedly, lashing out with one heavy boot and kicking the knees out from under Constantinus. The Tribune crashed to the ground, writhing onto his back just as the chieftain raised his axe. Jurian darted forward as Constantinus struggled to wrestle the axe away from the chieftain, to stop the inevitable blow from falling.

Thwarted by Constantinus's strength, the chieftain roared and turned the axe, trying to use the butt of the haft to strike Constantinus in the head. Constantinus jerked aside just in time. The haft barely nicked his forehead and sank into the soft earth instead, and the chieftain and Constantinus threw themselves into a frenzied contest to free it.

Jurian raised his axe and, with a great cry, swung as hard as he could at the chieftain's exposed neck. The blade struck true, and too suddenly the chieftain stopped fighting. His whole body went unnaturally still, then toppled sideways. The head rolled away into the grass, and Jurian shuddered when he saw its face frozen in that awful manic grin.

He let the axe fall and dropped to one knee beside Constantinus. The Tribune groaned and shook his head slowly, pressing a hand over the gash in his forehead, then accepted Jurian's arm to help him sit up.

"That's the second time you've saved my life," he said. "Are you ever going to give me a chance to return the favor?"

"Maybe someday," Jurian said. He rose and pulled

Constantinus to his feet.

The second division drew up around them and the centurion, his face streaked with sweat and blood and dirt, saluted Constantinus.

"We lost a dozen men in the woods," he said. "And the third division was destroyed. But—" he nudged the chieftain's body with his toe— "the day is ours, *Tribunus*."

Constantinus nodded wearily and laid a hand on the man's shoulder. "Go back for the wounded," he said. "Then fall back to the city." As the centurion turned away to bark his orders to his men, Constantinus turned to Jurian. "Where's Agapius?"

"Wounded badly," Jurian said.

"Get him back to the *castra*," Constantinus said. Jurian inclined his head and turned to leave. "And Jurian," Constantinus called. Jurian glanced back over his shoulder. "Thank you."

By the time Jurian got him back to the city, Agapius was fading. His skin was clammy and pale, his heartbeat weak and fast, and minute by minute he drifted in and out of consciousness. All Jurian could do was leave him in the care of the chief *sapsarius* with strict instructions that he should be called if his friend's condition worsened. Feeling utterly helpless, he wandered into the *atrium* and sat down on a low stone bench near the *impluvium*. He didn't dare look at his reflection in the water. Instead, he buried his hands in his hair and squeezed his eyes shut.

Sometime later—minutes, or maybe hours—someone sat down beside him. Jurian lifted his head. Constantinus, his head well-bandaged in clean linen, leaned on his knees and stared into the water.

"Victory," he said, almost spitting the word.

"Your father will be pleased," Jurian said.

"Of course."

Jurian glanced at him. "I thought I was the one with all the regret," he said.

"You? What do you have to regret? You saved the life of your friend. And mine. There is nothing to regret in that."

Jurian rubbed his hands together slowly. "You remember after Heraklea," he said. "To wash your hands and never feel like they are clean. To kill a man...even in battle..." He shook his head. "Those men today. They were just men. Like me. Like you."

"Don't let Rome hear you talk like that," Constantinus said wryly.

"But I mean it," Jurian said. "We could have been fighting Eilwen and Brigit. Or Menas, even. Is that what it means to be Roman? That anyone who is not under the rule of the Empire is...somehow less than human? Or deserves to be simply exterminated, like pests?"

Constantinus turned his head and met Jurian's gaze. "Yes. And it is true even of those who are under the rule of the Empire," he said, "but fail to follow her customs."

Jurian stiffened. "You see this, and yet you fight her battles?"

"And what should I do?" Constantinus asked, heat in his voice. "Everything is so simple to you, isn't it? If you don't like something, you think you can just stand back and refuse to take part. That somehow removing yourself from the conflict is the brave and right thing to do. Do you think that the games, the arena, all of that suffering and death has ended because you no longer see it? Do you imagine that one man turning away could change the fate of an Empire?" Constantinus got to his feet. "It isn't that simple," he said. "Sooner or later, you will understand that sometimes the only way to change anything for the better is to do the hard things...to bow your neck beneath the yoke, to shed the blood that Rome wants spilled, all so that one day—"

"The bridge builder will mark the sign in the sky?" Jurian suggested, quietly, while his heart burned with grief and shame at the Tribune's words. "And you can restore what has been broken?"

Constantinus's face darkened. "Do not dare to cast that woman's words in my face," he said. "And hear me well," he added. "I have risked everything for you—*everything*, do you understand?—to give you the opportunity to join me in this fight."

"I understand."

"Then make your choice, Lucius Aurelius Georgius, and do not look back."

35

Alexandria, Aegyptus — November, A.D. 301

Aikaterina stood at the top of the palace steps, flanked by the members of her court, and watched as the imperial procession threaded its way through the streets of Alexandria. Her people had all gathered on the walkways to watch, and some hung out their upper story windows to get a better glimpse. Nobody was cheering. There was a repressed hum of excitement in the air, but Aikaterina couldn't tell if the people were at all pleased that the Emperor Diocletian *Augustus* had come to Alexandria.

She was not. She had sent word to him about the troubles in Egypt, hoping perhaps that he would send money, or food, or troops. Instead he had sent word back that he himself was coming to survey the state of Egypt, and that he was bringing his own Legion with him.

The Legion had been left encamped outside the city, but Diocletian and his retinue would stay in the palace while he was in the city. The household had been buzzing with nervous anticipation since she had told them to expect the *Imperator*. She didn't blame them for their uncertainty. The last time Diocletian had been in Alexandria, he had sworn he would slaughter the city's rebels until his horse's knees were drenched in blood.

The procession stopped at the foot of the steps, and Diocletian swung off his horse with a sweep of his purple cloak. Aikaterina sucked in a breath through her teeth when she recognized the man dismounting beside him—Maxentius. Diocletian had said nothing about bringing him. Aikaterina couldn't blame him. He had probably guessed what she would do if he'd given her advance warning.

As Diocletian strode up the steps, Aikaterina dropped to a genuflection that all her people mirrored.

"Welcome to Alexandria, *Nobilissime Imperator*," she said.

He barely glanced at her. His gaze was roving over the palace, the streets, the awed but wary faces of the servants.

"I trust I find the city at peace?" he said. There was a note of warning in his voice, but Aikaterina refused to be intimidated.

She rose and lifted her chin, saying, "We are hungry, *Imperator*, but you will find no unrest here."

"I expect not," he said.

He stepped past her, striding into the palace as if it were his own, and Aikaterina stifled the urge to run in on his heels. Instead she waited where she was, watching Maxentius direct the Emperor's retinue and the servants who had approached to take their horses. Then he climbed the palace steps and gave her a shallow bow, pressing his lips to her offered hand.

"Ah, Aikaterina," he said, holding her hand longer than necessary. "We meet again."

"I congratulate you on your marriage, Maxentius," she said, withdrawing her hand.

His lips tightened in a thin line but he muttered a thank you before following Diocletian's example and making his own way into her palace. She gritted her teeth and gave a slight wave to her servants, and they all filed wordlessly back inside.

She didn't know how long the *Imperator* planned to stay, but she thought sourly that he had already overstayed his welcome.

THAT NIGHT, SHE HELD a splendid banquet for the Emperor and his retinue, but as she surveyed the spread the servants set out, she couldn't help but feel a little embarrassed—the drought had destroyed her country's crops, and everything had suffered as a result. Her servants had done the best they could, but the feast still looked rather like a poor man's meal compared to the extravagance of the feasts she had seen in Nicomedia and Antioch.

Diocletian turned to her midway through the meal. "I am sorry that your father could not join us tonight," he said.

"As is he," she replied. "But the *medicus* insisted he stay in bed. His health is very fragile, as you know. The least bit of excitement is disastrous for him."

"And your *medicus* is skilled enough? Would you permit me to send for my private physician?"

She held his gaze a moment. His concern surprised her, but there was no gentleness or compassion in his eyes. She couldn't quite make sense of his offer, so she only demurely inclined her head in a way that neither accepted nor refused anything. It was a gesture she had learned from her father.

"I am troubled to see how Alexandria is suffering," Diocletian went on. "I have brought a shipment of grain with my fleet. Tomorrow my Legion will oversee its distribution."

"*Imperator*, my people are suffering not just from hunger but from the troubles with the currency," Aikaterina said. She hesitated the barest moment, then added, "And the burden of taxation is too great. We have little wherewithal to buy grain from anyone."

His mouth lifted in an enigmatic smile. "I did not bring grain to sell it," he said.

She bowed her head, murmuring. "Thank you. But one shipment—"

"But I didn't say it would be only one," he said, and waved a hand in a gesture of dismissal. "Next week Maxentius and I will take the Legion to tour the rest of Egypt. The barbarians are still encroaching on your lands in the south, are they not?"

Aikaterina nodded.

"We will campaign against them and secure your southern

borders. Send your Legions with us if you choose."

"They are yours to command," she said.

THE GRAIN DOLE BEGAN the next morning. Aikaterina could hear the commotion in the streets even from within the sanctuary of the *Bibliotheka*, where she tried to distract her mind with reading Aristotle.

"Theokritos," she said suddenly, pushing the scroll aside.

Her tutor glanced up from his own reading, looking faintly surprised at her tone.

"He did it all on purpose, didn't he?"

"Who did what?" Theokritos asked through a frown.

"Diocletian. He knew about the drought. He knew our harvest would suffer. He imposed a grain tax anyway, which brought Alexandria to its knees. And now he marches in, resplendent in imperial glory, and graciously gives away grain to my starving people. Just watch, my senate will propose a monument to Diocletian before the winter is out, in gratitude for his generosity."

Theokritos smiled thinly. "He is a prudent statesman," he said.

"He manipulated my people," she protested, "to secure our allegiance to him."

"As I said, he is a prudent statesman."

Aikaterina bit her lip and pulled the scroll of Aristotle's *Politika* toward her again. "I just dread to discover what else he has in store for Alexandria."

36

Augusta Treverorum, Germania — December, A.D. 301

Jurian and Constantinus campaigned for two months against the Suevi around Ara Agrippinensium before returning to Augusta Treverorum for the winter. Agapius had recovered well enough to make the journey, but his wound had festered in Ara Agrippinensium and the sickness hadn't left him yet, so Jurian had left him under the care of an actual *medicus* in the palace. The man had clucked in disapproval at what he called the patchwork efforts of the field *sapsarius*, and promised to keep Jurian informed of his friend's recovery.

Not three days after their arrival, Constantius Chlorus held a banquet in honor of his son's victories over the barbarians. Jurian found himself once more surrounded by all the pomp and glittering smiles of Roman high society, and without Agapius there, he felt more alone than he ever had before. His mind and his heart were still far away, in the blood-drenched fields around the Rhenus, and all the spectacle of the court felt shallow and petty, and far, far beyond his reach.

To make matters worse, Julius Asclepiodotus kept eyeing him all throughout the meal, sidelong, the way a vulture might survey a bit of carrion. Jurian half-heartedly wished the man would choke on his wine.

"They say the Suevi eat their own dead," whispered a matronly woman on Jurian's left.

She was the wife of a retired Legion commander, who sat across from her and had drunk himself into oblivion before the meat had even been served. He was snoring peacefully now, his head cradled in a bread trencher. It was only after the woman stared at Jurian pointedly that he realized she had been speaking to him.

"What?" he said. "I...I don't think that's true."

The woman sputtered like a prodded hen. "Well, but my husband says that when he rode in campaign against them, they would drag off their dead!"

"That doesn't mean they ate them," Jurian said, irritable. "Perhaps they wanted to give them due burial rites."

"Burial!" snorted the woman. "As if they would do any such civilized thing! I think they eat them in a ritual to their horrible gods."

Jurian couldn't bring himself to argue. He wished in vain that the woman would bother someone else, but now that she had captured Jurian's attention, she seemed determined to keep it for as long as she could. Not for the first time that night, Jurian wished Agapius were with him—he would know how to put the woman off.

"It's just like that other cult, now," she said, her voice a conspiratorial whisper. "The Hebrews."

"The Hebrews?" Jurian asked with a frown.

"My husband says there's quite a settlement of them now in Ara Agrippinensium." She peered around Jurian to spear Constantius Chlorus with a narrowed gaze. "He's let them in. And no one seems to think anything of it! They're as bad as the cult of that Galilean...or worse. The *Augusti* mandated a purge of the army of their filthy numbers, but did he do it? No. And do we wonder why we are having so much trouble with the barbarians? The gods are displeased. I told my husband so yesterday. But would he listen to me? Of course not."

Jurian stared at her, completely at a loss for what to say, but she sailed past his silence.

"Of course you agree," she said. "My husband says they want nothing more than to overthrow the Empire."

"The...Suevi?"

"The Hebrews," she said, smacking the embroidered edge of her *palla* on the table. "And the Nazarenes. Both of them."

"Does he say why?" Jurian asked carefully. "Have they caused the *Caesar* trouble?"

The woman snorted again. "They haven't yet. But my husband says they are causing plenty in Rome and Nicomedia. Just wait. If he doesn't do something, it will spread. Like a *plague*. Haven't you heard about those strange followers of Mani in the south? Wait and see, if he doesn't stop this madness now, we'll have them to deal with here, too!"

Jurian glanced down the table at Constantius Chlorus, who was laughing with some ancient Legion *dux* Jurian didn't recognize. Asclepiodotus was still fixated on Jurian, even though another man sitting beside him was prattling on about the campaigns along the Rhenus.

Suddenly, Constantius Chlorus lifted his voice and his goblet. "Join me," he said, "and drink the health of *Tribunus* Constantinus and his cohort, who have finally brought us a sound victory over the Suevi, though dearly paid for!"

The assembly pledged Constantinus's health with hearty enthusiasm. And then, as talk swirled once more around them, Asclepiodotus turned to Constantius Chlorus, a deferential smile on his narrow face belied only by the sly look in his eyes.

"*Caesar*," he said. "Surely it does Rome credit for the Suevi to be challenged and beaten at every possible turn. But the cost was heavy for such an enemy, whom we surely ought to have been able to defeat far more quickly, and with far fewer losses. I wonder if perhaps choosing men more...acclimated to our ways might not result in a better outcome."

Constantinus set down the goose leg he was eating. "What are you implying, Asclepiodotus? Speak plainly or don't speak at all."

Asclepiodotus jerked his chin in Jurian's direction. "We know nothing about this man," he said. "Where he comes from, his parentage, his experience. And yet, *Caesar*—" turning once more to Constantius Chlorus—"your son seems very determined to keep him close."

"You think I know nothing of the men I choose to surround myself with?" Constantinus said, before the *Caesar* could reply. "I have my reasons for keeping him close, and it is well that I do. He has saved my life, not once, but twice now. If not for him, tonight you would be raising a tribute to the headless corpse of a tribune instead of the headless corpse of a Suevian chieftain and a decimated barbarian nation."

Asclepiodotus's face puckered. "How nice," he said. "And how is it, *Tribunus*, that you got yourself into such straits in the first place?"

Constantinus's sudden grin was void of mirth. "Why don't you come with me on our next campaign, and you can find out for yourself what happens in battle."

Asclepiodotus drew himself up. "I have fought in battles enough for three lifetimes of men," he said.

"It is incredible how quickly those fires turn to ash," Constantinus retorted.

"*Pax*," Constantius Chlorus said to his son, and then turned to Asclepiodotus. "I echo what the Tribune said. If you wish to say something, say it. You are wandering in the weeds."

"All I mean to say, *Caesar*, is that perhaps it is unwise to trust a man with your son's life when we know nothing about him, however much the Tribune claims to know him." He sniffed and added, keeping his voice off-hand, "One of my men in Ara Agrippinensium said that he regularly saw that man sneaking off into the district of the Hebrews the night before their battles. Who knows who he met there, or what schemes they hatched?"

A stunned silence fell over the table. Asclepiodotus seemed to enjoy the sudden attention, and he continued in an even more innocent voice, "I don't have to remind anyone of how the battles went ill for us."

"We were victorious," Constantius Chlorus said.

"But victory," Asclepiodotus said, "was a long time coming."

Jurian's heart hammered in his chest. He heard the woman next to him suck her breath in through her teeth, and he could almost feel her pull away from him as if he were a diseased thing. Constantinus's face darkened with barely suppressed anger.

"Last I checked," he said through clenched teeth, "it is not among the powers of men to conjure up mists and snow."

"Oh, so it was the weather," Asclepiodotus said, his voice biting as a serpent's. "I'm glad to hear it, because we never have to fight the enemy in anything but sunshine and moss flowers." He leveled a finger at Jurian. "*You*. Why don't you explain for all of us what you were doing in that district? Surely, if it was some innocent pursuit, you won't be ashamed to ease our minds on the matter."

Jurian didn't dare move a muscle, for fear that anything might give him up to suspicion. But even as he was trying to frame the truth in words vague enough to satisfy Asclepiodotus and protect Maternus—and Constantinus—the *Caesar* dropped his ponderous fist on the table.

"How dare you launch an interrogation in the middle of my feast!" he thundered. "You are as dour and pickled as a rotten apple! If you envy the boy's success, I suggest you get yourself to the *fabrica* and find yourself a sword. Now stop ruining my celebration with your conspiracies!"

Asclepiodotus pushed back his seat and rose. "I can see that my presence is not welcome," he said.

Constantius Chlorus waved a hand without even looking at him and returned to his conversation with the retired *dux*. Asclepiodotus tarried there for another moment, his face working in furious frustration, and then he turned on his heel and left the *triclinium*.

Jurian softly exhaled and took a sip of wine. The woman beside him leaned over, her earrings dancing in the firelight.

"Is it true?" she said. "Did you really go to such a place?"

Jurian shrugged. "Some men will say anything," he said. "Even when they do not know the truth."

The woman nodded her head, as if Jurian had just uttered pure wisdom. "Especially that one," she said, nodding her head toward the door where Asclepiodotus had exited. "If he hadn't made such a strong play against Allectus and Carausius, I doubt the *Caesar* would tolerate him." She lifted her narrow shoulders in a shrug. "But they say it is best to keep your enemies close to you."

"Yes," Jurian said thoughtfully. "They do say that."

His thoughts turned, against his will, to Casca, always too close for comfort, never close enough to be controlled. He'd heard nothing about Casca's activities since he had gone into exile, but the thought gave him no peace. If he knew anything about Casca, it was that he never stopped scheming, and his thirst for others' misery was never satisfied. He only prayed, as he prayed every night, that the people he loved would be safe from harm.

DAY WAS JUST BEGINNING to break, but Jurian, head in his hands and half asleep, didn't move from the low stool he occupied at Agapius's bedside. The night before, the fever that had tormented Agapius since the battle had finally broken and left him to sleep peacefully. Jurian had come as soon as the *medicus* sent word to him of his friend's improvement, and had stayed with him all through the night.

His head ached and his eyes were gritty, but he knew it was too late for him to get any sleep. In a few hours he would be reporting to the *campus* to drill with Constantinus and his cohort. Only this time he would not be training as a common *miles*, but in a new rank Constantinus had called *protector*, which he intended to ease Jurian back into a command role.

It was a test, Constantinus had said, to see if Jurian was ready for his return.

Constantinus, it seemed, envisioned Jurian riding into Nicomedia in some kind of triumphal procession, perhaps leading barbarian warriors by chains around their necks. At the head of such a column, he could stand before Diocletian and demand reinstatement as a citizen and a tribune, in repayment for his great service to the Empire.

Jurian sighed and the lamp next to Agapius's bed guttered. It had been his own dream, too, but what were a handful of battles against a remote barbarian tribe? Was he fooling himself to imagine his few accomplishments would impress Diocletian, who himself had waged countless wars against enemies far stronger than the scattered Suevian tribes?

"What am I doing here, Agapius?" he murmured to his sleeping friend.

"Bothering me?" Agapius said, his voice little more than a croak.

Jurian's head snapped up and he seized his friend's hand. "You're awake!" he said. "Praise God, but I thought you were going to sleep forever!"

"For a little prick in the shoulder?" Agapius mumbled. He cracked open one eye to appraise Jurian. "And anyway, I told you. No sword will end my life."

Jurian shook his head and smiled. "Well, you had me worried anyway. You've been ill for two months."

"I'm touched." He paused, then said, "Really, I'm touched. Please let go of my hand."

"You must be feeling better," Jurian laughed and released him.

"I won't be going into battle against screaming barbarian hordes anytime soon, if that's what you're hoping." He tried to move his arm and let it fall back on the pallet, exhausted. "In fact, I don't know if this arm will ever lift a sword again."

"Don't move it," Jurian cautioned. "It was badly infected for a long time. You'll need time to restore its strength." He paused, then said flatly, "The *sapsarius* wanted to cut it off."

Agapius muttered something under his breath, then said more loudly, "Maybe it would hurt less." He eyed Jurian again. "Two months?"

"Two."

Agapius closed his eyes, and stayed still and quiet for so long that Jurian thought he had gone back to sleep. But just as he was about to slip away, Agapius opened them again and heaved a deep breath.

"What did I miss?"

"A lot of marching," Jurian said. "And sleeping on wet ground."

Agapius made a noise of distaste.

"And some battles, and a lot of barbarians. We think we've finally routed the Suevi, but the Franks are stirring up trouble now, too, so we'll be heading out again once the winter breaks."

Agapius snorted. "So, what, two months? Or two weeks?"

"Something like that," Jurian said, smiling. "Hopefully by then you'll be well enough to come with us." He paused, then added, "Constantinus gave me command of a small troop."

Agapius studied him, forehead creased. "Well, don't sound so pleased," he said at last. "That's what you wanted, isn't it? The chance to prove yourself?"

"I…don't know. I suppose I do."

"Well, a word of advice," Agapius said, sounding suddenly wide awake, and very serious. "You might want to figure that out before you lead men into battle…and quite possibly to their deaths."

Jurian shot him a glance. "I know. Constantinus said the same thing."

"Constantinus gave you good advice? I suppose miracles do happen." He managed a grin and closed his eyes again. "Don't tell me you've had your fill of Legion life."

"It's my life," Jurian said, simply.

It was the best answer he could give—even he had a hard time explaining to himself how right it felt, being in the camp and out in the field with his men. If only he could be certain he could fight all Rome's battles with a clear conscience, he would have no reason for the doubts that always hovered, murmuring, in the back of his mind.

"Some men are called to live and die by the sword," Agapius said. "Perhaps you're one of them."

Jurian said nothing, but Agapius's words sent a chill over him. He rose silently and slipped from the room, and this time Agapius made no motion to call him back.

37

Ara Agrippinensium, Germania — February, A.D. 302

As Jurian had partly expected, the plan to winter in Augusta Treverorum was interrupted by new reports of hostilities from the Frankish tribes along the Rhenus. The new year had barely begun, and the snow was still thick on the ground, when Constantinus gave his cohort orders to prepare to march back to Ara Agrippinensium.

Agapius had recovered enough to travel with the cohort, but he still hadn't gotten full use of his arm, and Constantinus refused to consider him as part of the combat unit. The miserable journey to the Rhenus took a toll on him, and when they finally arrived at Ara Agrippinensium, he had relapsed into a fever.

Jurian left him in the care of the *sapsarius* and, with no other duties to occupy him, turned his steps toward the city. He passed the playhouse, quiet now in the afternoon, and felt a pang of remorse.

He's not dead, he told himself. *And, God willing, I will survive the battles in the days to come.*

Agapius seemed to have taken the Lady of Afallon's words as some kind of promise, but Jurian had no such reassurances. Everything he had heard since they had left Portus, so long ago, had been stone, and blood, and fire.

And still nothing from Sabra. Although he tried to keep himself busy to distract his mind, every day that passed made him more anxious. Each day made it harder for him to invent an explanation for her silence, and his heart was heavy with worry.

The road under his feet ended abruptly at a door, and Jurian stopped and glanced up. Without even realizing it, his feet had carried him back to Maternus's *domus,* and he rapped hesitantly, wondering if the presbyter would be in at this hour of the afternoon. After a moment, the door opened a fraction and a young man thrust his face out to look at him.

"What do you want?" he asked.

Jurian frowned. "That is no way to greet a—" He stopped, suddenly unsure what to call himself. He'd been about to say *a tribune*—but it had been a long time since he'd carried that title. Shouldn't he say *a fellow traveler?*

"A what?" the young man said, wrinkling his nose. "A *miles* looking for trouble? You're in the wrong district, I'm afraid."

"I'm a friend," Jurian said, making the *signum.*

"Who is it, Adalfuns?" came Maternus's voice from within the domus.

"A man who says he's a friend is at the door, *pater,*" said Adalfuns. "Shall I throw him out?"

"And what if he is Christ at the gate?" Maternus said. "And you throw him out in the street?"

Adalfuns's face shifted from wary suspicion to utter terror. He stared at Jurian—with special attention to his red hair—and scratched his own head nervously. "I didn't think the Christ would have red hair," he mumbled.

"I am not He," said Jurian, making the *signum* again. "Open the door and let me in."

Adalfuns finally stepped aside and held the door for Jurian. Maternus came forward to greet him and clasped his hand in both his own.

"I would say I'm surprised to see you again, but I'm not," Maternus said, leading him inside. He peered over Jurian's shoulder. "You've been gone a long while."

"We wintered in Augusta Treverorum. Or, that was the plan, until we got called out again."

"And Agapius?"

"He is here in the city, but not well. His fever has returned. Would you…might you come visit him? I think it would bring him comfort."

Maternus fixed him with a keen eye. "I do not usually go to the *castra*," he said. "I am no priest of Mithras, and even here, this far away from the heart of the Empire, suspicion of the followers of the Christ is growing."

"But Constantinus doesn't spread that kind of intolerance," Jurian objected. "Nor his father, from all I can tell."

"No," Maternus said with a faint smile.

They sat down at the small table and Adalfuns brought them wine and some fresh bread. As soon as he had disappeared once more into the *culina*, Jurian leaned forward.

"If not them, then who is spreading the hate? I have seen enough of men to know that most just want to be left alone to make their way in this world. Unless something, or someone, threatens them, they are mostly content to let others be."

"True," Maternus said. "Men are like bees in that way, I think. But there is one in the *Caesar's* court who would like nothing more than to see all the followers of the Christ driven out." He cocked an eyebrow at Jurian, as if prompting him to supply the name.

"Julius Asclepiodotus," Jurian said. He shook his head with a frown. "I don't understand it. Why does Constantius Chlorus keep him around? He is poison—everyone knows it, even the *Caesar*."

"Who am I to say what his motives are?" Maternus said with a shrug. "But Constantius Chlorus has plans for his son, and those plans require him to remain, at least in appearance, in line with the policies and attitudes of the *Augusti*."

Jurian made a face and tore off a piece of bread. "It all seems so…foolish," he said. "In my own town, where I was raised, I saw the cost of such ambition."

Maternus nodded as if he could see what Jurian did not say. "It is good you see it so," he said, "for you will one day be called to speak truth to kings."

Jurian started violently. "What did you say?"

"To speak truth to such men requires special grace," Maternus continued as if Jurian hadn't spoken. "You must ask for it."

Jurian's black horse snorted a cloud of steam in the cold morning air, almost dancing beneath him as they trotted over the open ground toward a distant line of trees. Jurian's spirits were just as high, and his blood sang with adrenaline and anticipation of the fight ahead.

He never would have imagined just how happy he would be to head into battle from the back of a horse, rather than on his own two feet. The week before, as preparations were underway for the upcoming campaign, Constantinus had taken him aside and informed him that he had been given a field promotion to *decurio*. He would be in charge of a small troop of horse—heavy horse, *cataphractarii*, which Constantinus claimed would put the fear of the divine in their enemies' hearts.

Since then, Jurian had often wondered if Constantinus's support and promotion had nothing to do with Jurian's quest to win back his honor, and everything to do with his own plans. Was Jurian simply a part of his larger scheme, like a piece to be played in a game of *latrunculi*? Either way, Jurian still couldn't quite believe his good fortune. Constantinus had given him a rare opportunity, and Jurian was determined to make the most of it.

Now his men rode at the head of the column of infantry, their horses' armor bright and jangling in the cold sunshine, and Jurian felt, keenly, all of their eyes fixed on him. He adjusted his seat in the armored saddle. Though he had been training in them for almost a week, he still wasn't accustomed to the weight of his heavy mail shirt and helmet, or the feel of riding with a short lance in his right hand. He had his axe strapped across his back as always, its weight a familiar comfort to him, but he had his doubts about how useful the weapon would be from the back of a horse.

At least, he thought, he would know the answer to that question before the day was out. The Suevi they had battled the previous autumn had regrouped, joining forces with some of their neighboring tribes, and the whole region was like tinder, ready to go up in flames at any moment. Messengers had come just the day before to report that other previously subdued tribes of Alemanni were also on the move, although it was uncertain whether they were massing a force for attack or simply moving to spring grazing grounds.

Jurian smiled grimly beneath his helmet. The Alemanni had once been allies of Rome, according to Constantinus—Roman in every way except official status as citizens. But Caracalla had betrayed their loyalty and sought to subjugate them instead, thus making them sworn enemies of the Empire.

And now the Empire was making the same mistake again, but this time with the Christians within its own borders.

They should have learned their lesson, he thought. *Repaying loyalty with betrayal and slaughter won't lead to peace.*

Constantinus held up a hand, and as the troop drew to a halt, the Tribune circled his horse back and reined in beside Jurian.

"Take your men into the trees," he said, pointing to their left with his sword. "Remember the maneuver we discussed. Wait for my signal."

Jurian nodded, his heart hammering. This was a new tactic that Constantinus had devised, and if it worked, it would win them all their fair share of renown.

And maybe this will be enough, Jurian thought as he spurred his horse and led his troop at a canter toward the treeline. *Finally enough for an end to this exile.*

Borrowing a tactic from the Suevi, they formed up within the shelter of the trees, angling their horses into the heaviest shadows of the canopy. The underbrush was enough to offer some concealment, but not so dense that it would impede them when they broke for the charge.

"How long do we wait?" asked a young soldier on Jurian's right. He was bright and quick, skilled with the bow on horseback, and Jurian had chosen him as his second in command.

Jurian pointed across the field at the black pennant held by one of Constantinus's men. It snapped in the breeze as the infantry continued their advance, and Jurian offered a silent prayer of thanks that there was no mist or fog this morning to confound them.

"As long as it takes, Servius," he said. "Make sure the men are silent, and keep the horses quiet."

Servius relayed the order and sat pensively beside Jurian. Jurian's horse champed on his muffled bit, tugging a little at the reins in his eagerness. Servius's mount seemed content to nose at the underbrush like a deer.

They didn't have long to wait. Almost before Constantinus had the chance to draw his men into formation, the Suevi were upon them with a deafening roar of shouts and screams, and both forces rushed into a charge. The lines met with a ferocious crash.

Jurian shifted in his saddle, eyes fixed on the pennant. It wavered as the battle raged, but did not drop. From their distance could just hear the shouts of the living and the screams of the dying. Jurian's hands tightened on the reins, and Servius glanced at him, every muscle tense and ready for action. It looked like Constantinus's cohort was being driven back, and then, suddenly, the Romans broke into full flight.

A shout of triumph went up from the Suevi.

"Wait," Jurian murmured.

As soon as the Romans got free of the Suevi, the pennant dropped.

"*NOW!*" Jurian shouted and drove his heels into his horse's side.

His cavalry broke the cover of the trees with one mighty

shout and launched into a full gallop. The Suevi stopped in confusion and swung to face them, but too late. The horses, hooves thundering on the turf, plowed into them like a battering ram. Men fell on all sides, bashed to the ground and then trampled by the iron-shod hooves.

As they broke through the line on the other side, Jurian wheeled his horse. It reared, and he threw his lance. It struck a Suevian warrior in the soft flesh of his neck, and he dropped to the ground in a pool of blood. Jurian unslung his axe, and lifted it high over his head.

Constantinus led the infantry at a run back into the fray, and they cut down the shattered Suevi without mercy. Jurian spotted a small group of barbarians fleeing for the trees, and he leveled his axe at them.

"After them!" he shouted. "To me!"

He drove his heels into his horse's side and galloped after the retreating Suevi, his troop forming up behind him. Just before the barbarians reached the forest, Jurian's men overtook them and cut off their retreat. The Suevi fought like caged animals, desperate to break free. Jurian cut one down with a stroke of his axe, and Servius took out several more with rapid shots from his bow.

"Surrender," Jurian said, leveling his axe at the survivors.

One of the Suevi spat at his feet. "We know what you do to survivors, Roman. We would die free rather than live out our days as slaves!"

He launched himself at Jurian with a shout, his *seax* knife gleaming in his hand. Jurian's horse shied away from him and Jurian, unaccustomed to the weight of his armor, lurched sideways, off balance. Just before the Sueve could plunge the knife into Jurian's side, an arrow hissed through the air and pierced through his matted and skull-beaded hair. He toppled noiseless to the ground. Jurian regained his seat and control of his horse, and gave a brisk nod of thanks to Servius.

Jurian's men dispatched the rest of the Suevi as they fought to escape the circle of horsemen, until not a single man of them was left breathing. Jurian maneuvered his horse out of the carnage and cantered across the field to where Constantinus was directing his men to look for the dead and wounded Romans among the fallen.

As Jurian rode up, Constantinus swung around and raised his sword, crying, "Victory!"

Jurian reined in beside him and pulled off his helmet, letting the cold wind sift through his sweat-soaked hair. "It worked," he said, clasping Constantinus's hand at the wrist.

"Well done, *decurio*," Constantinus said with a broad smile. "Let Julius Asclepiodotus choke on this."

38

Alexandria, Aegyptus — March, A.D. 302

In the brisk chill of a stiff spring wind, Aikaterina faced the harbor of Alexandria, her heart caught somewhere between joy and fear. Sailing into the harbor was a merchant vessel, and on board were two of Aikaterina's dearest friends. And yet she wished with a bitterness that choked her that they were not coming to Alexandria.

As the vessel was made fast, Sabra appeared at the rail, and Aikaterina's breath caught in her throat. Sabra looked radiant, and even clad in common garb, she looked more regal than Aikaterina had ever seen her. Even Hanno, standing close behind her, looked like he had been infused with new life, and he lifted a hand to wave when he caught sight of Aikaterina waiting for them below.

In the face of such joy, Aikaterina could do nothing but wave in return. Then the ramp was cleared and Sabra came down, throwing her arms around Aikaterina's neck.

"It's been too long, sister," she said, hugging her tight. "I've missed you!"

Then she released Aikaterina and stepped back, regarding her somberly. Aikaterina bowed her head under the intensity of Sabra's gaze, which, she thought, always seemed to see more than eyes alone could see.

"Diocletian is in the city," she said flatly, to forestall the inevitable questions.

Sabra started, and all the joy in her eyes was snuffed out, replaced by a hollow kind of fear. "What? Why?"

"Oh, he's been very good to us," Aikaterina said.

She waved for Sabra to follow as she turned toward her *lectica*. Once they were settled inside, with Hanno and some of the palace slaves following behind with the luggage, Aikaterina folded her hands in her lap and met Sabra's worried gaze.

"He raised a grain tax in the middle of a drought," she said, "but then was so kind as to give us a dole to ease our sufferings. We were failing to repel the barbarians from our southern *limes*, and he graciously came in with his Legion and routed them for us. We are all most grateful for his kindness. And now he is threatening to murder a segment of my citizens, and there is nothing at all that I can do about it. I've spoken to my senate. I've spoken to the people. And yet they are all cowed by Diocletian and fear the repercussions of denying him his wish."

Sabra, looking terrifyingly pale, said, "Threatening whom?"

Aikaterina waved a hand. "A man named Innai, in particular, and his followers. They preach a corrupted Christianity, saying that all matter is evil and only the spirit is good."

"That is the preaching of Mani!" Sabra exclaimed. "I know this Innai. I met him once, when I was going to Cyrene on a ship with Jurian and Menas. Innai was a passenger, and he and Jurian argued the whole time about spiritual matters."

Aikaterina stifled a sudden laugh. "I'm sorry," she said. "That amused me. Spiritual matters. Spirit…matter…never mind."

Sabra smiled and clasped Aikaterina's hand. "You never change," she said. "But why is Diocletian so opposed to them?"

"If he disapproves of Christianity, he absolutely despises the followers of Mani. They are in every way opposed to the Roman way of life, and they will not peacefully coexist with Rome, either. Not to mention that Mani was Persian, and that is a wound to Rome's pride that has not yet healed." She sighed and shook her head. "My people have just suffered through Diocletian's purges. Why is he tormenting us again? Does he truly believe that shedding our blood will make us tractable?" She frowned and added more softly, "Did he learn nothing the last time?"

"What did you say?" Sabra asked, leaning forward.

Aikaterina frowned—she hadn't spoken *that* softly. And then she heard the noise escalating outside the *lectica*, and at the same moment Sabra drew up like a startled doe.

"Do you smell that?"

Aikaterina slapped the back of the *lectica*. "Stop, stop!"

As the *lectica* settled to the ground, she pushed back the curtain and climbed out. They had come into the *agora*, and instead of the peaceful, day-to-day business of merchants and government officials, she faced an anxious mob. And there, across the way, were three pillars. She pressed her hand against her mouth and staggered back, as waves of noxious black smoke roiled above the pillars. Behind her the curtain twitched, and she spun around and ducked back into the *lectica*, startling Sabra as she was starting to climb out.

"Stay in," Aikaterina gasped. "Don't look—don't look!"

"What's going on out there?" Sabra cried.

"They're burning…oh, God have mercy…"

She hammered on the back of the *lectica* again, calling out to the slaves to move on. Then she bowed over her knees and wept. Sabra clasped her hands tight and didn't let go until they had reached the palace, and Aikaterina drew her hand free to wipe the tears from her cheeks. Then, not even trying to bridle her fury, she dismounted the *lectica* and strode up the palace steps, leaving Sabra and Hanno to find their own way inside. She had business with the *Imperator* Diocletian.

She found him—to her immense displeasure—pacing in her favorite garden, one hand folded behind his back and head bowed. He might have looked like a philosopher contemplating the form of the just, but all Aikaterina could see was his hands stained with blood.

"I was in the *agora*," she said, without preamble.

He rounded on her in surprise, and his guards took a few polite steps away from them.

"They had fair warning," Diocletian said. "I issued my edict, but they would not come to heel. And so they were punished. If Rome's enemies saw how we were incapable of carrying out our threats against an enemy as weak as these followers of Mani, what mischief would they not cause us along our *limes*? The same will happen to anyone who dares defy the edicts of Rome."

"But to burn them alive, in the public square? It's an abomination, *Imperator*."

"Have you listened to the preaching of this man, Innai?" Diocletian said. "He subverts the very foundations of Rome with his lies."

"And that may be!" Aikaterina protested. "But should you not have engaged them in intellectual debate, rather than with physical violence? When will you learn that you cannot extinguish an ideology with the sword?"

Diocletian's face grew very still, and very cold, and Aikaterina realized all at once that she had blatantly rebuked the Emperor—to his face. Flushing, she bowed her head and took a single step away from him, but she couldn't apologize for her words.

Then, to her surprise, Diocletian made a faint noise that she realized was suppressed laughter. "I should have sent you to argue with them."

Aikaterina glanced back at him, flustered and bewildered. "And I would have done it, gladly," she said. "Especially if I believed it might save their lives." She paused, then added earnestly, "Just because someone disagrees with your beliefs, *Imperator*, does not mean they have to die."

"Those must die who I say must die," Diocletian said, the anger in the words all the more terrifying for how calm his face was. "And today all the leaders of this cult of Mani have been put to the sword. The streets of Alexandria have run red with blood once more, Aikaterina. How am I to judge this place? Will Alexandria always be a thorn in my side?"

Aikaterina swallowed and turned aside. "That is not my wish, *Imperator*. In fact, you would find us most tractable if you would be as tolerant of us as we are of others."

"Ah," Diocletian said. "I remember. Your Library and its open embrace for all knowledge." He took a step closer to her, gesturing vaguely in the direction of the city *agora*. "Do you still believe that knowledge is not dangerous? Mani was not unlearned, but I would argue he wasn't learned enough. Such people are inherently dangerous, and your scattering knowledge before people incapable of receiving it only leads them astray." He nodded toward the palace and said, "Good day."

Aikaterina bowed and retreated into the palace, wounded and humiliated by the dismissal from her own garden. Her mind was still reeling when she found Sabra and Hanno in an inner chamber, Hanno with his head in his hands, Sabra trying to comfort him.

"God have mercy," Hanno said, over and over again. "Those poor souls."

"He saw it all, but won't tell me what happened either," Sabra said, looking up at Aikaterina. "What was it?"

"They executed Innai and his two companions. They burned them, Sabra. In front of all my people. And Diocletian says the rest of the leaders of that sect have been slaughtered as well. And if Diocletian would do that to the followers of Mani, what will he do next? To *us*?" With a shiver, she murmured, "Oh God, what is to become of Your people?"

"You think it was a warning?" Sabra whispered.

"Undoubtedly. Diocletian...he's never been very adamant about going after us, but I cannot help feeling that this was his warning, that if we don't *come to heel,* as he called it, we will be next."

Hanno shuddered, his hands tight around his head.

"You cannot stay here," Aikaterina said to Sabra. "I wish you could. I would've gladly kept you here for as long as you wished to stay, but my city is a tinderbox right now. And Cyrene will need you, too, in the days to come."

"I know," Sabra said, softly. "It's why I have come home."

SABRA AND HANNO LEFT the next morning, somehow managing to escape the palace and the city without Diocletian knowing that they had been there at all. Aikaterina felt strangely lonely without Sabra there, even though they'd had only a few hours in each other's company after more than a year of separation. Sabra had promised to write more often. Aikaterina wondered how either of them would find time for the luxury of cheerful correspondence.

She sighed as she walked through her garden—for once, blessedly alone. She had not seen the Emperor at all that day, but she wasn't sure if the thought made her more nervous or relieved. But the peace and quiet of the garden path was short-lived. The sudden sound of running footsteps made her jump, and she peered back down the path, straining to see who was coming in such a hurry.

A moment later, Diodoros came into view, and Aikaterina drew herself up, fear blanching through her at the sight of his wide, wild gaze, his tousled hair.

"What is it?" she said as he stopped in front of her, breathing hard. "What happened?"

"The *Bibliotheka*."

"What...what about it?"

"I'm sorry, *kyria*. Diocletian's men...they've raided it."

Aikaterina's world shifted around her, and she leaned a hand against the rough trunk of a date palm. "What do you mean, raided it?"

"Theokritos is there now...trying to assess... But half the scrolls on astronomy are gone. Medicine, geometry, physics..."

A great sob tore from her chest and she bowed her head, fury and grief battling within her. "Not again! We've only just rebuilt...how could they dare take those things?" she cried. "What did they do with them? Because such barbarians would certainly not read them!"

Diodoros shook his head. "One of the slaves, he said he saw them burning..."

"*No!*" Aikaterina cried, slamming her palm against the tree trunk. "My God, what have they done? What have they done? All that knowledge...the work of so many lives..."

Diodoros took her hands in his. "You are right. They are barbarians," he said. "Men who have no respect for life can have none for learning, *kyria*."

"I should have known," she gritted. "When I spoke to Diocletian and he rebuked me for Alexandria's tolerance...I should have known this was coming! Is he punishing Alexandria, or is he punishing me?" She looked up into his face, a sudden horror choking her. "What have I done, Diodoros?"

"It's all right," Diodoros said gently. "You are not carrying the whole world, or even the whole city, on your shoulders alone." He gave her a small, sad smile. "God will give you the strength you need for whatever will come of this."

Aikaterina bowered her head and squeezed her eyes shut. She wished she had his certainty.

She spent all the next morning in the *Bibliotheka* with Diodoros and Theokritos, trying to sort out which texts were left and which had been taken and burned. It made no sense to her, this fear of knowledge. What harm could come from astronomy? What danger did geometry pose to the Empire? It was not so very long ago that Diocletian had seemed to agree with her that cultivating virtue in the citizen should be the highest priority, and the most practical good a government could seek. What had changed his mind?

She sat on the stone floor in a ray of weak sunshine with a tray in front of her as she sifted through the charred remains of a dozen papyrus scrolls, hoping to find fragments intact enough for her scribes to recopy.

Virtue has become the equivalent of agreeing with the Emperor in all things, she thought bitterly. *He doesn't want citizens who can think and understand, but only those who will obey without question.*

She clenched her jaw and pushed the tray aside. She would never be such a one.

And she was certain that Diocletian knew it, too.

39

Ara Agrippinensium, Germania — March, A.D. 302

Night had fallen when Constantinus led his cohort back into Ara Agrippinensium, and the men were in high spirits. Jurian and his *cataphractarii* left their horses in the stables, and Jurian headed straight to the baths to rid himself of his heavy armor and all the filth of battle. As soon as he had washed and dressed, he made his way toward the officers' quarters, and the bed that awaited him there. But halfway across the courtyard he spotted a few of his men sitting around a smoking brazier, passing around a winesack, and bits of their conversation drifted toward him.

"He fights like Heracles," someone was saying. "It doesn't surprise me the *Tribunus* has given him command of the horse."

"You heard about the dragon, didn't you?" someone else asked.

Jurian's steps slowed, barely. The men hadn't seen him in the deep shadows, and he was torn between the curiosity that wanted to stay and listen, and the embarrassment that wanted to retreat into the barracks before he could hear anything else.

"Dragon!" one of his *equites* echoed. "Surely that's just a story."

"My father's cousin's brother is from Cyrene," said the

second soldier. "He said it was all true. The *Cyrenicus* defeated a dragon in the hills, and then rode to Nicomedia to face down the Emperor on behalf of his friend."

"Is he an enemy of Diocletian?" another asked, sounding faintly worried.

"I neither know nor care," said the first man. "All I know is I'll gladly follow that man into battle."

"So would I," said the second, warmly.

"We all know why *you* would follow him into battle," the third retorted. "Since, if rumors are right, you both follow the same God."

Jurian froze, but the men just laughed, and the conversation drifted to the quality of their rations, and the significant lack of fresh wine in the *castra*. A bemused smile flitted across Jurian's face. For all the scheming and malcontent of men like Asclepiodotus, he thought, the soldiers didn't seem the least bit concerned about the presence of Christians among them. It was like that among the common people too, who had no desire but to live out their lives in peace with their neighbors. As he had thought for some time now, men like Casca and Galerius, and Asclepiodotus, wanted to sow division where none existed.

He headed on into the barracks, but no sooner had he come into the vestibule than Constantinus caught up with him, his face troubled.

"Jurian, come with me," he said.

"Is something wrong?" Jurian asked, his thoughts darting instantly back to the men in the courtyard.

"The *Caesar* is here."

Jurian stared at him, puzzled, for a moment not making sense of the words. "Here, in Ara Agrippinensium? Why?"

"I don't know," Constantinus said. "I only just got word of it myself. But he has summoned us both, so, come."

Jurian nodded and fell into step beside him. They found the *Caesar* in a large *tablinum* within the *praetorium*, with Asclepiodotus standing in the alcove of the window, arms folded, watching and waiting like a hooded snake.

"*Caesar*," Constantinus said, greeting his father with a formal military salute. "I am pleased to report to you that we have routed the Suevi just north of the city." He paused, then said, "But I think you have not come to hear about our battles against the barbarians."

Constantius Chlorus never moved, and Constantinus shifted his weight, barely, his gaze drifting toward Asclepiodotus. Jurian could sense the Tribune's uneasiness, and he clasped his own hands, now slick with sweat, behind his back.

"You've done well," Constantius Chlorus said. "But as you say, that isn't why I am here. There is another matter that has come to my attention, which must be answered before anything else is said."

Constantinus stiffened, and Jurian felt his stomach turn.

He knows, he thought. *He knows.*

"What matter is that?" Constantinus said.

"You may go," Constantius Chlorus said, turning suddenly to Asclepiodotus.

Asclepiodotus sputtered. "But...*Caesar*, surely you require my presence, my advice, if there is any matter of weight to be discussed?"

"It is nothing that concerns you at the moment," Constantius Chlorus said, in a tone that brooked no argument. "If your advice is required, I will ask for it. Now go."

Asclepiodotus made a flustered little bow and exited the chamber, but his face as he passed Jurian was dark with frustration and anger. As the door closed behind him, everyone in the room exhaled.

"Now," Constantius Chlorus said, rounding on Jurian, "I want to know exactly who you are, and why you are here."

"He is with me," Constantinus said. "That is all you need to know."

Jurian stared at him in surprise. Constantinus was usually so genial with his father, but there was an edge in his voice now that was dangerous, and uncompromising. Constantius Chlorus flattened his hands on the table.

"I was not asking you," he said. "I'm asking him."

"Why?" Constantinus said.

"Because Asclepiodotus has sent word to Rome and to Nicomedia that this man is among us, and I need to know what to expect in reply. He seems to believe he has some reason to be suspicious. Why is that?" He glanced from his son to Jurian. "I follow my own mind in most things," he continued, "but I will not have everything I have worked for jeopardized for you."

"As I said, he's with me," Constantinus said, the edge in his voice even keener. "Don't worry about him causing you any trouble. How long has he been under your governance now? Has he caused any mischief for you yet?" He paused, then added, voice cold, "Gods forbid he get in the way of your *schemes*."

Constantius Chlorus sprang to his feet and slammed his fist down on the desk so hard that the parchments and the inkwell danced. "Do not take that tone with me," he said. "Everything I have done has been for your sake." He leveled a finger at Jurian. "Tell me who you are."

Constantinus made a move to step between them, but Jurian laid a hand on his arm. "Perhaps it is better this way," he said quietly, and thought, *Perhaps it is time to speak truth to kings.*

"My name is Lucius Aurelius Georgius," he said, turning to the *Caesar*. "I am the son of Lucius Aurelius Gerontios, former *Legatus* of Satala and friend to the *Imperator* Diocletian. I went to Rome through many hardships and eventually found a place for myself in Diocletian's court in Nicomedia. I was made a *tribunus angusticlavius* of the Jovians for my service in Heraklea. And after that..." He hesitated for the barest fraction of a second, breathing a prayer for guidance, and then he continued, "I gave up everything to save my friend—the giant Menas, whom you met in Britannia—from death in the arena. An old enemy of mine poisoned the mind of the *Imperator* against me, and I was banished under *interdictio ignis et aquae*."

There was absolute silence in the *tablinum*. Then Constantius Chlorus straightened slowly, leveling his gaze at his son.

"You knew this?" he asked in a low voice.

"I'm the one who escorted him into exile," Constantinus said.

Constantius Chlorus was very still. "You knew this," he said, "and you didn't think to tell me?"

"For what purpose?" Constantinus asked. "So that you could arrest him or execute him before he had the chance to show you how much he has to offer?"

"Offer! If Diocletian banished him, he should not even *be* here," Constantius Chlorus said. "What do you think is going to happen now that Asclepiodotus has reported his presence in my court? My position in the Tetrarchy is already precarious, and *Imperator* Maximianus will look for any excuse to undermine it further. Why do you think you spent so much time in the south, you foolish boy?"

Constantinus's face hardened. "There is no *boy* here, *Caesar*," he said. "And I know very well why. It's the same reason you pushed my mother away and married Maximianus's daughter. To protect your precious power!"

"Not mine!" Constantius Chlorus shouted. "Yours!"

Constantinus leaned on the other side of the desk. "I don't want your power," he said. "I will not grovel to lesser men and lick the ground they tread like you do."

"You imagine yourself wise," the *Caesar* said. "But you, who have seen so much, still know nothing of the way of this world."

"I believe that respect cannot be bought, but must be earned," Constantinus said. "And I know too that men who will do anything for power will commit the most abominable crimes to keep it from slipping away."

Constantius Chlorus straightened. "Respect that is not bought—and bought dearly—shrivels and dies at the first breath of displeasure," he said. He pointed again at Jurian. "If word reaches Rome and Nicomedia that I am harboring an exile—"

"Then send word yourself!" Constantinus said. "Tell them that he has distinguished himself in battle, and that he has once again saved my life at great peril to himself. Tell them that he has done all of this in service of the Empire, and that you recommend his immediate reinstatement as citizen and *tribunus*."

Jurian gaped at him, then quickly closed his mouth. He hadn't dared to interrupt the verbal battle between Constantinus and his father—a disagreement that seemed to be long-standing between them—but now he felt he had to speak.

"*Caesar*," he said, stepping forward. "I did not come here to cause trouble for you. I came because your son offered me the opportunity to earn my honor back after it was slandered and taken from me. I wish only to be at peace with the Empire, and to live out the days I have been given."

Constantius Chlorus regarded him a while in silence, then sighed and leaned his hands on his desk, head bowed. "I would be lying," he said at length, "if I said I did not value you. If I did not believe you are an honorable man, and a remarkable soldier. From all I have heard, your men admire and esteem you, and in all your dealings you exemplify what it means to be a son of Rome. For some time now, I've suspected that you carried something like this in your past, but I didn't want to face the possibility of its truth, because I didn't want to risk having to set you aside." He thrummed his fingers on the edge of the desk, considering, while Jurian held his breath and waited. Then he said, "This enemy of yours. He has done you great wrong?"

"He has taken everything from me," Jurian said, his voice shaking with suppressed anger and grief. "He killed my mother and my sister, tried to send my friend to his death, slandered my name, and has set himself to destroy anyone who has ever been close to me." He stopped, and then added, "And I fear every day that he may have succeeded."

"And would it wound this enemy to know that you are once more in the favor of the Tetrarchy?"

"I cannot think of anything that would pain him more," Jurian said.

Constantius Chlorus nodded once. "I will send the letter,"

he said. "But understand, I make no promises. I cannot control Diocletian any more than I can control the weather." He paused, studying Jurian thoughtfully, then continued more softly, "And if he does not summon you back to your position in Nicomedia, you will have a place here with me for as long as you desire it."

"Thank you," Jurian said, overwhelmed.

"Does that suit you?" the *Caesar* asked, turning to Constantinus. "Or is there something else you want?"

"You know what I want," he answered. "More than anything."

A look of pain flashed across Constantius Chlorus's face. "I want the same," he said. "But she must remain where she is, and I must play the part given to me." He smiled wistfully at his son and reached across the table. "Be a better son to her than I have been a husband," he said as Constantinus gripped his father's hand. "If you do nothing more than that in this life, you will be a great man in my eyes."

Jurian lowered his head, feeling the burn of tears behind his eyes. He thought of his own mother, of Varro, of the harshness of love in this world of hatred and ambition. And he swallowed hard, thinking of Sabra and her long silence.

Please, he prayed silently, *let her be safe. Let no harm come to her on my account. Protect her, since I cannot.*

40

Cyrene, Libya — April, A.D. 302

Two weeks after she had set out from Alexandria, Sabra stood before the doors of the palace in Cyrene, with Hanno close behind her. She had been anticipating this moment for months, but now that it was here, she felt a surge of uncertainty. Would she be welcome in the city, now, after she had been absent for so long? Perhaps they had grown accustomed to her absence. Perhaps the city had been better off without her there.

She recognized the voice behind that last thought, though, and pushed it aside with grim determination. Drawing a deep breath, she stepped up to the doors to knock. They swung open before she could touch them, and her father himself stepped out in front of her. He caught her in a warm embrace, almost lifting her off her feet, his hand stroking her hair as if she were still a child.

"Come inside and get warm!" he cried as he released her, ushering her into the palace and out of the chilly spring wind. "How were your travels? How is your friend in Alexandria?"

Sabra let him bustle her into an inner chamber and settle her in front of a warm fire, but his question brought grief stinging to her throat.

"Oh, Father," she whispered. "Alexandria...Diocletian was

there. He killed…he killed so many people. They were heretics, and they distorted our Faith with their strange teachings, but he slaughtered them like chattel in the middle of the streets. No one deserves to be treated like that. No one. And he said…" She pressed the backs of her fingers against her mouth. "He said the same would happen to anyone who dared defy the Emperors of Rome. It sounded like a threat, and I know he intended it for Aikaterina, because she is so bold when she speaks of the Truth."

Her father sat down on the bench beside her, wrapping his arms around her. "I am so sorry that you had to see that, Sabra," he murmured.

"I am sick of death," she said, leaning against his shoulder. "Is there nowhere I can go where it doesn't follow me?"

He said nothing, and as a few servants brought in some food for her, he released her to let her eat. Talking about the carnage in Alexandria had robbed her of her appetite, but she forced herself to eat a little for her father's sake.

"Well, and, what of your other travels?" her father asked after a while. "Did you find what you were looking for?"

Sabra smiled at that. "Yes," she said. "And more."

"I am glad to have you back," he said, but there was a strange note in his voice that made Sabra instantly uneasy. At her puzzled glance he patted her hand. "Cyrene is troubled," he said. "And I fear a storm is coming. It feels like there are forces at work in the city bent on causing discord and unrest, and with each day that passes, a chasm opens a little further."

"A chasm between what?" Sabra asked, though she thought she already knew the answer.

"The followers of Rome's gods, and the followers of the Christ," he said, reluctantly. "I had hoped we would have peace, and unity—that Cyrene would be a beacon to the world for tolerance and fraternity. But all my efforts are thwarted at every turn. And…"

"And?" Sabra prompted.

He shook his head. "Ah, don't trouble yourself about it

tonight. Get your rest, and perhaps in the morning things will look a little brighter."

But things did not look brighter in the morning. Sabra woke to the weeping of one of the palace slaves, and when she questioned the woman, she learned that, in the night, someone had broken into the house of the woman's cousin and slaughtered the entire family. The attackers had left a message on the walls of the *domus*, painted in blood—a warning to all Christians in the city.

"They blame Christians for everything," Sabra told Hanno a few hours later, sitting by the long pool in the peristyle with her knees drawn up. "The drought, the famine, the earthquakes, everything. Will there ever be an end to their hate?"

"Not until they are sated with blood," Hanno muttered, and Sabra suppressed a shiver.

"I need to protect them. They will be hunted down, one by one, and killed without mercy. There must be a way to keep them safe."

She leaned her chin against her forearms, desperately racking her mind for an idea. Then like a flash it came to her. She sat bolt upright, one hand darting out to grab Hanno's arm.

"I know what we can do! A safe place where they can hide if the storm of persecution comes." She scrambled to her feet. "Come with me. We're going to see Theodorus."

Theodorus received them gladly, showing them immediately into the inner courtyard and the benches that soaked up the mild spring sunshine.

"I take it you are not here to tell me of your visit with Nikolaos," he said, smiling, as he bade them take their seats. "You have that look about you like you've hatched some bold plan."

"I have," Sabra said. "I've heard about the violence in the city, and the unrest. There's a storm coming, isn't there?"

"It isn't just the people," Theodorus said quietly. "There are political schemes in play, and I fear for your father's safety. Rome is not pleased with the tolerance he advocates here, and

Dignianus has been chafing at his rule for some time now."

Sabra's head snapped up and she stared at him, horrified. "Was that what he refused to tell me last night?" she wondered. For a few moments she was lost in thought, fingers thrumming on her knees. "I had an idea about how to protect the flock from the slaughter," she said. "But political schemes are beyond me. Maybe Aikaterina will know how to proceed on that matter. She has a head for politics."

"And Alexandria's support would be invaluable to the governor," Theodorus agreed.

Sabra nodded.

"Well, and what is your idea for protecting the people?"

That brought a slow smile to Sabra's face, and she leaned over impulsively to clasp Theodorus's hand. "Can you cleanse a place?"

The *episcopus* studied her carefully. "I take you don't mean with brooms and wash water."

"No," she said. "I mean, could you consecrate a place that has formerly...had a bad use?"

"Yes..." he said, the word trailing off in uncertainty.

Sabra nodded. "That decides it, then. I want to consecrate the temple of the old god in the city, and make it a refuge for our people."

She heard Hanno suck in a breath through his teeth, and even Theodorus stared at her in shock.

"The temple? Where you used to..."

"Yes. The inner sanctuary is hidden at the heart of a labyrinth. Where could be a better place for our people to hide if the storms of persecution break upon Cyrene? Surely, you don't think that everyone is prepared to lay down their lives for the Faith. Their faith is an infant fire, still. Too much wind, and it will be extinguished. It needs time to be kindled, to grow, and then...who can say how far it will spread?"

Theodorus nodded slowly. "I think you are right. Many of my fellow *episcopi* have advised the same thing. Some are called to witness to the Faith with blood, and we will need their strength in the years to come. But not everyone is ready for that call. Very well. I'll consecrate the old temple. It can be our catacombs, like they have in Rome."

Theodorus and Sabra went to the temple the next day, with Hanno and a few presbyters, and two women named Cyprilla and Lucia who carried baskets on their backs laden with torches. Sabra took a deep breath at the top of the steps that led down into the underground temple. Once she had sworn she would never return to that place, but she stood there now like a conqueror, not a victim. Nodding to the people behind her, she took a torch from Cyprilla, lighted it in the brazier that stood at the top of the steps, and carried it down into the labyrinth that had never seen the light.

It had been over two years, she realized, since she had taken the path through the labyrinth, but it was as familiar to her as breathing. She closed her eyes as she walked so the torchlight wouldn't fool her, and every twenty paces or so she directed the women to leave a torch. Wherever they left a torch, they drew an *ichthus* on the wall. They would remove the torches again on the way out, but the etchings would remain, a clear path for those who thought to look for the markers.

Finally they arrived in the inner sanctuary, where the fire Sabra had once believed was truly eternal had once burned. It had gone out without her there to tend it. The hearth was cold and empty, like any ordinary hearth left too long neglected. Theodorus and the presbyters, who had been chanting prayers the whole way through the labyrinth, now set to work cleansing the sanctuary with incense and blessed water and prayers to drive back the forces of evil.

Sabra stood against a pillar to watch. She had feared that being in the sanctuary would shake the foundations of her faith and reduce her to ruin, but she felt nothing at all in that vast empty space. It was a room like any other. It held no terror. And it held no voices to torment her. Beside her, Hanno watched the proceedings with fascination, but he too seemed at peace.

He turned suddenly to her. "It's strange to stand here,

mistress," he said. "All those years, I wondered where you went, and what mysteries the temple must contain. But it's just...empty."

"It always was," she said softly. "It was never anything but a tomb."

41

Paraetonium, Libya — May, A.D. 302

Casca despised *tabernae*. He despised them most of all in port cities, and the port city of Paraetonium was quite possibly one of the worst places he had ever been. But he'd had no choice—the ship's captain had been forced into port by a squall, and Casca had decided to make the rest of the journey to Cyrene by horse than risk another stomach-emptying voyage by boat.

It was perhaps for the best, at any rate. Much to his dismay, and despite all his careful efforts, there were some people in Apollonia who had finally discovered his identity. If they reported his presence to Lucius Titianus before Casca was ready to spring his trap, all his work would be in vain.

Trying to avoid people in Cyrene who recognized him was already making his efforts difficult. But he would rise above the challenge, as he always did, and Cyrene would inevitably bow down, brought to its knees at his hands. It was only a matter of time.

Galerius had to be pleased by Casca's patient efforts. It would pay off soon enough, he was certain of it. Dignianus had subtly redirected a grain dole sent from Alexandria some months ago, and then Casca had produced a letter proving that Lucius Titianus had rejected it on principle. If that didn't turn the people of Cyrene against their governor, he couldn't imagine what would.

Patience, Casca, he told himself.

He was inordinately pleased at his own ability to bide his time. A year ago he would have rushed in and made a mess of things because of his own great passion for the glory of his Emperor. He was wiser now, and soon Diocletian would realize just how valuable a careful, clever advisor like Casca could be. And now, if the report he had received was true, Sabra had finally returned to Cyrene. That meant it was almost time for him to make his move.

"Thank the gods for a dry room and a warm hearth," someone said nearby, and Casca glanced up with idle interest to see a courier taking a stool by the fire.

It was still pouring outside, and the man was drenched from head to foot. Casca sniffed. He had taken shelter in the *taberna* before the squall had reached land, and was already pleasantly dry and warm.

"Bad time to be traveling," someone else said—another traveler, sitting on the other stool by the fire. "Are you on foot?"

"Boat," the courier said. "The storms drove us to port."

"Where to?"

"Alexandria." He wiped the inside of his cloak over his face and slouched a little closer to the fire. "Shouldn't have taken the commission at all, honestly."

The traveler laughed. "Why is that?"

"That girl—the girl who commissioned me—she terrifies me. I don't care how much they say she's changed. There's just something about her, like she sees right into your soul. Like she wasn't the dragon's priestess, but the dragon's daughter."

Casca froze in the middle of sopping sauce out of his bowl with a chunk of day-old bread. He turned his head a little to the side so he could catch the quiet conversation better.

"What girl are you talking about?" the traveler asked. "What priestess?"

"Haven't you ever been in Cyrene?"

"Of course. Many times."

"And you've never seen her? The governor's daughter? She used to be a priestess, but now, gods only know what she is. But apparently she is very close to Aikaterina of Alexandria."

"Oh, Sabra," the traveler said. "I suppose I've seen her before. Lovely, isn't she?"

"If you like that kind of look," the courier said. "I don't. Aikaterina is far lovelier, but she has a tongue like a whip, people say."

"Ah, they're far above the likes of you and me anyway," the traveler said, and hailed the innkeeper for another cup of *posca*. "At least you have the fortune of going to Alexandria. It's a better place to be than Cyrene right now, for all I hear."

"Cyrene is never a good place to be," the courier muttered. "But Alexandria is not much better these days. Too much blood."

"There's blood everywhere, it seems." He lifted his cup to the courier as the man got to his feet. "I wish you safe travels, *amice*."

The courier nodded and retreated up the stairs to the common lodging in the loft. Casca watched him go from the corner of his eye, then steepled his hands under his chin as he thought.

He waited in the main room of the *taberna* all night, wide awake. Early in the morning he watched the courier come downstairs and take a cold breakfast, then leave the *taberna* to continue his journey. Casca tossed a few coins onto the innkeeper's counter and followed the courier outside.

42

Alexandria, Aegyptus — June, A.D. 302

Aikaterina knelt at her father's bedside, her head resting on the coverlet near his hand. She had dismissed the servants, and she didn't know how long she had been there alone. Her father's slow breathing was almost inaudible, and the fire in the braziers was burning down to embers.

"Why is this happening, Father?" she asked softly. She had been asking the same question for hours, it seemed. "Why won't you get well?"

Her father's long, slow sickness was taking its toll on her, and all her household. One moment he seemed to be on the verge of recovery, and the next he would relapse into this long, unwaking slumber. Aikaterina had done her best to keep the government of Alexandria moving smoothly as her father's condition seemed to shift from one week to the next, but there was a corner of her mind that wished the senate would simply recognize her as *praefecta*, and leave her father to convalesce in peace. But that thought tore her heart with guilt, as if she were giving up on him. As if she expected him to die.

A light rapping at the door startled her, and she sat up slowly, her entire body stiff from her long vigil. There was a brief pause, then the door opened and Nenet appeared.

"*Kyria*," she said.

Aikaterina got to her feet and pulled her deep purple *palla* up over her shoulders. "I gave word I was not to be disturbed," she said.

"The physician says he must see your father," Nenet answered, apologetic. "And...I think you had better come."

Aikaterina nodded, feeling weariness in her very bones. Leaving her father's bedside, she slipped out the door to join Nenet in the corridor. A half dozen servants, all looking worried and somewhat desperate, were loitering outside the door.

"You may go in and tend to the fires," Aikaterina said. Then, to the physician, "Make sure he is comfortable. Send word immediately if there is the slightest change."

The servants bustled inside, looking relieved to have a task to do, and the physician, with a slight bow to Aikaterina, followed them. It was always the same. Sometimes Aikaterina felt the words were mere formality.

She took a deep breath and turned to Nenet. "Now, what is it really?"

"It really was the physician. He said you need to eat something. You've barely slept in three days."

Aikaterina looked at her sidelong. "I see," she said. "So he wasn't here for my father. That was a pretense."

"Well, he is...but he also told me to make sure you ate something."

"I'm not hungry, Nenet." When Nenet crossed her arms over her chest, Aikaterina smiled and waved a hand in defeat. "I know that look," she said. "Bring me something, then."

They went together to the *triclinium* and Nenet vanished in the direction of the *culina* to find her some food. Aikaterina sat alone at the table and suddenly, for no reason at all, her thoughts drifted back to the dinner they had given in Jurian's honor, that first night he had come to Alexandria. She had been so prickly with him. Testing him in Greek, prodding him about the love of friendship that could drive him to track down his friend in the face of such great danger. She sighed and ran her finger along the wood grain.

I thought I was so wise then, she thought. *And really, I knew nothing much at all. And Jurian...he said so little. And yet he was wiser than me all along.*

She glanced up as Nenet returned with a silver tray piled with fruits and nuts and some flatbread. Another servant followed in her wake, carrying a pitcher of wine and a goblet.

As soon as the food was placed on the table, Nenet dismissed the other servant with a wave of her hand, then turned back to Aikaterina. "There is a messenger just arrived," she said. "I thought you should know."

"A messenger?" Aikaterina said, tearing a piece of flatbread. "From whom?"

"From Cyrene."

Aikaterina stopped with the bread halfway to her mouth. "Send him to me at once!" she cried. "What are you standing here for?"

"You need to eat," Nenet protested.

"I can eat and receive a messenger at the same time," Aikaterina said, crossly. "I'm sure my father used to."

Nenet nodded and left the room. Aikaterina nibbled on the bread, her heart beating wildly in anticipation. She hadn't heard much from Sabra since she had seen her four months ago, but the last news she had received had been good. Aikaterina had started a reply, but then her father had fallen ill again, and she had not had time to send it.

She finished the flatbread and sipped a bit of the watered wine. Already her head was clearing, and the heavy fog that had lain over her heart for the last two days began to dissipate. *Maybe Nenet was right after all,* she thought with a smile. *Food is good.*

Nenet reappeared some minutes later with the messenger walking briskly at her heels. When Nenet pointed to a spot on the floor where he should stand, the man dutifully stepped onto it and saluted Aikaterina. He was covered from head to toe in dust and sand, road-weary, and his gaze lingered just a moment too long on the tray of food. But when his eyes drifted back toward Aikaterina, she thought he looked faintly nervous.

No, she decided. *Not nervous. He looks afraid.*

"Thank you, Nenet," Aikaterina said, and Nenet bowed her head and withdrew.

"Would you care for some wine?" Aikaterina asked the messenger in Latin. "You look like you have ridden hard."

"No thank you, *domina*. You are very kind."

But still he stood stiffly, head bowed, and now he wouldn't look at her at all.

"Well?" she said. "You come from the lady Sabra?"

"From her, yes."

"What is your message?" Aikaterina repeated.

The courier reached into a pouch at his hip and drew out a scroll, hesitating just a moment before he handed it to her with a low bow.

The seal was broken.

Aikaterina scowled at him and unrolled the parchment. She scanned it quickly, and her pulse hammered in her temples.

"Do you know what is in this message?" she asked, her voice low. The messenger swallowed but did not answer. Aikaterina got to her feet and drew herself up to her full height. "Answer me!"

The messenger startled at her tone and shook his head.

"This was sent under seal," Aikaterina said. "Who broke it? Did you? If it was you, I can assure you that you will never again be able to fulfill your duties as a courier."

The messenger's mouth flapped and his face turned ghastly pale, but he still did not answer. Aikaterina stepped toward him, brandishing the parchment like a weapon.

"Did you break this seal and read the contents of this message?" she said. "Who else knows what is in this?"

The courier finally broke down. "*Domina*, it wasn't me...I swear it! I met a man on the road, in Paraetonium. He said...he ordered me to hand over all correspondence. He said it was for the Empire. That there were spies...and a plot against the Divine

Imperator himself..." He hung his head, and his fingers drifted up to touch the corner of his lip, which Aikaterina suddenly noticed was swollen and purple. "He...I didn't give it to him, *domina*. He...took it from me."

He lifted his gaze then, and Aikaterina saw all the signs of a beating that she had missed before—the cut at the corner of one eye, the slight swelling under his lock of hair, the way he favored one arm.

Aikaterina slowly lowered the letter. "This man," she said. "Who was he?"

"A tribune, *domina*. He said he was on his way to Cyrene. Something to do with the *praefectus*. He didn't elaborate. But he ordered me to hand over...and I—"

"Was his name Marcus Valerius Casca?" Aikaterina said. The man winced and looked away. "Was it?"

"I don't know, *domina*." He clasped a hand against his breast, shuddering all over. "There wasn't...there wasn't much conversation. But he was not very tall. Very pale, though, with large eyes. Dark hair. I don't know...he never said his name."

That was definitely Casca. Aikaterina was certain of it.

She turned away from him and paced the room. Sabra's message was full of fear—she had spoken of unrest in the city, and her fear that there were plots in motion against her father, and herself. She spoke of Jurian's warning about the storm from the north, and her hope that God would deliver them from the ancient evil she could feel stirring in Cyrene. Then she asked Aikaterina to send advice. It was all just vague enough.

Not vague enough for eyes like Casca's, she thought.

Aikaterina quickened her steps, tapping the parchment against her palm. If they had been compromised, who knew when Casca would decide to use the knowledge against them? What was the best plan against such an enemy?

Out of the corner of her eye, she saw the messenger still hovering where Nenet had planted him, his face pale and etched with terror.

She sighed and turned back to him. "When did you receive

your commission?" she asked.

"A...month ago, *domina*," he said. "Or a little more. I apologize...I came as quickly as...as I was able."

She pressed her mouth in a thin line, torn between pity and frustration. "Go now," she said. "Take care of your injuries. And in the future, don't be so careless."

He bowed low and stumbled from the *triclinium*.

"What am I going to do?" Aikaterina murmured as soon as he had gone. "What is to be done?"

A small voice in the back of her mind wondered what she could possibly do, with her own city so precarious, and Cyrene so far away.

But she pushed the thought away with a defiant question to herself: *What can't I do?*

A passage from the Scriptures slipped into her mind on its heels: *I can do all things through Him who strengthens me.*

She only needed time to think.

If she knew anything about Casca, she doubted he would go straight to Diocletian and Maximianus with whatever evidence he thought he had. First he would make sure. He would dig for evidence—build his case carefully. If he wanted to see her and Sabra condemned, he would do it in a way that would inflict maximum pain on Jurian.

"So we have a little time," she said to herself.

She moved to the brazier burning in the corner and tossed the scroll into the flames, watching the parchment curl and shrivel in its death glow. As soon as it had faded to grey ash, she wiped her hands on her chiton and took a deep breath. Things could not stand as they now were, but there was no cause for immediate panic.

"Nenet!" she called.

As soon as Nenet appeared in the doorway, Aikaterina turned to her and folded her hands behind her. "Bring Diodoros to me," she said.

Nenet bowed and disappeared again. Aikaterina paced the length of the *triclinium*, measuring her thoughts. She could not leave Alexandria, not now, even though she wanted nothing more than to run instantly to her friend's aid. Things were too unstable here, and, thanks to Diocletian's actions, growing more volatile by the day. She couldn't leave her city.

But if she couldn't go herself, she could do the next best thing.

"You received a message from Cyrene."

Aikaterina spun around, only to find her mother standing in the doorway behind her, the deep purple of her *palla* managing to convey both mourning and power. Her face was very quiet, a little tired about the eyes as Aikaterina had seen so often in recent months.

"Did you see it?" she asked, warily.

Her mother shook her head. "I saw the courier, and asked where he hailed from. You've heard the rumors about Cyrene. If word got out that you were in frequent contact with the governor's daughter...it could cast suspicion on your position here in Alexandria."

"Oh Mother," Aikaterina said, feeling suddenly weary. "Don't speak to me about my position. My friend is danger. What am I to do? Do you advise me to leave her to the wolves?"

"You are my only daughter, and I want what is best for you."

"Best for me?" Aikaterina echoed. "Or best for you?"

Her mother stood very still, and Aikaterina immediately regretted the words.

"I did not deserve that," her mother said softly. "It is what is best for us both, and for Alexandria. You know that."

Aikaterina heard her mother's footsteps retreat from the room, and she blew out all her breath at once. Was it best for Alexandria for Aikaterina to ignore her friend's sufferings? She couldn't believe it would be so. She would not accept it.

"You wanted to see me, *kyria?*" came Diodoros's rich voice behind her, some moments later.

Aikaterina smiled as she turned to greet him. "Yes," she said. "There is something I need you to do for me."

43

Cyrene, Libya — June, A.D. 302

The murmur of low voices outside her chamber roused Sabra from her troubled dreams. They had returned—those visions of blood in the streets, the spring Kyre running dry in the hillside. But now, there were tremors in the earth, and they shivered the stones of the temples of the gods until all the works of Rome were in desolation.

Sabra sat up. Her hair was damp with cold sweat, her body racked with shivers. The grey twilight before dawn crept through the lattice over her window and stained her stone floor silver, and she rubbed a hand over her face, wondering what hour of the morning it was. Then she realized what had woken her—not the murmur of voices, but a light rap on her chamber door. Her slave Acenith must have still been sleeping too, because Sabra heard her muttering as she got up from her pallet in the adjoining room.

"Hanno," Acenith said as she opened the chamber door.

"Is my mistress awake?" he asked.

Sabra pulled her woolen blanket up to her chin. "Let him come in," she said.

Acenith nodded and stepped aside, and Hanno edged into the room, keeping his gaze fixed on the floor.

"I don't wish to intrude, but...your father wishes to see you."

"At this hour?" she asked, frowning, but Hanno didn't answer. "Very well. I will come at once."

Hanno bowed and left the room. Sabra rose and Acenith helped her to dress, muttering to herself in annoyance as her own sleep-heavy fingers fumbled uselessly with Sabra's dark hair. When Acenith had finished, Sabra made her way through the palace to her father's *tablinum*. Her heart was hammering strangely in her chest. Some terrible thing must have happened—her father would never waken her so early in the morning otherwise.

Hanno waited for her just outside the *tablinum*, between the peristyle and the *atrium*. "I will wait for you, mistress," he said.

Sabra opened the door and slipped inside the room. Her father stood at the window, staring out into the peristyle, his arms folded tightly across his chest.

"Father," Sabra said. "What has happened?"

Lucius Titianus turned slowly and managed a half-smile. "We had a visitor arrive yesterday," he said.

Sabra waited, but her blood seemed to slow to a crawl. Something prickled the hairs on her neck, and somehow she knew what he was going to say before the words came out of his mouth.

"One Marcus Valerius Flaccus Casca, I think he said his name was." Her father watched her like a hawk. "He claimed to be an old friend of yours, from your stay in Rome."

"What does he want?"

"I wouldn't know," her father said. "He's been holed up with Dignianus since he arrived. I've barely seen him."

"Father..." Sabra tried to swallow, but her throat felt impossibly tight. "That man..."

Her father's eyes crinkled in a smile. "You think I can't pick out a court serpent when I see one? I know what he is."

"No," Sabra said. "You don't. The things he's done—" She took a step forward. "Why is he here?"

"I just told you that I don't know. He was pleasant enough to me. I was afraid—" He stopped abruptly and shuffled through some of the parchments on his desk.

"Afraid of what?"

"The *Imperator* Diocletian has been busy in Africa of late, as you yourself have witnessed. Perhaps this visit from his Tribune is meant to reassure him that we are loyal."

"But Father," she whispered. "Are we? Are we truly, in all respects? If Casca is here to perform some kind of imperial audit, are you sure Cyrene will pass his scrutiny?"

Her father held her gaze. "No," he said.

Sabra closed her eyes, trying to shut out the vision of the bloody streets, the skies black with roiling clouds, the desiccated spring.

"Dignianus is dangerous," her father continued. "He has always been subversive, and his thoughts quickly turn bloody. He's been more dangerous of late, and I fear he will spring at the chance to impress our imperial guest."

"It is coming," she whispered, the words escaping against her will. "It's coming, and I cannot stop it."

She opened her eyes and found her father watching her intently, his face creased with concern. "What?"

"Surely you must have pieced it together," Sabra said. "Casca coming here, now...meeting with Dignianus, who needs just the slightest push from Rome to usurp your authority and bring the terror of persecution to Cyrene."

Her father's eyebrows flew up in surprise. "Persecution?"

"That is Casca's favorite game," she said. "And please believe me when I say that he has come to play. None of us are safe."

Her father came around the desk and pulled Sabra into a tight embrace. "You are tired," he said. "And Hanno tells me that you have been busy. The temple, Sabra?"

"It's not a temple any more. It is a safe place now for our people. We have been making it comfortable, in case..."

"Safe?" he interrupted. "From what? In case of what?"

"People are being slaughtered in their homes, Father, and—"

"Those were the actions of a few, and they have been punished. That is all over now."

"No, it isn't over." She shuddered. "It is all coming to pass. The evil has returned, and the storm will break here first. Casca's coming makes it certain. Please...you have to believe me."

Her father stepped back and held her arms. "I believe you," he said, but to Sabra it sounded like the hollow reassurance given to a hysterical child.

"Why did you bring me here so suddenly, so early, if you didn't fear the hammer stroke from Rome?" she said, her voice sharp.

For a moment her father only studied her, his eyes grave and gentle, then his gaze shifted abruptly to the door.

"Hanno!" he called, and Hanno entered the room immediately. "I want you to take my daughter to safety."

"Safety!" Sabra cried. "Then you admit that we are in danger!"

"I see that *you* are in danger, from this snake of a man whose intentions I cannot judge!"

"You know he will come after you," Hanno said softly. "Because of Jurian."

"No!" Sabra protested, whirling back to face her father. "I cannot abandon our people! You sent me away once. Don't do that to me again. Don't make me—"

"This is not a conversation we are going to have," he said. "You will leave before the day is out." Sabra shook her head, once, fiercely, but her father's eyes suddenly darkened and he took her hands in his own. "I love you, Sabra, and I need you to live," he said. "Please. Go."

For a moment she just stared at him, then she turned and strode from the room, shaking with grief and anger.

"How can he do this to me?" she asked Hanno as she paced across the peristyle. "I won't go! If that snake is here...all our people are in danger."

She heard a slight breath of laughter from Hanno and turned

to glare at him, which only made him smile more broadly.

"He told me to get you to safety," he said.

She scowled at him a moment, trying to figure out what had him so amused, and then understanding dawned on her.

"Hanno, I believe you may be a genius," she said. "Come on, let's go warn Theodorus. We'll get as many people underground as we can. And then let Casca fret as he tries to track down a non-existent community of Christians."

THE RAGGED EDGES OF a disastrous dawn were tinged with the red of the rising sun as Sabra and Hanno slipped around the walls of the palace and made their way down into the city. The *agora* was empty save for a few merchants setting up their stalls for the morning market. They eyed Sabra and Hanno curiously as the two hurried past, but they said nothing. Sabra had spent most of her life as the object of awe—the dark priestess who was never liked and not quite trusted, but always feared. And since the defeat of the dragon and the liberation of Cyrene, that awe had grown as the people learned to love her and forgive her. But they still did not approach readily.

That might work to our advantage, Sabra thought, *or it might not.*

There might still be some in the city who had not forgiven her...who would be willing, for a price, to betray her to the Romans.

She lifted her dark *palla* over her head and quickened her pace, weaving through the alleys swathed in shadow with as much certainty as she had ever walked the labyrinth of the old god's temple. When they arrived at Theodorus's house, Sabra reeled to a halt, snatching Hanno's arm. The sturdy door lay in splinters on the stone floor. Sabra's throat turned dry, as if she had swallowed ash.

"Theodorus!" Sabra called, hoarse, as she stepped through the wreckage of wood into the silent house.

The air was thick with smoke, and there in the *atrium*, surrounding a brazier glowing with dead embers, drifted the ashen remains of Theodorus's priceless manuscripts.

"He is gone, mistress," Hanno said, his voice clipped. "We must go, now. If they find us here..."

Sabra retreated to the street, grief tearing at her heart, her thoughts scattering a million directions at once. Casca, and even Dignianus, would have no way of knowing the identities of all the Christian followers in Cyrene. She had to get word to them quickly, but how?

What would You have me do? she prayed silently.

"Mistress," Hanno said. "Where shall we go?"

She racked her thoughts for an answer, then suddenly snatched Hanno's arm. "I need the women," she said. Hanno frowned, uncertain. "What is the quickest way to spread a bit of information around the city?" she prompted, and that, finally, brought a smile to his face.

"Cyprilla, then," he said. "She knows everyone."

Sabra nodded. "Do you know where she lives?"

He just touched her elbow and set off into the winding streets, back in the direction of the *forum* where some of the more well-to-do merchants and their families lived.

"Across the way," Hanno said, pointing at the *forum*.

Sabra stepped out from the shelter of the narrow street, then drew up short. There, directly in front of her as if he had been waiting for her, stood Casca. He was cloaked in scarlet, blood red in the early light.

"There you are!" he said, then quieter, sinuous, "Thank the gods."

His lips twitched in a smile as she gasped, "Casca!"

"I'm delighted to see you as well," he said, giving her a slight bow. "You're out and about very early this morning." He glanced at Hanno, who stood with his arms crossed on his broad chest, looking like he had been carved out of stone. "Where have you been? They said they'd seen you—the merchants in the *agora*."

Sabra lifted her chin and said nothing. Casca gave a low laugh and shook his head.

"Hanno," Sabra said, as indifferently as she could. "This doesn't concern you." She turned and met his gaze briefly. "You may return to your duties."

He bowed, and with just a faint look of worry, he pushed past Casca and strode across the *forum*. Sabra let out her breath and turned back to Casca.

"Oh, Sabra," he said. "What am I going to do with you?" He folded his arms and tapped his chin with his long forefinger. "Do you know—have you heard—that we detained your father this morning?"

"What?" Sabra cried, all her blood rushing to her feet, making the street swim dizzily around her. "Casca—no! Why?"

"Just some questions. Nothing terrible, I hope, but you know how these things go."

She struggled to collect her breathing, but her heart would not slow its frantic pace. When she thought she could speak without her voice betraying her, she asked, "On what charges did you dare lay hands on the governor of Cyrene?"

"On what charges," Casca repeated, and idly smoothed a stray lock of dark hair back from his forehead. "Well, it seems that quite the little flourishing colony of vipers has sprung up here, under his very nose, and he has done nothing about it. Did you know about that? These followers of the Christ, that nuisance to the peace and prosperity of the Empire." He regarded her with a strange and burning intensity. "But I think you had some notion of trouble, because otherwise why would you have sent word to Aikaterina of Alexandria?"

Sabra started, feeling her world suddenly tip sideways. "What?"

Casca glanced up at the sky, watching the ragged clouds scudding in from the north. "I believe a storm is coming," he said. He stepped closer to her, so close that his breath stirred her hair. "And when it breaks over your head, to whom will you turn for shelter? Your precious Jurian can't save you this time. So who will it be? Who will be your savior when the world comes to darkness?"

"One whose love is unfailing," Sabra said quietly. "Who has loved me from the very beginning, though I have only lately known it."

Casca dragged a breath in through his teeth, and he stepped back. "And who would that be?"

Sabra tilted her head and smiled at him. "But you're so clever, Casca. I should think you would have guessed that by now."

Casca took another step back, and such a strange expression came into his face—hatred mixed with extreme pain and a wild, frantic hope—that it took Sabra's breath away. He opened his mouth and Sabra froze, sure that he would call his guards. But then his mouth snapped shut again and he turned away, heading not toward the palace, but farther into the city.

Sabra waited until he had disappeared from view, then ran all the way to the old temple.

Hanno was waiting for her nearby, keeping an eye on all who approached the temple steps. He straightened at once when he saw her coming.

"Hanno," she sobbed. She grabbed his arms, and he steadied her, his face wrought with worry. "They've taken him. They've taken my father."

"Be strong, mistress," he murmured, and guided her gently down into the labyrinth.

44

Ara Agrippinensium, Germania — June, A.D. 302

Jurian woke to a commotion in the *castra aestiva*, far too early in the morning, when all but the perimeter guards should have been asleep. For a moment he thought about rolling over and going back to sleep, but then, as his mind shook off its fog, he remembered he was a *decurio*. Whatever happened in this part of the camp was his responsibility. Swallowing back a grumble of annoyance, he rose and dressed, and stepped out of his tent.

He almost walked into Servius, who had a hand raised like he'd been about to pull back the flap himself.

"What in the name of all that's holy is going on out here?" Jurian asked.

"You'd better come quickly," Servius said. "That man is here."

Jurian frowned but followed Servius without a word, toward the small *forum* where a sparse crowd had gathered. In the center stood Julius Asclepiodotus, and in front of him knelt one of Jurian's *equites*, a man named Parmenion—not the brightest of Jurian's troops, but a man with a fierce heart and unfailing discipline. He was dressed in only his *subligacula*, as if he'd been pulled from his *striga* in the middle of the night.

"What is the meaning of this?" Jurian asked, pushing his way through the crowd.

Asclepiodotus turned to him as he approached, arms folded. "Don't you speak to me like that, Georgius."

Jurian stopped directly in front of him, fire hot in his veins. "I am *decurio* here, and you are holding one of my men. You have no authority in this *castra*, Asclepiodotus."

The man's lip lifted in displeasure. "Perhaps we should call your *tribunus* here to help mediate this conversation?"

"That's not necessary," Jurian said, with a certainty that surprised even himself. Every muscle in his back and shoulders was tight. "He has no authority over my *cataphractarii*, and neither do you. If you have something to say about this man, you will say it to me, or you will leave this camp."

"Well, haven't you become overly sure of yourself," Asclepiodotus sniffed. "I happened to come to the camp in time for the evening rituals, and I went to your *arae* to participate. This man was absent from the sacrifices."

For a moment there was absolute silence. Jurian could feel the gazes of several of his men fixed on him, and Asclepiodotus never took his eyes from Jurian's face—they were bright and hard, with a keen look that reminded Jurian, once again, of a vulture. Jurian's pulse picked up. He knew exactly the game Asclepiodotus was playing. After all, the unspoken accusation was there, all too clear. Jurian had also, notably, been absent from the sacrifices, as had Servius and Agapius, his two highest ranking subordinates. And all the men knew it.

So far, none of them had ever raised an issue with it. Jurian wondered, briefly, if someone had informed on him to Asclepiodotus, but he quickly dismissed the notion. His men were not only tolerant of their Christian brethren, they were also loyal, and would sooner betray Jurian to the Suevi than a snake like Asclepiodotus.

And Asclepiodotus was more than capable of coming up with a scheme like this on his own to draw Jurian out.

He barely had to consider his answer. "Very well," he said.

"I will deal with him."

Asclepiodotus made a brief, almost impatient gesture with his hand.

"I don't require your presence," Jurian said, "or your assistance."

"But...I will need to report to the *Caesar* that the discipline has been provided," Asclepiodotus sputtered.

"No, that really isn't necessary. If the *Caesar* requires a report, I will report."

Some of his men shuffled their feet behind him—he could feel their breathless anticipation as they waited to see who would break, who would back down. Asclepiodotus tightened his thin hands into knots, his cheeks puffed out in indignation. His gaze darted from Jurian down to Parmenion. He looked like he had half a mind to grab Parmenion bodily and inflict some punishment on the man himself. Jurian took one step to the side, placing himself between Asclepiodotus and the *eques*.

"I will ask you one more time to leave, *Praefectus*, or I will have my men remove you from this *castra*."

"You can't treat me like that!"

Jurian regarded him in unperturbed silence. The man was acting more like a child throwing a tantrum than a Roman official, and Jurian almost felt embarrassed for him. But not quite.

He said nothing to Asclepiodotus, and finally the Prefect backed a few steps, turned, and strode away like an angry diminutive rooster. Jurian heard someone in the crowd stifle a laugh.

Not wishing to encourage blatant disrespect for Rome's officials, he turned, suppressing his own humor, and leveled a fierce glare at the guilty *eques*. The man sobered immediately. Then Jurian shifted back to face Parmenion.

"I will see you in my tent," he said, and strode away without another word or glance at anyone.

Parmenion arrived a few moments after Jurian, escorted by one of the other *equites*, a man Jurian knew had a deep piety for the Roman gods. But his face was carefully neutral as he delivered Parmenion into the tent, and he withdrew with only a bow and salute to Jurian.

Parmenion stood before him with head lowered.

"Asclepiodotus expects me to punish you," Jurian said, folding his arms. Parmenion was at least ten years his senior, and perhaps four inches taller than him, but he still managed to look up at Jurian. "The entire cohort heard the accusation, and the edict does stand."

"*Domine*—" Parmenion began, but Jurian lifted a hand to silence him.

"You know of course that I don't believe your actions deserve any punishment," he said, very quietly. "Nor, I think, does Constantius Chlorus."

"Yes, *domine*," Parmenion murmured.

Jurian sighed and paced a few steps. If he let the man go without any punishment, would Constantius Chlorus turn a blind eye? He had shown clemency to his own soldiers in the past—everyone knew that. But perhaps he would take it as an excuse to finally cast Jurian out of his service and let Asclepiodotus send word to Rome of his treason.

"I heard that the rains have caused part of the surround to collapse," he said after a while.

"Yes, *domine*."

"Get back to your *striga* and get dressed, then report to the southern perimeter. You will assist there until the officer in charge of the fortifications dismisses you."

Parmenion nodded, looking a little crushed.

Wishing he could offer the man some consolation, some word of encouragement or solidarity, Jurian could only lift a hand to dismiss him. Parmenion saluted and retreated from the tent. Already late for the morning's briefings in the *praetorium*, Jurian grabbed his light cloak from his stool and headed back into the *castra*.

The meetings went on interminably. The Suevi were on the move, and the supply caravan from Lutetia had been delayed, which meant that Constantinus's cohort and the *cataphractarii* had no campaign to prepare for. Jurian gritted his teeth as he left the *praetorium*, trying to formulate the announcement to his men. They would undoubtedly be disappointed in the news.

He sent Servius to round up his *cataphractarii*, who had scattered to different parts of the camp for training or work. The few who were already nearby gathered closer in the *forum*, watching him expectantly. He could hear a few of their murmured conversations, however hard he tried not to listen.

"He sent Parmenion to fortify the ditch," one man said.

"Well, he couldn't very well do nothing," said another. "Not with that *perfectus abominosus* breathing down his neck. And it's barely even a punishment. I was there yesterday doing the same thing."

"What useless Roman law did you break?" one of his companions said.

At the same time another jibed, "Obviously you didn't do your job. Its walls are still caving in."

"*Vah*, I think the officers go down there in the night and undo all our work, just so they have something to tell us to do every day."

"Shh," said the first man, and Jurian caught a few hasty glances in his direction.

When they erupted in a bout of hearty laughter, Jurian turned a little aside in case he hadn't managed to stifle his own smile. The rest of his men gradually straggled in until his full force was there present in front of him.

"*Equites*," he said, and they grew quiet to listen as he explained their circumstances.

There was a bit of grumbling when he announced that there was no campaign immediately in sight, but his men mostly just seemed disappointed that they would have nothing to do.

"All this means that we will have more time to train, and more time to perfect this *castra aestiva*," he said, to more groans. "So, this afternoon, I want the first half of you to fill in the southern ditch. The rest of you, working behind them, go ahead and dig it all over again. Understood?"

The men roared with laughter, and Jurian let them laugh for a few minutes before raising his hand to quiet them.

"No, you are free to attend your scheduled training and duties. Continue in your current roles for now, but if, by the end of the week, we are still in place here, I will be rotating assignments." He scanned the rows of faces before him as they nodded acceptance. "Where is Parmenion?"

"Still at the wall, *domine*," someone piped up. "The officer in charge wouldn't let him come away."

Jurian let out a faint breath. "Who was the officer?"

There was a fractional pause, then, "Constantinus."

Jurian lifted his brows, unsure whether he was more surprised that the Tribune was in charge of the ditch, or that he had purposefully detained one of his men.

"Very well," he said, fighting to keep the annoyance from his voice. "See that Parmenion receives the information I just passed on to you. Dismissed."

The group broke formation and returned to their duties, and Jurian, after a moment's hesitation, set off for the southern perimeter of the camp. There he found Constantinus overseeing the soldiers who were repairing the ditch wall.

"Ah, *decurio*," he said, as Jurian joined him.

"*Tribunus*," Jurian said, matching his formality.

A ghost of a smile flashed over Constantinus's face. "You're angry with me."

"I ordered my men to report for a briefing, and you detained one against that order."

Constantinus regarded him in momentary surprise. "You did place him under my charge, Jurian," he said gently. "And as I am your superior officer, Parmenion could not violate my orders to obey yours."

"Are you trying to teach me a lesson, Constantinus?" Jurian asked. "If you think I was wrong in what I did, just tell me."

"I don't think you were wrong at all," he said, voice low. He studied Jurian a moment longer, then turned back to watch the soldiers in their work. He said, "You should understand. It's the appearance of the thing."

When he returned to his tent that night, Jurian was startled to find a man sitting on the ground beside the entry. He looked road-weary, but he sat in expectant silence, rigid, like a soldier in the presence of his officer, yet he was clearly not one of the *milites* from the *castra*. As Jurian approached the man glanced up, looked him over from head to toe, and got slowly to his feet.

"Are you the man called Jurian?" he asked.

Jurian swallowed. There was nothing about this person to give any indication of who he was, or what he wanted with him. Was he friend or enemy? Neither? He wore no insignia, no badge of office. And yet he was here within the camp, and he had called Jurian by his familiar name, not by rank, not by family title.

"Yes," he said.

The man closed his eyes in relief. "Finally," he breathed. "I've sought you from Londinium to Augusta Treverorum."

"Who are you?" Jurian asked. "What is it you want with me?"

The man smiled and, folding his hands behind his back, took a step closer to him. "A message. *For Jurian, carissime. I have at long last received your letter, and only wish that it had come sooner, that it had come a hundred times, that it had been you yourself and not only your words of comfort. I am sending my message to Britannia, because I do not know where else to send it. I trust it will find its way to you. There is a storm gathering in Cyrene, but we shall weather it, as we always have. Do not fear for me. I am stronger now, knowing that you are still with me. There is no evil I fear. I remain yours forever. Signed, Eva.*"

Jurian listened, heart hammering, as the man delivered the entirety of the message, and didn't move until the man had given a polite bow and cleared his throat gently, twice.

"Thank you," he murmured at last. The courier bowed again. "When did you receive your commission?"

"In *Aprilis*," he said.

"You were in Cyrene?" When the man simply nodded, Jurian asked, "Was there trouble in the city? Any cause for concern?"

The courier shook his head with an understanding smile. "All was well, as far as I could tell. I..." He hesitated, then bowed his head a little and said, "I do not know what this storm is that she speaks of, *domine*."

Jurian let out all his breath in a sigh of relief and pressed a handful of coins into the man's palm. The messenger tucked them into a pouch on his belt with a nod of thanks.

"You are a fortunate man. She is very beautiful." He turned to go, then added over his shoulder, "And I could see she loves you greatly."

45

Cyrene, Libya — July, A.D. 302

"Mistress!" Hanno called.

Sabra turned from the group of children she had been trying to persuade to go to sleep, in one of the recessed rooms just off the main sanctuary of the old temple. Since Casca's arrival, she and Hanno had been working tirelessly to convince the Christians of Cyrene to take refuge there, but many still refused to come. She lived in a constant fear of hearing that someone had been killed or imprisoned. And those reports, it seemed, came almost daily.

Fearing that Hanno brought such news, Sabra hurried over to the mouth of the labyrinth to meet him. But when she got there, she found not one of the spies they kept on the streets of Cyrene, but a young man with tousled dark hair and luminous eyes, covered in dust from a long journey.

"Diodoros!" she cried, instantly recognizing the scholar from Alexandria. "What are you doing here? How did you know where to find me?"

Her voice trailed off and she watched Diodoros, expectant, breathless. But Diodoros said nothing immediately, only leaned wearily over his knees. When he straightened, Sabra's smile faded at the expression on his face.

"What is it?" she asked. "What's happened?"

"I came as fast as I could. My lady Aikaterina sent me."

"What's happened? The *praefectus*—"

"Still alive," Diodoros said. "But still caught in that living death. This time I'm...not sure he will ever awaken."

"Oh," Sabra gasped, and laid her hand on his arm. "I'm so sorry. Is Aikaterina..."

"She is managing, as she always does."

Sabra exchanged glances with Hanno. "She got my letter?" she asked. "Do you bring a message from her?"

"I do. My lady sends a single word."

Sabra swallowed. "And what is that?"

"Run."

For a moment there was absolute silence between them. Sabra clenched her hands in fists, her mind a jumbled with confusion and weariness.

"No," she said. "I will not run." Her hands, like her voice, were shaking against her will. "I did not run before, and I will not run now. Not with my father imprisoned and..."

Her voice caught in her throat and she glanced away. Diodoros looked helplessly at Hanno, who merely lifted his hands in a resigned shrug.

"*Kyria*," Diodoros said, "you have been compromised."

"Compromised how?" Sabra asked.

"The letter you sent. It was...seen by unfriendly eyes."

A damp horror swept over Sabra, and the night breeze felt suddenly chilling. "What do you mean?"

"My lady says that it was opened and read on the road."

"By whom?"

"By a man named Casca."

Sabra's pulse pounded in her ears and she swayed unsteadily on her feet. Hanno surged forward to help her, but she held up a hand to stop him.

"I should have known," she murmured. "When he first came to Cyrene he spoke to me, and mentioned the coming storm. Why didn't I realize then that he'd actually read the letter?"

"If he knows, mistress..." said Hanno, and in the guttering light of a nearby torch, his face was ghastly pale.

"That is exactly why I will not run," she said. She turned to Diodoros. "You may go back to Alexandria. Tell Aikaterina... tell her that I chose to stay."

Diodoros set his jaw. "My lady was very clear that I was not to come back to Alexandria without you."

Sabra smiled and laid a hand on his arm. "If you tell her, she will understand."

"What will you do?" he asked.

Sabra said nothing for a long moment, but let her gaze drift over the little knots of people huddled along the walls of the temple.

"I will take care of my people," she said. "Whatever it takes."

"Please, mistress, do as he asks!" Hanno pleaded. "God spared you once...who is to say that He will do it again?"

Sabra didn't answer. In her heart, the answer was clear: He would save her as long as it served His will, and she trusted without a doubt that it would be so.

There was a sudden commotion farther down the labyrinth, and then a boy came streaking toward them, his face perfectly white and eyes wide with horror. He collapsed on the ground when he reached her, and Sabra's heart turned to lead.

"What is it?" she asked, gently lifting the boy to his feet.

"Something's happening!" he sobbed. "I saw the soldiers going into the *carcer*. And they're going house to house...they said it was time for the trial!"

Sabra caught in a sharp breath and nodded, wrestling down a rising tide of panic. She laid her hand on the boy's shoulder and pointed into the inner sanctuary. "Tell them to stay here," she said. "And keep watch outside. Don't let anyone find this place!"

He nodded bravely and she turned without a word and headed into the labyrinth. As she picked her way carefully through the darkness, she could hear Hanno and Diodoros following behind her, speaking softly together. Hanno, she knew, would never desert her, no matter where she decided to go or what danger presented itself. But Diodoros's staunch persistence surprised her.

They emerged onto the streets and Sabra led the way through dark alleyways, following the cacophony of shouts and clashing armor. The noise grew suddenly louder, and Sabra flattened herself against the wall of a tall building, deep in its shadows. Gradually she distinguished the sounds—the tromp of footsteps marching in cadence, barked orders from a commanding officer. Then they appeared, a troop of Legionaries under an unfamiliar emblem, marching down the street directly in front of Sabra. In the midst of them they hauled two men, weighed with chains and bloodied almost beyond recognition.

Sabra pressed back against the wall, Hanno and Diodoros close beside her, as the troop drove the men past them. As she watched, one of the men turned his face in her direction.

It was her father.

Sabra watched, frozen with fear and horror, her legs like stone, her heart pattering madly against her ribs. Hanno's hand circled around her wrist, steady and firm, and she closed her eyes. When she opened them again, the troop had disappeared farther into the city.

"Where are they going?" Diodoros asked.

"The *agora*," Sabra said. Without another word, she abandoned the shadows and trailed after the soldiers. Hanno and Diodoros followed close on her heels.

They eased their way into the *agora*, tracking through the deep darkness along the wall of one of the buildings. The *agora* was lit by dozens of torches, and the furtive light chased shadows across the imposing statue of the *Imperator* Diocletian. And the raised dais that had always been the place for civil justice and public debate had become a stage for the executioner. There were two stone blocks at the center, already stained dark with blood. A pair of guards stood near the back of the dais, armed with *flagra*, and at the front was a burly man, bare-chested, holding a naked sword across one shoulder.

A shred of cloud scudded across the moon and the torches guttered. The wind was shifting—Sabra could feel it in her bones. Her breath came in short gasps, and she felt as helpless as she had the day she'd watched Ayzebel slaughtered for her faith in this very place.

A huddled crowd of sleepy-eyed and confused townsfolk had begun to gather at the edges of the torchlight, driven from their homes by imperial command. As they realized they were about to witness an execution, they began to murmur—quietly at first, then louder, like a mountain stream swollen by rain.

And do they realize whose execution? she wondered. *They love my father. If they knew…would they rise up to defend him?*

Caius Dignianus stepped up onto the dais and lifted a hand. A movement just behind his shoulder drew Sabra's attention, and she saw that Casca was there too, watching, scanning the crowds. With awful certainty, she knew exactly what he was looking for.

He was looking for her.

"Citizens of Rome," Dignianus began, and Sabra shuddered. He threw back his shoulders, trying to give himself an imperial air of authority, but he only looked small and petty and pinched. "You have long known me as vice-governor, but it is not in that office that I stand before you tonight. As of this morning, I have formally relieved Lucius Titianus of his title, under the sanction of Rome, and now humbly accept your recognition of my authority as *praefectus* of Cyrene. For Cyrene is at a crossroads, and Lucius Titianus was prepared to stand back and let her sink into infamy and ruin. Cyrene has long harbored subversive and dangerous elements within her walls, and Rome has been more than tolerant. But no longer. Plans against the very life of our *Nobilissime et Sacratissime Imperator* Diocletian have surfaced—plans originating here."

A murmur broke out again in the gathered crowd, and people tried not to look left or right—as if catching someone else's eye would be an admission of guilt. Dignianus held up a hand again to quiet them, and they subsided with a nervous shuffle of feet.

"We should be thankful," he continued. "Thankful that Rome is so dedicated in its care of our corner of the Empire! To supervise our efforts to purge the threat from our city, the esteemed *Tribunus* Marcus Valerius Flaccus Casca has journeyed directly from the imperial court in Antioch."

There was a half-hearted smattering of applause as Casca stepped forward to join Dignianus at the *rostrum*. Sabra hardly dared to breathe. All of this, she was certain, was Casca's doing—planting in Diocletian's mind the idea that there was some threat against his life, and that the Christians were responsible for it. And it was no accident that he had chosen Cyrene as his opening target.

He was still scanning the crowd as Dignianus stepped back, and Sabra wondered if he could sense the changed mood of the crowd as she could. The uncertainty and fear were almost palpable.

"Citizens," Casca began, his voice like oil over water, "subversion cannot be tolerated. Unity and devotion are the pillars upon which our great Empire stands. Cyrene has long been suffering from famine and hardships, and the loss of its trade, all because of this man."

He gestured to the guards, and they dragged Sabra's father to one of the stone blocks.

"And because the gods have been angered by the outrages committed against them by *this* man, whom your former governor tolerated, if not condoned."

Another gesture, and the *episcopus* Theodorus was led forward. He went silently, like a sheep to the slaughter. Sabra's hands clenched into fists, her heart sick with fear and grief.

"See how this treachery has poisoned even the highest places," Casca said, pointing at Lucius Titianus. "But it runs deeper still, like your mountain, stretching to the sky, dropping its roots deep into the earth. We must purge it. We must purge it all. First the dragon. Next the dragon's daughter."

Sabra's heart fumbled a beat.

Turning abruptly from the rostrum, Casca approached the prisoners with a single nod to the guards. They shoved Theodorus down so that his neck rested on the block. The executioner, his naked sword leaning lazily over his shoulder, stepped forward, and a shuddering gasp ran through the crowd.

"Now," said Casca, in a voice loud enough to carry across the *agora*. "Tell me where she is. I know she has been tireless in protecting your little cult. Turn her over to me, and I will spare your life."

"You looked for treason here, and you couldn't find it, could you?" Lucius Titianus cried. "Where is your claimed nest of vipers waiting to strike the heart of the Empire? Have you found it, Tribune?"

Casca's lips tightened in displeasure, then he whirled toward Theodorus and shouted, "Tell me where she is!"

Theodorus stared straight ahead, his mouth a firm line. There was no hatred in his face, nor fear, only a calm, steady resignation. Casca pointed a finger at one of the guards holding a flagrum, and the man stepped forward and delivered three harsh blows across Theodorus's back with the whip. The *episcopus* gasped and his hand clutched vainly at the stone, but he said nothing.

"Tell me," Casca repeated, bending low over Theodorus's shoulder as if to whisper in his ear, but his voice never fell too soft for the crowd to hear. "Is such a small thing really worth dying for? You know what she is capable of. Is protecting her really worth so much?" Casca glanced up, but never straightened, and stared at the crowd below. "First she led you, falsely, in worship of the dragon. Now she leads you to false worship of that Galilean. Will you sacrifice so much to protect her?"

Sabra's teeth were chattering now. She clenched and unclenched her hands, trying to work feeling back into them. Every nerve in her body was buzzing.

Theodorus didn't move, and still he didn't speak. The crowd shuffled, and Sabra thought she heard someone weeping. The guard delivered three more fierce lashes with the *flagrum*, and another voice in the gathering began to sob.

"Do you know how we found you?" Casca went on. "Hidden so well in the city, with your precious books and your outlawed rites, drawing the people of Cyrene away from the worship of their true gods?" He placed his fingers under Theodorus's chin and tipped his head up, pointing into the crowd. "See there? Do you see him? How quickly he gave you up when he realized he would no longer be threatened by Lucius Titianus's traitorous regime."

Theodorus's eyes shadowed, and Sabra could barely hear the name spoken on a sad exhale, "Leontius."

"Do you have any parting words for your father?" Dignianus asked the man at the front of the mob.

"Words for him? He never had words for anyone but his God," Leontius said.

"My Leo," Theodorus said, his voice gentle, full of love. "I have always loved you above every gift. You are my masterpiece, the greatest of all my works."

"Still?" Casca asked, voice etched with skepticism. "After he denounced you to our most excellent Governor Dignianus?"

Theodorus's eyes never left Leontius. "I forgive you, my son. I pray one day…you may forgive yourself."

Casca spun on his heel and paced a few steps away, then reeled back and grabbed Theodorus's jaw. "No words? No words? Speak just one, and I will release you. *Where is she?*"

Theodorus closed his eyes and said nothing.

It happened almost too fast for Sabra to see. One minute Casca was leaning over Theodorus, gripping his jaw as if to pry out an answer, the next a knife blade was in his hand, flashing in the torchlight, and blood was pouring from Theodorus's mouth.

Someone in the crowd screamed. Sabra's stomach roiled and her knees quavered, sending the world spinning beneath her feet.

"Then you will never speak again," Casca hissed.

He turned away from the episcopus, the bloody blade

blazing like fire at his side, then jerked his chin at the executioner.

The sword flared in the torchlight and fell, and Theodorus's severed head rolled to the edge of the dais. Brutal, quick, clean.

Wailing broke out in one corner of the crowd, a child sobbing. Sabra saw her father sag in his chains, miserable horror and fear flooding his face.

The executioner tumbled Theodorus's corpse off the dais and onto the stone pavement, where it landed with a sickening thud. He cleaned his blade on a cloth that hung from his belt, and then stepped back, his sword once more across his shoulder. Someone from the crowd tried to dart forward to minister to the body of the *episcopus*, but he was forced back by the guards.

Casca turned to Sabra's father and motioned for the guards to drag him forward.

"Please!" her father shouted. "You don't have to do this. You don't have to—"

"Don't I, though?" Casca asked, his voice like iron. "If you had kept better control of your city and not polluted your office with sacrilege, I would not be here. Under your rule, Titianus, Cyrene has become a city of strange rites."

"You have no right, Tribune. You have no right to execute me without trial."

Casca regarded him thoughtfully, head tipped like a bird's, then he *tsk*ed softly and pulled a narrow scroll from his belt. He unrolled it and held it, just a moment, before the governor's face, then snatched it back again and tucked it away.

"Oh, but in this case I do, Governor," he said. "In this case I do. I am your judge here. I am the law, and the appointed hand of the *imperium*. This is your trial—these your witnesses. And I am offering you…mercy."

He gestured to the guards, and Lucius Titianus's body shook with silent sobs as the they forced him down before the stone block.

"Let's not have any more unpleasantness," Casca said. "Just tell me where she is. I promise you, I will not harm her."

"Even if I did know, I would never tell you," Lucius Titianus said. "And I don't believe a word you say. So kill me and be done with it."

Casca rubbed a hand across his jaw. Sabra could almost feel his frustration. "No," he said thoughtfully, after a brief silence. "I think not just yet. Because sometimes, with the right persuasion, men will come to see things in the proper light."

Sabra pressed her hands against the wall, desperate to steady herself. Beside her, Diodoros was murmuring something in a language she had never heard before, but she knew the intonations were those of prayer. Hanno was mute, but when she glanced at his face, it was ashen with horror.

"Hanno—" she said in the barest whisper. "I cannot stay here and watch this…"

His hand clamped around her arm. "You will not move," he murmured. "Mistress, do not move. They'll see you."

Hot tears spilled over Sabra's lashes and burned down her cheeks as she forced her gaze back to the *agora*. Casca made a sign to the guards standing at the edges of the crowd. Instantly they were on the move, weaving their way into the throng. A commotion broke out in the corner where Sabra had heard the wailing.

"No!" a man shouted. "No!"

The crowds parted like a troubled sea and the guards emerged, dragging three women with them. They had scratched their faces in their grief, and their hair was tumbled around their shoulders. Two men were trying to shove through the crowd after them, but their fellow citizens held them back.

"She has done nothing!" one of the men shouted. He was half-wild with fear and grief. "Let her go! *Aroa!*"

The soldiers dragged the women onto the dais, where they clung to each other, sobbing with fear. Sabra felt nausea wash over her in a warm wave. She knew—as if the curtain of the future had suddenly fluttered aside—she knew what was coming. Those women…they had been safe in the temple before. Why had they come out? Why?

Casca linked his fingers behind his back and bent down to

bring his mouth close to Lucius Titianus's ear. "These women seem very unhappy with me," he said. "I think they must be members of your foul sect. Guilty of impiety and traitors to the Empire, I'd say."

"Is this also Rome's justice?" Lucius Titianus growled. "To drag innocent women from a crowd and condemn them without evidence and without a trial? What does your scroll say about that? Does it condemn Cyprilla and Lucia for unnamed crimes? Does it account Aroa among your traitors?"

"You're right," Casca said. "Absolutely. We need evidence."

He gestured to the guards, and they dragged forward one of the women—the widow Cyprilla, who had worked so tirelessly to help usher their flock to safety. They forced her to her knees, and one pulled her hair roughly away from her face. Casca drew a long knife from his belt and contemplated its edge.

"You," he said to the woman, who was shaking with terror. "Are you a follower of this man they call the Christ?"

Cyprilla glared up at Casca. "Murderer," she spat. "You are an abomination!"

Casca chided her with a soft cluck of his tongue. "That's not what I asked you, is it?"

He drove the point of the knife into her shoulder and tracked it down the outside of her arm, opening a long, ugly gash. The woman's blood-curdling scream of agony shuddered the crowd and Sabra fell to her knees.

"Oh God, have mercy," Sabra whispered. "Mercy...Hanno, let me *go*..."

"Mistress, I'm so sorry," Hanno said. Even without looking at him, Sabra heard his voice thick with tears. "I cannot."

Blood soaked Cyprilla's chiton and stained the dais. She sobbed and tried to place her other hand over the wound, but the guards jerked on her hair and pinioned her arm behind her. One of the guards scored her upper back with half a dozen stripes from his *flagrum*.

"Stop!" shouted Lucius Titianus. "Stop, please. What is it you want from us?"

"But I told you that already," Casca said, turning to Sabra's father, the bloody knife in his hand. "Tell me where she is hiding, and all of this can end."

"You lie like a coward and a child of Hell!" he shouted. "There is no plot against the Emperor's life in Cyrene! This is the worst and basest form of tyranny!"

"In You, O Lord, have I hoped—" Cyprilla said, the words falling in broken melody.

Casca's arm flicked, and the knife slashed across the woman's throat. Blood sprinkled the hem of Casca's toga as the guards released her and she fell, lifeless, to the dais.

For a moment, horror darkened Sabra's eyes. She could barely see the stone wall in front of her face, could barely feel the stone beneath her knees. Gasping for breath, she opened her mouth to cry out, but no sound escaped the noose of her throat.

"I'm growing weary of this," Casca said. "You know I will find her. I will find her, or I will rid this city of its plague, one abomination at a time."

"God will protect her," one of the other woman said suddenly, her voice clear and loud.

Sabra lifted her head and dug her fingers into the stone wall. She knew that woman, too. It was Aroa, Elissa's mother—Elissa, the last child to die in sacrifice to the dragon.

And am I to have her mother's blood on my conscience too? Sabra thought, pulling herself to her feet.

"Surely," Casca said, "you mean the gods."

"You must not have heard me," Aroa said, dragging against the guards. "I mean God—Jesus Christ, our Savior."

Casca turned toward the crowd, arms outstretched. "You see?" he said. "We have evidence."

The other woman, Lucia, pulled away from her guard and threw her arms protectively around Aroa. Below the dais, the crowd was in a tumult, weeping, writhing with horror, hemmed in on all sides by a score of Roman soldiers.

"Look, Aroa," Lucia said, pointing upward. Sabra followed the gesture, and saw, impossibly, a pale dove roosting on top of the pillar in the center of the *agora*, bright under a slant of moonlight. "Don't be afraid! Theodorus is watching over us still, and God has visited us in our time of need."

The guards pulled them apart and kicked their legs from under them. Almost before their knees had hit the dais, the executioner's sword had done its work, and two more heads fell to join Theodorus's.

"And you," Casca said to Lucius Titianus. "I want you to die in the certain knowledge that you have failed. You have failed your people. You have failed your Emperor. You have failed your daughter. And you have failed your God."

He stepped back and the executioner took his place, sword raised. Sabra sagged against the wall, and she felt Hanno's strong arms encircle her.

"I love you, father," she whispered, the words broken and tangled with grief, as the sword flashed in the torchlight. "Be at peace."

She closed her eyes as the sword fell.

"So ends the abomination of Lucius Titianus, traitor to the Empire," Dignianus said. His voice rolled over the crowd, which had finally been stunned to silence.

Far in the distance and still faint, thunder rumbled in the north.

46

Alexandria, Aegyptus — July, A.D. 302

Aikaterina paced the path that wound through her palace gardens, her eyes fixed on the white paving stones. All around her, the sun blazed on the bright flowers and the wind sighed through the fronds of the date palms, but she barely registered her surroundings.

It had been a little more than a month since she had dispatched Diodoros to Cyrene, but she had heard nothing from him. She tried to tell herself that she shouldn't expect word—that Sabra herself would soon be safely in Alexandria. Together, they would weather whatever storm was coming. But the knowledge that Casca was on the road somewhere between Alexandria and Cyrene made her gnaw her lip in worry. There was no predicting the man's tactics, and she didn't know what to do.

And then there were the murmurings in the streets. When Nenet had come to help her dress that morning, she'd told Aikaterina that crowds were beginning to gather in the *agora* and at the Temple of Serapis. And more troubling still, the people were finally beginning to fear that their *praefectus* would never recover from his illness. Everything felt as unsettled as a storm-tossed sea.

For two weeks, Aikaterina had gone dutifully every morning to study with Theokritos in the *Bibliotheka*, as if carrying on with the routine of her old life would somehow bring it back. But today, finally, Theokritos had rolled the parchment, folded his wrinkled hands, and sent her away.

"You must have peace inside to study and learn, *kyria*," he had told her. "I will be here waiting when you are ready."

His voice had carried none of his usual sternness, just patient understanding. But somehow it still stung like a rebuke.

She blew out her breath and turned at the end of the walkway, then drew up when she saw Nenet hurrying toward her. Seized with a sudden fear, she ran forward to meet her and caught her hands in a tight grip.

"What is it? Is it Father?" she asked, breathless.

Nenet shook her head and a wide smile blossomed across her face. "Come and see."

She led Aikaterina back through the garden and down a little path to a secluded spot, well out of sight of the palace. There Aikaterina could just make out three figures standing in the shade of a great date palm. And then, with a little cry, she recognized them.

She left Nenet's side and raced toward them. "Sabra!" she cried. Sabra turned, and Aikaterina caught her in a fierce embrace. "Thank God! I've been so worried about you. I hoped you would get the message and come right away…"

Sabra said nothing, but only clung to her friend, and Aikaterina suddenly realized she was shaking all over. Exhaustion? Or…grief? Aikaterina's heart chilled, and she held Sabra more tightly. This was not the happy meeting of separated friends that she had expected.

After a moment she drew back and glanced at Diodoros. His face was drawn and a little ashen, and his clothes were caked in dust from the road.

"We rode as hard as we dared," he said, his voice raspy. "I am sorry I didn't send word ahead."

Aikaterina shook her head. "There was no need for you to

send word," she said. "But...has something happened?"

Sabra took Aikaterina's hand, and there was such sadness in her face that tears stung Aikaterina's eyes. "It has begun," she said softly.

She sank down on the low stone bench near the trunk of the tree and buried her face in her hands, body racked with sobs. Hanno sat beside her, a hand on her shoulder, silent but steady.

"It's been a hard journey," Diodoros said. "And we witnessed horrors before we escaped Cyrene."

Aikaterina's stomach pitched. "What horrors?" she asked. She could barely force the whisper. "What happened?"

"They...murdered her father," he said. "And Theodorus, the shepherd of the people."

"Who did?" Aikaterina asked, even though her heart had already told her the answer.

"Dignianus," he said. "And Marcus Valerius Casca."

Her hand flew up to cover her mouth, then she drew a thin breath and lowered it again. "*Casca.*"

"There's more," Diodoros said. "They were looking for her. They interrogated her father...tried to torture her location out of him. He died protecting her."

"Yes, I'm sure Casca was looking for her," Aikaterina murmured. "It is exactly what he would do."

"He's coming here, *kyria*," Hanno said suddenly. "He said... after it was all over, he said he would make Alexandria bow just the same. We are not safe here. You are not safe."

Aikaterina glanced from Hanno to Diodoros. "None of us safe are anywhere now," she said. "So what point would there be in running away?" Diodoros's face settled into resignation, and Aikaterina lifted her hand. "That does not mean that we won't defend ourselves," she added. "And Sabra must be hidden where Casca cannot find her."

Sabra lifted her head. "Do you think I would abandon you to meet him alone?" she said, her voice ragged with tears.

Aikaterina knelt in front of her and took her friend's hands tightly in her own. "Of course not," she said. "But if he finds you here, you know what will happen. You know why he is looking for you."

"I know."

"We cannot let that happen."

"I know," she said again. She heaved a shaking sigh and squeezed Aikaterina's hands. "Where am I to go?"

Aikaterina smiled as she glanced up at Diodoros. "I know a place."

THE SUN WAS SINKING behind a dark rack of clouds gathering in the west as Diodoros led Aikaterina and Sabra out of Alexandria, crossing the river Draco into the city of the dead. Sabra stayed close to Aikaterina's side, and Aikaterina could feel her trembling beneath the dark cloak Aikaterina had given her. Only Hanno was missing from their group—Aikaterina had taken him into her own service, since he could not be welcomed in *Amma* Synkletika's community.

"Why is it everywhere I go death surrounds me?" Sabra whispered, her eyes haunted. "Why can I never find a place among the living?"

Aikaterina tried to smile reassuringly. "You know better than I," she said, "that those who are dead to the world are truly the most alive of us all. You'll see. It will be all right, Sabra."

Sabra said nothing, and Aikaterina gave her hand a gentle squeeze. She remembered that she had felt exactly the same way when she had first come here so long ago, looking for Diodoros's sister. She'd found not only the little community of faithful women that day, but also someone else altogether—someone she could never have expected.

"Do you know," she whispered to Sabra, "this is where I first met Jurian."

Sabra's head snapped up, and for the first time, Aikaterina saw something like hope flickering in Sabra's eyes. "Really?"

"Yes, really. And I think...I must have been rather rude to him."

Sabra laughed out loud, and the sound flitted among the

tombs like a sudden ray of sunshine. "Oh, I can only imagine how that must have gone."

"And then Agapius had to show up. So irritating. He was always following me around." Aikaterina stopped, suddenly and strangely lonely. But it was a feeling she could not quite comprehend, so she pushed it roughly aside. "I thought they would come to blows, those two."

"How strange it all is," Sabra said.

"Yes," Aikaterina agreed, then, after a moment, she added softly, "No coincidences."

They followed Diodoros along a narrow path between two tombs and came at last into a large central square bounded by a low wall. To their right, the maw of a massive tomb opened into darkness. Aikaterina stopped, the waves of memory catching her by surprise. This was exactly the place she had stood when everything in her life had changed.

Sabra gasped suddenly and caught Aikaterina's arm. When Aikaterina glanced at her, she found her pointing, open-mouthed, eyes bright with wonder or fear. A lynx crouched on top of the wall, watching the courtyard as if it, too, were made of stone.

"It's all right," Diodoros said softly. "She will not harm us. She is here to watch the path."

"You bring a stranger to us, *adelphe*," said a woman's soft voice behind them.

Aikaterina and Sabra spun around and found two women on the path, as if they had just gathered from the shadows between the tombs. Diodoros moved to greet one of them with an affectionate embrace.

"Theokleia!" Aikaterina gasped suddenly, recognizing the younger of the two women.

The girl turned her head in the direction of Aikaterina's voice, and a smile brightened her face. "Ah!" she cried. "The truth-seeker. You returned to us, like you said you would."

"This is *kyria* Aikaterina of Alexandria," Diodoros said.

"We have met before," Theokleia said, and turned to

Aikaterina. "The ring I gave you?"

"It has gone to another," Aikaterina said, catching a sharp breath. "A just man, bold as a lion."

Theokleia simply nodded, then shifted her attention to Sabra. "And you," she said. She paused, and took a step backward. "I must find Amma."

Almost without a sound, the *monacha* vanished into the darkness of the tomb.

"Who is she?" Sabra asked, and then, her voice wondering, "She is blind."

"Yes," Diodoros said. "But she sees more than most who have sight." He turned to the other young woman, who was standing quietly to the side and watching them with a bright and curious gaze. "Aikaterina," he said. "You wanted to meet my sister. This is Irene."

The girl came forward and clasped Aikaterina's hands with a gentle smile. "You bear many burdens, but you are not alone. I will pray that you may find your peace."

Aikaterina, shaken, could think of nothing to say in reply, but the girl didn't seem to be expecting one. She tightened her grip on Aikaterina's hands briefly, then nodded to them all and faded away between the rows of tombs.

The lynx jumped down from the wall and padded softly after her, westward through the necropolis. Aikaterina watched them go, then turned as Theokleia returned with *Amma* Synkletika.

"You see," Theokleia said. "She is here, just as I promised she would be."

Sabra frowned. "How did you know I would come? Did someone send word?"

"Only the Lady," Synkletika said with a crinkle around her eyes and a fond smile at her sister.

"She has seen much of darkness," Theokleia said, her unseeing eyes fixed on a point just over Sabra's shoulder. "So much darkness. And—" She stopped with a sharp little gasp.

"Yes," Sabra said softly. "But that is all past now."

"I expect you have come for a reason," Synkletika said to Aikaterina. "Not just to pay us a visit."

"She is in danger," Aikaterina said bluntly. "And she needs somewhere to hide."

Synkletika's eyes narrowed. "In danger? What sort of danger?"

"The darkness follows her," Theokleia said. "Even now, I can see it coming."

"We are not accustomed to offer sanctuary," Synkletika said. "We are a community for women who have chosen a life of sacrifice and prayer, not for those running away."

"I am not running away," Sabra said.

"Please," Aikaterina said. "I asked you once to let me stay, to learn the ways of Truth. You refused me and said I was not yet ready. But I have seen the Truth since that day, and we have both of us watched men die for its sake. Not two weeks past, she watched her own father and the *episcopus* of her community in Cyrene fall to the sword." She turned to Theokleia. "You are right. Darkness is coming. So be the light that drives it back."

She stopped. Diodoros, close beside her, was watching her with a glimmer of approval in his eyes.

Amma Synkletika hesitated. "I have my daughters to think about," she said softly. "If you bring this danger here, they will all suffer the sword...and that would be a mercy." Her lips closed into a tight line.

"No one but Diodoros and myself know she is here," Aikaterina said. "And you have my word that no one else shall. There are not many who would come willingly to the city of the dead."

Theokleia laid a hand on Synkletika's arm. "Did not Our Lord say that we should shelter those in need?" she asked softly.

Amma Synkletika finally yielded with a nod of her head. "Very well," she said. "But if her presence here in any way becomes a danger to our community, I must ask that you find another place for her."

"You have my word," Aikaterina said with a faint smile,

then turned to Sabra and embraced her fiercely. "I will come and visit if I can."

"Kat, wait." Sabra stepped back. "Can you…send a message for me?"

"It's too dangerous," Aikaterina said. "There are things in motion in my father's household that make correspondence of any kind a risk, and with the roads being watched…I'm sorry. I can't."

Sabra sighed and nodded. "I know." She hesitated, then added, almost in a whisper, "But you know as well as I do that I don't actually have to be dead or imprisoned for Casca to spread that report."

47

Ara Agrippinensium, Germania — September, A.D. 302

THE TURN OF THE SEASONS WAS ONCE MORE SHIFTING THE HEAT OF summer to autumn's burnished chill, and Jurian had seen little of Constantinus after a series of campaigns against the Suevi around Ara Agrippinensium. He assumed that the *Caesar* had sent him out to patrol farther down the frontier, and at first Jurian wondered if Constantinus had been ordered to leave him behind. But nothing happened—no soldiers came to arrest him, and Constantius Chlorus, though his manner was chilly, seemed content to leave Jurian alone for the present.

Jurian had spent the quiet weeks between campaigns with his unit, taking them out each morning to train in the open fields outside the city. But in the afternoons, when his duties were finished and his *equites* were busy with their own, he rode out into the forests surrounding the *castra*, either alone or with Agapius if the camp could spare him.

They tracked through the deep forests, each day going a little further, learning the paths that led deep into the heart of the countryside. The strategic advantage the barbarians had over the Romans was their native knowledge of the terrain, and Jurian reasoned that if the Legion could develop a solid knowledge of the region, they could use their superior military tactics more efficiently. That was the reasoning he gave to anyone who asked, but he knew that deep inside, he was simply glad of the peace and contemplation the woods provided.

One afternoon, late in September, Jurian and Agapius found themselves in a dense wood, far north of any region they had explored so far. Sunlight filtered through the golden and red-mottled leaves of the oak and beech trees, casting the air with a soft amber light. The leaves that had already fallen lay like a mosaic mat on the forest floor and muted their horses' hooves, while in the lofty branches strange northern birds chirped their cheerful songs. With every breath of chill air they caught the crisp, fragrant scent of pine needles, and the earthier smell of fallen leaves.

Agapius let out an audible sigh, and when Jurian glanced at him, he saw his friend grinning.

"What?" Jurian asked.

"I love it out here," Agapius said. "We've been places, you and I...but Germania is my favorite by far."

"Better even than Alexandria?" Jurian asked.

Agapius shrugged and took a deep breath of the pine-spiced air. "Different. Wilder. And...newer somehow."

"I doubt that. Do you see the height of those trees?"

"Well, it feels newer," Agapius said. "Like a place untainted by the Empire."

"That's because it is."

"Not for long, if the *Caesar* has his way," Agapius muttered. "Do you think one day there will still be wild places in the world? Places that no human has ever seen?"

Jurian considered that briefly. "I don't know," he said. "I've never—"

A sudden shout fractured the peace of the forest, and overhead the birds exploded into the air with cries of alarm. Both horses shied, and Jurian, after calming his own, reached over to take the reins of Agapius's horse. When it settled down, Agapius flashed Jurian a grateful smile. His right arm had never fully healed from his shoulder wound, though he never liked to admit the pain and weakness it still caused him. Jurian was careful not to bring attention to it if he could help it, but he was always watchful.

For a few minutes they sat side by side, in perfect silence, waiting and listening for another sound to make sense of the first. None came.

"We're probably closer to the Suevian encampment than we thought," Jurian murmured.

"Should we turn around?"

"Probably," Jurian said, which made Agapius laugh.

"So, no, then."

Another cry came from somewhere ahead of them—like the first shout, it sounded close. Terrifyingly close. And it sounded like pure pain.

"Jurian…"

"Come on," Jurian said.

He couldn't ignore the nagging fear in his gut, so he set his heels to his horse's flanks and drove him ahead into the trees. All too soon they arrived at a broad clearing edged by towering pine trees, and both Jurian and Agapius drew to an abrupt halt. A score of Suevian warriors were gathered in the open space around a blazing campfire. And near the center of the group, two men knelt on the ground.

Two Romans.

They were stripped to the waist, and their backs were a tapestry of stripes and burns. As Jurian watched, a Suevian warrior stepped up behind one of the Romans and did something that Jurian couldn't quite make out, but the Roman immediately cried out again, writhing and collapsing forward on his hands.

"Stop!" Jurian shouted, nudging his horse again.

The Suevi turned of one accord, weapons drawn and held at the ready.

"Jurian…" Agapius said again, through his teeth, but Jurian ignored him.

The two Roman *milites* murmured in relief when they saw

the approaching horsemen. Jurian didn't recognize either of them, but they were clearly soldiers, so he assumed they were reinforcements to Constantinus's cohort. With only a quick breath of prayer that he wasn't actually as insane as he felt, he rode directly into the midst of the Suevi and dismounted in front of the man who was obviously their leader.

"Georgius!" one of the Romans called. "*Decurio*, please, help us!"

Jurian said nothing. He just met the Suevian warrior's gaze, and held it. The Sueve lifted his *seax* knife, its edge glinting red with wet blood, and held it directly under Jurian's nose. Jurian didn't flinch, even at the coppery stench of blood, and finally the Sueve's mouth lifted in a feral smile.

"I will treat with you, Roman," he said, in broken Latin. "Them I will not talk to. You...you have something of the barbarian in you."

Jurian suppressed a noise of surprise. Instead he nodded and drew his own *seax* knife, using it to create some space between himself and the Suevian warrior.

"What have these men done, that you are subjecting them to such tortures?" he asked. He kept an iron edge on his voice, even when every prudent part of his mind wanted to feel terrified at being surrounded by a score of barbarian warriors.

"They have violated our sacred spaces," the leader spat, "and desecrated our holy lands."

Jurian held up a hand. To his astonishment, the warrior actually fell silent and watched him, curious, to see what he would do next. Fixing him with a brief look, Jurian moved around him and went to stand in front of the two Romans.

"Is he speaking the truth?" he asked them.

"No!" one cried, face white with terror. "Honestly, we had no notion we were in any sacred space. It looked like any ordinary grove, with a spring. We were thirsty. We drank from the spring."

Jurian nodded and straightened. "Is that the accusation against them? That they drank from your sacred spring?"

"Yes, and they must die for their impiety!"

Jurian considered that a moment. "Do you accept that these Romans, ignorant of your ways and of this region, might not have known that it was a spring sacred to your people?"

"No," he said, eyes narrowing.

"How did you know it was a sacred spring?" Jurian asked quietly. "When your people first arrived in this region?"

"Because some drank of it and were filled with visions of the divine," he said, face reddening with rising anger.

"Ah," Jurian said, and the man deflated a little to watch him, as if Jurian were some kind of curiosity that fascinated him. "So some of your people drank from it, not knowing it was sacred. And did you punish them?"

"No…" he said, but there was uncertainty in his voice now.

"And is it possible that you might, at this very moment, be burning a sacred tree in that fire pit?"

The Sueve spun around, paling rapidly, as if he expected the whole grove to erupt into flames of divine vengeance.

"Do you think," Jurian went on, "that the divine—God, or His spirits who watch over the earth—would simply expect every human to know all the divine mysteries, without being taught them?"

The Sueve shook his head, rattling the bones woven into his long red-gold beard.

"My men meant no dishonor to you, or the places you hold to be sacred. I, for my part, apologize that they were encroaching on your lands." *Without an official Roman order*, he added mentally, bemused.

"Georgius," the Sueve said, startling him. "We have heard many tales of your skill as a warrior. I did not expect to find you wise and just as well." He snapped his fingers at a few of his men, who loosed the ropes that bound the Romans' wrists. "Take them and do what you will with them." His lips lifted in another ferocious grin, and he gave Jurian a faint gesture that looked almost like a salute. "Perhaps I will have the joy of battling you with steel instead of words, one day."

"Perhaps you will," he said. He backed a step toward his horse. "And most people know me as Jurian."

Jurian and Agapius escorted the two men back to the *castra*. The soldiers were overflowing with relief for the first five minutes or so of the journey, but they quickly settled into a quiet focus, and marched doggedly behind the two horses.

Jurian turned to them as they neared the *castra*, saying, "Steer clear of the Suevian lands from now on. I may not always be available to rescue you, or speak in your defense. And, for the love of all that is holy, if you find yourself in Suevian lands, don't touch anything."

The men nodded, one of them suppressing a laugh.

"But you're Georgius, Dragon-Slayer," the other said. "Everyone knows you will come to the aid of your soldiers, no matter where they are."

They had reached the camp, and the two men went on alone to visit the field *sapsarius*, leaving Jurian and Agapius still on horseback at the entrance to the *castra*. Jurian watched them go, feeling strangely at peace.

"Agapius," he said after a long silence.

"Yes, Jurian?" Agapius said, gently mocking.

"I don't ever want to be unable to take care of my men."

It was hard, trying to put into words exactly what he felt. How could he explain how complete he felt in that role, as an officer in the field, surrounded by good men and skilled fighters...*his* men? Suddenly he realized that he wasn't just using these men to win back his private honor, so that he could retire and live out a life of peace. He wanted to go on serving with them. He wanted to keep leading them out on campaigns, fighting for them and alongside them. It was one of his dearest dreams from as long as he could remember, but it was no longer a childish fancy.

He was a soldier. It was a part of him, written in his blood, as dear and necessary to his life as breathing.

48

Aegyptus, Africa — September, A.D. 302

Sabra sat in the back of the crypt, listening to the haunting voices of the women as they chanted their evening prayers. She couldn't make out the words, and the melody seemed dark somehow, and sad. For two months now she had dwelt in that forsaken place, and most of the melodies the women sang had become familiar to her. But this one was different, and as note followed note, Sabra felt them pierce through her heart, making it ache with a keen sorrow.

"What troubles you?" came a soft voice behind her.

Sabra startled and spun, only to find Theokleia standing there, staring over Sabra's shoulder with that milky gaze that still seemed to see for ages.

"How did you know I was here?" Sabra asked, her voice strangely hoarse. "I made no noise."

Theokleia smiled. "I may be blind, but I am not deaf," she said. "And besides, you've seemed sad to me lately. The darkness you carry is heavy, especially tonight."

Sabra's shoulders slumped. There was no point in arguing with the *monacha*, who clearly could hear and see far better than anyone else in that place.

"Yes," she murmured.

"And still you find no peace here," Theokleia continued, as if Sabra had not spoken at all. "I think your friend hoped you might find comfort among us."

"This place is built for death," Sabra said. "And I have spent too long in its service to welcome this place as my home, even if just for a little while."

"Death is not an evil," Theokleia said, so bluntly that Sabra stared at her in surprise.

"You don't...you aren't afraid to die?"

"I would gladly embrace it," she said, and her face lit with a rapturous joy that shook Sabra to the core of her heart. "If only I could die tomorrow!"

"How can you say that?" Sabra asked. "Have you ever seen death?" And then the wrongness of the words struck her, and she bit her lip. "I'm sorry, I didn't mean—"

But Theokleia only laughed. "I take no offense. I have known death, certainly. But think of what it is—what it *truly* is. Finally to be at peace, and resting in the heart of the Lord that loves us so much, He who chose death as the way to save us for Himself."

Sabra bowed her head. Ever since that awful day in Cyrene, she had clung with desperate force of will to Nikolaos's teachings. Now, more than ever, she felt the presence of that evil hovering around the corners of her mind, waiting for the least break in her focus to worm its way back in.

"I don't know that I have any right to that love," Sabra said.

"Do you think you are the only one who has done wrong?" Theokleia asked. "What about blessed Paul, who persecuted the church of Christ in its infancy? What about the Magdalene?"

Sabra smiled at that—she couldn't help it. The name brought back the memories of that peaceful year in Cyrene, when Nikolaos had taught her the story of Mariam, and she had found, finally, someone in the Scriptures who felt like a kindred soul.

"Thank you," she murmured.

The girl turned and made her way back to where, Sabra

supposed, the others must be concluding their evening prayers. Sabra watched her go, feeling loneliness creep into her heart once more. She wished Hanno were there, even if all he did was sit beside her without speaking.

She couldn't understand Theokleia's joyful acceptance of death. For as long as she could remember, death had been the one evil, the thing she hated and feared above all else...even more so because she had been dedicated to its service. She'd seen no great glory in the death of her father or Theodorus, or Varro and his soldiers in the arena, just as she'd never seen beauty in the sacrificial deaths of the children outside the dragon's cave— no matter how she had tried to persuade them of it.

Of all the teachings of the Faith, it was the folly of the Cross that she most struggled to embrace. How could death ever be considered a victory? How could anyone, ever, consider it a good?

Sighing, she rose and made her way back into the main corridor. In one direction it led to the spiraling staircase to the night above, and in the other direction...that room. That room swathed in shadows, always filled with gloom despite the constant flickering of an oil lamp somewhere inside it. The one room she had never dared to go into. Now, almost against her will, her steps turned toward it. On either side of the doorway, crowned serpents leered at her, mocking her, daring her to go further.

Another step, then another, and she was standing inside the burial chamber. She held her breath as her eyes adjusted to the dim light, then let it out again. The niches for the dead were empty, here.

Bitterness filled her mouth, her heart.

She didn't even have the company of the dead.

And then, as she watched, one of the hollows seemed to fill and darken slowly. Sabra stared, frozen with horror, as the torchlight flickered over the niche and glimmered off the brightness of blood. It ran over like a cup filled to the brim, and slipped down the bare face of the rock to pool over the stones at her feet, higher and higher, drenching the hem of her chiton in crimson.

Sabra screamed and scrambled backward, tripping over the lip of the threshold and falling hard on the stone floor.

Amma Synkletika and several of the other *monachi* came running at her cry, and Synkletika helped her to sit up. Sabra stared at the niche in the wall, which was bare and clean once more.

"Did something happen?" Amma Synkletika asked.

Sabra wrapped her arms tightly around herself, shivering uncontrollably. She kept her eyes riveted on the stone, as if at any moment it might start to bleed again.

"The storm of fire and blood," she whispered.

"What is she talking about?" asked one of the younger women.

Vaguely, Sabra saw Synkletika wave a hand to shush her. "What storm?" she asked Sabra. "What happened to you, child?"

"The beginning," Sabra said, "and the end."

The world spun into darkness, and she slumped forward in Synkletika's arms.

49

Alexandria, Aegyptus — September, A.D. 302

A light rapping on her chamber door roused Aikaterina from deep thought. Her surroundings came back to her in a rush—the open window where she sat with her arms resting on the stone ledge, the mild autumn breeze disheveling her hair. It had been late afternoon when she had settled there to think, but the sun had long since set, the last splashes of color already fading from the western sky. She rubbed her hands over her face as the knock came again.

"Yes?" she called. And then she unfolded herself from her cushion and went to open the door, muttering to herself, "Where has Nenet got to? Why should I have to answer my own door at this hour? Isn't she supposed to be helping me dress for dinner?" Then, "Did I miss dinner?"

She pulled open the door with a frown and stepped back in surprise. Diodoros stood in the corridor, his face as pale as if he had just witnessed a murder. His expression made her heart jerk in sudden panic, and her hand flashed out to grip his arm.

"Tell me nothing has happened to—to—"

He shook his head. "Worse."

Aikaterina scowled at him, her relief making her angry. "What could possibly be worse than that? Stop being dramatic."

"No, it is worse." Diodoros glanced down the corridor and lowered his voice. "He's here, *kyria*."

Her breath froze in her throat. "When?"

"Just now. With his whole cohort."

Aikaterina snatched her hand from Diodoros's arm as if it had burned her. "Nenet!" she cried. "Nenet!"

Nenet came running, and when she reached the door she glared daggers at Diodoros. "What did you do?" she snapped.

Diodoros backed away, hands raised. "Nothing! I did nothing!"

Aikaterina seized Nenet's arm and dragged her inside. "Leave him alone. He's done nothing wrong." Just before she closed the door, she turned back to Diodoros, murmuring, "Thank you."

He nodded, and as the door closed on him, Aikaterina confronted Nenet with hands on her hips.

"Now Nenet," she said. "There is someone very important who has come to visit Alexandria."

"Yes, I know." Nenet made a face. "He looks like a pickled fish left too long in the sun. I don't like him."

"Nor I, but these things are irrelevant." Aikaterina turned to pace the floor. "Where is he now?"

"I believe your mother received him."

Aikaterina let her breath escape in a hiss. Her mother had no idea what sort of snake Casca was, and Aikaterina suddenly doubted whether she would be able to handle him. What might Casca do, or say, to her?

"It is almost time for dinner," Nenet said. "I believe your mother arranged a *deipnon* for our imperial guest."

"Very well," Aikaterina said, suppressing a surge of irritation that her opinion had not been consulted on the matter. "Then we have work to do."

A short while later, Aikaterina stepped into the *triclinium*. Her mother had requested an intimate dinner, with just Casca and his chief officers, and a few select noble families of Alexandria. The smell of roasted meats, fish in creamy sauces, and hot bread filled the room, and servants with pitchers of wine and trays of dates and aged cheeses made the rounds, refilling plates and goblets wherever needed. Lamps and torches glimmered everywhere, so that the whole room seemed drenched in languid golden light.

Aikaterina lifted her chin and waited just inside the doorway to make her entrance. Nenet had piled her dark hair high and studded it with blue and white gems. She wore twisted golden arm bands adorned with matching gems high on her bare arms, and her simple white chiton and *palla* were set off by a belt of twisted gold.

Casca sat next to her mother, pulling apart a piece of bread and laughing insipidly at whatever she had said. And then, as he turned to take a handful of dates from a passing tray, his eyes caught hers.

Aikaterina felt a surge of satisfaction as he fumbled the dates. They cascaded onto the table with a series of dull plunks and rolled onto the floor. As Casca rose awkwardly from his seat, everyone followed his gaze to see what had called his attention.

"Ah," said one of the noblemen nearest to her. He was Petillius Tiberius, a Senator and a kind man who was a dear friend to her father—almost an uncle to Aikaterina. "My dear Aikaterina, what a joy to see you."

"Here," Casca said, finally finding his voice. He indicated the empty seat on his left. "There is a place for you here, *domina*."

Aikaterina lifted a brow. As if Casca had any right to dictate where she sat at her own table. Without a word to him, she swept past him, head high and shoulders thrown back, and seated herself, as if it were the most natural thing in the world, in her father's own place of honor.

As she sat, she heard one of the ladies whisper, "She looks like an empress."

And that, she thought as she smiled across the table at Casca, *is precisely the point.*

As the servants poured Aikaterina a goblet of wine and

offered her food, her mother leaned forward and said, "The Tribune was just telling me how much time you spent together in Rome when you went abroad. I didn't know that you were acquainted!"

Aikaterina sipped her wine, regarding Casca thoughtfully. Her mother apparently had not been able to smell the snake behind Casca's easy politeness. She likely saw Casca as a possible ally, whose good opinion of Alexandria could somehow influence the Emperor.

"It's true," Aikaterina said. She looked up at Casca. "I'm sure I didn't expect to see you in Alexandria. Do your duties not keep you close to the Emperor?"

Casca's mouth settled in a thin line for just a moment, and Aikaterina knew she had struck a nerve there. "I have many duties," he said. "And you know how much Alexandria is in the Divine *Imperator*'s care."

"Our dear *Imperator*," her mother said, with a carefully neutral glance at Aikaterina. "He shows us such concern. Did he send you to look after us and make sure that the city is stable and peaceful?"

Casca glanced at Aikaterina's mother, a frown creasing his forehead. "Should he have cause for concern?"

Aikaterina stiffened.

Her mother faltered and said, "Well, with my husband…"

Casca's frown deepened. Before Aikaterina's mother could finish speaking, he turned to Aikaterina and asked in a low voice, "Did something happen to your father? I'd heard he was ill, but—"

Aikaterina tilted her head. There was something odd in his voice. If she didn't know him better, she would have thought it was genuine concern. But it was Casca…and it couldn't be.

"My father has relapsed into his illness," she said simply.

"But when did this happen?" he asked. "Why was no word sent to Nicomedia?"

"It was very sudden," said her mother. "We all thought he was on the verge of recovery." She darted a glance at Aikaterina and went on, "Of course, you know that Aikaterina holds herself very capable in managing affairs during his illness."

"I'll drink to that!" cried Petillius Tiberius from the other end of the table. "Without *domina* Aikaterina's steady hand to the reins, the chariot would have wrecked at the turning post."

All of the Alexandrian nobles raised their goblets to her with smiles and murmurs of commendation, and Aikaterina felt a warm flush spread into her cheeks. For much of the last year, she had done what she thought she must, spending hours away from her beloved library in council with her father's many advisors. Alexandria's operations were so much more complex than she had ever imagined, and she understood now, far better than she had when they had traveled to Nicomedia, how valuable it was to the Empire.

After they drank her health, Casca regarded Aikaterina with a guarded smile.

"Well," he said, "you have done well for yourself."

"I'm sure I don't know what you mean," Aikaterina said. "Everything I have done has been for Alexandria, and for my father."

"And for Rome, of course," Casca supplied.

Aikaterina held his gaze and said nothing. Casca's careful smile faded as she remained silent.

"Of course, for Rome also," her mother said, sounding anxious.

"Oh," Casca said, with an airy wave of his hand, "I know very well how much Rome means to her, and how much she would be willing to give for its sake."

Careful, Aikaterina told herself as she nibbled a date. *You are dancing once more with a serpent.*

"You see, Mother," she said. "True loyalty never goes unnoticed."

Casca snapped his fingers. "That is absolutely right, *domina*. We have just come from Cyrene, and that was a terrible business." He shook his head. "Such a pity. I know the *Imperator* had such hopes for Lucius Titianus, but some can govern with a steady and loyal hand, and some, it seems cannot."

"A pity," Aikaterina echoed. She made sure her voice was loud enough to carry. "I've heard rumors, of course, but no official report. What happened? Was there a trial?"

Casca's face shifted just slightly. "Roman justice was duly served," he said.

Aikaterina nodded as she swept her gaze around the table. "It is as I always tell my people," she said. "So long as Rome is just, there is nothing to fear." She lifted her goblet, and the Alexandrian nobles joined her. "As long as justice reigns, so long may Rome stand."

They pledged once more and Aikaterina set down her goblet. "So," she said sweetly, leaning forward and lowering her voice to keep their conversation once more private, "what really brings you here to Alexandria, Tribune?"

"I should think you would have guessed that by now," Casca said, just as softly. He touched her hand, resting on the table, and smiled at her. "I'm looking for the one who got away."

Aikaterina clamped down every impulse within her that wanted to snatch her hand away or shudder at the heat of his touch. He withdrew his hand, his eyes never leaving her face.

"You know whom I mean, of course," he added.

"After two years? I should think you'd have given up that hunt by now," Aikaterina answered. "He is serving out his exile, just as you wished."

Casca chuckled. "Oh, that was not my wish. Not at all. That was due to the meddling of your uncle Constantinus. But that's no matter just now. And you mistake me—that's not who I meant at all. I meant another."

Aikaterina shook her head at him. "It really is appalling," she said, chiding, "how you seem to lose people. I wonder if Diocletian knows what actions you took in Cyrene? Did you dispatch a message? Who did you set up in Lucius Titianus's place?"

"That was already arranged," Casca said. "Don't pretend to play innocent with me, and don't you dare think you can imply that I took action without Diocletian's express approval."

Aikaterina regarded him steadily. "I'm sure the way you arranged that transfer of power was exactly what he had in mind."

Casca drew back, looking almost exactly like a snake readying itself to strike. "And how would you know anything about that if you didn't also have what I am looking for?"

"You perhaps forget where you are," Aikaterina said. "My father is the *Praefectus Augustalis*. Do you honestly think anything happens in this region that we do not know about?"

"I think you are misleading me. If I called your advisors to me right now and questioned them, I would lay a handsome wager that not a single one of them knows what happened in Cyrene. Perhaps the *domina* has forgotten her geography, for the last time I looked, the reach of Egypt did not extend quite so far as Libya." His eyes narrowed. "And did you not say yourself you had only heard rumors?"

Aikaterina didn't dare move for fear that she would give herself away. He had her there, and she didn't dare push him further in that direction. She had to be more careful.

"So this is why you have come here?" she asked. "What does it possibly serve you to pursue this one who got away?"

"Oh, Aikaterina," Casca said, chuckling. "I'm really almost offended. I thought you understood me better than that." He tapped a finger against his chin. "No. You will tell me what I want to know, or I will make it very unpleasant for you. I will. You know I can."

Aikaterina leaned toward him and gestured discreetly at the assembled nobles with her goblet. "I should be very careful with making threats if I were you," she said. "If Diocletian found out that your personal scores were responsible for division between Alexandria and the Empire, I think you might find yourself headed for the untamed places of the world…or worse."

Casca smiled at her, and her stomach curdled. "Once again," he murmured, "you underestimate me. I would never be so foolish as all that."

Aikaterina straightened in her chair. He had gotten cleverer since the last time they had met, and that was unsettling. Either that, or the heavy cares of her father's illness and ruling the city by proxy had slowed her wits.

"And fortunately," Casca continued, his voice like a serpent's hiss, "right now, my interests and those of the Empire line up exactly."

"And what will happen, I wonder," she said, "when they no longer do?"

A courtier Aikaterina could not name approached before Casca could answer, bowing low to Aikaterina and excusing himself from the feast. Aikaterina glanced around in surprise, realizing that many of the guests had already retired, and the small crowd in the *triclinium* was slowly dwindling. Casca took his cue, rising from his seat and clasping her hand as he gave her an elegant bow.

"Tomorrow, you will have to show me your fair city," he said. "I have never been here before."

Aikaterina withdrew her hand and inclined her head. "Goodnight, Tribune," she said.

As soon as he had disappeared from the hall, she rose and bade a goodnight to the rest of her guests. Then, shaking with anger and nervous energy, she strode down the long corridors to her own *cubiculum*. Once within the safety of the chamber, she stood a long while in the middle of the floor, in a patch of patterned moonlight, hands clenched and head bowed.

"Deliver me out of the hands of my enemies," she whispered, "and them that persecute me. Make Your face to shine upon Your servant, save me in Your mercy."

50

Augusta Treverorum, Germania — October, A.D. 302

As autumn peaked and began to shift toward winter, Constantinus's cohort and the *cataphractarii* made an end to their campaigning season, dismantled the *castra aestiva*, and retreated to the permanent fortress at Augusta Treverorum. The daily routine of briefings, training, and drills gradually gave way to a more relaxed pace of life, and Jurian found his thoughts drifting to the south more and more often. He longed for the day when he could send one last letter to Sabra, inviting her to come north to Britannia, to join him there.

Soon, he told himself, one evening as he and Agapius were returning to the fortress. *Soon this exile will be over.*

They entered the vestibule just behind a man wearing the badge of an imperial courier, who was moving almost at a run. Jurian and Agapius exchanged a brief glance, and of one accord they turned their steps to follow the messenger. They almost lost him in the winding corridors, but then Jurian saw him stop in front of Constantius Chlorus's *tablinum*, where he was instantly admitted. A few moments later, he emerged, stumbling a little as he came into the corridor. He almost smiled at them as he passed, and Jurian caught his arm.

"What news?" he said.

"That's for the *Caesar*," he said. "Trouble in the South."

"What kind of trouble?"

The messenger shrugged off Jurian's grip. "My message wasn't for you, was it?"

Jurian stood aside and let the courier pass, then jerked his head toward the *tablinum*. There was a low murmur of voices inside the chamber, and Jurian hesitated just a moment before rapping cautiously on the door.

"Come!" bellowed Constantius Chlorus.

Jurian opened the door and saw Constantinus standing next to his father's desk. He swung to face Jurian, and Jurian froze. He hadn't seen a look like that on the Tribune's face since Varro's trial.

"What is it?" he asked. "Constantinus?"

Constantinus left the desk, making his way slowly toward Jurian, while Jurian felt all the blood in his heart turn to ice.

"Jurian," Constantinus said, laying a hand on his shoulder. "Jurian...it's Cyrene."

Jurian's breath caught in his throat, and for a moment, everything in the room seemed to darken. Agapius came beside him and gripped his other shoulder tight.

"What happened in Cyrene?" Agapius asked.

"There was a change in power," Constantius Chlorus said.

Constantinus's mouth twitched, but his gaze never left Jurian's face. "He deserves to know the truth, *Caesar*," he said. "Lucius Titianus was murdered in the public square, Jurian, along with one Theodorus, reported to be a Christian *episcopus*." He stopped, face ashen, then finished, "Three women were also publicly killed."

"No," Jurian gasped. "No...no..."

He staggered a step. Vaguely he saw Constantius Chlorus rise from his chair.

"I'm so sorry, Jurian. The reports are vague, but...at least two witnesses say that one was the governor's daughter. The official report I have just received confirms it."

Jurian stumbled, leaning heavily on the desk. Rage and grief flared through him like wildfire, clouding his vision. Agapius tried to clasp his arm but Jurian shook him off. A voice roared with a fury that shattered the sudden silence—his own. He barely recognized it.

"No!" he gritted. Every muscle in his body was taut, tense, strained to the point of breaking. "It wasn't her! It can't—it wasn't—"

Constantinus lowered his gaze and said nothing.

"Jurian," Agapius said gently.

"It wasn't her!" He slammed his fists against the desk so hard that the wood cracked. "You know the truth!" he shouted. "Tell them it wasn't her!"

Constantius Chlorus shook his head once, and Jurian reeled back, breathing hard. Nothing around him made sense. He heard Agapius say something, but he couldn't figure out what the words were. His hand was on the hilt of his *seax*, and before he knew what he was doing, the knife was in his hand.

Someone called his name—he didn't know who. He didn't care. With a terrible cry, he slammed the knife through the parchment on the *Caesar*'s desk.

"Jurian!" shouted Constantinus, and Jurian came back to himself with a rush.

He stumbled a step back. "Who?" he mumbled. "Who was it?" He saw Constantinus's eyes flicker at Agapius, and he pushed away from his friend. "Tell me!"

"Dignianus, now governor," Constantinus said. "And Marcus Valerius Casca."

Jurian just stood there, shaking from head to foot.

He knew it.

Constantinus glanced again at Agapius, and then at his father, who cleared his throat. Constantinus dislodged Jurian's knife from the wood of the desk and handed it back to him, hilt first.

"Everything I have, he has taken from me," Jurian said quietly, turning the knife over in his hand, pondering its cruel edge. Then he looked straight at Constantinus and said, "I'm going to kill him."

"No," Agapius said, gripping his arm. "That's grief talking, and wrath."

Jurian rounded on him but Agapius stood his ground. "The blood of my mother, my sister, and my beloved is on that man's hands," he said, his voice shaking. "Why should I not take his life?" He shook off Agapius's hand. "I ride for Nicomedia. If I know anything about that snake, he won't be far from the Emperor's knees."

He turned to leave but Constantinus stepped between him and the door.

"Get out of my way," Jurian said in a low voice. "You of all people should understand. If you hadn't stopped me…she would have been safe! *She would have been safe!*"

"If you return now, your life is forfeit," he said. "Think, Jurian. She's dead. There's nothing—"

Jurian grabbed him by the tunic and drove him back. "Don't say that!" he shouted. "Don't you say that." He released him with a shove. "If my life is forfeit, then let it be forfeit."

He pushed past the Tribune and hauled open the heavy door. Behind him, Constantinus said, "You will throw away your life for nothing, Jurian," he said. "Is that what she would want?"

Jurian glanced at Constantinus and Agapius over his shoulder, feeling a cold heaviness settle its weight in his stomach.

"She's dead," he said. "And I will make him pay."

51

Alexandria, Aegyptus — October, a.d. 302

"If I may be so bold," Nenet said, "I am heartily sick of the sight of that Tribune. What is he still doing here?"

Aikaterina closed her eyes and leaned her head in her hands, earning her a half-hearted rebuke from Nenet, who was trying to comb out her hair.

"My thoughts precisely," she muttered. "He just won't...*go*. And I don't trust him lurking about the palace, or his soldiers wandering my streets. God only knows what spies he's drawing into his service." She sighed heavily. "He's clever, Nenet."

"Not as clever as you are."

"I appreciate your confidence in me," Aikaterina said, with a bitter smile. "But I think he knows that Sabra is here, and he is prepared to go to extreme lengths to find her. I'm not sure I can keep her safe. Every time I see Casca I am afraid he will tell me that he's found her. But I don't know where to send her."

Nenet said nothing, but the swift movement of her hands through Aikaterina's hair was strangely calming. As her thick curls came down, Aikaterina traced a pattern on the coverlet. Circles within circles.

Suddenly, she sat up so abruptly that the little tray of jeweled hairpins tumbled off the bed.

"*Kyria!*" Nenet said in exasperation.

"I have an idea," Aikaterina said. "I just need to find some way...some pretext for getting him called back to Diocletian's court. If he's summoned away, he can't be here sniffing around for Sabra!"

"But how will you manage that, *kyria?*" Nenet asked. "Every day that passes it's more dangerous that he is here!"

"Perhaps I should send Sabra back to Myra. I doubt Casca would ever think of going there."

"But that would require you sending word to her, and somehow smuggling her out of the port. And if Casca has as many spies about as you imagine..."

Aikaterina blew out her breath in frustration, shoulders slumping. Everything seemed so clear in her mind, but as soon as she tried to arrange the details, it all fell apart. Perhaps, she thought, Diodoros would be able to help her think clearly.

Once Nenet had finished with her hair and helped her change into fresh clothes, Aikaterina headed out to the gardens to see if Casca was lurking there, waiting for her. She had almost reached the reflecting pool when she caught sight of two figures on the path, and she slipped instinctively behind a tree. One was Casca, which she had expected, but the other was her mother, which she had not. Casca was walking slowly beside her, his head bent attentively toward her. Her mother's hands moved earnestly, as if making a case for something she felt passionate about.

As they rounded the corner of the pool and began making their way toward her, Aikaterina retreated further into the shadow of the tree.

"She is stubborn on the matter, though," her mother was saying. "And her father never insisted. Does Diocletian have anyone in mind? She is of age, and Alexandria is no small enticement, but she will have none of the usual suitors. She once told me she will only consider marrying a man who is her equal in all things. And I was at my wit's end trying to find one."

Aikaterina frowned. Her mother had, for months now,

given up trying to persuade Aikaterina to enter a marriage, but now the tables had turned, and it wasn't her mother seeking to settle her future, but Diocletian himself. Just as he had warned.

Was that why Casca was in Alexandria? Had Diocletian tried to turn him matchmaker? The notion would have made Aikaterina laugh if Casca had been anyone else. But Casca, she realized suddenly, would find a way to use this as his leverage point, and his knowledge—or suspicion—of her faith made the situation that much more dangerous for her.

"She is enticement enough on her own, I promise you," Casca said, with a warmth that unsettled Aikaterina strangely. "But Alexandria, as I do not have to tell you, is the jewel of the eastern Empire, and it will make the Divine *Imperator* very happy to have it more securely bound."

"She does her best," Aikaterina's mother said, and there was a plaintive note in her voice. "I only fear what the people might do to her, if they ever begin to doubt the strength of her rule."

"I understand perfectly," Casca said, then turned to her with a slight bow. "But now, if you will excuse me, I do have other pressing matters to attend."

Aikaterina's mother inclined her head to him and then swept back into the palace. Aikaterina just glimpsed her face as she turned away—there was fear in her eyes, and a sick look like she had just committed some kind of treachery.

Casca linked his fingers behind his back and paced thoughtfully around the reflecting pool. He didn't look particularly busy, as he had claimed. Aikaterina waited, frozen and hardly daring to breathe, to see what would happen next.

She didn't have to wait long. Only moments later, one of Casca's men approached at a run. He stopped, breathless, and saluted Casca.

"Well?" Casca said.

"We found him," the soldier said. "And if he's here, she's bound to be here somewhere."

Aikaterina placed a hand on the tree trunk. Her pulse galloped in panic, sending the world reeling around her.

No, she thought. *Hanno...*

Casca nodded once. "Hold him in custody and wait for me," he said. "You can make him uncomfortable, but keep him alive. I want to question him myself."

52

Aegyptus, Africa — October, A.D. 302

Sabra sat in a pool of crisp sunshine beneath the wall of the large tomb, watching the other women weave baskets out of rushes. The lynx slept nearby—so close that if she stretched out her arm, she could touch its fur. But peaceful as the animal seemed, Sabra still eyed it with distrust, and hardly dared to move for fear of disturbing it. Instead she closed her eyes and let the warmth of the sunlight drive back the briskness of the morning air. Even though she was still surrounded by the houses of the dead, somehow being out in the sunlight made her feel the chill of death a little less. But she was restless, and nothing she did could settle the turmoil in her mind.

Already this morning she had formed and discarded seven different plans for what she should do next. She thought about returning to Cyrene, where she was sure Dignianus was hunting down each and every member of her little community of Christians. How long could they stay hidden? Sooner or later they would have to leave the labyrinth, and what then?

She thought she could lead them to the necropolis, where they would be safe. Or, rather, since *Amma* Synkletika had made clear that sanctuary was not their mission, she could set up her own community. From what Aikaterina had told her, there was a section of the city where the Hebrew people kept to themselves and lived in peace. Perhaps in Alexandria they could build a community of Christians, tolerated by such a ruler as Aikaterina.

But she had quickly dismissed that thought as well. If Casca wasn't in Alexandria already, he would be soon. And Aikaterina had her own set of troubles burdening her, with Alexandria itself tottering from instability.

And then Sabra had thought about the Magdalene, and how she had faithfully followed the Savior in all His earthly wanderings, and she had tried to come up with a plan to follow Jurian beyond the *limes* of Britannia. Perhaps the man in Myra was right, and she should have gone with him from the beginning. But in all of her other adventures, she'd had Hanno with her. She had never attempted anything like this alone, and she didn't know if she had the courage to try now. If only she could get word to him in the palace...perhaps it was not impossible.

She plucked at a scrubby plant near her foot and sighed. The lynx's ear twitched, and she inched a bit further away from it. And then, suddenly, the cat lifted its head. It blinked its tawny eyes once at her, then it leapt to the top of the wall, where it sat with its tail curled around its paws. A moment later, a young woman in a dark chiton and *palla* came hurrying through the tombs.

"*Amma!*" she cried. "Someone is coming."

Instantly, all work in the courtyard stopped. The *monachi* gathered their things and scattered, disappearing into the houses of the dead like ghosts. Sabra got to her feet and touched the young woman's arm.

"Who is it?" she asked. "Who is coming?"

Then she heard it: the steady pounding of the hooves of a troop of horsemen. She met the girl's frightened gaze as *Amma* Synkletika approached them with Theokleia by her side.

"Go inside, daughters," she said. "We will watch and see what happens."

The young woman took Sabra by the hand and pulled her into the deep shadows of the tomb. She tried to pull Sabra down the curved staircase with her, but Sabra shook her head. The girl finally gave up, leaving her in the darkness inside the doorway and hurrying into the catacombs alone.

From her vantage point, Sabra watched Theokleia and Synkletika slip into the maw of one of the other tombs. The courtyard was silent and empty now, save for the watchful lynx. The wind caught the dust off the stone and eddied it into little drifts against the sides of the tombs.

A moment later, the horsemen came into view. A man dressed in Legion armor rode at their head, and already he was staring up at the tomb where she was hiding—the largest of the tombs in the necropolis. The horses seemed nervous in this place, troubled by the scent of death. They tossed their heads, their legs in constant motion.

The man drew his horse to a halt and dismounted, tossing his reins to another *miles*. As he scanned the courtyard, his gaze caught in surprise on the lynx, who watched them with unblinking eyes.

"What are we doing here?" the *miles* asked.

His commander crouched suddenly and picked up a sliver of a rush off the bare stone. He turned it over in his fingers, then slowly stood, staring intently in the direction of the large tomb.

"Why should we look for the living among the houses of the dead?" the *miles* continued.

"Shut up," the commander snapped. "We aren't alone."

The soldiers backed their horses at this, many of them casting a sign to ward away evil. Several of them spotted the lynx and one drew his *spatha*.

"Put that away," the commander ordered.

"Let's get out of here," muttered the *miles*. "This is no place for us to be."

His commander ignored him and swung back into the saddle. "I have seen what I need to see," he said.

He spurred his horse and the troop followed him back

up the rocky path. As soon as the sound of hoofbeats faded, Theokleia and Synkletika emerged from their place of hiding. Sabra left the tomb to meet them, her palms slick with sweat.

"I cannot stay here," she said. "I have put you all in danger." She clenched her hands into fists. "It is exactly what I feared would happen!"

"What makes you think they were here for you?" Synkletika asked. "Do you think this is the first time soldiers have come here?"

Sabra frowned. "Isn't it?"

"No."

"But this is different," Sabra said. "Aikaterina told you I was in danger. They must be searching for me. And they will slaughter all of you to get to me."

This made Synkletika smile. "We live among the dead," she said. "Do you think we fear to join them?"

Sabra shuddered, thinking of Theokleia's joy at the thought of her own death. All she could see was the *agora* in Cyrene, and the stones of the dais soaked in blood.

"You don't understand," she said. "Please, *Amma*...you must let me go."

"I do not hold you here," she said.

"If they were here for you, how did they know to come here looking for you?" Theokleia asked.

Sabra glanced at her, and then the question hit her. How indeed, unless they had found out from someone who knew she had come here? Aikaterina, she was certain, would die rather than betray her.

A sudden, horrible gnawing fear spread through her, and the vision of blood in the burial niche edged into her memory.

"Oh," she breathed, "no...no..." She turned to *Amma* Synkletika. "I have to get to the city. I must go—I must—"

"And what will you do there?" Theokleia asked.

"What I must," Sabra said sharply. "What I should have had the courage to do in Cyrene. I will not have more blood on my hands...not if I can prevent it this time."

Theokleia caught Sabra's arm, her grip astonishingly strong. "Walk the path of the Magdalene," she said.

The lynx rose to its feet, and all three women riveted on it.

"Are they coming back?" Sabra asked. "Oh, God, please…"

But then Diodoros, covered with dust and looking ashen, rounded the tomb and pelted into the courtyard. As soon as she saw him, Sabra's strength abandoned her, and only Theokleia's arm around her waist kept her standing. If he was standing here, then…

"*Kyria,*" he said to Sabra.

His voice was taut with anguish, and Theokleia stepped closer to Sabra to support her weight.

"I'm…I'm so sorry," Diodoros said.

Sabra's breath caught in a sob. "Hanno…?" she whispered.

She could barely say his name. If she said it, if she said his name, it would make her fears true… Hot tears spilled down her cheeks, grief knife-sharp in her heart. She clung to Theokleia, shaking uncontrollably.

"No, God, please…please don't let this be happening…"

"My lady sent me," Diodoros managed. "I'm so sorry… someone identified him…"

"But he's alive…he's only imprisoned, isn't he?"

He only looked at her, lips pressed in a thin line, and then he gave the faintest shake of his head.

Sabra collapsed on the rocks. "Hanno! What did they do to you?" she wept.

"Is that how the soldiers knew?" someone asked—she couldn't tell who.

"No!" she cried, the word broken like shards of clay, but her heart tremored with fear, with horror. Was it true? Could it possibly be true? "Oh, no," she whispered, her throat on fire. "How they must have hurt you to make you give me away… You would never…you would…" She balled her hands into fists and pounded the stones until they cut into her skin and drew blood. "You never deserved this! You never deserved any of it! My sins…my sins made this happen! My sins…" She leaned forward. Her whole world rocked beneath her like a ship tossed in a storm.

Theokleia crouched beside her and laid a hand on her back. "God will bring all things to good," she said gently.

Sabra scrambled away from her. "Don't!" she cried through a fury of tears. "Don't you dare speak to me of the good! What good can ever come of death? Death begets only death!"

Theokleia sat back on her heels, and one slow tear trickled down her cheek. Sabra scrambled to her feet, her breast heaving.

"I have to go to him," she said wildly. "You! Take me. Take me to him."

"*Kyria*, you can't."

Sabra rounded on him. "Why not? I must! He would do the same for me! Take me to him!"

Diodoros took her hands in his and gripped them tight. "*Kyria*," he said. "There is nothing left."

For a moment, the words made no sense. Then, with a strangled cry, Sabra reeled away from him. She dug her hands into her hair, her nails digging into her scalp. Her stomach heaved and she staggered a few paces before she fell to her knees. Vaguely, she heard Synkletika calling for someone to bring water mixed with wine.

"Hanno," she whispered. The rough stones cut into her hands. "Oh, Hanno…Hanno…."

A great emptiness opened within her, and she folded herself like a child and wept.

53

Alexandria, Aegyptus — October, A.D. 302

"On whose authority did you do these things?" Aikaterina asked.

The guard shuffled his feet in the sand of the prison yard. The bright morning sun beat down on them with a ferocious intensity, unnaturally warm in the late autumn month, and there wasn't even the ghost of a breeze. Sweat beaded on the man's forehead and trickled slowly down his nose, but he apparently didn't dare reach up to swipe it away.

Just behind Aikaterina's right shoulder, her personal *lictor* Kleitos folded his arms across his chest. He was a massive man, with corded arms that looked like they could snap a man in half. He had been her father's most trusted attendant for as long as she could remember, and now that Agapius had gone with Jurian, Aikaterina had asked him to serve her in his stead.

The guard watched Kleitos nervously for a moment, and then dropped his gaze once more to the sand.

Aikaterina scanned the courtyard. Save for the three of them, it was empty and unnaturally quiet. And then she caught sight of a charred stump, half-buried in the freshly raked sand in the center of the yard. Her chest tightened until she could hardly breathe, and memories of the *agora* in the city swarmed behind her eyes. She lifted a finger and pointed.

"What is that?"

The guard shifted again and Aikaterina took a step forward. Kleitos laid a hand on her shoulder to stop her.

"You do not need to do this, *kyria*," he said. "I will do this."

At that, the guard backed in a panic, but not fast enough. Kleitos stepped around Aikaterina and seized the man's tunic, his other hand knotted, ready to strike. The guard wilted and snatched desperately at Kleitos's arm.

"No! Please!" he gasped. "Please!"

"Tell my mistress what she wants to know, or you won't have teeth left in your head to chew your meat."

Kleitos dropped the man roughly and he sprawled a moment in the sand before scrambling to his knees before Aikaterina. She folded her arms and held herself tightly against the rising tide of grief and fear.

"They brought him here—he wouldn't answer them. They kept asking about a woman. Said she had escaped? He wouldn't tell them. They tortured—"

Aikaterina's mouth went dry and she closed her eyes. The guard stopped abruptly. For a moment, it was all she could do to keep from vomiting. As soon as she thought she could speak, she opened her eyes again.

"And," she said, her voice acid, "did they succeed?"

The guard stared at her. He was breathing hard, and Aikaterina couldn't make sense of the tumult of emotion behind his eyes.

"No," he whispered at last. "He...never broke. No matter what they did."

"I know what you did." She pointed again at the charred stump. "On whose authority did you do such a thing?" she asked again, but her voice was little more than a whisper.

"The *Tribunus* who arrived from Cyrene."

"We do not allow such tortures here," Aikaterina said. "To burn a man alive. How could you dare obey such an order?"

The guard's brow wrinkled. "He said it had been approved

at the highest levels," he said. "And he said that the house of Alexandria stood united with Rome in expunging traitors and blasphemers, like when we purged out the followers of Mani. Could I argue with him? Could I…"

Aikaterina turned away from him and stalked from the courtyard. Behind her, she heard Kleitos order the man to get up and return to his duties, and then his long, quick strides brought him beside her before she'd reached the gate.

"Is that all you needed to know?" he asked.

"Yes."

They left the prison and Aikaterina stepped into the waiting litter. Kleitos drew the linen curtains for her, and then walked beside the litter in silence as they made their way back to the palace.

In the shadows of the *lectica*, Aikaterina clenched her hands and shook with an anger and grief she had not felt since Varro's execution. But this was different. This had happened within her own city walls. And Hanno had been under her personal protection as part of her household. Hanno, who loved Sabra so dearly, whom Sabra loved more than any other person, save one… How could Casca embrace, sanction, require that much pain?

And how could he dare be so bold as to usurp her authority?

This was a side of Casca she had never seen before. In Rome, he had worked by subterfuge, laying traps and snaring even the Emperors into doing his bloody work for him. But not now. From what Diodoros had told her, he had swept into Cyrene in much the same way as he had here. He had used the tool Dignianus to supplant Lucius Titianus, but Diodoros had told her, in words broken by horror, that Casca personally had blood on his hands from that night's work.

And now, here in Alexandria, he was borrowing torments from the days of Nero.

What is he becoming? she wondered. The thought of seeing him at the palace made her stomach clench like a fist. She didn't understand him. She had never understood him.

Was he testing her? If she protested his treatment of Hanno, would he report to Diocletian that Alexandria was now sympathetic to the Christian cause? She shuddered as she remembered the bloody days of Diocletian's purge of the Manichaeans. His siege of the city after the uprising of Domitianus. Both events were burned in her memory like a nightmare. She could not subject her people to such horrors again.

Since her father's illness, she had managed to maintain order in the city and she had the love of her people on her side. But none of that mattered to these cruel men, who could see nothing beyond the edges of their own ambition. She was a woman, and hardly more than a girl. Her experience with Diocletian in Nicomedia had taught her that, as amusing as he found her impudence, he would never tolerate her independence.

She rubbed her icy hands over her flaming cheeks. Her eyes burned with tears she could not shed. She felt the jaws of a trap closing around her, inexorable as death. If she said anything about Hanno's execution, she would endanger not just herself, but her entire city. She would give Casca all the evidence he needed to leverage against her…and she knew what choice she would be given.

And if she did nothing?

She shivered and her teeth chattered, even though the air within the litter was pleasantly warm.

She could not do nothing.

She dug her nails against her palms as anger burned out her fear. *If Father were himself and whole*, she thought, *he would have Casca executed in the public square for usurping his authority.*

But then she remembered how unhappy he had been in Nicomedia, how endlessly worried. He feared the displeasure of the *Imperator* Diocletian, and with good reason. If Casca were here as the official arbiter of Nicomedia, her hands were tied even more tightly than before.

She squeezed her eyes shut and drew in a deep breath, trying to soothe her hammering heart with the words of the

Scriptures. *Strengthen me, O Lord God of Israel, and in this hour look on the works of my hands.*

A breeze stirred the curtains, and she opened her eyes.

I must go carefully, she thought, *but perhaps there is still something I can do.*

THE LITTER CAME TO a stop, and Kleitos helped Aikaterina disembark. She almost ran up the steps and strode into the palace like a fury, and the servants who encountered her stepped aside and flattened themselves against the wall. She caught the look in one young woman's face—something of a mix between awe and fear.

Let them be afraid, Aikaterina thought, clenching her jaw.

She glanced in the rooms she passed, but she didn't see what she was looking for. Finally, as she stepped out into the peristyle, she saw him.

Casca stood at the far end of the long reflecting pool, speaking in a low voice to two of his soldiers. Aikaterina closed her eyes for a moment, reaching for God in a moment's silent prayer, and then made straight for him.

She was halfway across the peristyle when he dismissed his soldiers and turned to face her.

For a moment he seemed to catch himself, the color staining his cheeks a brilliant crimson, but in the next breath he had wrestled himself under control.

"*Domina* Aikaterina," he murmured, sweeping her a low bow. "You honor me this morning."

Aikaterina stopped a few paces from him. A warm breeze lifted, stirring the water in the pool into gentle ripples, fluttering the edges of her *palla*.

"How could you?" she said softly.

Casca's mouth opened, but no sound came out.

"Casca," she said. "How could you do such a thing?"

"I…I don't know," he said. His hand reached for hers and then he checked himself. "Perhaps, *domina*, you could clarify… What have I done?"

Aikaterina turned away, letting tears spill over her lashes.

"You have no idea," she said, "what I have been through. My father..."

"Yes. I am so sorry," Casca said, too quickly.

Aikaterina glanced at him over her shoulder. "Are you? Are you really? Because now I think perhaps you have come here with no other purpose than to wound me."

Casca's mouth opened again as he struggled for words. She could see that he wanted desperately to deny it...and she knew he couldn't and tell the truth. She shook her head at his silence. Casca had never shied away from a lie before.

"You see?" she said. "I am right."

Casca took a step towards her. "I am only here to see justice done," he said. "I serve the Empire."

"So I well remember."

"There is another way," he said. "It doesn't have to be pain."

Aikaterina took a small step toward him. "But you always make sure there is pain," she said. "No matter what I do...or what I say. It would never be enough for you, would it?"

Casca looked for all the world like a man adrift on the ocean, and Aikaterina felt a small thrill of triumph. She might not be able to execute him in the public square for what he had done, but she could make him wretched...and she could make him leave.

"It would," he managed. He took another step toward her, and again almost reached for her hand. "If you only knew..." He struggled with himself for a moment, and then said, "I don't understand you."

Aikaterina tilted her head. "Perhaps, Tribune, you could clarify. What puzzles you?"

"Before...in Rome. You were..." He stopped, fumbling for words. "You were my enemy."

"And whose choice was that?"

He looked even farther adrift than before. "The company you chose to keep...enemies of Rome...and..."

My enemies, she could almost hear him think.

Aikaterina turned to walk slowly down the length of the pool, and after a moment she heard Casca following behind her.

Careful, she told herself. *Careful*.

"You didn't even know me," she said. She turned, opening her arms. "This is the only world I have ever known. And I have seen the price of rebellion against Rome. Perhaps you do not know your history."

"I know enough." Casca stopped a few paces from her.

"Do you? How can you know what it is like to see the lifeblood squeezed out of your city?" she said, lowering her arms to her sides. She let tears fill her eyes again. "To see innocent men and women and children paying the price for one man's disgusting lust for power."

Casca flinched.

Almost, Aikaterina thought.

"Casca," she said, taking a step closer to him. "Do you really think that is what I want for my people?"

"I don't...understand," he said. "I thought..."

"You thought what?"

He cast about desperately for the words. "You harbor enemies of Rome," he faltered. "That man I...*we* executed. He was an escaped criminal."

She caught his gaze and held it. "Oh, Casca," she said with a little sigh. "What would displease the *Imperator* more, I wonder? Failing to capture, torture, and execute a eunuch and a woman? Or causing civil unrest and riots against the Empire in Alexandria?"

Casca caught himself. "What?"

Aikaterina reached out and touched his hand. He started as if lightning had suddenly lanced through his veins.

"You really should have asked me first," she said softly, and stepped back.

At that moment, a soldier came running and saluted Casca. "*Tribunus*, there is a mob outside the prison. If we don't do something, and quickly—"

Casca's gaze slowly tracked from the soldier to Aikaterina's face. "What have you done?" he asked, his voice low.

Aikaterina ignored him and addressed the soldier. "He is not in charge here, *miles*. Call my *lectica*. At once."

The soldier saluted her and raced to obey. Casca's hands twisted in the folds of his tunic.

"You set this up," he said.

Aikaterina drew herself up. The top of her head almost reached Casca's shoulder, and she wished—as she had so many times before—that she could have a stature as imposing as Helena's, or even Nenet's. But something in her bearing seemed to affect him.

"There are consequences to choices," she said. "Word spreads fast in Africa, *Tribunus*, and my people do not take well to brutality…even if it is sanctioned by Nicomedia." She turned away from him and headed for the palace. When he did not follow immediately, she glanced over her shoulder. "You really should come," she said. "If you want Alexandria to see how united we are in these matters."

She left him standing there speechless, but she had barely passed the threshold into the palace when she heard his running footsteps behind her. She never paused to acknowledge him, but swept through palace, the slaves scattering around her as she passed.

Kleitos met her at the bottom of the palace steps and handed her silently into the litter. As he stepped back Aikaterina let the curtain fall into place, and then, bitterly, she smiled.

THE GATHERING MOB HAD already filled the street to overflowing, and Aikaterina could feel the *lectica* slowing down as its bearers and Casca's cohort pressed their way through the throng to the prison gates. People were shouting all around them. Aikaterina peeked through the curtains, her heart tripping in her chest. She only prayed that her plan would work, that the crowd would be willing to listen.

Finally the litter came to a stop. Kleitos helped her down, and followed close by her side as she ascended the steps to the prison. She motioned for Casca to join her, and as soon as he was standing stiffly beside her, she lifted her hands to quiet the crowd.

It was growing by the moment, she noticed. Some of the men carried their tools like weapons, and the whole square seethed with anger and suspicion.

"Men of Alexandria!" Aikaterina said, lifting her voice over the crowd. "I beg you to hear me!"

The crowd subsided into a low murmur, but they kept their eyes warily on Casca's men. Aikaterina could feel Casca's tension—it was as if he were a lyre string pulled too taut, and then plucked.

Give me the words, Aikaterina prayed silently. *Lord God, please...just give me the words.*

Toward the back of the square, she saw Diodoros. His face was drawn, but he managed an encouraging smile when their eyes met. She took a breath.

"Citizens," she said. "We all—all of us—remember too well the days of siege."

The murmuring swelled again, and she felt Casca shift, almost imperceptibly.

Let him squirm, she thought. *For just once, let him know what this feels like.*

"We remember too well the days when the innocent were caught in the flames of strife," she continued. "When our city was overrun...when blood was spilled in the streets."

The men in the crowd roared and raised their tools above their heads. Casca's soldiers cast each other nervous and sidelong glances, and Casca's hands twitched at his sides.

"What are you doing?" he asked through his teeth.

Aikaterina ignored him. "Last night," she said, lifting her voice once more, "a servant from my household was taken, and he was tortured. He was doused in pitch and set afire, and his ashes scattered on the very stones where you now stand!"

The men's murmurings grew dark now, and they all shifted their feet, as if afraid they were desecrating the dead. A man with a jagged scar that pinched his top lip pushed through the crowd and leveled a finger at Casca.

"Him!" he shouted. "It was him! I saw him! Is this the justice of Rome?"

The crowd surged forward behind him, and shouts of "Death!" and "Bring pitch and fire!" echoed through the square. Aikaterina had seen a storm whip the sea into a frenzy in mere heartbeats, and she could feel the crowd hovering on the edge of madness.

Casca took a single step back, his face drawn.

Aikaterina moved between him and the angry mob and lifted her hands once again.

"My people!" she said. "There is no need for further bloodshed."

The crowd drew up like a wave crashing against a seawall. All of Casca's men were watching her as if she were their Pharos, their sole beacon in a ravaging storm.

"But they spilled our blood readily enough!" another man shouted. "It's time to send a message to Nicomedia! Or when will it be too much?"

"A message has been sent," Aikaterina answered. "I wrote it myself and dispatched it this morning. What happened here was not by order of Diocletian *Augustus*, nor even by order of *Caesar* Galerius. As for this man—" She stepped aside, revealing Casca once more to the full fury of the crowd. "He has agreed to take his men and depart Alexandria immediately."

Casca made a noise deep in his throat, and Aikaterina turned to him. "Unless," she said in a low voice that only he could hear, "you would prefer me to release the crowd."

For one awful moment, they faced each other. Casca's fingers curled, seeking something to strangle. "You will regret this," he murmured.

Aikaterina smiled at the crowd and lifted a hand, as if she were presenting Casca to them as a gift. "Alexandria stands with Nicomedia and the Empire," she said. "So long as the Empire stands with Alexandria."

The crowd erupted into cheers. Chants of *"Kyria, kyria!"* rang out from all corners of the square. Aikaterina dropped her arm and Kleitos returned to her side to escort her back to the litter.

"I want you and your men out of my city," she said to Casca. "And if you ever dare to show your face here again, I will not protect you."

"I promise you," Casca said. "I will find a way to make you pay for this."

Aikaterina lifted her chin. "I look forward to seeing you try," she said. "*Vale*, Casca."

She left him standing there with his men and swept down the stairs. The crowds parted to let her through, but as she reached the *lectica* she paused, her gaze fixed on the stones. Her heart ached with a terrible and gnawing grief.

I'm so sorry, Hanno, she whispered to him in her mind. *I should have protected you, as you protected her.* Her throat choked with bitterness. *Well done, good and faithful servant.*

She grasped Kleitos's hand and stepped into the litter before anyone could see the tears that clung to her lashes. Just before the curtain fell, she glanced back and saw Casca's face turned toward her, dark with hatred and rage.

With a shuddering sigh, she let the curtain fall closed and leaned back on the cushions. The litter made its tortuous way through the crowds, and she listened to the people shouting her name. She had won this battle, and Casca would retreat to Nicomedia to lick his wounds. But she feared that he would come back for her. She just didn't know how or when.

54

Alexandria, Aegyptus — October, A.D. 302

Casca and his men were gone before noon. The city settled itself back into an uneasy peace, and Aikaterina, sitting in a dusty shaft of sunlight at the long table in the *Bibliotheka*, waited to be summoned before the Alexandrian Senate. She had been bold and done what she had to do to rid the city of Casca's hateful presence, but she was not so foolish as to think that her actions would not be questioned.

"I can't believe you did that," Diodoros said, taking a seat across from her.

Aikaterina stirred and glanced at him, and managed a faint smile. "It was the only thing I could think of," she said with a lift of her shoulders. "How is she?"

Diodoros shook his head, and Aikaterina sighed. For a long moment neither of them spoke, but Diodoros regarded her with deep sympathy in his eyes.

"I think sometimes," Aikaterina said slowly, "that I do not understand suffering."

"I think the problem is that you try to. There is no understanding it. There is only the strength to endure."

Aikaterina lifted her eyes to his. "I don't think I have the strength," she said.

Impulsively, he reached out his hand and laid it over hers. "You do," he insisted. "What I saw today... No, *kyria*, you have strength. I think perhaps you don't realize just how much."

Aikaterina cleared her throat and drew her hand from under his. "Thank you," she said. "Did you dispatch my letter?"

"First thing this morning. It is already on its way."

"Good. Then it should reach Diocletian before Casca does. That is all that matters."

"And do you think he will listen?"

Aikaterina lifted her shoulders again and let them fall. "Who can tell? Diocletian is...a mystery to me. But if he can hear reason, then I have a chance."

"I pray it be so," Diodoros said. He set three *codices* on the table. "I thought you might like these for your study. I know you don't have much time for such matters these days, but..."

Aikaterina laid her hand on the volumes like a caress. "My heart longs for the days when we had nothing but time," she said. "And peace." She gritted her teeth and shook her head fiercely. "I don't know if we will see such times again. We are caught at the heart of the storm."

He caught his breath and cleared his throat. "Then we will endure," he said.

Aikaterina closed her eyes, feeling the warm sun on her face. Now that, for the moment at least, the danger had passed, a wave of sudden, bone-weary exhaustion swept over her. She wished in vain that her father were awake, so that she could run to him and let him take all of these cares and worries and fears from her shoulders.

But it was for her to comfort now, not to seek comfort. She pursed her lips and met Diodoros's concerned gaze. "I must go to her," she said. "Will you come with me?"

"Of course."

THE LONG AFTERNOON SHADOWS stretched among the houses of the dead as Aikaterina and Diodoros made their way down the path, and the breeze had turned chilly. As they reached the courtyard before the large tomb, Synkletika and Theokleia came forward to meet them.

"She has been asking for you," Synkletika said to Aikaterina. "I am glad you could come."

"I had...matters to attend to in the city," she said. "I came as soon as I could."

Synkletika gestured for Aikaterina to follow her, and Theokleia took Diodoros to a flat stone in the shade nearby, where he could sit comfortably and wait.

Aikaterina and Synkletika took the winding stair down into the catacombs, and Aikaterina could hear soft wailing.

"They all mourn," Synkletika said. "But they also honor him. He died for the Truth that sets all men free."

Aikaterina swallowed hard. *Cold comfort*, she thought, feeling the wound in her heart left by Varro's death begin to weep.

Synkletika showed her to a small room, where Sabra sat huddled on a stone bench facing the wall. The room was lined with niches and filled with bones, and, to Aikaterina's surprise, bits of graffiti in Christian symbols. She shivered and nodded once to Synkletika, who bowed her head and left them alone.

"Sabra?" Aikaterina said, taking a few steps into the chamber. "Sabra..."

The rest of the words would not come. Sabra turned, her face pale and stained with dust and tears, her hair loose in a torn and tattered cloud around her shoulders. Aikaterina rushed forward and threw her arms around her friend, holding her close as sobs racked her body.

"I don't know what to do," Sabra said when her tears finally subsided, and her voice was hoarse from crying. "I've never been...he's always been..." Her breath caught and she buried her face in her hands. "I haven't seen him...I hadn't seen him in so long. If only I'd seen...if only I'd told him..." Her voice broke, shoulders racked with sobs. "I...I'm all alone, Kat."

"No," Aikaterina murmured. "Not alone. Not ever."

Sabra lifted her head a little, managing a faint smile through her tears. For a moment she couldn't speak, but finally she managed to say, "Thank you for coming."

"I had to get rid of Casca first," Aikaterina said.

"However did you manage that?" Sabra asked, straightening and wiping a fold of her *palla* over her cheeks.

Aikaterina told her what she had done, and Sabra's eyes widened as she listened to the story.

"He will come back for me," Aikaterina finished. "Whatever he was before, he is my sworn enemy now. He will not forgive what I did to him today."

Sabra squeezed her hands. "God will…" she began, and then stopped abruptly and looked away. "Best to leave tomorrow's troubles for tomorrow," she said. "Today's strife is enough."

"Sabra," Aikaterina said, and bit her lip, wondering how to proceed. "I don't know what you heard, or what you suspect, but Hanno…Hanno did not betray you to Casca." Sabra caught in a breath, her eyes filling again with tears, and Aikaterina laid a hand on her shoulder. "I know it's a small comfort, but…I just wanted you to know that. He loved you too well to ever give you up. In the end he found death sweeter than the thought of betraying you into danger."

A storm of emotion flooded Sabra's face, part relief, part wonder…part rage. Then the bitter rage surged until nothing else was left in her fire-gold eyes.

"I almost wish he *had* betrayed me," she said, "if it would have spared his life. I wish he would have given me up, because in the end it didn't even matter. They found us anyway. Somehow. I would rather have him alive, and broken like me, than…"

Her voice caught and she crumpled, head buried in her arms, shoulders shaking. Aikaterina wrapped an arm around her and leaned her cheek on Sabra's shoulder, and let her weep. When Sabra's grief had spent itself, they sat a long while in silence, side by side, staring at the Christian graffiti and memorials on the catacomb walls.

Aikaterina said, "The danger has passed. You can stay here

as long as you wish."

Sabra shook her head. "I can't stay," she said. "There is too much pain here." She flung a hand toward the bones in the burial niches. "Too much death." She drew in a shuddering breath and glanced up at Aikaterina. "I'm lost," she said. "I must wander for a bit until I find my way again."

"But where will you go?" Aikaterina asked. "And…" She stopped. She had been about to say, *and all alone.*

Sabra seemed to guess her meaning, because her lower lip quivered treacherously. "I was thinking of going home, but I know I can't, not with Dignianus in power. He will turn me over to Casca as soon as he sees me. So, perhaps I will return to Myra. To Nikolaos. I thought I was strong enough to endure all things, but these last few months…I don't know that I have the strength to endure any more." She hesitated, then smoothed her hand over her *palla* and said, "Perhaps I might go to Ephesus, and see the tomb of the Magdalene."

"She died in Ephesus?" Aikaterina asked, curious.

Sabra nodded, wiping her palms over her cheeks. "After traveling all over the Empire. Nikolaos told me she stood up to the Emperor Tiberius, and preached the Resurrection of the Christ, before she returned to Ephesus."

"And did she find peace then?" Aikaterina asked.

Sabra met her gaze, understanding perfectly all that Aikaterina couldn't bring herself to say. Then she drew a shaking breath and said, "I think she did."

Aikaterina nodded quietly. "Perhaps you will find peace with Nikolaos, at least for a time," she said. "But you cannot go alone. I won't allow it—it's too dangerous." She cast about for a moment, trying to think. "I'll send Diodoros with you."

"No," Sabra said. "His place is here. He is a scholar, Kat, not a soldier or a servant."

Aikaterina folded her arms. "Then you must take Kleitos."

"Who is that?"

"My personal *lictor*." Sabra looked at her, and Aikaterina continued, "Well, Agapius ran off with Jurian, so I had to replace him. But I trust Kleitos with my life, and he will make sure you are safe."

"Is he...of the Faith? I don't want to put anyone in danger... least of all Nikolaos."

"He is not, but he is no lover of the Empire, and he is very discreet. You will have no trouble from him on that score. And anyway, from all I know of Nikolaos, I think he can take care of himself." She stood, and as Sabra rose to join her she pulled her into a tight embrace. "When will you leave?"

"Soon, I think. I must make some preparations."

"I will give you anything you need. Just send word, and Kleitos will be ready with all the supplies."

Sabra smiled at her through sudden tears. "I don't deserve a friend like you," she said. "You shouldn't be so kind to me, Kat. If you knew..."

"Hush," she said, scowling faintly. "It's the least I can do." She hugged Sabra again and then drew back. "I will come and see you again," she said. "Don't you dare leave without saying goodbye."

"I won't," Sabra said.

Aikaterina left the chamber, feeling strangely lighthearted, strangely at peace. A stay with Nikolaos in Myra sounded like exactly what Sabra needed, and she only hoped that Kleitos wouldn't be too upset about the unexpected change of scenery.

She saw *Amma* Synkletika speaking with two other dark-veiled women at the foot of the spiraling staircase, and she hurried forward to meet her. Synkletika dismissed the other women and turned to meet her.

"Did you convince her to stay?" she asked.

"No," Aikaterina said, surprised. "I actually think she should go." The drawn expression on the woman's face made her heart lurch. "Is there some reason she should not?"

"Ask Theokleia," she said. "It is none of my affair."

They returned to the surface of the necropolis and Aikaterina found Diodoros exactly where she had left him, sitting on a flat stone in the courtyard with Irene and Theokleia. He rose as she approached, but Aikaterina waved him back.

"Why should Sabra not leave this place?" she asked Theokleia.

The blind girl tilted her head and her eyes seemed to look straight through Aikaterina. "Darkness follows her," she said. "And darkness awaits her."

"And you think she is safer if she stays here?"

"None of us are safe," Theokleia retorted, echoing words Aikaterina herself had said, not so very long ago.

Aikaterina and Diodoros exchanged glances. "Then what?" Aikaterina said. "She cannot help it that darkness follows her, as you say. Should that paralyze her?"

The lynx got to its feet on the top of the wall and arched its back in a stretch. Then it sat, tail wrapped around its paws, and watched them with unblinking eyes.

"It is difficult to see," Theokleia said. "We sail into darkness."

Aikaterina tossed her head. "Well, then," she said. "It's a good thing we have a lighthouse."

55

Augusta Treverorum, Germania — November, A.D. 302

Jurian paced the courtyard like a caged beast. He'd never felt so desperate and so powerless all at the same time, not even when he'd seen Mari's body floating in that pool of lilies in Rome, or when he'd seen his house go up in flames with his mother, so weak and vulnerable, trapped within.

He ground his teeth. For weeks now, Constantinus had caused him no end of difficulties. He wouldn't give him discharge from his position as *decurio* and so Jurian was faced with another impossible choice: to violate his duty and hunt down Casca to exact justice for the blood he had spilled, or to obey his commanding officer and sit here in Germania, fighting for the Empire...an Empire he now hated with every fiber of his being.

"Listen to me," Agapius said from his perch on the stone wall, "I understand. I do. I'd like to take a piece out of that man myself for the things he's done. But you *have* to think."

"I am thinking," he gritted. "Thinking about whether the axe, the sword, or the knife would be a better end for him."

Agapius sighed. "Spilling that man's blood won't bring her back."

"I know that."

"Have you been to see Maternus?"

"No. I haven't. I think I can move ten paces without asking his permission."

"You haven't gone because you know what he'll say."

"I just told you. I don't need to hear what he has to say."

"Jurian."

Jurian pivoted to face him. "What?" he snapped. "What? You tell me not to be angry. Not to bring the wrath of God down on this man who has murdered…how many? Do you know? Can you count them all? I can. I see their faces…" He dragged in a ragged breath. "I will squeeze every drop of blood out of his body."

"Jurian," Agapius said again. "And once you have bled him dry, what then?"

"I don't care."

"Yes, you do."

Jurian spun away from him and resumed his pacing. He felt that if he didn't stay in motion, he would burst, or tear apart in a thousand pieces.

"No, you're right," he said. "You're right. I need to be practical. Casca may have been the murderer, but he is not the root of the problem."

Agapius jumped down from the wall and crossed to his side in two bounds. "Hush," he said, shoving his shoulder. "Are you insane?"

"You know it's true. Constantinus knows it's true." He shrugged Agapius's hand off his arm. "The Romans betrayed the Alemanni," he said. "And they are looking for the chance to take their revenge. I could give them exactly that."

Agapius's hand knotted as if he had half a mind to punch him. "Stop," he said. "Whatever you're thinking, *don't*. This is madness!"

Jurian stared at him for a moment, then his shoulders sagged. What would it matter, in the end? If he mustered an army of Rome's worst enemies and descended on them like fire, he would be just like them—a murderer and a betrayer.

"That's right," Agapius said, nodding. "You're starting to see straight again. Put the pieces together."

"I can't." Jurian looked at Agapius, feeling that surge of helplessness tearing his heart again. "She was the one who made sense of everything. I can't...I don't know how to live if she's not here to show me the way."

Agapius glanced over Jurian's shoulder at something, and Jurian, heart sinking, turned to see Constantinus coming toward them. Agapius stepped back as the Tribune stopped beside them.

"Are you ready to do something with that grief, *decurio*?" Constantinus asked.

"I don't think that's a good idea," Agapius said.

Constantinus studied him a moment, and then turned back to Jurian. "Are you ready or not?"

"What did you have in mind?" Jurian asked.

"I have obtained permission from my father to take you south."

Jurian seized Constantinus's arm. "What?"

"Listen. Let go." He pulled his arm free. "There are forts all the way down the border of the Empire. We can inspect them as we go, direct fortifications where needed, engage any enemies if they arise. And we can slowly build your *cataphractarii* to a force worthy of a *tribunus*, not just a *decurio*, so that when you enter Nicomedia, you will compel attention to your cause. What do you think?"

Jurian hardly knew what to think. The prospect, which opened in front of his mind like a shimmering vista of possibility and hope, was almost too much for him to bear. And the thought that Constantinus would once again shepherd him—this time on his triumphal entry into the heart of the Empire—stunned him to silence.

But he knew exactly what he would do. He would bring his *cataphractarii* to the very steps of the palace, and he would denounce Casca for all the atrocities he had ever committed. He would lay him bare before the Emperor's scrutiny, and let

Diocletian himself hand down punishment. And that would wound Casca more than if Jurian himself were to bring him down, because he knew that, if there was anything Casca loved more than himself, it was the *Imperator* Diocletian.

Jurian studied Constantinus in curious silence, then asked, "Why would you do this for me? I don't deserve it."

"I don't know about that," Constantinus said with a smile. "You've saved my life twice now—at least. You have a strength and conviction about you that I admit I almost envy. Also, I would be lying if I didn't also admit that I have my own plans. If Rome is ever to regain its former glory, men like Casca and Julius Asclepiodotus need to be driven out. They are a poison." He glanced back at the *praetorium*. "And besides, you have been gravely wronged by this man and I would help you set it right, if I can. I stood by and watched a dear friend tried, convicted, and executed for crimes he did not commit, and I did not defend him." He placed his hand on Jurian's shoulder. "I will not abandon my friends like that again."

Jurian's heart caught strangely at his words, and he exchanged a long look with Constantinus. When he finally glanced away, the Tribune was still watching him, a tormented look in his eyes.

"Well said," Agapius interjected, missing that wordless exchange. "I can just see it now—the shining cavalry in the streets of Nicomedia, and Casca's nasty little face all pinched up with fear. He has to know that you will come for him, don't you think?"

Jurian sighed. "I think he's counting on it."

"But the way you will return won't have entered his wildest imaginings," Constantinus said. "Now, I want to leave within the week, so make your preparations, and give your orders to your men."

"I will," Jurian said. "Thank you."

THE NEXT FEW DAYS passed like a whirlwind, filled with all the preparations that attended a deployment. The forges and anvils of the *fabrica* were never idle, and great wagons were loaded with provisions. Jurian drilled his men hard, until the precision of their movements was the envy of the entire *castra*.

Jurian and Agapius made one more visit to Maternus the night before they were to set out for the south, but Jurian could not bring himself to mention what had happened in Cyrene. He didn't know how to speak the anger that he felt, the gnawing, consuming fire that blazed up whenever the memory of Sabra flashed through his mind. But Maternus seemed to sense something of it, for as they were leaving the house, he laid his hand briefly on Jurian's head.

"We cannot always choose how we feel," he said, "but we can always choose how we respond to it." He held Jurian's gaze for a long moment, until Jurian had to look away. "Don't let it consume you," the presbyter added. "Pray for the grace to make the right choice when the time comes."

Jurian nodded, feeling the battle between peace and hate spark again in his heart. Then Maternus turned to Agapius with a smile.

"And you, brother," he said. "Listen for the call, and follow it with joy."

"Thank you," Agapius said.

They left the house and ambled back through the streets. Once more, they passed the playhouse, which was blazing with light. Street performers tumbled and danced, and one—a great swarthy Parthian—juggled sharp and gleaming swords. Men handed out playbills, inviting any who passed to come inside for the show.

Agapius sighed as he took a *libellus* from a gap-toothed man with bow legs. "I suppose," he said, "it's too late for the play."

Jurian dropped a few coins into the man's hand and propelled Agapius toward the playhouse.

"No," he said with a smile. "A promise is a promise. And this is the closest you'll ever be to *Miles Gloriosus* anyway."

56

Antiochia ad Orontes, Syria — November, A.D. 302

When Casca entered the Emperor's *tablinum* in Antioch, Diocletian stood with his back toward him, a parchment gripped tightly in his hands. *Caesar* Galerius sprawled in the Emperor's own *sella*, watching Diocletian with a hawk-like, predatory gaze. Casca's hands twitched and he folded them behind his back. He must not show fear. Not here. Not ever.

"It seems you have been busy," Diocletian said at last.

Casca wavered. He wished Diocletian would say what he meant. Was busy a good thing or a bad thing? Was he happy or not? Who could tell? He glanced at Galerius, whose expression had not changed. No help from that quarter, then. No help from *Galerius*, who had always been there, always quick to put in a good word for him to the *Augustus*. Galerius, who had sent him on this mad mission in the first place.

Casca swallowed back a sudden surge of bitterness. "Yes, *Imperator Augustus*," he said.

He opened his mouth to add something else and then shut it again. Best to wait and see if he could better gauge Diocletian's mood first.

"Dignianus is securely in place in Cyrene?" Galerius asked.

Casca risked a glance at the *Caesar*, who was watching him

with a sharp, meaningful stare. For a moment Casca's chest tightened, then he gave Galerius a subtle nod.

"Yes, *Caesar*," he said.

Galerius held his gaze a little longer, then twisted around to face Diocletian.

"Well, at least he didn't make a mess there," the *Caesar* remarked.

Casca's gaze snapped from Galerius to Diocletian's back. Did the Emperor think he had made a mess? That parchment in his hand...

Casca's mouth went dry. Of course. Aikaterina had told the crowds on that horrible, humiliating morning that she had dispatched a letter to the Emperor with her complaints against him. That must be the letter in his Divine *Imperator*'s hands, polluting the name of Marcus Valerius Flaccus Casca in Diocletian's mind. He tamped down an almost irresistible urge to snatch the parchment from Diocletian's hands and cast it into the fire.

"I only wish to serve," Casca said, placing his hand over his breast and bowing low.

Diocletian half turned to face him and held up the letter. "Is that so? And you serve me by invading the household of the *Praefectus Augustalis* of Alexandria?" he asked, his voice horrible and low. "By desecrating the body of a dead slave?"

"I...can explain, *Sacratissime Imperator*," Casca stammered. "I understand that the appearance of the thing is unfortunate, and that you have had a report from—"

"I don't think you understand at all," Galerius remarked. "Do you have any idea how difficult those people are to manage? How much trouble they have caused the Empire in recent years? Gods, they are like the heel of Achilles. Julius Caesar had Cleopatra, and we, it seems, will have Aikaterina of Alexandria."

"I know something of the history," Casca said, remembering Aikaterina's fevered words to the mob.

"Then you should know that we must always tread carefully

in Egypt," Diocletian said, his voice so smooth, too smooth. "We certainly don't invade the governor's private household and execute his slaves, and then dishonor the holy goddess Libitina by scattering their ashes in the street. What could possibly have entered your mind to make you think this was a good idea? Alexandria is on the tipping point. Do you understand how much careful work I laid out there this last year, trying to bridle that people's unruly temper?"

Casca's mouth flapped open, and Galerius snorted softly. "I don't think anything entered his mind," he said.

"No, he...he wasn't just any slave! He had escaped us in Cyrene," Casca said. "He and the governor's daughter. Sabra. We tracked them to Alexandria. They are friends, you know. Sabra, and Aikaterina." He bowed to the *Caesar* and added, "My understanding was that we should not leave loose ends."

Galerius's gaze sharpened, a cold, warning look. Casca fidgeted with the edge of his toga, not sure if he felt more terrified or gleeful at the *Caesar*'s discomfort. If Galerius would not defend him, then Casca would defend himself.

"In Cyrene, yes. But if they were under the jurisdiction and protection of the governor of Alexandria, that becomes another matter," Diocletian said. "That is a den of asps, and it requires careful thought and prudent action."

Casca's mouth edged up in a careful smile. "On that we can absolutely agree, *Imperator*," he said. "But in spite of this present...difficulty, I think there may yet be an opportunity."

"An opportunity for what?" Galerius said.

"If I may be so bold," Casca replied, turning to Diocletian, "summon Aikaterina to your presence, *Imperator*."

Diocletian turned fully to face Casca. "Why would I do that?" His mouth twitched, and he added, "The last time the girl was in my presence, she caused quite a stir. Every time she is in my presence, she causes a stir."

Casca checked himself. Was that *affection* he saw in the Emperor's eyes? It was repulsive. Aikaterina infuriated him. She drove him mad in every way he hated, like an unquenchable fire that he could never quite freeze out of his veins.

"You have an astonishing weakness for letting dangerous people close to you," Galerius said to Diocletian. "First it was Marcellus, then Gerontios, then Georgius. Now you tolerate the audacity of Aikaterina of Alexandria, who is like wildfire. It will come to no good."

Diocletian leveled a dark and enigmatic stare on his *Caesar*, but said nothing. The silence drew out far too long.

Casca licked his lips. "Alexandria is on the verge of collapse," he began, trying to redirect the conversation. "And—"

"No thanks to you," muttered Galerius.

Casca took the barb without flinching. "The governor is incapacitated by illness. Although Aikaterina has been managing affairs in his stead, with the help of the Alexandrian Senate, I think we can all agree that Alexandria needs the firmness of a man's hand to guide it, and—"

"Ah," said Diocletian. "This again."

He turned away and paced to the other side of the *tablinum*. The windows looked out over his private *hortus*, barren and ugly now in the late autumn chill.

Galerius sat up in his chair and leaned forward, that hawkish look back in his eyes. "Well, she is a pretty young thing. Her temperament may leave something to be desired, but all that can be easily overlooked." His mouth lifted in a twisted smile. "I can't say I was sorry to miss her when she came to Antioch the last time. Wasn't there talk of marrying her off then?"

"She was not disposed to listen to that notion at the time," Diocletian said drily.

"Has that changed?"

Diocletian's mouth twitched and he didn't answer.

"She is of marriageable age, *Caesar*," Casca said. "And securing her hand would bind Alexandria's loyalty to Rome." He paused, and then added, "It is not the first time marriage has been used to ensure, how shall we say, congenial relations between the *Caesars* and the Empire."

Galerius rubbed his jaw and sat back in his seat, and Casca

nodded approval to himself, knowing he had struck a nerve there. Diocletian, of course, remained silent, unmoved.

"Knowing how your mind works," Galerius said to Casca, "I'm sure you already have someone in mind."

"The matter has been considered already," Diocletian said, waving generally at Casca.

"I apologize if I haven't occupied my thoughts with the fate of Aikaterina of Alexandria," Galerius said. "Who is the lucky man?"

"We had thought—" Casca began, and waited for Diocletian's nod of approval. "What of your sister's son, *Caesar*? Maximinus Daia."

Galerius's gaze sharpened, but Diocletian had turned away, and would not favor them with a word or a glance.

"He is a man of distinction," Casca said. "His reputation in the army is outstanding."

"And you think my nephew would make a good match for that Egyptian firebrand?" Galerius asked with a snort of laughter. "He's done well enough in the army, to be sure, but the boy is as dull as a ploughshare."

Casca smiled. *So much the better,* he thought. *Let her be shackled to a man who marries her only for her position, and whose dull mind will wear her down to a shadow.*

He thought of her standing there on the steps before the prison, her dark curls piled high on her head, her bright eyes flashing and her bare arms, adorned with simple silver bracelets, raised against the mob. His heart hammered and he forced the image out of his mind.

"With respect," Casca said, "the intention is to secure Alexandria for the Empire, not make her eternally happy."

Diocletian turned at last. "I had intended to introduce them myself, when Aikaterina was last in Antioch, but Daia was called back to the frontier. Is he in Nicomedia now?"

"I—don't know," Casca said.

"If he isn't, send for him," Diocletian said to Galerius. "In the meantime, I will extend an invitation to our little *praefecta* of Alexandria to join us there. I am curious to hear how she has managed affairs since my visit. Casca, you may go."

Casca inclined his head, trying to keep the Emperor from seeing the heat that rushed suddenly to his face, and retreated from the room.

He wanted to congratulate himself that Diocletian finally seemed to be listening to his advice, but even he had a hard time persuading himself of that truth. Diocletian had been mulling over the matter of Alexandria's prefecture for over a year now. Casca had just managed to remind him of it at a strategically valuable time, when he could use it to distract Galerius's focus from his blunders in Africa. But the way Diocletian had called Aikaterina *praefecta*—half mockingly, half fondly, as if he would ever contemplate such an absurdity...it would have been laughable if it weren't so repulsive.

Still, it was settled now—Aikaterina would be called to Nicomedia to meet her future spouse.

Casca smiled smugly as he imagined her sitting at table with Maximinus Daia. He had met the man only once—he was a round, flaccid man with a mind like sodden oats, and yet, he knew how to use his power to get what he wanted. That, at least, was something Casca could respect. And he was nephew to Galerius, and Galerius had vision. More than that, Galerius had the strength of will to do the hard things...to sacrifice whatever needed to be sacrificed for the good of the Empire.

Yes, Casca thought. *Galerius understands that sometimes blood and fire are necessary.*

He could almost feel sorry for Aikaterina, condemned to a life with such a man, but when he remembered how she had threatened him, the spark of pity was choked in a black ash of anger.

She should have been more careful, he thought, and then, with a flash almost of regret, *Even after everything we have been through together, she still does not realize who I am.*

He stopped in the peristyle, trembling. What strange thoughts were teasing his mind? Why should he feel anything but scorn for her, when she felt nothing but hatred for him?

A hushed voice in the back of his mind whispered that perhaps Casca did not know who he was. The Oracle had held up a mirror for him, once. He just hadn't wanted to look.

He silenced the voice. He did not need any gods to tell him who he was, and he didn't need any mirrors either.

And he certainly didn't need Aikaterina of Alexandria.

Yes, Maximinus Daia would do beautifully. Casca chuckled to himself as he wondered how Constantinus would like such an arrangement. *He* was another one Casca would love to bring down, if he could. And perhaps this would do well enough, for present.

He could just picture it now: the expression on Constantinus's face as he read the letter from his tearful niece, lamenting that she had been condemned to marry a man more than twice her age and less than half as intelligent. The thought made Casca almost want to dance with glee.

Too bad for him, Casca thought. *He shouldn't have thrown in his lot with Jurian. They will all get what they deserve, every single one of them.*

57

Nicomedia, Anatolia — December, A.D. 302

Aikaterina dressed for the night's banquet with special care. A week now she had been in Nicomedia, summoned there by imperial invitation—or command—and yet Diocletian had not yet once granted her an audience. He was preoccupied with *Caesar* Galerius, by all rumors, but she'd heard no news of what they were discussing, locked away in the Emperor's *tablinum*. The barbarians to the north, she imagined, who had been the focus of the *Caesar*'s recent campaigns.

The other person she had not seen since her arrival, much to her relief, was Casca. If he was in Nicomedia, he was staying out of sight of the palace, which made Aikaterina wonder if he had somehow fallen out of favor with Diocletian. If he had, she thought, she just might esteem the *Imperator* a little more highly.

But tonight she was finally to be in the Emperor's presence, and her nerves were raw as Nenet worked her hair into ornate little braids pinned up with precious gems. She had to be strong. She knew what she meant to ask Diocletian, and she needed all her wits about her to make her case persuasively.

"The sooner we are out of this viper's nest, the better," she muttered, to no one in particular. "I don't even know why the

Imperator summoned me here."

Nenet leaned around, her mouth full of jeweled pins. "Perhaps," she said, forming the words with difficulty, "he likes your company."

Aikaterina snorted. "That is certainly not true," she said. "After all, if that were the reason, surely I would have seen him even once this week. No, I feel more like he is testing me. And I have heard nothing at all from home…and maybe that is the other reason I'm here. To get me out of the way. What if Casca tries to do in Alexandria what he did in Cyrene? And with my father already so vulnerable…"

"I think you're too suspicious for your own good," Nenet said, the pins wobbling as she spoke.

Aikaterina said nothing. Nenet, she knew, wanted desperately to believe that everything was as it used to be, and she wanted Aikaterina to believe it too.

But I know better, Aikaterina thought. *It is just the calm before the storm.*

Nenet finished dressing her and Aikaterina made her way slowly to the *triclinium*. It was all the same—every night, the same faces, the same hollow laughter. The Empress Alexandra's worried face, which seemed to have more lines every time Aikaterina saw her. Maxentius's endless gallantries, his wife Valeria's pouts.

She longed to return to Alexandria—to the cool *Bibliotheka*, the lush gardens, and her father, far from the false glitter of the imperial court.

But tonight was different. A slave escorted her not to the grand *triclinium* but to a smaller dining chamber. She paused in the doorway. There were no raucous crowds, only a single small table lit with oil lamps. Diocletian reclined with Alexandra on his left and Galerius on his right. Casca had the place next to Galerius, and opposite him sat Maxentius. His wife Valeria was there, of course, and the place beside Casca was empty.

Aikaterina took a breath and lifted her chin. This was dangerous, and she would have to be especially on her guard.

What could be worse than a tribunal over roast lamb with herbs, and judgment passed during dessert?

"Ah, our lovely Egyptian ambassador," Maxentius said as she entered the room and took her place. "I hope you are well?"

"Well enough," she said. "But anxious to be home again, as I seem to have been brought away from my affairs for no good reason."

She glanced at Alexandra, who seemed even more on edge than usual. At Aikaterina's bold complaint, the *Augusta* turned almost white. Aikaterina couldn't blame her. Her own pulse was shaky, and it was all she could do to keep her hands from trembling.

"Where are all your guests, *Augustus*?" she asked, turning to Diocletian. "I am surprised to see so few gathered tonight."

"We have much to discuss," Diocletian said. "A more intimate gathering seemed appropriate."

Aikaterina's heart jumped. She lifted her goblet of wine and sipped slowly, keeping all her movements deliberate so as not to give away her anxiety.

"Of course," she said. "As it pleases you, *Imperator*."

Diocletian seemed to appreciate her deference, and she hazarded another glance at Alexandra. The Empress gave the tiniest shake of her head, and Aikaterina felt herself slipping from momentary relief back into a jangle of nerves.

"Tell the story yourself," Maxentius said suddenly, leaning forward. "I want to hear from your own lips how you threw him—" he pointed at Casca— "out of Alexandria."

Valeria folded her arms, her face red. "Oh yes," she said. "Let's hear the story. Again."

Aikaterina managed a smile and shook her head. "No," she said. "If it's been heard already—and I have no desire to dwell on such unpleasantness. That is all in the past, and it is the future we must look to now."

"Indulge us," Galerius said, his voice frigid.

Aikaterina glanced at him. His face was inscrutable, but there was something in his eyes that she didn't like at all. She turned to Diocletian.

"That is as the *Imperator* would have it," she said.

He made a gesture for her to continue, and Aikaterina took a breath. She didn't dare look at Casca, but she could feel his tension in every fiber of her being. It was like being squeezed by an invisible hand.

Her thoughts drifted in a slow panic. She had assumed they had summoned her to discuss her marriage—and she had prepared to cast their plots back in their face by asking the *Imperator* to publicly acknowledge her as *Praefecta Augustalis* of Alexandria, as official regent of her father if not his actual successor—someone who could rule Alexandria without interference from anyone else.

This was not the conversation she had anticipated.

"A servant was removed from my household without my knowledge," she began. "A young man, a faithful servant, true and devoted. But he was taken and tortured without cause or warrant, and finally he was executed by being set ablaze in the courtyard of the prison. And then his ashes were scattered in the street to be trampled."

She stopped abruptly, a surge of tears burning her throat and her eyes. She closed her right hand into a fist on the table, as if that could trap and hold her grief.

"That's the most horrible thing I've ever heard," Valeria said suddenly.

Aikaterina, startled, looked up. Valeria's eyes glittered with tears, and her face was as white as Aikaterina's chiton. She was staring at Casca, her breath hitching.

"Did you do that?" she asked. "Did you really?"

Casca's hand twitched, tremoring more violently than it usually did. "It's such a pathetic story, the way she tells it," he said quietly. "What she doesn't say is that the man was a criminal who had escaped justice. I had pursued him across the desert all the way from Cyrene. *Domina* Aikaterina was giving aid and shelter to an enemy of Rome and of the gods."

Valeria gasped and swung her gaze to Aikaterina. "Is that

true?" she breathed. "You were giving shelter to the enemies of the Empire?"

Casca, Aikaterina saw out of the corner of her eye, was smiling into his goblet of wine. He thought he had her pinned.

"If you please," Aikaterina said, turning to Casca, "I've been meaning to ask you. Can you explain to me and to all here on whose authority you deposed and publicly murdered the governor of Cyrene?"

At that, Valeria's mouth dropped open and Alexandra drew in a sharp breath through her teeth. Galerius's face was like stone, but his murderous stare was directed not at her, but at Casca. Maxentius seemed to be enjoying himself as much as if he were watching the gladiators in the arena. Diocletian alone gave no indication of his thoughts, but there was a deep smoldering in his eyes.

Aikaterina could not help the thrill of triumph that shivered through her. She felt fairly certain—though she did not know—that Diocletian would have preferred a bloodless transition of power in Cyrene. And she felt certain as well that Galerius opposed that view, and that he was not above giving Casca a special set of orders. But she could be mistaken.

Guide my words, she prayed silently. *Set my feet upon the path of righteousness.*

"I had my orders to see to the transition of power," Casca said. "And I was vested with the authority to try Lucius Titianus and the other conspirators with their crimes, and to carry out their just sentence."

"I see," Aikaterina said. "In the middle of the night? When your soldiers dragged women and children out of their beds, out of their homes, and drove them like chattel into the *agora*? When they forced the people to watch as their fellow citizens were tortured in the most brutal and inhumane ways imaginable? What child should have to see such cruelty? Is this Rome's justice now?" She felt the heat in her veins now, giving her courage, and she leveled her gaze at Diocletian. "Is this what I can tell my people in Alexandria that they can expect from the *imperium*? Fear, and blood running in the streets, and knife work in the dark, all in the name of a so-called justice?"

Alexandra looked like someone had her around the throat and was slowly choking the air out of her. Valeria gaped at her with eyes agog, as if she expected some kind of thunderbolt of Jupiter to singe Aikaterina in her seat. Even Maxentius was staring at her as though he had never seen her before.

Good, she thought. *Let him see me for who I really am.*

"It would be irresponsible and reckless of you to speak so," Galerius said, the edge in his voice unmistakable now.

He would kill me in my sleep if he could get away with it, she thought, *and never feel the least hint of remorse.*

He added, "Would you destabilize your city even further than it already is? Would you have riots in the street?"

"Would you?" Aikaterina fired back. "Contrary, perhaps, to the belief of some here, people see with their own eyes and hear with their own ears. Word of what happened in Cyrene traveled quickly, and it did not need my help to spread. Yes, Alexandria is in a precarious position. I would be lying if I said otherwise. But when those who are supposed to keep her secure begin engaging in tactics that resemble tyranny more than justice, the people quickly lose trust and become restless." She turned to Diocletian. "That is why I wrote to you, *Imperator*, of Casca's actions. Because surely that is not what you want for my city... nor any other city in the Empire."

Diocletian's eyes flickered. "And what would you suggest we do, then, with those who follow a faith that profanes and angers our gods, who keep our gods silent so that we cannot know their will? Must not such a pestilence be burned out, like a wound that must be cauterized? What is the just course of action to take?"

Aikaterina caught herself. She had not expected that question. All at once, she saw Varro's body being dragged around the arena, and she battled down the lump that once more formed in her throat.

"*Augustus*," she said slowly, "I would ask just one question.

Do these people do violence against the Empire? Have they rebelled openly, or caused civil unrest in the streets? Do they murder your soldiers or your representatives?" She lowered her voice and added, voice cold and taut, "As far as I recall, *Imperator*, the only people sowing violence in the streets of Alexandria march beneath the *aquila* of Rome."

For a moment there was perfect silence.

Then Galerius struck his fist on the table. "This is intolerable," he said. "These people are an abomination! They refuse to honor the Emperor with his due rites, or to sacrifice to the gods as is our custom. They have angered the gods, and their very existence is a stain on the Empire!"

Aikaterina regarded him for a moment, and then turned back to Diocletian, who was staring at her in stony silence. "*Imperator*," she said, "humbly, I beg you to explain this to me. You conquer barbarian tribes, who have raised up arms against the Empire, and when you have brought their people into the Empire's fold, you also bring their deities into her pantheon—the very gods in whose names those barbarians were fighting against your rule. And yet the Christians have no desire but to live peacefully as Romans, and they do not stir up discontent. How is it, then, that you refuse to allow them the worship of their God?"

Diocletian grew very still, and Aikaterina didn't dare to move or speak. Casca was holding his breath, and out of the corner of her eye, she could see that his face was mottled.

Galerius was livid. "I cannot believe," he said to Diocletian, in a low voice that set Valeria shivering, "that you are entertaining this...this interrogation."

"You mistake me," Aikaterina protested. "I am not interrogating...I only wish to understand. These matters are high and veiled in mystery, and I look to my Emperor for guidance. It is my sincere belief that the *Imperator* wishes more than anything to do right by the divine, so that the Empire may prosper in peace."

"That is my wish," Diocletian said at last. "But answer me

this—how am I to tolerate their God, when He refuses to share honor with mine? The God of the Hebrews and the Christians is a jealous God, they say, who would cast down the statues and temples of Rome's gods to secure all honor for Himself. How can I allow that within my borders?"

"When Nero burned Rome, the whole city suffered," Aikaterina said. "A plague of fire will only eat the foundations of the Empire, regardless of where you order it to burn."

Diocletian looked at her long and hard through narrowed eyes, but Aikaterina never believed for a moment that she had persuaded him.

"Then I would ask again," he said, "what you would propose as a solution instead?"

"You know my belief about that, *Imperator*," Aikaterina said. "The last time I had the honor of being in your presence, I spoke of our great *Bibliotheka*, and the open arms with which Alexandria welcomes knowledge and learning—an offered embrace that recent events have only strengthened. By analogy, I believe the same can be true of the Empire. Peaceful coexistence is in fact possible, where there is no threat. That is why I asked whether the Nazarenes have engaged in open and violent conflict with the Empire…because if they too desire nothing but peace, then what barrier is there to—"

Galerius slammed his hand down on the table again so that his goblet tipped, spilling the blood-red wine all over the white linen. "I've heard enough!" he shouted. "You are on dangerous ground, Aikaterina of Alexandria. If you condone tolerance for these impious, how are you different from Lucius Titianus?"

Aikaterina stared at him. She didn't need anyone to spell out the threat implied in his words.

"Galerius," Diocletian said, his voice very quiet, his gaze barely drifting in his *Caesar*'s direction. Then he turned to Aikaterina. "You are right about one thing," he said. "The workings of justice must be apparent to all."

Aikaterina nodded, but felt strangely unsettled. She had gotten the Emperor to evaluate his own tactics and possibly to reconsider them—the thought should have thrilled her. But as she studied the faces of the *Augustus* and Galerius, and even Maxentius, she saw nothing there to reassure her.

But Casca—he was breathing again, though only shallowly. His eyes were fixed on his plate, but somehow Aikaterina wondered if he saw it at all. What was he thinking that had him so disturbed?

And then, suddenly, she felt it, as palpably as if the metal had bit into her flesh.

The trap had been sprung.

58

Nicomedia, Anatolia — December, a.d. 302

Aikaterina woke in the middle of the night to the smell of smoke.

"Nenet!" she called, coughing. "Nenet!"

There was no answer. She threw off her covers and slipped out of bed, feeling strangely disoriented. The room was almost completely dark. No moonlight shone through the window, but a strange orange glow stained the sky. Stumbling to the window, she peered out, desperate for the sight of something that would reassure her, but she couldn't see anything at all. The smell of smoke was getting stronger by the moment, and her lungs began to seize in protest.

"Nenet!" she called again, and her voice crumpled in a racking cough.

Without waiting for an answer, she grabbed her *palla* from the low couch and wound it around herself, using it to better shield her mouth and nose.

She went to the door and put her hand on the iron handle.

Instantly she snatched it back with a cry of pain. The latch was scalding hot to the touch, and smoke was pouring in beneath the door. She reeled back dizzily, coughing and gagging, her heart hammering for want of air. Her hands shook so much that she could hardly grasp her *palla*. Grabbing the blanket from her bed, she tried to use it to block the gap beneath the door, but it was no use. The smoke was everywhere.

Aikaterina ran to the window again, dragging away the wooden lattice so she could look out more easily. Her room was high off the ground—there were two other levels of the palace below her—and it overlooked a stone courtyard below. The walls of the palace were perfectly smooth. There was no way for her to climb.

She turned away from the window and raced into the small adjoining room where Nenet usually slept. Her bed was unmade but empty, and Aikaterina frowned, wondering where she could possibly have gone in the middle of the night.

Please let her be safe. Please let her have gotten out before the fire started, she thought.

Shouts, hoarse and laced with fear, carried up from the courtyard below her. She hurried back into the main room of her *cubiculum*, but flames were edging under the door now, toying with the fringe of her blanket, and the room was filling with smoke faster than it could escape through the window. Holding her breath, she raced to the trunk that held her belongings and rummaged through it until she found her precious *codex*. She could hear the roar of flames in the corridor, and tears of fright ran down her cheeks.

Her thoughts strayed against her will to Hanno, burned to death in the prison yard, and her whole body shook. Above all things, she was terrified of dying by fire.

"Please," she prayed through her tears. "Please, don't let me die here."

She scrambled back to the window and saw men running with buckets of water, women with their hair unbound, wailing with fear, and slaves scurrying to carry precious valuables out of the path of the flames. The whole palace had emptied, it seemed, poured out like water.

"Help!" she screamed. "Someone help!"

Several men turned to glance up. One pointed and she

waved frantically.

"Help me!" she screamed again, but no one seemed in any hurry to do anything for her.

She spotted Nenet on her knees in the midst of a crowd of servants, her hands and face lifted in supplication. Diodoros and Theokritos were beside her, and Aikaterina cried out with relief. Diodoros saw her and he ran to the men with the buckets, gesturing at her frantically, but they only pushed past him as if he weren't there.

The pale hope that had surged in her heart when she saw him withered. Behind her, the wood creaked, and flames licked now at the thick rug with its intricate Persian design.

Then, suddenly, the wood collapsed and a blaze of fire roared into the room.

Aikaterina dropped to the floor beneath the window, covering her head with the *palla*. The heat was overpowering as it beat against her in waves. She shook with helpless sobs.

"Father," she murmured. "I'm so sorry. I'm so sorry…"

Her thoughts began to stray, drifting in confused snatches, revolving over half-formed prayers of supplication. And then, suddenly, rough hands grabbed her by the arms and hauled her to her feet. Her *palla* slid to the floor and with it the *codex*, its leaves scattering over the stone as it hit the ground.

Aikaterina lifted her face, fearing she knew who had come to her rescue.

She was wrong.

"Casca?" she gasped.

She almost couldn't recognize him, covered as he was with the grime of smoke and ash. He met her eyes for one moment, and she couldn't tell if the look was full of regret, or fear, or grief, or anger. Without a word, he bent and lifted her in his arms, and then he turned and charged through the flames.

The corridor was an inferno of heat and smoke and fire. Aikaterina buried her face in Casca's shoulder and tried to breathe, but the smoke was around her and within her and all she could do was pray that they would make it out alive.

Somewhere behind them came a tremendous crash as wood caved in, and Casca stumbled. Aikaterina screamed something that was lost in the roar of fire and wind, and clung to his shoulders like a frightened child.

And then, by some miracle, they were through. Casca hurried down the stairs, his breath coming in wheezing gasps, and stumbled with her out into the open air of the courtyard.

Then Diodoros was there, kneeling beside her as Casca set her gently on the ground. Nenet came running like a cyclone, wailing with relief. She flung her arms around Aikaterina and held her like a mother would, rocking her and saying broken words in Egyptian.

Aikaterina glanced up at Casca, who stood awkwardly to the side now, twisting one trembling hand in his toga as he watched the fuss everyone made over her. She smiled at him, for once, in sincerity.

"Thank you," she said, her voice hoarse and broken.

Casca inclined his head, then turned abruptly and disappeared back into the palace. Aikaterina took a deep breath that ended in a fit of coughing, and dissolved into exhausted tears. Nenet hugged her close and she clung to Diodoros's hand.

Through the clamor of shouting servants and distraught residents, Aikaterina heard the sharp clatter of boots marching on stone, and the smoky night blazed bright in a sudden wash of torchlight. A troop of Legionaries circled into the courtyard in a tight formation.

"Where is Eleutherius?" shouted the man at the head of the file. "Find him!"

Aikaterina lifted her head and swiped at her cheeks. Her fingers came away grimed with ash. "Eleutherius?" she croaked, frowning at Diodoros.

"They think he set the fire," Diodoros said, grave.

"Why?" Aikaterina said.

"Hush," Nenet said. "Stop bothering her with such nonsense. It doesn't matter."

Aikaterina pushed away from her as the soldiers wove

their way through the assembled crowd, peering into faces and interrogating the servants.

"It does matter, Nenet," she said. "Eleutherius...I know that man. He was a friend of Jurian's. He..." She stopped and pressed a shaking hand over her mouth. "Oh...Nenet...what have I done?"

Her eyes swam with heavy tears as the horror crashed down on her. It was so clear, so obvious.

The soldiers wrestled one of the servants to the ground under a rain of heavy blows. Gorgonius, Aikaterina realized as they dragged him away, the *lictor* who served in Diocletian's personal guard. Her gaze strayed over the frightened faces in the courtyard. Petrus Cubicularius and Dorotheus, the other Christians she knew in the household of Diocletian, were nowhere to be seen. She wondered bleakly if they had perished in the fire.

"What have *you* done?" Nenet echoed. "Nothing, that's what. This is none of your doing, *kyria*. Theokritos! Stop gawking and fetch some water."

Theokritos took off on his spindly legs, and Aikaterina turned to Diodoros. "You have to warn them," she said, seizing his hand again. "Warn them all..."

"What are you talking about?" he asked. "Warn who?"

"You stay where you are," Nenet ordered, planting her finger in his chest. "Don't you dare go running off. We are leaving this accursed place, and I won't have you getting lost!"

Aikaterina reached for Diodoros's other hand. "Please," she said. "Warn them. Before it's too late."

59

Nicomedia, Anatolia — December, A.D. 302

Casca hurried back inside the burning palace. Nothing made sense to him. He knew that the *Caesar* had cleared that wing of the palace before he'd had the fire set, so how was it that Aikaterina's rooms had been in the path of the flames?

Unless…unless it had been Galerius's intention that she perish.

He could still hear her words echoing in his mind, oddly portentous. *When Nero burned Rome, the whole city suffered…*

His thoughts reeled, desperate to escape the suspicion. The *Caesar* would not be that bold. Could he? It was one thing to fabricate a destruction that would finally push Diocletian into action on the matter of the Christians, but it was quite another to deliberately assassinate the daughter of the *Praefectus Augustalis* of Alexandria. If Diocletian had trusted Casca to handle it, this would never have happened.

He would never have needlessly murdered someone just to—

His steps faltered and a wave of nausea roiled in his stomach. With a wretchedly tremoring hand he swiped his grimy face, slick with ash and damp with sweat.

Focus, Casca.

There remained one task for him to do, and then he could put all of this wretched business behind him. But his feet would not move. He sagged against the wall and pulled the pages from Aikaterina's *codex* out of the folds of his tunic. One was half-charred already. So much the better. But as his eyes skimmed the words, a phrase jumped out at him as if the words themselves had been scribed in fire.

Shall not God search out these things: for He knows the secrets of the heart. Because for Your sake we are killed all the day long: we are counted as sheep for the slaughter.

Casca reeled back as if a great hand had struck him. He tried to catch his breath, once, again, but it caught in his throat like ash and his chest tightened until his vision swarmed with shadow all around the edges.

What am I doing? he thought. He stared at the pages in his hand, wanting to drop them, unable to loosen his fingers.

"What are you doing?" hissed a voice.

Casca spun around, but no one was there.

You made your choice, the voice said again, winding its way through his thoughts. *Are you a coward, that you will not see it through?*

Casca's hands trembled treacherously. He remembered the look on Aikaterina's face when he'd found her, the flames curling all around her. It suddenly occurred to him that maybe she had prayed for deliverance, and it was he who had come to find her…

Don't be a fool, came the voice again. *You think her God would ever use a disgusting tool like you? You have plunged yourself in blood. You are drenched in it. There is no power in this universe that could ever make you clean.*

Casca shook his head, once, again.

"*Tribunus!*" someone called.

Casca winced and hid the pages behind his back. A small troop of Legionaries was making its way toward him, dragging the limp and half-unconscious body of the soldier Eleutherius between them. The *tesserarius* at their head saluted him.

"We found him, *Tribunus*," he said.

"Lock him up," Casca said. "And find the others. Petrus Cubicularius and Dorotheus."

The *tesserarius* bowed and motioned for the troop to move off. Casca watched them go, and then drew the pages out from behind his back once more. He didn't need them. He didn't even know why he had taken them. They had enough evidence against the three household slaves without them, and they could manufacture more than enough circumstantial testimony against Eleutherius. He wasn't well-liked—at least, not by people whose opinions mattered. And as for the rest, well, men would say anything for the right price.

Casca crinkled the pages in his fingers.

He could use them against Aikaterina.

He had Sabra's letter, which he could argue proved that they were in conspiracy with one another. And now he had this: proof that Aikaterina was reading the Christian scriptures.

But he couldn't banish the memory of her face, smeared with ash and tears, as she had thanked him in the courtyard.

He crumpled the pages in his hand and turned on his heel, and as he headed past a corridor that was still on fire, he tossed the wad of parchment into the flames.

HE DIDN'T SEE AIKATERINA again. She and her attendants departed for Alexandria at dawn the next morning, and in a way he was glad. Galerius had set things in motion that could not be undone, and she was safer away from Nicomedia.

There would be time to deal with her, but later. And he had made sure that there would be a welcoming party waiting for her in her palace, which should keep her occupied until he had time to figure out what to do with her.

He pushed her out of his mind as he entered Diocletian's *tablinum*.

"How long have you known?" Diocletian asked as soon as he stepped through the door.

Casca paused. He had never seen Diocletian so livid and...

afraid. That was the look in his eyes, Casca realized, hidden deep behind that enigmatic mask he wore. Fear.

Caesar Galerius, as usual, seemed in his element, sprawled in a *sella* and leafing through some parchments on the desk, completely unmoved by the events of the night before.

"You knew," Diocletian repeated. "How long?"

Casca closed the door as he stepped into the room. "I suspected, *Imperator*," he said smoothly. "But without evidence, I did not want to disrupt your—"

"They could have murdered me at any moment! And they have been close to my deepest counsels. Petrus *Cubicularius*, my own chamberlain..." Diocletian's face hardened, white as marble. "Who knows what secrets they have spread?"

"We will find out," Casca said. "I have already ordered that Dorotheus and Gorgonius be executed. And Petrus *Cubicularius* will discover how painful betrayal can be, I promise you."

Diocletian glanced at Galerius. "Truly," he said, "he is a man after your own heart."

"I have been saying for months now," Galerius replied, tossing the parchments onto the desk, "that you have been too soft on these apostates. By the gods, when will you learn that your tolerance is going to destroy all that you've worked for?"

Diocletian pursed his lips. Casca's gaze darted from one man to the other, but wisely, he held his peace.

Galerius went on, "So now, will you listen to reason? Simply banning these Christians from the military and public office is not sufficient to bring them back to the truth. Now they have set fire to your palace—and they almost murdered the daughter of the *Praefectus Augustalis* of Egypt! How would that have harmed relations with Alexandria? And she is all but promised now to my nephew, which makes it a personal insult to me."

Diocletian leaned on his desk, head bowed, the firelight from the nearby brazier casting his face in mercurial shadows. He looked like a statue of a mourning god, Casca thought, flawless even in the depths of uncertainty.

"What are you suggesting I do, Galerius?" Diocletian asked,

and his voice was so low Casca almost couldn't hear it.

"It is time for you, like Jupiter, to unleash the storm of fire and blood," he said, rising from his *sella* and leaning on the table across from Diocletian. "Let it begin here, and let it make such a statement to the world that none will dare profess faith in that false god ever again."

"You are once again advocating the wholesale slaughter of countless Roman citizens."

"Citizens! They are as unworthy of that title as any barbarian I've ever fought. Diocletian, they will only be brought to heel by the blade of a sword."

Casca shifted his weight. By the anger that blazed in both men's eyes, he knew this was a long-standing argument between them. He'd heard that as soon as they both arrived in Nicomedia, they had holed up in this very *tablinum*, and spent hours every day arguing over what to do about the Christian problem. Casca was only glad that he'd been gone for most of it. If there was such a thing as a dragon, Diocletian was the very embodiment of one when he was angry.

Diocletian measured Galerius stonily for a moment, but Casca could see the turn of his thoughts as he considered the situation. Diocletian turned suddenly to Casca.

"A solution to my many problems then," he said, and Casca's stomach curdled as he realized he was counted among those problems. "You once brought me the message of the Oracle, and her words have often been in my thoughts. The sword she spoke of."

"Excalibur?"

"Georgius took it into exile, presumably. But by all reports I have heard, the ferocious red-headed *miles* who travels with Constantinus fights with a battle axe of a rather barbarian style."

Casca snorted. "Of course he would."

"So, where is the sword?"

There was a silence, and Casca shuffled his feet. "I don't...I don't know?" he ventured.

"I want you to find out." Diocletian glanced across the room at Galerius, and Casca almost thought he saw the ghost of a smile at the corner of his mouth. "Go. Find it for me, and bring it back to me. The next time I see you, if you don't have that sword for me, I will kill you myself."

Then he turned to Galerius. "Do what you will."

Nicomedia, Anatolia — December 24, A.D. 302

A few days later, Casca left the private *tablinum* where *Caesar* Galerius had summoned him, his thoughts churning in a thick daze. He had thought the *Caesar*'s plan with the palace fire had been bold, but this...

This was not bold. It was something else.

Once outside the palace he called for his horse, and the whole time he wove his way through the bustling streets, he battled with himself, fighting to bolster his nerve. Galerius had told him to see to the matter of Petrus Cubicularius before he departed for Britannia, and Casca had all but promised him that he would make the man suffer.

He heard the chatter of voices, the loud back and forth of barter in the market, and it drew his mind back to his surroundings. The *forum* spread around him in a riot of color and noise. Women with laden baskets wandered between the market stalls, and children wove in and out of the crowds, laughing, thieving baubles and coins from unsuspecting shoppers. But the men stood in tight little knots, talking in low voices. Their shifty eyes watched Casca as he rode past, and he clenched his jaw.

They should not look at him like that. Didn't they realize

who he was? Didn't they know the power he commanded over their very lives?

I wonder how many of them will not last the night, he thought.

The wind had shifted, and a cold, damp breeze was bringing with it a dark rack of clouds that would soon blot out the sun. Casca stared a long time at the troubled sky, daring it to unleash its fury, and a warm, languid sense of power flowed through his veins.

Yes, I walk the road of blood, he thought. *And there is no other road that I would choose.*

He soon arrived at the amphitheater, where once, so long ago, they had made a mockery of Jurian's battle with the so-called dragon of Cyrene. The memory of the farce made him smile, and he was still smiling as he approached the contingent of guards stationed outside the arena. They bowed low to him and let him pass, and the centurion in charge came out to meet him. He was a hard man, and the pale, knotted scars on his bare arms bore witness to his long experience in battle.

"We executed the two as you requested," he said. "But you asked that the other—Diocletian's chamberlain, Cubicularius—be kept aside."

"Yes. I have something special in mind for him," Casca said. "But I have another task for you tonight, Anatolios."

The centurion folded his arms across his broad chest. "Oh?"

"At sundown, bring your cohort to the palace. And make sure each man brings a torch."

Anatolios snorted. "I would have thought they'd have had enough of fire at the palace after the other night."

Casca scowled at him. "Watch your tongue," he said. "Or you may lose it."

"Don't threaten me, *Tribunus,*" Anatolios said. "Especially not here, where you are my guest."

Casca and Anatolios faced each other for a long moment, and then Casca decided it was best to keep the man appeased. After all, he needed him.

"Just be there at sundown," he said. "Fail me and you fail

the Divine *Imperator*, on whose orders I am here. And now, take me to Petrus Cubicularius."

CASCA COULD NEVER UNDERSTAND the strength of these Nazarenes' wills. It was the same with Theodorus and Lucius Titianus, it was the same with the Libyan eunuch Hanno. Casca had seen far stronger men, far mightier men, break under the scourge. More powerful men than a mere chamberlain had found their tongues loosened by the salve of salt and vinegar. How could these simple men be so unrelenting?

It was nearing midnight, and Casca sat in the courtyard of the palace, staring into the glassy water of the reflecting pool. The smell of char stung his nostrils, and still the man's screams echoed in his ears.

And what was the point? Petrus Cubicularius had preferred to die than give him any information. Casca couldn't imagine preferring death to anything. And he had only wanted a location from the man. It wasn't as though Casca had asked him to betray his friends. Not exactly, anyway.

But he deserved to die. Even if his death was useless, it was deserved. And at any rate, Casca had succeeded in getting the information he needed—that Galerius needed—from another slave they had captured the night of the fire. That man had broken much more readily. So all was well.

Now all that remained was to wait.

Casca didn't know how long he sat there, but then he saw the torchlight in the water and knew that the hour had come. He turned and saw Anatolios striding toward him.

"It is time," he said.

Casca left the pool and followed Anatolios to the courtyard in front of the palace. Another soldier held their horses, and Casca swung up beside Anatolios. Galerius was already mounted, waiting, fierce and implacable, like the statue of avenging Jove himself.

They set off through the empty streets, the light from the torches scattering the darkness. The air was oppressive with the threat of a storm, and a fitful, cold wind snapped at the awnings and tangled the men's cloaks in icy fingers. Galerius rode at the head of the column, and Casca and Anatolios followed just behind him. The priests of the Temple of Jupiter came next, bearing a great tripod and an *amphora* of incense.

Everything seemed a blur to Casca. He had relayed the slave's directions exactly to Galerius, but now he couldn't remember a single detail of it. His horse seemed to sense his agitation—its ears kept flattening on his head, and it startled at every sound.

Finally, Galerius reined in his horse and held up a hand, calling the troop to a halt. They had reached a quiet square in the midst of the city, and the building before them was as unobtrusive and peaceful as a stable on a winter's night. It looked like a temple, and it seemed utterly abandoned.

Casca's heart jumped into his throat as a sudden clammy terror washed over him. The slave had promised that the followers of that Galilean would all be gathered here for the "great feast," as he'd called it. But if he had lied, and Casca had been misled, Galerius would probably slit his throat on the spot.

But then, faintly, Casca heard the sound of singing coming from within the building. He wanted to stop his ears. It was even more horrible than the screams of that traitor slave, Petrus Cubicularius. It made his flesh crawl.

"Open in the name of *Caesar* Galerius!" shouted the herald.

The singing stopped as abruptly as if it had been cut off by a sword. After a long moment, the doors opened and an old man stepped outside. His long beard reached almost to his waist, and he carried his many years on straight shoulders.

"If you have come to join us," he said, his voice carrying across the square, "then enter and celebrate the birth of the Christ with us."

A ripple of uneasy laughter ran through the ranks of soldiers, and even Galerius seemed amused by the man's boldness. But Anatolios sat rigidly beside Casca, regarding the ancient with something like respect. Casca narrowed his eyes. Was he a sympathizer?

But then Anatolios raised his arm and the soldiers came to attention. Anatolios gave another signal and they fanned out around the building, taking up positions on every side. Their torches guttered and then blazed.

The old man watched the proceedings with uncanny calm. Casca almost envied him. His own stomach was roiling, and his hands were damp with sweat. A scattering of snowflakes swirled down into the square on the uneasy wind, like pale flakes of ash.

"Who are you?" Galerius demanded of the old man.

"I am Anthimus," he said. "*Episcopus* of Nicomedia."

Galerius turned to Casca. "Go inside," he said. "Tell these unbelievers and blasphemers what awaits them. Tell them to come out and offer incense to save their lives."

Casca nodded once and dismounted. Slowly, he paced the distance from the *Caesar* to the steps. He felt like he was walking through sludge. His feet dragged, and the only thing that kept him moving was the inexorable and invisible force of Galerius's power driving him from behind.

He reached the top of the steps and glanced at Anthimus. The *episcopus* didn't seem angry, or surprised, or even afraid. He just stood there, and met Casca's eye.

And smiled.

Casca snapped his gaze away and entered the *ekklesia*.

He froze as if his feet had taken root in the floor. So many people. He had never imagined so many. Women, infants, children, old men, all staring straight at him with wide eyes.

Like sheep to the slaughter.

Casca shivered uncontrollably. Sweat trickled down his temples and burned in his eyes, but he couldn't move to wipe it away.

He had to speak to them. His mouth opened but nothing would come out. He hated them. Hated them and their staring lamb eyes, their peace, their...*joy*. His hands, shaking fitfully, twisted in the length of his wool cloak.

Why would they not fight? Why did they not charge him? They were so many. They could trample him if they wished. There were not soldiers enough in the square to take down even a third of the men in that gathering. They could all be free. But they just stood there.

What kind of shepherd lets his flock be eaten by the wolves?

He loathed them all. If they would not fight and they would not run, they deserved death, if for nothing other than their stupidity.

"You are surrounded!" Casca shouted, hatred giving his voice power. "If you would live this night, the *Caesar* Galerius is prepared to grant you mercy! Come out and renounce your blasphemy. Burn incense to Jupiter, and go in peace!"

No one moved. Two men had been chanting in Greek when he had entered the building, and their song still carried on against Casca's words, but softly now, persistent and patient.

Casca clenched his jaw to keep his teeth from chattering. Anthimus appeared beside him, and Casca turned to face him. "Tell them," he said. "If they do not come out, they will all be burned to death." He flung his arm wide to encompass the whole crowd. "Down to the last infant, they will all perish."

Anthimus regarded him with something like pity. Casca seized him by the arms and shook him.

"Tell them!" he shouted. And, as Anthimus still said nothing, he whispered, "Please tell them."

Behind him, the solemn chant began to swell, until the ancient stone echoed with it.

"Show us, O Lord, Your mercy, and give to us Your salvation. Lord, hear my prayer, and let my cry come to You. Let me listen, now, to the voice of the Lord God; it is a message of peace He sends to His people; to His loyal servants, that come back, now, with all their heart to Him. For us, His worshipers, deliverance is close at hand; in this land of ours, the divine glory is to find a home."

As the echoes died away, Anthimus left Casca and went, slowly, back up the main aisle to the simple altar. He knelt down on the steps and raised his own voice.

"*Judge me, O God, and distinguish my cause from the nation that is not holy: deliver me from the unjust and deceitful man. For You are God, my strength: why have You cast me off? And why do I go sorrowful while the enemy afflicts me?*"

The people knelt on the cold stone, and the two men who had been singing before took over the chant, "*Send forth Your light and Your truth: they have conducted me and brought me unto Your holy hill, and into Your tabernacles.*"

Casca turned away and headed slowly toward the doors. He wanted to crawl. The voices continued behind him.

"*There I will go up to the altar of God, the giver of triumphant happiness; You are my own God, with the harp I hymn Your praise.*"

He heard the sound of weeping, but the voices carried on. He reached the door and laid his hand on the wood frame.

"*Soul, why are you sad?*" thundered Anthimus's voice from the altar steps behind him, and Casca stumbled on the threshold. "*Will you never be at peace? Wait for God's help; I will not cease to cry out in thankfulness, my champion and my God.*"

Casca left the *ekklesia* and stepped out into the night. Galerius sat astride his white horse, unmoving. Beside him, Anatolios waited, hand raised.

"They will not come." Casca heard his own voice roll across the square.

"Bar the doors," Galerius ordered.

Two *milites* shouldered past Casca and dragged the doors closed. Just before they shut, Casca heard Anthimus's voice.

"May almighty God be merciful to you, and forgiving your sins, bring you to everlasting life."

Casca's legs shook as he made his way down the steps, while a small troop of soldiers marched past him carrying wood braces. The sound of hammer on iron nails thudded in Casca's head. Thunder growled and lighting forked in the sky, blazing off the swirl of snowflakes in some bizarre cacophony of the skies. The wind gusted, guttering the torches.

And then, when the hammering stopped, he heard the

singing again.

Anatolios's hand dropped, and the torches arced through the night sky. Casca turned, barely able to force his body into obedience.

A great pyre had been built before the doors and soaked in pitch, and now one of the soldiers drove a torch into its belly. It blazed up like an inferno.

Casca found his horse and clung to the saddle. He didn't have strength in his legs to mount. Vaguely, he thought he heard Galerius say something like, "Stay here and see that none escape."

And then Galerius wheeled his horse and cantered away with his personal guard.

Casca stood there, staring at the flames until his eyes watered. So long ago—it felt like so long ago—he had ordered a fire like this. How had two become two hundred, or two thousand, or twenty thousand?

He stood there, listening to the wailing and the screams, until the fire devoured them all and the rains and the sleet came.

Anatolios and his soldiers had gone, and the square was empty.

Thunder rolled overhead and lightning spit the darkness.

61

ALEXANDRIA, AEGYPTUS — JANUARY, A.D. 303

Aikaterina stood on the quay of Alexandria, tilting her face into the pale winter sun, and inhaled the stinging salt of the chill sea breeze. She had never been so grateful to be home.

They had returned with almost nothing, because the fire had ruined almost all of her clothes. Nenet carried one small chest containing what jewelry she had managed to salvage, and Theokritos and Diodoros each had a small bundle of *codices*—which, thankfully, had all been at the palace *bibliotheka* when the fire broke out. All, that is, except for the *codex* Diodoros had given her.

Nenet hailed a slave and ordered a litter to be brought, and soon the little party was disembarking at the palace gate. Diodoros and Theokritos took their own way to the *Bibliotheka*, and in spite of Aikaterina's protests that she wanted to see her father immediately, Nenet bustled her away to the baths and soon had her dressed in fresh clothes.

Now, looking once more like the governor's daughter instead of a ragged runaway slave girl, Aikaterina hurried through the corridors to her father's *cubiculum*.

The door was ajar, and Aikaterina pushed it open quietly and peeped inside. Her mother sat in a chair under the window, and even in the sunlight that glowed through the linen drapes, she looked faded. There was no sign of the *medicus*.

Aikaterina slipped into the room and her mother looked up swiftly, relief flooding her face.

"We had word of the fire," she said. "Aikaterina—are you all right?"

"Well enough," Aikaterina answered, voice thick. "How is Father?"

Her mother shook her head. "The doctors don't have much hope that he will ever recover," she said. "There are many reasons—I don't understand them."

She turned her face away, and Aikaterina's heart ached at the grief and weariness drawn in her mother's eyes. For a moment she hesitated, wondering how to comfort her, then went and knelt by her father's side. She took his hand in both her own and laid it against her cheek. It felt dry as dead leaves in winter, and it brought the tears to Aikaterina's eyes.

"Oh, Papa," she mumbled. "Please wake up."

"We have a guest," her mother said after a while, that pale fatigue still etched in her voice. "He is meeting with the senate this afternoon."

Aikaterina sniffled and set her father's hand gently back on the coverlet. "What?" she said, glancing at her mother over her shoulder. "What guest?"

"Come," her mother said. She rose from her chair, graceful as ever, and led Aikaterina out of the chamber.

"What guest, Mother?" Aikaterina said as soon as they were out in the corridor.

"The nephew of *Caesar* Galerius, Maximinus Daia. Apparently, the *Imperator* asked him to come and see to things here. He came while you were still in Nicomedia."

"I know why he is here," Aikaterina said, pressing her fingers to her forehead. "Is this not what you have been hoping for? A suitable match for me?"

Her mother sighed, looking inexpressibly weary. "I believe that is why he is here, but please, believe me when I say that this was not of my doing. He says that he was sent by imperial command." She drew her shoulders up and tried a faint smile at Aikaterina. "Chin up," she said. "Face this Maximinus Daia with courage. Perhaps he will not be as awful as you imagine. He may even be a friend."

Aikaterina sniffled. "I doubt it, considering that it was probably Galerius and Casca who conspired to get him here."

"There is always hope," her mother ventured.

WHEN AIKATERINA ENTERED THE *triclinium* that evening, she found her mother and a tall, round man already there, speaking in low voices. Her mother glanced up when she came in and forced a strained smile at Aikaterina, and the man turned around with ready congeniality.

He had a kind enough face, Aikaterina thought, even though his eyes bulged a bit like a fish's. For the first time since her mother had mentioned his presence, she felt a glimmer of hope that he might not be the monster she feared.

"Ah, Aikaterina," her mother said. "This is Maximinus Daia, nephew of the *Caesar* Galerius."

Aikaterina inclined her head in courtesy, but Maximinus Daia came forward eagerly and seized her hand. He bowed over it and pressed it to his lips.

"I have been to the senate this afternoon," he said. His voice was sonorous but carried the slightest lisp. "They are all very fond of you, *domina*."

"I am sure they are not all fond of me," Aikaterina said. "But thank you. It is kind of you to say so."

"Oh, no, they speak very highly of you. Your mind, they say, is quite remarkable. And there are not many in the Empire who have not heard how you threw Marcus Valerius Flaccus Casca out in disgrace." He chuckled and Aikaterina flushed. "Quite something, that. Very bold."

"She is much too bold for her own good," her mother said with a cautious smile.

Maximinus Daia held Aikaterina at arms' length. "We shall

see," he said. He crooked his arm and offered it to Aikaterina. "I hear you have a menagerie," he said.

"We do," Aikaterina said, taking his arm.

She led him back through the gardens and down the path that led to the menagerie. She hadn't been there herself since all their adventures with Menas in Rome, and to her surprise, the *Caesar*'s nephew was as eager as a child to see what she had to show him.

"A tiger!" he exclaimed when she paused in front of the enclosure. "Quite the beast. I saw one in the games in Sirmium. Tore apart some of those followers of the Christ like it was—" He stopped suddenly as Aikaterina stiffened. "I'm sorry," he said. "Such talk is not for delicate ears."

"You mistake me," Aikaterina said, spearing him with a glance. "I too have seen such bloodsport, when I was guest of the *Augusti* in Rome."

Maximinus Daia arched his eyebrows, which gave his comical face an even more exaggerated look of surprise. Aikaterina turned away from the tiger, which watched them out of its unblinking tawny eyes, and followed a small path to the aviary. He hurried to catch up with her, but she did not wait for him.

When he finally reached her, she was watching the brightly-feathered birds flit here and there in the great mesh net that kept them trapped. It always made her marvel how those creatures could seem so joyous, and sing so bravely, with the sky so close and yet forever out of their reach.

"You're angry with me!" Maximinus Daia marveled, studying her, and not the birds. "Aren't you? Gods, but you are beautiful when you are angry!"

Aikaterina decided it would only provoke him if she reacted, so she ignored him. But now he was chuckling to himself in the most aggravating way, and finally she turned to him in exasperation.

"What is so funny?" she demanded.

"Nothing is funny," he lisped. "I am just in amazement at

my good fortune. I thought when my uncle adopted me that I had emptied the *amphora* of the gods' blessings. But it seems they have more in store for me, and I cannot even believe it."

Aikaterina held his gaze until his eyes wavered and he turned to look at the bright birds in the cage. It wasn't long before he was chuckling to himself again.

"These birds," he said. "Why are they colored like that?"

Aikaterina linked her fingers through the fine mesh and watched one—a great bird with red and green and yellow feathers, as bright as if they had been painted.

"I think it makes the heavens happy," she said.

"But—they aren't practical."

"What?"

"Birds like that. You don't eat them, and they're not for sport. So what is the use of them?"

"You think everything must be useful to be valuable?" Aikaterina asked. "That there is no place for beauty in this world, in its own right?"

Maximinus Daia scratched his blond head. "I'm not sure I see the point of all that. What's it got to be beautiful for? Does it help it kill its enemies?"

I wonder what's wrong with him, Aikaterina thought. Aloud, she said, "A moment ago you said I was beautiful. Am I similarly useless?"

He studied her for a moment in a way she didn't quite like. "No, not useless," he said. "It pleases me to look at you…so that means your beauty has a purpose."

Aikaterina's hopes plummeted like a bird caught through the heart by an arrow. The man, if it was possible, was even more self-centered than Casca.

"If you will excuse me," Aikaterina said coldly. "I have matters to attend. I trust you can find your way back to the palace from here?"

She turned on her heel without waiting for his answer and headed back up the path, struggling to tamp down the rage fuming inside her.

"Wait!" Maximinus Daia called from behind her. She heard him huffing as he trotted after her. "Where are you going? Can't I come too?"

Aikaterina whirled to face him and he almost tripped over himself in his haste to stop before colliding into her. "No," she said. "I'm going somewhere where they keep useless beautiful things. I'm sure it would bore you."

"How could I be bored if I can look at you?" he said with a simpering smile.

Aikaterina left him standing in the middle of the path.

He must go, she thought. *He is odious, and if he follows me around staring at me all day like some stray cur, I will...I will...*

She didn't know what she would do. But she was certain that he didn't belong in Alexandria, and since she couldn't very well incite another riot to throw him out, she would have to come up with something else.

62

Sirmium, Pannonia Secunda — January, A.D. 303

After weeks of hard riding through the mountainous regions between Augusta Treverorum and the milder southern provinces of Pannonia, Jurian saw the walls of the great city of Sirmium rising in the distance. He glanced at Agapius, who rode on his right, unarmored, his dark hair grown long in a rather barbaric fashion. Agapius had proven himself an invaluable asset as a scout on their passage through the mountains—more than once, his keen senses had saved them from ambush. He carried no weapon now except for a *pugio*, and he seemed completely content in his new role.

The stiff breeze caught their horses' manes and the *draco* over Jurian's head snapped and unfurled. He grinned at Servius, whom he had elevated to the position of *draconarius*. When word had gotten around—perhaps through Agapius's doing—among his men that he was the Dragon-Slayer of Cyrene, they had asked the *custos armorum* to have a *draco* made for their unit. The dragon's head was copper molded around a frame of ash wood, and the long banner was red as flame.

While at first Jurian had thought it was a joke, Constantinus had surprised him in Summontorium by recognizing Jurian's unit officially as the *Ala Draconis* and promoting him to the rank of *Praefectus Alae*. Even though his ranks weren't quite numerous enough yet to merit the title of *ala*, Constantinus had assured him that they would recruit the rest in Sirmium.

Jurian spurred his horse and trotted ahead to join Constantinus at the head of the column. The Tribune looked even more grim than usual.

"Luckily for us," he said as Jurian approached, as if he were continuing a longer conversation that Jurian hadn't been part of, "Galerius is currently in Nicomedia." He glanced at Jurian. "There is no turning back once we ride through those gates."

"Why would I want to turn back?" Jurian asked, and glanced over his shoulder at the almost three hundred men he now commanded. "I'm looking forward to surprising the Emperor."

"Do your men know that?"

Jurian regarded him in some surprise. "I'm not intending to overthrow him, Constantinus," he said. "It's not like we're riding to invade Nicomedia." He paused, then, "What would you have me do?"

Constantinus's jaw tightened but he said nothing.

"Constantinus," Agapius said, nudging his horse up alongside them and pointing to a long bridge that arched over the river Sava. "I think we've finally found your bridge of destiny!"

Constantinus turned and leveled a ferocious glare at him, which only made Agapius cackle with delight. After a minute he fell back to his former position, and then Jurian dropped back to ride with his unit once more.

As they rode through the city gates, Jurian couldn't help but marvel at the expansiveness of the place. The river port was surrounded by workshops of all kinds, and a great *forum* with market stalls bustled with people. It reminded Jurian more of the stable and prosperous trade cities in the south of the Empire than the *coloniae* in the north, which were at peace, but precariously so. Even Augusta Treverorum had more the feel of a military fort than a flourishing city.

They passed a large building near the *forum* and Agapius

pointed. "Look!" he said. "A theater!"

Jurian groaned. "No more plays," he said. "You subjected me to that once already!"

"You didn't appreciate Plautus?" Servius said from his other side.

He leaned across to share a look with Agapius, and they both shook their heads at Jurian.

"No, I didn't," Jurian said.

"Well, we probably won't have time for such things," Servius said. "From what I hear, we'll have our hands full."

"Why is that?" Jurian asked.

"Didn't you say we were going to build out a full *ala* here? That's another two hundred men to recruit, and right under the nose of *Caesar* Galerius too."

Jurian frowned, wondering if this was another part of Constantinus's plans that he had failed to tell Jurian. He'd had no idea—or had forgotten—that Sirmium was Galerius's imperial seat, but now he understood why Constantinus had mentioned the *Caesar*'s absence. He glanced up at his *draco* and blew out his breath.

He's led us right into the heart of the beast, he thought. *That's what he must have meant when he said there was no turning back.*

They passed the great hippodrome, which was one of the largest structures Jurian had ever seen, daring to rival even the great Colosseum in Rome in its grandeur and sheer size. Shortly after they arrived at the *castra*, and Jurian left Agapius and Servius in charge of settling the men and the horses while he and Constantinus continued on alone to the palace.

"Watch yourself," Constantinus told Jurian as they clattered into the courtyard of the palace. "Valerius Licinius is close friends with Galerius—they served together in the Persian campaign, and Galerius has since shown him great favor. He leaves him in charge any time he is called away by the *Imperator*." They swung down from their horses and Constantinus added, "For now, you are Lucius Aurelius Georgius, *Praefectus Alae*, and nothing else."

They ascended the steps of the palace and Valerius Licinius himself came forward to meet them. He was a stocky man—not at all what Jurian had expected—but he obviously had seen his share of military service.

He has the look of a man who would knife you in the back when you least expected it, Jurian thought, *if he believed it would advance his own cause.*

"You should have sent word of your coming," Licinius said to Constantinus. "But no matter. It has been too long."

"Not nearly long enough," Constantinus muttered under his breath, and Jurian hid a grin. There was obviously no love lost between the two men.

Licinius turned on his heel and led them into the palace's inner courtyard. Jurian gaped as they passed a massive structure that dominated the courtyard. The stones used in its construction were so large that Jurian wasn't sure how anyone had managed to stack them. A small grove grew beneath the arches, and Jurian could see an altar stone in its center.

"What is that?" he asked.

Licinius glanced at him over his shoulder as if Jurian were nothing more than an ignorant peasant. "The *Caesar* has a great devotion to Jupiter," he said. "This commemorates his victory over the Sassanids in Satala."

Jurian felt a great surge of excitement, and he wanted to tell Licinius that he was from Satala himself and knew the battle well. But then he glanced at Constantinus, who gave the barest shake of his head. Jurian closed his mouth again and contented himself with admiring the workmanship of the arches.

It's so strange, he marveled as they moved past the grove, *how everything in my life seems to move in circles, especially lately.*

He felt strangely unsettled as he considered what that might mean, tracing circles in his life, moving ever closer to his own origins.

He hurried to catch up with Constantinus as they passed into the great *vestibulum*. The floors here, like in Londinium and Glevum, were like a great woven carpet of tessellated stone—

interlocking shapes and figures in all different colors.

"Your father is well, I trust?" Licinius said over his shoulder.

"He sends his greetings," Constantinus replied.

Licinius took his seat in the *sella* and Constantinus and Jurian stood respectfully before him. For the first time, Licinius seemed to notice Jurian as something more than an ignorant gawker. Perhaps it was the sight of Jurian's *lorica squamata*, or the way he stood confidently next to Constantinus, but Licinius sat straighter in his *sella* and studied him with interest.

"Who is this?" he asked Constantinus, indicating Jurian. "You are experimenting with the *cataphractarii* now?"

"Yes, I thought I might," Constantinus said. "This is Lucius Aurelius Georgius, my *Praefectus Alae*."

Licinius nodded slowly, but if he was impressed, he didn't show it. "I'm surprised that you thought it necessary to ride so far south with a full *ala*," he said warily. "I thought you were helping your father."

"We did," Constantinus said. "But we have business in Nicomedia."

"Is that so?" Licinius said, his voice even colder now.

Constantinus laid a hand on Jurian's shoulder. "I'm going to present him to the *Imperator*," Constantinus said, as if he were a proud father showing off his son.

All the wariness went out of Licinius's face, and he gave a short laugh. "You had me worried there," he said. "But of course, I had no cause, did I?"

"None at all."

Jurian felt something pass between the two men, but neither of them said anything further.

"You may find Nicomedia less than hospitable at the moment," Licinius said after a moment. "After what happened last month, the *Imperator* is in little mood for celebration."

"What happened last month?" Constantinus said. "We've been on the border battling the *barbarii*, and news reaches us late if it reaches us at all."

Licinius lifted a shoulder in a gesture of careless indifference.

"Someone set fire to the imperial palace. Some of those followers of that foul cult of the Nazarene, they think it was."

Jurian stiffened as a chill shivered through him, and he swallowed hard. He didn't dare speak for fear he would give himself away.

"I'm surprised you didn't hear," Licinius said. "Your niece was almost killed."

"My niece?" Constantinus said, the question more like a bark. "What was she doing in Nicomedia?"

"How should I know? But that was the report I heard. Don't look like that, by Jupiter. She's safe, and back in Alexandria now, I think. *Caesar* Galerius had summoned Maximinus Daia to go there and oversee things—make sure she is in no danger, and ensure the security of the city."

"Is that so?" Constantinus's voice carried an edge that Jurian hadn't heard in a long time.

Licinius leaned forward. "That isn't the half of it," he said. "The Divine *Imperator* was so angry that he put *Caesar* Galerius in charge of ferreting out the perpetrators. And you'll never guess what he did."

"I can't even imagine," Constantinus said.

"They were all together in their *ekklesia* for some feast. He sent in a tribune to try to persuade them to burn incense to Jupiter, and when they wouldn't come, they barred the doors to trap them inside. Then they burned them all to death."

A tribune, Jurian thought. *Casca.*

His hands closed into fists. Cold sweat beaded on his forehead, and he could barely breathe. "How many?" he asked, his voice hoarse.

"Who knows?" Licinius said, leaning back in his *sella*. "Two hundred? Two thousand? I even heard twenty thousand."

"Twenty. Thousand." It was all he could do to say the words. "That's...that's impossible."

"I know!" Licinius agreed. "How could Diocletian have been so foolish as to let that cult fester so long that it could grow to those kinds of numbers? Did he not know it was growing right under his nose? How could he have been so blind?"

"How could he be so foolish," Jurian repeated.

He wanted to drop to his knees and weep, or retch. He couldn't even fathom it. A dozen in the arena, that he could imagine, because he had seen it. Two burned to death in a house...he had seen it. But twenty thousand men, women, and children?

His stomach roiled and he closed his eyes against another wave of nausea. Vaguely, he heard Constantinus's voice through the fog that clouded his mind.

"Are you questioning the wisdom of your *Imperator*, Licinius?"

And Licinius's hasty reply, "No, no. Of course not. He is guided by the hand of the gods. Can I judge him?"

Jurian blinked and gritted his teeth, and stared at the imperial *signum* behind the *sella*.

Constantinus said, "It seems we ride for Nicomedia not a moment too soon."

63

Sirmium, Pannonia Secunda — January, A.D. 303

"How can you just sit there?" Jurian gritted, one hand tight on the hilt of his *seax* knife.

They had returned to the *castra* after the feast at the palace, and Constantinus sat with Agapius and Servius in Jurian's *cubiculum*. No one spoke, but Agapius's face was drawn and pale, and Servius seemed stunned out of his wits.

"I just told you that twenty thousand men, women, and children were burned alive," Jurian went on, "and all you can do is sit there?"

"What do you want us to do, Jurian?" Servius asked, raising his wide eyes to Jurian's. "I can't...how is such a thing even possible?"

"It's possible," Constantinus said. He leaned on his knees, fingers laced tightly together.

"Your mother wasn't in the palace when the fire happened, was she?" Jurian asked.

Constantinus shook his head. "She's away—I think the last letter I received from her, she was in Aelia Capitolina."

Jurian blew out his breath and paced the room. "I can't do nothing," he said.

"She's safe?" Agapius asked Constantinus. "You're sure?"

"I just told you. She's in Aelia Capitolina." Then he stopped and glanced at Agapius. "Oh, you mean Aikaterina. Yes. He said she made it out alive, and that she is back in Alexandria." He shifted his gaze to Jurian. "No one said you should do nothing. But there is the very real question of what you *can* do." And then, bluntly, he added, "They're all dead, Jurian."

"I know that."

"And with five hundred men, what do you think you would accomplish—other than suicide—in attacking Nicomedia?"

"Who said anything about that?" Jurian snapped. "Why do you think everything has to be solved with an army?"

Constantinus regarded him in surprise. "You're the one who wanted to disembowel a man out of vengeance," he said. "Perhaps I just think on a grander scale than you."

"If we were talking about murdering one person, or two, or even three," Jurian said, "I can believe Casca would be capable of that. But twenty thousand?" He shook his head. "I can't even fathom such a thing…much less imagine that he would have a hand in something of that magnitude."

"You'd better start fathoming it, I think," Agapius said. "Because it has happened. The storm is upon us, Jurian."

Jurian nodded in silence and went to the window to look out. The courtyard below was quiet save for a few sentries, who patrolled lazily about, stopping under the torches to talk in low voices and share a drink from a wineskin. Everything was at peace here, and the stars twinkled as if nothing of consequence had happened on their watch. How was it possible that the heavens had not split open and swallowed the whole of the Empire for such a crime?

"Diocletian has to be told," Jurian said, leaning on the sill. "It's not right. Whatever happened at the palace, it wasn't the fault of the Christians."

"How can you be so sure?" Servius asked.

"I just am." Jurian put a hand to his tunic and gripped the pyx hidden beneath its folds. "Licinius said they caught four men in the Emperor's household…but I know those men. They would never cause harm. Even Eleutherius, for all his obsession with fire...he would never do such a thing. It's not our way." He shook his head. "Diocletian may not like Christians, but he has been fairly reluctant to take drastic action against us so far. But someone wants to turn him against us completely...and it looks like he may have finally succeeded."

He pushed off the sill and turned to face his friends. They regarded him in silence, somber in the guttering lamplight.

"We stay only long enough to gather the rest of the men," he said, meeting Constantinus's gaze. "And then we ride for Nicomedia."

"But Jurian," Servius said, as Jurian started for the door, "what are you going to do when you get there?"

He paused, his hand on the latch. "I don't know yet."

He lay awake all that night, staring up at the ceiling. His heart still burned in anguish and anger over Sabra's death and Casca's actions in Cyrene, but this business in Nicomedia... whatever hurt had been done to him personally, it was time to put that aside. How many fathers and mothers, brothers, sisters, lovers had lost someone in that fire? How many, just like him, were left to grieve?

And his heart grieved for the heart of Christ, already pierced once by a lance...with what sorrow would He not weep to see His people slaughtered for their love of Him? And would no one stand up to defend them? To defend His honor?

He closed his eyes as if he could hear their screams, and then it was as if he was standing there. The darkness, the rolling thunder, the lightning that forked the sky, and before him, the inferno of fire as it consumed the building and everything—and everyone—inside. Then the heavens opened and poured down a balm of rain and sleet, and vaguely, from the corner of his eye, he thought he saw someone standing in the street.

As he strained to see if it was really a person or just a trick of the light, he saw a man who was not a man come toward him. He stopped between Jurian and the smoldering remains of the *ekklesia*. He was mail-clad like a soldier in Jurian's *ala*, and he held a great sword in his gauntleted hands. He held it point down, just resting on the stone. The hilt was like Excalibur's, and Jurian's heart leapt with joy.

He held out his hand to receive the sword, but the man who was not a man did not move. Slowly, Jurian lowered his hand again and waited.

"Lucius Aurelius Georgius," the man said, but his voice seemed not a voice—neither high nor low, soft nor loud. It was resonant, like the plucked string of some great instrument, and Jurian felt everything within him vibrate in response.

"I am here, *Domine*," Jurian said.

The man who was not a man did not speak again for a long time, but then he raised the sword and pointed it toward the heavens. A blinding flash of lightning arced from the sky and struck the sword, and the blade gleamed as if set on fire.

Then the man who was not a man said again, "Lucius Aurelius Georgius."

"I am here, *Domine*," Jurian repeated.

The man lowered the sword, point downward once more, to the stone, and the fire seeped from the blade and ran between the cobbles like tiny rivulets of blood. They flowed toward Jurian's feet and Jurian wanted to run, but he could not. Rooted to the spot, heart hammering, he watched as the streams snaked closer and closer.

"Lucius Aurelius Georgius," the man who was not a man said a third time.

"I am here, *Domine*," Jurian said again.

The flames reached him, and Jurian felt a great shock shiver through him from the soles of his feet to the roots of his hair.

The man who was not a man raised his eyes and met Jurian's. They were deep and fathomless, ancient and new, and under that gaze Jurian felt as if his soul had caught fire.

"Rise!" the Man called in a great voice.

And then He lifted the sword and drove the point down into the stone.

64

Alexandria, Aegyptus — January, A.D. 303

Aikaterina was hiding in the *Bibliotheka*. At least, she told herself that she was busy cataloging some new manuscripts that had recently arrived from Corinth, but the truth was that she was hiding from Maximinus Daia. He had no use for libraries, he had told her. She hadn't said a word in reply.

Her peaceful work was suddenly interrupted by a scattering of footsteps, and she glanced up to see Diodoros hurrying toward her. Seeing his face she started to her feet, because his eyes were glassy and rimmed with red, his hair disheveled as if he had been tearing it in grief.

"Oh, no," she whispered, running to meet him and clasping his hands. "Is it...is it Father?"

"No," he said. He closed his eyes and bowed his head. "I came to tell you something else... We just received word..."

The look on his face made Aikaterina's stomach seize. "How much worse can things get, Diodoros?" she asked, but she was afraid of his answer.

"After we left Nicomedia...*Caesar* Galerius, he...all the Christians who were gathered for the vigil of the Nativity..."

Aikaterina gripped his arm. "What did he do?"

"*Kyria*, he—" His voice failed, and he glanced up at the windows as if that could hide how they shone. "He burned them all alive."

She staggered. "All—"

"The courier said twenty thousand."

Something burst inside her. Her vision clouded, until she couldn't even see Diodoros's face. Everything inside her felt numb and cold, and for a moment she wasn't even sure she was still breathing.

"*Kyria*," came Diodoros's voice, as if from somewhere far away. "I'm so sorry…"

"How? How could he do such a thing?" she mumbled. "How could anyone? What kind of evil…what kind of evil…"

It was incomprehensible. Her teeth chattered with horror and she couldn't stop shaking. She raised her eyes to Diodoros's face, her hand tight on his arm.

"Diodoros," she murmured, "Is this the end? Is this the end of all things? Will the world end in fire and blood?"

He shifted his gaze to the shaft of sunlight angling through the high windows, and shook his head. "I don't think it is the end," he said. "I fear it is only the beginning."

Aikaterina sagged and he caught her, and then guided her to a bench at one of the tables. She sat there, staring at the grain of the wood, her mind utterly blank.

"I can't think," she said, and her voice sounded thick in her own ears. She took one shuddering breath, and then another, focusing on the feel of her heartbeat against her ribs. "What am I supposed to do? What can I possibly do? I will never allow that to happen in Alexandria, but if he comes, if he tests me… what should I do?"

"I don't know."

She didn't think she had any tears left, but they burned in her eyes and in the back of her throat. "I wish…I wish Father would wake up," she said. "I can't do this alone. I don't know how. I don't know—" Her breath caught in a sob. "I want my city to be a haven. Why can't I protect my people?"

Diodoros shook his head. "They are not yours to protect, *kyria*," he said gently. "They are God's first."

"But He has given me charge of them," Aikaterina protested. "I am responsible...I cannot do nothing."

"He will show you the way," Diodoros said, laying his hand over hers. "You will know what to do when the time comes, I am sure of it."

Aikaterina shifted her gaze to his face, but at that moment, the great door opened and Nenet appeared in a burst of watery sunlight. She bustled toward them when she saw Aikaterina, and Diodoros released her hands and got to her feet. Nenet speared him with a suspicious look and then turned to her mistress.

"You've been weeping! Have you?"

"No," she murmured. "Tears are useless in times like these."

Nenet gave her a reproachful look, then nodded once and said, "You are asked for in the palace," she said.

Aikaterina heaved a sigh and rose. "Is it my mother?" she asked.

"No, *kyria*."

"Then it must be that wretched imbecile Maximinus Daia."

Nenet's face quirked in a small smile. "Your words, not mine, *kyria*."

Aikaterina glanced at Diodoros, hoping he would recognize her dismay and tell her that they needed her help with the catalogue. But he said nothing, and Aikaterina gestured for Nenet to lead the way.

"If I am not back within the hour," Aikaterina said to Diodoros, "please summon me, would you? On urgent business."

Diodoros smiled faintly and nodded. "We will."

Nenet led her outside and back up the path to the palace. When Aikaterina entered the *atrium*, she found Maximinus Daia sitting on a low stone bench, poring over a letter and scowling.

Aikaterina's heart leapt in sudden hope. Perhaps he was being summoned away.

"Not bad news, I hope," Aikaterina said, dismissing Nenet with a wave of her hand. She came forward and stood near the bench, but Daia didn't seem to realize she was there. "*Domine?*" she said. "Have you received bad news?"

He startled and glanced up. "Oh," he said. "I sent your slave for you."

"I am here, as you see."

"Yes, I see that."

Aikaterina waited patiently for a moment, but he only went on scowling at the parchment. "Is there something wrong?" she ventured.

"Yes and no. At least, I hope not." He lifted the letter, waving it like a pennant at her. "Read, if you like."

Aikaterina snatched it from him and scanned it quickly. It was a dispatch from Sirmium, reporting that an *Ala I Draconis* of *cataphractarii* under the command of one Lucius Aurelius Georgius was preparing to ride for Nicomedia, accompanied by Constantinus, son of *Caesar* Constantius Chlorus.

Jurian. Commanding an *ala* of heavy horse, riding for Nicomedia. It was almost beyond belief.

He knows, she thought in a rush of joy. *He is coming home to set all wrongs to right.*

"Is this true?" she asked Daia, holding out the letter. "Is it true, about this *ala*?"

"That's what it says," he answered sourly. "But I don't know what it means."

"Then perhaps you should return to Nicomedia at once," Aikaterina said. "To meet my uncle Constantinus and this Lucius Aurelius Georgius—"

"You want to be rid of me," he said suddenly, cutting her off. He seized her by the wrist. "Is that it?"

Aikaterina winced and tried to pull her hand away. "What?"

"How convenient for you," he continued. "Have you written to your uncle? Is that why he is bringing an armed force against Nicomedia?"

"I haven't, and he is doing no such thing." His grip on

her wrist tightened and she bit back a cry of pain. "Let me go, *domine*. This does not become you."

Maximinus Daia got to his feet but did not let her go. "You belong to me," he said. "The *Imperator* promised you to me."

Aikaterina shook her head, feeling the sudden rush of courage that always left her breathless. "I belong to no man," she said and pulled her hand free. "Least of all to you."

He held her gaze for a long moment, but she didn't waver. "He cannot protect you, you know," he said. "If that's what you are hoping."

"The one who will protect me is greater even than my uncle," Aikaterina retorted.

Daia laughed at her, as if she were a precocious child he found amusing. Placing his forefinger beneath her chin, he said, "I do not need to have you to have Alexandria, you know."

Aikaterina's heart pounded against her ribs. "Do not threaten me, Daia," she said, keeping her voice even. "I know well who rules this world, and it is not you. Every move you make or don't, every word you say or don't, it is all by someone else's direction. And you and I both know what will happen to you if you throw Alexandria into chaos."

Daia pulled his hand back as if he would strike her, but when she did not flinch, he laughed and lowered it to his side. "That may not always be the case," he said.

"Perhaps not," Aikaterina agreed. "But we don't live in a hypothetical world, do we?" She raised the letter under his nose. "Now, what are you going to do about this?"

He took the paper from her and creased it. "I will return to Nicomedia," he said. "But when I come back, I will come for what is mine."

He tapped her under the chin with the letter and then left the *atrium*. As soon as he was gone, Aikaterina sank down on the bench, tears of relief gathering on her lashes.

Maximinus Daia was leaving, and Jurian was coming home in triumph. The tide was turning, she was sure of it. The storm was almost past.

65

Maridunum, Britannia — February, A.D. 303

Casca looked over his shoulder at the soggy hill country stretching endlessly away behind him. Britannia was a wretched place, he decided, and the sooner he could be done with his troublesome task, the sooner he could ride back into Nicomedia in triumph. He had been chasing rumors for two weeks, and had finally gotten a report that sounded more plausible than most—that Jurian had arrived in a place called Glevum with a great sword across his shoulders, and then a few weeks later, had returned without it.

Finally, as the afternoon was wearing on and Casca was beginning to fear that he would be stuck another night on the side of the road, he caught sight of a shabby little town squatting on the edge of a river. No one was out, and no wonder. Who would be out in the muck if they had a dry place by the fire? On a low hill, he saw a Roman fort, but it was clearly vacant. He wondered how long it had been unoccupied, and why. Not that it mattered—it only mattered that it could afford him no comforts.

As his horse plodded down the street, the door of one of the hovels suddenly opened, and a young man burst outside. Casca reined in his horse, and the boy stopped and gaped at him.

"Oh," he said, in heavily accented Latin. "You're not—"

"Albanus!" came a young woman's voice, and the next moment, she appeared in the doorway.

Casca sucked his breath through his teeth. It was impossible. He watched, frozen, as another girl appeared, pushing past her sister. These girls—he remembered them. How could he forget the twin lionesses who had fought so brilliantly in the arena? They had disappeared after Jurian had spirited Menas out of the arena. No one knew what had become of them, and yet, here they were.

Casca's stomach roiled with distaste. Of course, Jurian would have to play the hero and return the stolen girls to their home. It was so perfectly typical of him.

One look at Casca and the girl who had stepped out of the hut reeled back with a cry of alarm. Everything seemed to happen at once. Albanus jumped in front of the girls with a wooden broom—as if it would do anything against Casca's *spatha*, then an old man shouldered his way outside, yelling at the top of his lungs in some language Casca didn't understand. And the bolder girl, standing directly behind the boy, just stared at Casca as if he had personally betrayed her. As if she had been expecting to see someone else.

Clearly, this situation was a bit more volatile than he had anticipated. He held up his hands, empty of any weapons.

"*Pax!*" he said, the word strange in his mouth. "I'm not going to hurt anyone."

At that, the old man came forward and bowed. "You will forgive our uproar, *domine*," he said in Latin. "We do not often get visitors here, and my daughters have only just recently been returned to me—"

"After their escape from the games, you mean?" Casca said, his eyes on the bold girl's face. She was staring at him with murder in her eyes. She, he knew, had the skill to end his life—and probably would do it without a moment's hesitation

The old man laughed nervously. "What would have given you such an idea?" he asked. "Of course not! They were only just visiting a cousin in the south, and—"

Casca looked from the old man back to the girls, calculating. What would it gain him to make enemies of these people? He recognized the girls, but they likely had never seen him before, certainly not in any way that they would recognize him now. But if they were here, they had come with Jurian. Which meant they were more likely than anyone else to have information about him.

"Of course," he said. "I am mistaken. I'm trying to find a friend of mine, who was rumored to have passed this way a little over two years ago. Like me, he traveled from the south, so perhaps you would remember him? Lucius Aurelius Georgius was his name, or perhaps you would know him as Jurian. He traveled with three companions—another soldier, a giant with a single eye, and the *Caesar*'s son Constantinus."

There was absolute silence, and Casca shifted his weight uncomfortably, all their eyes riveted on him.

Then the boy Albanus took a step forward with a defiant lift of his chin. "I saw him, *domine*, but it was, as you say, two years ago. He's long since gone."

"What was he doing in these parts?"

The boy's eyes narrowed. "He spouted a lot of nonsense about some mystical sword. Was he really a friend of yours? I think he was a little mad."

"Well, that may be," Casca said placidly. "Did he really have a mystical sword?"

Albanus shrugged. The bolder girl was watching him fixedly, her hand toying with the plait of her long braid. Casca's gaze flitted over her, and then snapped back, because she wore an unmistakable silver ring styled with two clasped hands—a *fide* ring. So, the lioness had found herself a mate. Casca's lip lifted in displeasure.

"He had a sword," Albanus said with careful indifference. "Think he lost it somewhere, though."

"Somewhere in these parts?"

The girl speared Albanus a sharp glance, then stepped past

the old man. "We have not seen him in years," she said. "Surely, if he is friend to you, he would have sent word to you."

"Are you questioning me?" Casca asked.

The girl lifted her chin. "What are you looking for, Roman? The soldier or the sword?"

Clever, Casca thought.

He drew his *spatha* and edged his horse closer to her, pointing the tip of it toward her throat. "Perhaps both," he said.

No one moved. They almost didn't dare to breathe. But she just glared at him, terrible and cold and utterly unimpressed by his threat.

"Maybe you *should* go looking for that sword," Albanus said suddenly. "Maybe it'll drive you mad too. Ask her. Ask her what he did with it."

"Ask who?"

"The Lady of Ynys Afallon."

"Albanus!" the girl hissed, but he ignored her.

"Thank you for that." Casca sheathed his sword and tugged his horse's head toward the road.

"I hope you do find Jurian!" Albanus shouted after him.

"Don't worry," Casca said over his shoulder. "I will."

As he rode away he heard the girl say to Albanus, "Why did you tell him?"

"Because he won't be able to do anything with that sword even if he finds it. And I really hope that place drives him mad."

Casca gritted his teeth and drove his horse down the Roman road toward Glevum.

66

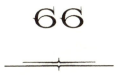

Sirmium, Pannonia Secunda — February, A.D. 303

Jurian sat astride his black horse above the plain outside the walls of Sirmium. The *draco* snapped in the wind over his head as he surveyed his assembled *ala*. Five hundred heavy cavalry waited for his orders, the burnished plates of their armor glinting in the midwinter sun. The horses snorted clouds of steam, and the lifted long lances marched back in even rows, like a forest of saplings.

He couldn't help smiling. He had been around Legions all his life, but he had never seen anything so splendid—or fearsome—as that assembly.

"I think it will be very convincing, don't you?" Constantinus asked from beside him. Jurian glanced at him and saw that he, too, was grinning. "Hard to argue with a man who has five hundred *cataphractarii* at his command."

"If the weather holds, we should reach Nicomedia in three weeks," Agapius said, cantering up and reining in his horse beside Servius. "They've lit the signal fires, so every fort and *colonia* from here to Philippopolis knows we're coming."

"I had Licinius dispatch messages to Nicomedia and Alexandria," Constantinus said. "Just to make sure a warm welcome is waiting for us. I also took the liberty of sending word to Coel back in December, before we left Ara Agrippinensium—I thought Menas could meet us in Nicomedia. I am sure he would want to be there to see your triumphal return home."

"Thank you," Jurian said, his heart strangely moved. He glanced at Servius and Agapius, then turned back to Constantinus. "Shall we ride?"

"Let's ride," he said.

Jurian nodded to Servius, and he raised the *draco* and signaled for the *ala* to prepare to move out. They cantered down the hill and took their places at the head of the column.

"Three weeks?" Jurian asked to Agapius as the thunder of hooves picked up behind them.

"Three weeks."

THE THREE WEEKS PASSED like an eternity. The roads were good and the weather did hold, but still their pace felt agonizingly slow to Jurian. Agapius and Servius had become good friends, and they spent much of the journey discussing what they would do when they reached Nicomedia, but Jurian quickly wearied of their jovial conversation. He couldn't shake the sense that they were riding into darkness, and he felt rudderless. Whenever he could, Jurian rode with Constantinus, but the Tribune, like Jurian himself, seemed lost in his own thoughts and had very little to say. Jurian couldn't help wondering what was preoccupying his mind.

His own thoughts were in a constant turmoil. He had intended to win back the favor of an emperor, but twenty thousand now stood between them. How could he reason with a man who could sweep away the lives of so many of his people? How could he even try?

The closer they came to Nicomedia, the heavier his doubts grew.

Still, he did his best to conceal the tumult in his mind, for the sake of his men, and for the sake of the people who came out to greet them. The signal fires from Sirmium had done their work, for in every town they passed through, a crowd of people had gathered to cheer them on.

Shouts of *"Cyrenicus!"* and *"Draconis!"* rang in the streets, and women gathered to throw flowers in their path. Wherever they stopped, they were feasted as if they had just come from a great victory. Jurian couldn't understand it, but Constantinus seemed content, and Jurian wondered if this, too, were all part of his calculations.

They stopped in the town of Serdica to rest their horses and reprovision the *ala* for the final ten days of their journey to Nicomedia. Jurian found Constantinus on the walls, leaning on the battlement and staring out over the rough terrain to the south.

"Is this what you had planned?" he asked, leaning on his elbows beside him. "The cheering and the flowers and all that? Were you expecting it?"

Constantinus shrugged. "Not at all," he said. But then he glanced sidelong at Jurian with a quirk of a smile. "It may prove to be better."

"Or not," Jurian added.

"Or not." He was silent a while, looking out toward the horizon, then he turned back to Jurian and said, "I thought you always wanted to be a hero. This is a hero's welcome."

"But I haven't done anything to deserve it," Jurian protested. "A few skirmishes with the barbarians, Constantinus. It's not like it was the Battle of Vindonissa."

That made Constantinus chuckle. "How my father loves that story," he said. Then he waved a hand as if to dismiss Jurian's concerns. "The people love a hero…and they especially love one who rides a horse in splendid armor."

"That's not true!" Jurian laughed out loud.

"You'd be surprised."

"But to what purpose are you dragging these people out of their homes to gawk at me?" Jurian pressed.

"Because word spreads faster than you might think, and if Diocletian thinks you have the hearts and souls of the people all the way from Nicomedia to Augusta Treverorum, then he will be very willing to accede to any demands you might care to make."

"You honestly think a bunch of parades and cheering are going to give me the bargaining power to sway an emperor?" Jurian asked.

Constantinus shrugged. "It's worth the hazard. You'll have five hundred heavy horse to toss into the balance…and, by the time we're done, almost legendary status among the people of the East. Surely that puts you in a stronger position than a disgraced *tribunus angusticlavius* crawling back out of exile to beg pardon at the knees of the *Imperator*, don't you think?"

Jurian couldn't argue with that, but he also couldn't help wondering if Constantinus might be overestimating the effect it would have on Diocletian.

I guess I'll have to wait ten days to find out, he thought.

The cheering crowds were there to greet them again in Philippopolis and even as far south as Perinthus. They skirted the edge of the Propontis, the gateway of water between *Mare Nostrum* and the great inland sea that bordered Anatolia, and then the walls of Nicomedia were in sight.

As they thundered through the city gates under a lowering sky heavy with rain, another crowd gathered to meet them. But this one, Jurian thought, had none of the lighthearted and cheerful attitudes of the towns to the north. Instead, there was an almost breathless anticipation pulsing in the streets, as if the people here harbored some secret hope that Jurian had come to liberate them.

Before the gates of the palace, Jurian drew his *ala* up into parade formation, and then he, Constantinus, Agapius, and Servius, who bore the *draco*, dismounted and ascended the steps. Diocletian himself, dressed in brilliant purple, waited there to receive them. He was flanked by several other men, only a few of whom Jurian recognized. Galerius was there, of course, and a young man he had met before in Rome, *Imperator* Maximianus's son Maxentius. There was no sign of Casca, and Jurian felt a twinge of disappointment. He had secretly hoped that the snake would be there to see his triumphal return.

Jurian's party stopped a few feet from Diocletian, and they all presented the *Imperator* with a formal military salute.

"Constantinus," Diocletian said smoothly, "news of your coming has preceded you."

Constantinus stepped to the side and lifted his arm to present Jurian. "*Imperator*," he said, "I bring back, as one risen from the grave, Lucius Aurelius Georgius, *Praefectus Alae* of the *Ala I Draconis*."

Jurian waited, hardly daring to breathe, as Diocletian's gaze snapped from Constantinus to him. It took him a moment to realize that, with his helmet on, the Emperor had not yet recognized him. He pulled off his helmet and stepped forward.

A low murmur rippled through Diocletian's assembly, and white-hot anger simmered in Galerius's eyes. But Diocletian's face was like marble, and his gaze unreadable.

"So," he said finally. "It seems you have made a name for yourself in the north."

"My only wish is to serve," Jurian found himself saying, as if he had rehearsed the words.

Diocletian said nothing for a long, tense moment. Thunder growled in the distance, and behind him, his horsemen sat straight and perfectly still. This was the moment it could all come crashing down.

"Welcome back to Nicomedia, *Praefectus*," Diocletian said. "Your men are welcome in the *castra*." He moved as if to go inside, but paused and fixed Jurian with an enigmatic stare. "You are an exile no longer, Georgius *Cyrenicus*."

Jurian's knees almost buckled with relief, and he turned to Agapius and Servius. "See to it," he said. "And then rejoin me here."

Agapius and Servius bowed and returned to the *ala*, and Jurian heard Agapius calling the order to move out.

An exile no longer...

His heart wrenched strangely. *But I am, more than ever*, he thought.

"You may find our hospitality somewhat diminished, *Praefectus, Tribunus*," Diocletian said. "We are still recovering from the attack on the palace. But whatever comforts we can afford you, you will have."

He turned without another word and led the way into the palace, and Constantinus and Jurian fell in behind his assembly.

Servants came forward to escort them to their chambers, and Jurian was glad of the chance to remove his armor. After he had bathed and dressed in fresh garments, another slave came to summon him to an audience with the *Imperator*.

Jurian found Constantinus waiting for him in the corridor. He, too, had washed and traded in his military gear for his court toga.

"Tread carefully," Constantinus said to Jurian as they followed the slave. "Remember, you may have earned the temporary respect of the Emperor, but not everyone here is friendly to you."

Jurian nodded, though he didn't need Constantinus to warn him of that.

They entered the Emperor's *tablinum* and found Diocletian with *Caesar* Galerius and Maxentius in attendance. Diocletian was standing near the window, but he didn't turn as Constantinus and Jurian entered. Maxentius wore a look that might have been admiration or envy, but Galerius watched Jurian with ill-concealed displeasure, and as soon as the door was closed securely, he leveled a finger at him.

"You are in disgrace," he said. "An exile. How dare you come back here, and dressed as a Roman officer, receiving the honors of a Roman officer?"

Constantinus made an almost imperceptible gesture with his fingers, so Jurian said nothing.

"He has earned the right," Constantinus said. "He distinguished himself in battle for the Empire against the Alemanni in my father's service, and—"

"Your father," spat Galerius, "should know better than to cross the decree of our *Imperator Jovius Augustus!* How dare he allow this man into his service? How dare he allow him within his province?"

Constantinus's jaw tightened. Jurian knew that this was the battle he had anticipated. But to Jurian's surprise, before Constantinus could answer, Diocletian lifted his hand.

"I appreciate your zeal for our commands," the *Imperator* said. "But I am not above mercy for those who demonstrate their loyalty." He turned and leveled a look at Galerius, heavy with hidden meaning. "I have already lifted the *interdictio*."

Galerius flung himself moodily into the *sella* and clapped his mouth shut. Maxentius, Jurian noticed, was watching everything, as if he could devour the room and everyone in it with his gaze. Diocletian clasped his hands behind his back and turned to face Jurian.

"I have received reports of your activity," he said. "Julius Asclepiodotus first sent word of your coming into the court of Constantius Chlorus. Constantius Chlorus himself wrote to me, advising me of his tolerance for your presence in light of your honorable deeds in service to the Empire. And then Licinius sent a courier to tell us of your plans to return to Nicomedia with your *ala*." His eyes sharpened ever so slightly. "That was a cunning play. You have learned something of the arts of— how shall we say?—*persuasion* in your exile, Georgius son of Gerontios."

Jurian said nothing. He wanted to tell the Emperor that that plan wasn't any of his doing, but he decided that might only send Galerius into another rage.

"And since you have made a name for yourself," Diocletian continued, "you undoubtedly expect me to honor it. But what if I refuse?"

Jurian hazarded a glance at Constantinus, but the Tribune kept his own eyes fixed on the Emperor.

"Why would you wish to refuse, when I only wish to serve?" Jurian said, echoing the words he'd used on the steps outside the palace. "I risked my life for Rome when I could have betrayed her, *Augustus*," he added. "Is that not proof enough of my loyalty?"

Diocletian angled away from them and paced the room. "That remains to be seen," he said. "But it is enough to save you from being immediately arrested and executed."

That, at least, is something, Jurian thought.

"These are difficult and dangerous times," Diocletian said. "There are traitors lurking even in my own household. We must consider carefully how best to test for loyalty."

Jurian's throat tightened. *Like you tested the loyalty of the twenty thousand in the ekklesia?* he thought. *Like you tested Varro's?*

Diocletian lifted a hand in dismissal. "You may go," he said. "Tonight, we will feast your return as our honored friends. And tomorrow, we will begin."

67

Aquae Sulis, Britannia — February, A.D. 303

Impatient as he was to reach this Ynys Afallon, Casca had to stop at nightfall and make camp in the damp woods just off the road, where he spent a bitterly cold night sleeping on uncomfortable ground, cursing the Emperor who had sent him on this fool's errand every time a hooting owl startled him from sleep. Two days later he passed through Glevum, but he didn't stop for the night, only a brief meal at a cheerless *taberna*.

By the time he had reached Aquae Sulis, though, he had to stop. His horse was exhausted and he—he was so weary he nearly fell three times from his saddle. In Glevum he had asked the innkeeper the way to Ynys Afallon, and the man had informed him loftily that he would never find it on his own. At the *thermae* in Aquae Sulis, he asked a guard if he had ever heard of the place, and the man had squirmed and made the sign against evil. Casca had ordered him to lead the way under imperial command.

They set out the next morning, with the clear sunshine taking the edge off the chill breeze. They rode in silence until the midmorning sun had almost reached its zenith, and then the man reined in his horse and pointed. A tall peak rose out of a sea of mist like an island in the clouds.

"That's the Tor," he said. "Go that way. The boat is always waiting."

"Boat?" Casca asked. "What—"

But the man was already galloping north as hard as his horse would go. Casca gritted his teeth and spurred his horse forward. As the beast plunged into the mist, Casca felt his skin beginning to crawl. This place reminded him of the Oracle at Didyma, and he had the sudden urge to turn his horse around.

Tamping down the sudden, desperate need to escape, he rode through the clinging fog for what felt like hours, until finally he heard the gentle slapping of water against a rocky shore. Gradually the mist thinned and lifted, and he saw the crescent of a dark lake and, a short distance away, a tiny coracle tied off at a ramshackle pier. A boathouse, scarcely more than a skeleton, hunched on the shore, and Casca guided his horse toward it. After securing the skittish beast to a ring in the weathered wall, Casca turned to the boat.

He stepped carefully into it, grasping its edges as it rocked beneath his weight. Then he faltered, his gaze riveted on the water beneath him. He could see his reflection there, too clearly...but then his blood turned cold, because that was not his face staring up at him. It looked like a woman's face, beautiful and haunting, and he was sure he didn't imagine it. But when he twitched his head, the reflection did not.

Shuddering violently, he seized an oar and drove it into the water, shattering the illusion. With a few sound strokes he had pushed off from the shore, leaving the horror behind. The oars cut through the water, the sound muffled by the heaviness of the mist that hung just above his head.

Slowly the opposite shore materialized out of the mist, like an apparition of another world.

Almost too soon, the boat ground on the shore, and Casca, shipping the oars, stepped out of the boat and dragged it up onto the rocks. Everything inside him was tense and drawn, shuddering with fear and apprehension. What would he find on this gods-forsaken place? What if there was a guardian?

Who was that Lady that the boy named Albanus had spoken of? Perhaps she was nothing more than that illusion in the water, the figment of his own imagination.

At the top of the hill Casca came to a wide ring of standing stones, so heavily blanketed with mist that he could not see the stones on the other side. There was no sound at all, and Casca couldn't even hear the lapping of the water on the shore below. It was as if this were the only place in the entire world, and the only way forward was through the gateway of stone.

He drew a shallow breath. Every impulse inside him begged him to turn and flee, and leave this cursed place far behind. Was finding that sword worth this terror?

Would Diocletian even care, if Casca succeeded and brought it back to him?

Casca ground his teeth and stepped past the boundary of the stones. The ground within the circle was mossy, and his footsteps made no sound as he paced toward the center of the eerie space.

Halfway across the glade he glanced back, but the mists had shrouded the stones, and for a moment he thought he could imagine what it would feel like to be the last person left alive in the whole world.

Casca took a deep breath. *If Jurian went through this trial, so will I.*

He edged forward. All at once, he saw a great stone, like an altar, cold and stark and unadorned. On the stone rested the sword Excalibur, and there, just on the other side of the altar, stood a woman.

Casca reeled back, his heart hammering. This woman was nothing like the Oracle. She was not terrible but beautiful, but the power that radiated through her seemed not of this world.

"Marcus Valerius Flaccus Casca," the woman said, her voice low and musical like the flutes he'd heard once in the Emperor's court. "Come forward."

Casca swallowed hard and took a step forward.

Now is not the time to run, he told himself. *Stand, and wait.*

His gaze wavered from her face and fell on the sword.

"You have come for the Sword of the King," she said.

"Yes." He took another step toward the altar. "Who are you?"

"I am the Lady of Ynys Afallon," she said. She raised her hand and pointed at the stone. "Once the sword has been taken, only blood will bring it back again." The woman's eyes bored into Casca's, and he felt everything inside him shiver. "Do you understand the consequences of what you are about to do?"

"I must obey," he said, taking another step and stretching his hand toward the hilt. But just before he took hold of it, he hesitated and looked up at the Lady.

"Casca," she said, her voice soft. "From a little spark will spring a great flame, and the song your heart sings will not always be silent."

Casca reached out and gripped the hilt of the sword, and as he drew it from the table, the Lady of Ynys Afallon stepped back and vanished into the mist.

In his hand, the sword felt strangely light.

68

Nicomedia, Anatolia — February, A.D. 303

True to his word, Diocletian held a sumptuous banquet in the palace that night, the *triclinium* showing almost no signs of the recent conflagration. It reminded Jurian of the first time he had come to this place, when he had swirled through the glittering dignitaries only to come face to face with the *Imperator*. He remembered the feast when Kat had challenged him on the matter of the library. When Sabra had come with her father to answer the imperial summons.

The memory of her watching him from the ship's deck, so sad and beautiful, made his heart burn with fresh grief.

"I should send word to Alexandria at least," he told Constantinus as they took their seats at the long table. "Don't you think? Or, perhaps you should."

"I think we must wait a bit for that," Constantinus said. "Be patient. If the gods so will it, you will have plenty of time to write letters and visit friends."

Clearly, Jurian realized, Constantinus was not easy about the way things were going. On the surface, everything seemed as it had been before, but the way *Caesar* Galerius and Maxentius watched them was still far from friendly. And no matter how hard he tried, he could guess nothing of Diocletian's thoughts.

The *Imperator* was as remote and enigmatic as ever.

As the chatter swirled around the table, Jurian's thoughts revolved back to the Lady of Ynys Afallon. She had told him that he would need the courage to speak truth to kings, and try as he might to convince himself that he had already done it, his heart whispered otherwise.

The longer the evening wore on, the more he began to dread whatever was in store for the next day. When he finally managed to slip away from the feast, he went down to the *castra* to see Agapius, desperate for his friend's clear-sighted, if simple, wisdom. He found him sitting in the courtyard with Servius and several other men from the *ala*. They had a fire going in a large brazier, and they were sharing a flask of strong wine. As Jurian stepped into the light, Agapius jumped to his feet and came forward.

"Jurian!" he said. "You'll never guess."

"Guess what?" Jurian said, rubbing his forehead to try to banish the ache that had started behind his eyes.

Agapius turned back to the group around the brazier with a dramatic flourish. After a moment, one of the men rose, and when Jurian saw his massive size, his heart jumped into his throat.

"Menas?" he said, hardly daring to believe it. His friend stepped fully into the light, and Jurian laughed aloud. "Menas!" he cried. He circled the brazier and seized the giant in an embrace. "I didn't think you would make it here so quickly!"

"Boats," Menas said, making a face. All the men roared with laughter, and Jurian gripped his shoulder.

"We didn't have a horse big enough for you anyway," he said. As they settled again around the fire, Jurian grinned at him. "It is so good to see you again. How did Coel's court suit you?"

"Very well," Menas said. "He is a good man, Coel." He surveyed the courtyard and hunched up his shoulders. "The last time I was here," he said, "the company wasn't nearly so pleasant."

"It may not be pleasant for long," Jurian said with a short laugh.

Everyone hushed, and all eyes turned toward him.

Agapius frowned at him. "What do you mean by that?"

"Nothing. I'm just tired, and it's the wine talking."

He sat with his friends as they continued their conversation, but he couldn't bring himself to join in. Not even the unexpected arrival of Menas could lift the heaviness that continued to weigh on his heart. He clasped the pyx that lay under his tunic and tried to pray, but no words beyond "please" would come.

He passed another sleepless night. He was haunted by fragments of memories of Sabra—over and over again, hearing her harsh rebuke of his determined efforts to ascend through the Legion to the rank of *tribunus*. Had he committed the same folly again, thinking that armor and a title and a force of men behind him would make any difference to Diocletian? In the end, he realized, it all came down to two men: himself, and the Emperor.

He only prayed that when the time came, he would be strong enough to stand his ground.

All night long, thunder rolled in the distance, but no rain came. The dawn arrived clad as if in mourning, and the sun pulled ragged gray clouds around himself as if to hide his face. Jurian rose, splashed his face with water, and dressed.

The palace was oddly quiet as he made his way to the *triclinium*. As he stood there, wondering where he might get something to eat, a slave approached and bowed low.

"*Domine*," he said. "The Divine *Imperator* requests that you dress and bring your *ala* to the *forum*."

Jurian scowled. "Dress? In armor?"

The servant bowed again and departed.

Strange, Jurian thought, but he returned to his *cubiculum* and armed himself. He slung his battle axe over his shoulder and then left the palace to gather his men.

By the time they reached the *forum*, it was almost noon. A great crowd had gathered in the square, and in the very center sat a large tripod. Diocletian and Galerius sat on a raised dais, with Maxentius behind Galerius's right shoulder. Constantinus, Jurian noticed, stood with the crowd just to the left of the dais.

"What is this?" Agapius asked.

Jurian shook his head, dread roiling through him. "Stay here," he said. "If anything goes wrong here, I want you to go. Do you understand? Take the men and go."

He glanced over his shoulder and then nodded at Servius, who raised the *draco* and brought the *ala* to a halt. Jurian cantered forward into the square, alone. His horse snorted, ears pinned, and tried to rear, as if some stench in the square made him nervous. Jurian had to circle him twice before he would calm down enough to stand.

"Lucius Aurelius Georgius, *Praefectus Alae* of the *Ala I Draconis*," Galerius said, raising his voice so the entire assembled crowd could hear. "Come forward."

Jurian swung off his horse and Agapius darted over to take him. Jurian pulled off his helmet and strode forward until he stood before the dais, then bowed his head with a sharp salute.

"Come," Diocletian said, indicating the dais. "Join us."

Jurian mounted the steps to the dais, heart pounding.

A herald came forward and stood at the edge of the dais, facing the people, and unrolled a papyrus scroll.

"The edict of the *Divinus Imperator* Diocletian *Iovius Augustus*," he cried, his voice loud in the hushed square. "Be it declared that henceforth any senator, *eques, decurio, miles*, or veteran of military service who acknowledges himself to be a follower of the man called the Christ shall henceforth be stripped of his rank. That any found to be a follower of the Christ shall be deprived of rights in the court. That no gathering for worship shall be permitted to any followers of the Christ. That all scriptures and places of worship belonging to the followers of the Christ shall be henceforth destroyed."

Jurian listened to the words roll over him, his heart numb. So this was what the *Imperator* had been hinting at the night before. This was to be the test of his loyalty.

"And that any slave who was declared free and who acknowledges himself to be a follower of the Christ shall be brought back into slavery," the herald concluded.

A low murmur rippled through the crowd, and the people looked at Jurian's *ala* with fear in their faces. Jurian's heart lurched. They were afraid that Diocletian would use his men to round up anyone suspected of being a Christian. Jurian was afraid that they might be right.

Galerius came forward to the edge of the dais and raised his hands. The murmuring subsided and an uneasy silence took its place. Then the *Caesar* turned to Jurian with a disarming smile and gestured for him to approach and stand beside him.

"As *Praefectus Alae*, newly returned from exile, Lucius Aurelius Georgius is invited by the Divine *Imperator* Diocletian *Augustus* to burn incense to Jupiter, and to lead his men in public sacrifice."

Utter silence fell on the square. Jurian shifted his gaze from Galerius to Diocletian. The *Imperator* sat very still, his eyes riveted on Jurian. Was there a silent plea in their depths? It was impossible to tell.

Thunder rolled overhead, and the first drops of rain drizzled down.

Rise, Pendraig, and find the courage that will speak truth to kings. I cannot do nothing.

Jurian took a deep breath. He turned and walked slowly toward the tripod. The herald, he realized, was walking with him, that abominable scroll still spread open in his hands. A priest in elaborate hooded robes waited by the tripod, holding a carved bowl of incense ready for him.

Jurian set down his helmet, every motion precise and deliberate. Out of the corner of his eye, he saw Constantinus, tense and speechless at the edge of the crowd, flanked by Menas, whose shaggy head was bowed. In front of his *ala* he saw Agapius, face drawn, grief and horror in his eyes. Servius beside him, eyes averted, blinking away the rain.

Jurian stood for a moment, staring down at the grains of

incense. The priest moved forward a step, as if Jurian were hesitating because he couldn't reach the bowl. His face was cold and pale as marble, dark eyes like pools of ink under the dismal sky. He lifted one hand and pointed, deliberately, toward Diocletian.

Rise.

Jurian lifted his eyes to the priest's face. And then he slapped the bowl of incense out of his hands.

It skittered across the stone, the incense spilling everywhere. The priest dropped to his knees and scrambled after the bowl, trying to dig the grains of incense out of the crevices in the stone.

Then Jurian turned and snatched the imperial edict from the herald's hands. Before the man could react, he tore it down the center and tossed the fragments on the blazing tripod.

A gasp rippled through the crowd.

Jurian turned back to the dais. Diocletian was on his feet now, eyes blazing with wrath. For once, Jurian thought wryly, there was no mystery to the Emperor's mood.

"I will not," Jurian said, raising his voice over the thunder that threatened to split the sky.

"Do you acknowledge yourself to be a follower of the Christ?" Galerius said.

"You say it," Jurian answered. Then he turned to Diocletian. "For the slaughter of twenty thousand innocent and loyal Roman citizens here in this city, I denounce you as a murderer, a tyrant, and an abomination in the sight of God and the Roman Empire. For the torture and murder of Lucius Titianus, governor of Cyrene, and four other Roman citizens, I denounce you! You are unworthy of your office and the trust of the people of Rome, and unworthy of the power that God has seen fit to give you."

He pulled the tribute coin from the pouch he carried always on his belt, the coin that Diocletian had tossed him a lifetime ago, in another world.

"I have always been willing to render to *Caesar* the things that are *Caesar*'s," he said, holding the coin up briefly, hoping that Diocletian could see his own face in the tarnished metal from that distance. Then he dropped it on the ground, where it rattled a moment on one edge, and then toppled. "But you have usurped the things that are God's."

Chaos erupted in the square. From every side, soldiers flooded in, and amid the screams of the people, Jurian thought he heard Agapius calling for his men to stand their ground.

"I will not stand by and allow you to torture a peaceful people for refusing to betray their God," Jurian cried, his voice ringing out, silencing the crowd. "I will not stand by and allow you to raze their *ekklesiae* and homes, and imprison them on false accusations, and subject them to barbarous tortures that blacken the very name of Rome herself. I will not stand by and allow you to strip honorable men of their ranks and offices for fabricated crimes. Let them go in peace. End this madness. You don't need their blood on your hands."

Jurian, his eyes never leaving Diocletian's face, knelt on the stone and raised his hands. The soldiers seized him and pinioned his arms behind his back. Diocletian stepped down from the dais and came close to him.

"Somehow, I knew," he said. "I knew from the moment I first saw you. But I had hoped you would change when you realized the truth."

"What truth?" Jurian asked.

Diocletian opened his hand and then closed it tight. And when he spoke again, his voice was like oil on water. "That all power on this earth is given to me." He struck a blow to Jurian's face with his closed fist. "For your betrayal of my trust," he said.

Jurian winced at the blow, but raised his head again. "You're wrong," he said. "What power you think you have will be stripped from you. One is coming who will tear down this Empire and rebuild it."

Diocletian measured him for a moment and then turned. "Take him away," he said to the guards.

They dragged him to his feet and hauled him from the square.

69

Myra, Anatolia — March, A.D. 303

Sabra stared at the man on the docks of the Andriake port, feeling as if all the blood had been dragged from her veins. He wouldn't meet her gaze.

"How recent is this news?" she asked, trying to keep her voice even.

"Two months ago," he muttered. "I've been sailing since. I've heard no more recent news than that."

Two months, she thought.

It was over two months now that she had been back in Myra, with Miletta and Chloe and Nikolaos, trying to heal the wound in her heart, but none of them had heard any news of this nature in all the time she'd been there. Part of her wanted to deny the sailor's words, but he claimed to know a man who had seen the report with his own eyes.

"You don't know if this...Georgius...has arrived in Nicomedia? How he was received?"

"For all I know, *kyria*, he is still on his way to Anatolia," the man said sharply. "I am sorry that I cannot give you any more news than that."

Sabra shook her head and turned away, everything inside her reeling with horror and fear. Jurian, according to official report, had been riding south toward Nicomedia with an *ala* of *cataphractarii*. The sailor on the dock had no idea if he were coming in peace or hostility, but Sabra's heart was sick with a certain fear—that if Jurian had dared to breach his interdiction, he was riding straight into a trap.

And if the news is already two months old…

She left the man staring after her and hurried through the streets of the town, making her way toward Nikolaos's house. Moving in a blind panic, she almost didn't see the Legionaries standing outside the gate before she stumbled into one of them.

"Mind your step!" the man snapped, spinning around. She stared at him, speechless with shock, and he regarded her in surprise. "Apologies, *kyria*."

Her gaze drifted away from the man to Nikolaos's home. "Can I go in?" she asked.

"You know the man who lives here?"

Her heart stammered, and she felt as if the breath were being slowly choked out of her. "I had a message for him…"

"He is not here."

"Where is he?"

He smirked a little. "He's at the *phylake, kyria*."

"Visiting someone, perhaps?" she asked, though she knew perfectly well what his answer would be. She just didn't want to hear it.

"He has been taken into custody, on charges of being a follower of that cult of the Nazarene."

She staggered, trying to maintain her composure, trying not to betray her horror to the guards.

Drawing a steadying breath, she asked, as calmly as she could, "Then will you take me to see him, *stratiota*?"

The soldier looked at one of the other Legionaries, who nodded briefly. The man gave Sabra a little bow and stepped away from the gate. "Follow me," he said.

Sabra walked close behind him, her hands tight on the folds of her chiton. This couldn't be happening. Nikolaos, in prison? Who could possibly have turned him in? Who would do such a thing? Everyone in Myra seemed to know him, and know what he was, and they all loved him with a jealous sort of love. No one would do such a thing. It was impossible. The soldiers had made a terrible mistake.

They finally arrived at the *phylake*, which was no more than a small, narrow building with only one or two holding cells—nothing like the prisons in the larger cities in the Empire. Nikolaos was in one of the cells, kneeling in the corner of the room with his arms folded and his head tipped back, and—impossibly—a smile on his face.

"Ah, Sabra," he said, jumping to his feet and clasping her hands as soon as she came in to join him, as if he were greeting her in his own courtyard. "It is good to see you, daughter. Did you hear anything interesting at the docks?"

"How did you—never mind." Sabra folded her hands and bowed her head. "Jurian is going to Nicomedia. As far as I know, he may already be there. He was riding there at the head of an *ala* of heavy horse, but the man I spoke to had no notion of what he meant to do there."

"Rebuke the Emperor, I imagine," Nikolaos said calmly. "For the lives of twenty thousand. For the lives of others."

"It's a trap, isn't it?" Sabra asked. "He's walking straight into a trap. Casca will never let him get away with that!" She bent her head, pressing her fingertips against her lips as she tried to collect herself. "I thought he would be riding for Nicomedia to request the Emperor to revoke his interdiction. To reinstate him as a citizen. To…come for me."

Nikolaos put a hand on her shoulder, and when she glanced up at him, his face was oddly serious.

The last time she had seen him look anything but joyful, it was on the day of the Nativity, after they had both been woken the night before by the same nightmare. When she had gone to his house in the morning, she had found him weeping in his courtyard. She had wept with him over the dream of fire and blood, the countless lives lost. The horror too terrible to even grasp. And then, a week later, they had learned that it had all happened, just as they had dreamed.

It was not the last nightmare that Sabra had suffered. But her dreams now were vaguer, and she always woke herself choked with sobs.

"I fear the same thing," Nikolaos said suddenly, and he took his hand from her shoulder to cover his face, and paced a few steps away. "He is in very great danger."

Sabra caught in a sharp breath and grabbed his hand. "Nikolaos! You have to warn him!"

He waved generally at his surroundings. "I cannot, as you see."

"But you…you can…"

"Sabra," he said, with a gentle smile. "I told you once. I have no power on my own but what is given me, when it is given me."

For a long moment she stared at him, willing back the indignation that God would not consider this a fitting time to bless Nikolaos with his peculiar gift. It was hardly fair. But if Nikolaos could do nothing…

"Then I must do it," she said. "I will go to Nicomedia and wait for him there, and if he is already there…then perhaps I can stop him from…whatever it is he means to do." She turned to go, but stopped and glanced back at him. "Will you be all right?"

He laughed softly. "Prisons are just a place like any other. I am content."

She took his hand and pressed it to her lips. "I will pray for you."

"And I for you." He held her hand tightly for a moment. "Stay strong, Sabra, and remember the Magdalene."

She hesitated a moment, suddenly disquieted, then nodded and fled from the *phylake*.

70

Nicomedia, Anatolia — March, A.D. 303

Casca disembarked at the docks in Nicomedia to find the city in an uproar. He could feel it in the air as soon as he stepped off the boat—that hum of anticipation, the tang of fear, that nervous energy straining at every sinew of the city.

"Has something happened?" he asked one of the guards posted at the quay, staggering under his burden.

The sword Excalibur hung at his back like a leaden weight. As light as it had been when he had taken it up, it had grown heavier ever since, and now he could barely keep himself upright with it across his shoulders.

The guard didn't seem to notice his discomfort. "Everyone's still talking about what happened in the *forum*. Something to do with the Emperor's new edict."

"Edict!" Casca echoed, stunned. "What edict?"

"That's right. They finally decided to do something about those Christians. But someone tore the edict in half almost as soon as it had been announced, right in front of the *Augustus* himself, and *Caesar* Galerius."

Casca gritted his teeth and nodded his thanks. He made his way to the palace, going by side streets and back alleys to avoid the crowds, but even when he arrived, he keenly felt that something was amiss. The servants clustered together in the corridors and spoke in hushed whispers, and no one seemed to notice Casca when he entered the *atrium*.

He finally shouted at one of the slaves to get his attention, and the man scurried forward and stooped in a low bow before him.

"Take me to the *Augustus*," he said.

The slave nodded and motioned for him to follow, but as soon as they reached Diocletian's *tablinum* he left Casca at the door and hurried away, not even bothering to announce the Emperor's visitor. From inside the room, Casca could hear raised voices—he recognized Galerius's. The *Imperator* Diocletian had never raised his voice in his life, he was sure.

He rapped once and the door opened, and Casca found himself face to face with Maxentius. Exactly the man he had hoped never to lay eyes on again. But still, he might have his usefulness, if he was anything like Galerius. A man of blood, like the *Caesar*.

And like me, he thought.

"What do you want?" Maxentius snapped. "No one is permitted in here."

"I am. I bring a mighty gift for the *Augustus*," Casca said. "Step aside."

Maxentius caught sight of the hilt at Casca's shoulder, and he opened the door wide to admit him.

Galerius stood in the center of the room, arms raised. Diocletian sat rigid in his *sella*, a look Casca had never seen on his face. He was terrible as an avenging god, and for a moment, Casca regretted coming into his presence.

"You should burn him alive!" Galerius shouted. "Right in the *forum*! Sprinkle him with incense and make *him* the offering to the gods!"

Diocletian snapped his gaze to Galerius's face. "We are not worshipers of Molech," he said sharply. "Or the barbarian gods of the Alemanni. Such sacrifices are an—" He stopped and closed his mouth.

"They are an abomination," Casca said smoothly, striding forward.

He didn't mention the Christians they had burned within their *ekklesia*, or the three prophets of Mani whom Diocletian had burned at the stake in Alexandria, or Casca's own variation on that theme with Sabra's eunuch. Those, of course, were different.

Diocletian startled at the sound of his voice, and Galerius spun around.

"Who let you in here?" the *Caesar* snapped. He saw Maxentius by the door and glowered at him. "I thought I told you to open the door for no one."

"He said he brings a mighty gift," Maxentius said.

At that, Diocletian started to his feet. "You have it?" he asked, coming to meet Casca.

Casca reached up and unsheathed the great sword. Its edges glinted in the light from the brazier, the plain hilt glowing as if it were on fire itself.

"I don't believe it," Diocletian murmured.

Casca's blood cooled at the words. *So, you never believed I would succeed? You thought you were sending me out on an impossible mission? You wished to rid yourself of me forever?*

Will you rethink my worth now?

Diocletian held out his hands and Casca, bridling his indignation, laid the sword across them. The weight seemed to catch the *Imperator* by surprise, because he almost dropped the blade. He caught the hilt just in time, and the point struck the marble floor with a hollow clang.

"Truly," he said. "A sword of divine power...a sword of kings."

Casca backed toward the door, vaguely unsettled. Something had happened to the *Imperator's* face. That beautiful face, perfect as the carved marble of a god's statue, was greedy and grasping and...ugly. As if a cruel hand had reached down and twisted his regal features into a mockery of their former terrifying splendor. Only his blue eyes were as Casca remembered—too blue, too piercing, fathomless and paralyzing.

Diocletian spoke first to Galerius. "Not burned alive," he said. "He is a Roman." He eyed the sword with a cruel smile. "And he is, after all, an officer. It seems only fitting."

Casca tried to slip out the door without being noticed, but Maxentius blocked his way. "You were not dismissed," he said.

Diocletian heard him and turned. When he saw Casca by the door, he nodded once. "You have done well," he said. "I shall not forget this."

Casca bowed, and swallowed. If Maxentius had not stepped aside to let him through, he would have pushed him over to get out. He staggered into the corridor, gripping his head between his hands.

Something had happened in the square. Someone had defied the Emperor. And Diocletian wanted him to die by the sword.

By *that* sword.

Casca sucked in his breath through his teeth and stumbled down the corridor, his thoughts as chaotic as the city itself.

71

Alexandria, Aegyptus — April, A.D. 303

Maximinus Daia, true to his word, had left for Nicomedia, and Aikaterina had heard nothing more from either him or her uncle for weeks. No word had come from Sabra either, and the silence that followed such glittering hope was too much for her to bear.

To make matters worse, her father's condition seemed to be worsening, and there were whispers among the household servants that a malignant power held him from the gateway of death. The physicians who attended him day and night wagged their heads when she arrived each morning to check on him, and every hour she expected him to slip away.

As the spring warmth began to loosen the bands of winter's chill, Aikaterina made up her mind to return to Nicomedia in spite of her father's condition. She found Nenet folding her chitons in her chamber, and she pulled out her traveling trunk and opened it.

"What do you think you are doing?" Nenet asked, planting a fist on her hip. "Put that away."

"I can't wait here forever," Aikaterina said. "Pack my things. We are going to Nicomedia."

"You should wait here forever, if that's how long it takes,"

Nenet said staunchly. "If you return to that place, who knows what will be waiting for you? That horrible man with eyes like a chameleon's, that is certain."

"Nenet," Aikaterina said with a laugh. "I will be under my uncle's protection while I am in Nicomedia. And Maximinus Daia will have grown bold indeed if he thinks he can cross Constantinus and live."

Nenet scowled, but she started laying Aikaterina's clothes in the trunk.

"Thank you," Aikaterina said.

She turned to leave, but froze. Her mother stood in the doorway, her face drawn and ashen. "Aikaterina," she said, her voice hollow and broken. "It is time."

Aikaterina ran from the room. Servants were scurrying toward her father's chamber from all directions, but they crushed against the corridor walls and bowed almost to the ground as she raced past. She shouldered her way inside her father's chamber.

Thick candles burned at every corner of the room and at the four corners of his bed. The physicians stood at the foot of the bed, hands folded.

There was nothing more they could do.

Aikaterina fell to her knees by her father's bedside. "Papa," she mumbled, her shoulders shaking with sobs. She seized his hand and pressed it to her lips. His breathing was rasping like the hull of a boat on the rocks, and his skin was thin and brittle as papyrus.

"Please don't leave me here alone," Aikaterina whispered. She chafed his hand gently, then tightened her fingers around his. "Wake up! Wake up!"

Vaguely, she heard a stirring behind her and saw her mother take her place at her side. She thought she heard her crying, or it might have been one of the servants.

Her father took a breath and exhaled, and his hand stilled in Aikaterina's. She barely felt the change, but one moment, she had felt the frail life beneath his skin, and the next...nothing. She stared at his face—it was still as marble. Desperately grabbed his hand again and pressed it to her cheek.

"Papa," she said. "Papa!"

Behind her, a low chanting began. Aikaterina, her eyes streaming with tears, leaned forward and kissed her father's forehead. Then she laid her head on his breast and sobbed until she was spent.

Someone gently clasped her shoulders and pulled her away, but she clung to her father's hand as long as she could. As she was ushered toward the door, she saw her mother lift her hands and speak in a low voice. Then each of the servants in their turn stepped forward.

Aikaterina stumbled and the hands caught her. It wasn't until she was lifted and carried into the corridor that she realized it was Nenet who held her.

They laid her father in state in the *atrium* of the palace on a great *lectus funebris*. Torches burned at each corner day and night, and large candelabra sat to either side with oil lamps. One held a small figure of Persephone, goddess of the underworld, and the other a figure of Hades. Her father's body was draped with rich linen edged with gold, and a crown of laurel rested on his brow.

People from Alexandria and all the surrounding cities processed past all day, some weeping, some just solemn. At night, guards stood silent watch over the body.

While the people came to pay her father the honors due to the dead, Aikaterina stood against the wall and looked on, feeling as cold and numb and unmoved as a marble statue. She would have much preferred to let her mother handle the funeral rites, but she could not stand aside now. Alexandria needed to see her there. Her people needed to see her there.

But she had never felt more alone.

She had thought that her uncle might come on the news of her father's passing, but he did not. Aikaterina's fear that something had happened to detain him in Nicomedia grew by the day, but she did not have the strength or the courage now to think about the journey. Her traveling chest stood open and half-filled, exactly as it had been the day her father died.

At last, the night came for the burial. Aikaterina, dressed all in black and with her hair unbound in loose curls all down her back, followed the eight bearers of the *feretrum* out of the palace. The sky was overcast and the torches carried by the slaves guttered and flared in the furtive breeze, which smelled of a coming storm. Behind them, all the household was emptied, and the street to the royal necropolis was lined with people. They tossed flowers on the street in front of the bearers as the ribbon of sorrowful music from the pipers rippled through the procession.

Her mother held tightly to Aikaterina's hand.

They reached the tomb and the bearers slowly carried the *feretrum* inside and laid her father to rest. As they sealed the tomb, the rain began to fall.

Slowly, the great procession of mourners broke away, and as soon as they had enough distance from the tomb to be respectful, they scurried for their homes. Aikaterina and her mother, with their closest household servants, stayed behind. Her mother's thin shoulders were bowed with grief, but Aikaterina stood quiet and still.

It was done. There was no more waiting, and no more hope. Whatever was to come in the wake of her father's death would be set in motion, and she could no sooner stop the storm or hold back the tide.

She tilted her face up into the pelting rain, feeling the cool drops mingle with her hot tears.

Hear, O Lord, my prayer: and let my cry come to You, she prayed silently. *Turn not away your face from me: in the day when I am in trouble, incline Your ear to me. I am become like a pelican of the wilderness, I am like a night raven in the house.*

Her mother let go of her hand and her servants ushered her away, but Aikaterina still did not move. Behind her, she heard Nenet speak softly to Diodoros and Theokritos, who had come with her to the tomb.

Aikaterina opened her arms as lighting forked in the sky over the ocean. "I will accept the bitter cup You give," she cried. "Not my will, but Yours."

She lowered her arms and faced her father's tomb once more. "So they buried Constus, *Praefectus Augustalis* of Egypt," she murmured, echoing the words of Homer. "Be at peace, Father."

Aikaterina turned away and Nenet and her tutors received her. Nenet wrapped her in a dry cloak, and together they made their way back to the palace.

Whatever would come, would come. But for the first time in many weeks, as she felt Nenet's arm around her shoulders and the silent strength of Diodoros and Theokritos, she did not feel that she faced her future alone.

When they arrived at the palace, Senator Petillius Tiberius was standing in the *atrium*, waiting for her arrival.

He bowed low before her, and said, *"Praefecta."*

72

Nicomedia, Anatolia — April, A.D. 303

Jurian would not be swayed. Diocletian had sent messengers of every variety to the *carcer* to try to persuade, bribe, threaten, or cajole the former Tribune into giving up his impiety, and the man would simply not give up. The *Imperator* had concocted the worst possible tortures, and Jurian refused to bend.

Casca loathed his stubbornness, his bull-headed dedication to his beliefs.

It was late in *Aprilis* when Diocletian summoned Casca to the courtyard outside the palace. When Casca arrived, he was surprised to find the Emperor simply dressed, without his typical trappings of imperial splendor. An *agaso* held his horse at the ready, and another held a smaller horse that Casca guessed was meant for him.

"*Imperator*," Casca said, bowing as he joined him.

"Ride with me this morning."

Diocletian mounted his horse without another word and wheeled him toward the palace gates, and Casca stumbled in his haste to follow him. Soon they were out in the city streets, flanked by a mere handful of imperial guards, and Casca realized too late where they were going. It was a place he had been one too many times, and had never wanted to return. The city *carcer*.

He gritted his teeth and halted his horse beside Diocletian's, resenting at every moment that the *Imperator* had commanded him to accompany him. He had not seen Jurian once since his return to Nicomedia, though he had often contemplated going to visit him, to mock him, to taunt him for his failure. To see how Jurian was enduring the new tortures he heard some of the Legion guards discussing in hushed voices. By all accounts, no one could believe that the prisoner was still alive.

"My messengers have done no good," Diocletian said as they swept into the *carcer*. "Perhaps I myself can convince him to give up his foolish beliefs."

Casca wanted to say that he doubted Jupiter himself could persuade Jurian of anything. Part of him wanted to ask the *Imperator* why he was even trying to change Jurian's mind. Jurian had made his position very clear. As far as Casca was concerned, they ought to just honor his decision and be done with it.

They arrived at a dingy cell at the far back of the cell block, where the air stank of fetid straw and old blood. Jurian was sitting against the wall. His face was mottled with bruises and lacerations, and one eye was almost swollen shut. He didn't move when Diocletian stopped in front of the cell, but when the jailer opened the cell door and the Emperor stepped inside, he finally lifted his head to look at him.

Casca was only glad that, for the moment, Jurian hadn't noticed him lingering just inside the cell door.

"Georgius," Diocletian said. "What am I to do with you?"

Jurian shifted his position painfully. Casca was about to rebuke him for not standing in the *Imperator*'s presence, but then he saw the metal band circled around his waist, chaining him to a ring at the base of the wall. It had chafed through the thin fabric of his tunic, which was already shredded by the stripes of a *flagrum*. Jurian's feet were bare. Casca realized after too long that he was staring at them, because they were swollen, and mottled with purple bruises, and the soles were torn so badly that Casca couldn't even imagine standing on them.

"Whatever you will, *Imperator*," Jurian said after much too long. His voice lisped behind the swelling of his lip. "I am here at your command."

Impudent to the end, Casca thought.

"You are here because you violated my commands," Diocletian said.

"I obeyed the commands of your superior," Jurian said, and Casca thought, strangely, that he was smiling.

"I have no superior," Diocletian said, his voice frigid.

Jurian bent his head and said nothing.

"Is there nothing I could give you that would bring you back into my service?"

"You have nothing that I want," Jurian said softly. "There is nothing at all in this world that I want."

Casca flinched. What about Sabra? Surely he still wanted a life with her…

Diocletian shook his head, folding his hands behind his back and pacing a few steps in the cramped space. "Such a tragedy," he said. "You set out with so much to prove. Georgius the man. Georgius the hero. Georgius the *failure*."

Jurian's head snapped up, and he stared at Diocletian with a haunted look in his eyes, his face terribly pale.

"What did you say?" he asked, hoarse.

Diocletian only stared at him, impassive. "Do you think your God has any place in His court for failures like you? You're a disgrace to your faith."

Casca winced.

"But you could be so much more. Let me guide you, raise you up, and you could stand at my right hand."

Jurian tipped his head back against the filthy wall. "Are you offering me all the kingdoms of the world?" he asked, mumbling the words a little, a half smile playing around the corner of his mouth.

Diocletian hesitated. Casca guessed it was some reference

to a Christian scripture, but Diocletian seemed to be honestly considering the question—as if he *would* offer Jurian all the kingdoms of the world.

"I would not take them if you did," Jurian said, before Diocletian could reply.

"You think yourself wise, but you are a fool," Diocletian snapped. "What will your death profit the world?"

"All men die," Jurian said. "One Man's death changed the world."

"And you would die for that?"

"Would you die for Rome?"

"Gladly."

"Rome is a lesser master than mine."

Diocletian's mouth twitched. "Rome will last forever."

"One Rome will," Jurian said. "Not yours."

Diocletian moved so fast neither Jurian nor Casca had time to flinch. His fist slammed into Jurian's jaw, and Jurian's head snapped back, cracking against the wall.

Casca took a half step forward.

Jurian rolled his head to the side, and then looked back up at Diocletian. His mouth was split, blood matting the sparse beard he had grown in his imprisonment. He didn't move to wipe it away. Then, after a moment, his gaze drifted past Diocletian, and landed on Casca.

"Here I am," Jurian said simply, and bowed his head.

Casca turned and fled from the *carcer*.

73

Nicomedia, Anatolia — April 23, A.D. 303

Jurian walked slowly across the *forum*, the heavy shackles dragging at his ankles and his wrists, splashing in the little puddles gathered amongst the paving stones. The guards pushed at him and he stumbled. Pain lanced like brands from the soles of his feet.

Just before he fell he managed to steady himself, and they forced him, step by painful step, up onto the dais. Vaguely, he realized that a crowd had gathered to witness the scene. Their faces were like damp petals against the darkening sky.

Diocletian sat in a *sella*, imperial and cold as a stone effigy. He didn't look at Jurian, but that was just as well. Whatever love had existed between them for his father's sake had died with the proclamation of the edict. Now, Jurian felt only sadness. A verse his sister used to read flitted through his mind, and his thoughts drifted to Aikaterina, alone at the helm in Alexandria on a storm-tossed sea. There was nothing he could do for her now. He prayed that she would be strong in the days to come.

She, like all else, I give into the hands of the God who sees all things.

He shuffled across the dais and stood with head lifted to hear his sentence. There would be no trial. The edict had made it clear that he had no right to one. This was merely an opportunity for spectacle.

Galerius stepped forward and lifted his hand for silence, even though no one in the crowd had made a sound.

"Lucius Aurelius Georgius, whom some style Jurian, sometime *Tribunus Angusticlavius* of the Jovians, sometime *Praefectus Alae* of the *Ala I Draconis*, you stand condemned of blasphemy and treason against the divine person of the *Imperator* Diocletian *Iovius Augustus*." He paused, and then swept on, "What have you to say?"

Jurian tried to swallow, but his throat was so parched it hurt. "The fool said in his heart: There is no God. They are corrupted, and become abominable in iniquities: there is none that does good."

Galerius swept his arm toward the crowd. "He does not deny it!" he cried.

"Why do you glory in malice, you who are mighty in iniquity?" Jurian said, staring at Galerius as another verse flowed through him and out of his mouth. "All the day long your tongue has devised injustice: as a sharp razor, you have wrought deceit."

"He calls me a liar!" Galerius said, lifting his voice. He leveled his finger at Jurian. "You have heard it from his own mouth!"

Jurian turned to Diocletian and saw, for the first time, the sword Excalibur across his knees. A great shock shivered through him. How was it that he held the sword of kings, which he had left in quiet rest in the mists of Ynys Afallon?

He wanted to ask how it was possible. But when he opened his mouth, different words came out, his voice swelling with power as lifted his gaze to the sky.

"You have protected me from the assembly of the malignant, from the multitude of the workers of iniquity. For they have whetted their tongues like a sword." He looked straight at the *Imperator* and went on, "You have loved all the words of ruin, O deceitful tongue. Therefore will God destroy you forever: he will pluck you out, and remove you from your dwelling place, and your root out of the land of the living."

There was something about his voice that seemed to make even Galerius hesitate. But then the *Caesar's* anger overcame his fear.

"Lucius Aurelius Georgius, I hereby sentence you to death by the sword for your crimes!"

Soldiers flooded the dais, and they dragged him down from the platform and through the *forum*. At the front of the crowd stood Alexandra, the Emperor's wife, veiled in dark purple. Jurian thought he could hear her weeping. Behind her, he glimpsed someone moving deliberately through the crowd. Caught a glimpse of his face. Agapius.

I told you to run, he thought. He wanted to shout it, but no sound would come out of his mouth.

The guards marched him through the streets, and the crowd followed. He fell once and they hauled him to his feet, lashing his legs and back with their whips, as if that could make him steadier on his feet.

They left by the city gates and followed the wall to the place of execution. It was a narrow courtyard, bare of anything green or beautiful, with a small pillar of stone in the center, only about a foot tall and just wide enough for a man's neck. It was scarred with dozens of grooves, and Jurian wondered how many had gone before him, and how many would suffer the same fate after him.

The soldiers pulled him to a stop. Diocletian took his place on the other side of the courtyard, where he was flanked by Galerius and Maxentius. Casca was there too, Jurian realized, standing beside Galerius in his tribune's toga, his face unreadable.

Another man stepped forward to take his place on Maxentius's left. Constantinus. Deep in his heart Jurian wished he could have made him proud. He had never wanted anything as much as he had wanted that man's respect, and he knew that his profession of faith had probably cost him that forever.

God, he whispered in his heart, *for You, all things. You have always held my life in Your hands.*

Jurian turned his head to look out at the crowd. They were silent, looking on with eyes wide with grief, all of them clad in the dark robes of mourning. He saw Agapius again, and wished only that he'd had the chance to say goodbye. Then Agapius shifted slightly, and Jurian saw Menas just behind him. The giant stood as still as a great oak, his one eye fixed on Jurian. As soon as Jurian's gaze locked with his, he smiled solemnly and nodded once.

As the soldiers stripped him to his waist, Jurian kept his gaze turned toward the crowd, but suddenly a figure stepped in front of him, blocking his view of his friends.

It was Casca.

"What are you doing?" he hissed, hovering beside him, ignoring the executioner who tried to nudge him away. "Jurian, look at me! What are you doing?"

Jurian met his gaze and smiled, feeling a peace like the unwinding of a river ripple through his soul.

"Casca," he said. "I forgive you."

Casca stumbled back. And as he moved, Jurian saw her.

There, moving through the crowd like a vision, was Sabra. She was dressed all in white, with a crown of flowers twined in her hair, just as she had looked when Jurian had found her chained to the pillar outside the dragon's lair in Cyrene.

She had come to welcome him home.

Then she took Menas's hand in both her own, and the giant bowed his great head to kiss her hair. Draped over her arms, Jurian saw a scarf of perfect blood-red wool, and on her finger, a signet ring set with scarlet.

His heart caught in his throat.

Sabra was alive.

74

Nicomedia, Anatolia — April 23, a.d. 303

Sabra clung to Menas's hand, great sobs welling in her chest. She dared not weep. She would not let Jurian see her weep. But it took all her strength to keep the tears from spilling over her cheeks.

She watched as they forced Jurian down to his knees in front of the execution stone, and from the corner of her eye she caught a sudden movement near the place where Diocletian and his retinue stood. A flinch, no more. When she looked, she found Constantinus standing like a man stricken, staring at her. His eyes glittered with tears, but he didn't say a word.

Please do something, Sabra thought at him. *Please...you can stop this. Stop this...make it stop.*

But he didn't move.

The executioner stepped forward and took the great sword Excalibur from Diocletian's hands, swinging it effortlessly in his scarred hands.

Jurian's gaze never left Sabra's face, and she smiled at him through her tears. The smile he returned was radiant, and it stole her breath away, like the wind at sea. Then she saw his lips move, saying three words,

"*Viva, et ama.*"

Menas's hand tightened around hers. "Strength, child," he murmured softly.

Sabra's breath was racked with silent sobs.

I love you to the uttermost, she thought. *And I will never let you go. You are not alone. Father of mercy, please...accept the soul of Your servant.*

The sword flashed up, pointing straight down for a soldier's death, and the rain began to fall again. Jurian held Sabra's gaze one last moment, then he closed his eyes and bent his head to bare his neck to the blade. Casca, crouching close by him, never moved.

"I cannot bear it," Sabra whispered to Menas. "I cannot."

Then the sword came down, and it was finished.

Sabra closed her eyes and the hot tears spilled from beneath her lashes. Thunder rumbled once and was silent, but the rain came steadily down.

After a long moment, Menas squeezed her hand and she opened her eyes again. Casca was standing beside Jurian's lifeless body, the hem of his white toga soaked with the martyr's blood. The sword was half-buried in the stone.

As if suddenly released from paralysis, Casca moved. He reached out, and staggered to his knees. His hand trembled violently, and his shoulders shook, and everything about him was taut as a bowstring. Sabra wondered if he were happy. If his lust for blood had finally been sated. If he finally counted himself victorious.

His hand stretched out further, and gathered something up from the pool of blood beneath the stone pillar. Then he stumbled to his feet and rounded on Diocletian, and Sabra's heart caught in her throat. In his clenched and bloody hand he held Jurian's pyx.

"No," Sabra whispered. "No, not that...Menas, don't let him—"

But then she saw Casca's face.

She saw the wonder in his eyes. The grief. The fear. The rapture of joy.

"Leave him," *Caesar* Galerius commanded.

But Casca stood rooted, staring at him and Diocletian both, his fingers tight on the pyx. His hand wasn't shaking any longer.

"What," Diocletian said. His voice was low and sinuous. "Don't tell me, Casca. Have you lost your mind? Are you infected by this madness too?"

"Casca the Christian," Maxentius mocked.

Casca said, his voice taut and hollow, "I am."

Pale with anger, Diocletian nodded at the executioner, who tried to pull the sword from the pillar. It wouldn't move. He tried again, all the corded muscles in his arms and back straining against the sword.

The *Imperator* himself stepped forward then, and the executioner moved aside. Diocletian pulled at the hilt but it would not come free. His face darkened with rage, and he turned toward Casca.

"This is the sword of the king!" he said, his voice rolling across the courtyard. "Should it not obey my commands? Why will it not come free?"

Casca only smiled. "Because you are not the King."

Galerius stepped forward, knife bare, and without a word he slit Casca's throat. He fell, lifeless, beside Jurian.

Sabra caught in a shaking breath.

Somewhere in the front of the crowd there was a commotion, and Sabra tore her gaze away from the sight of the bodies in the courtyard. Alexandra, the *Imperator*'s wife, staggered forward and fell to her knees beside Jurian's body, her hair torn with grief, her *palla* stained with rain and blood. Two of the soldiers knelt beside her.

"Will there ever be enough blood shed for you?" Alexandra said to Diocletian, voice hoarse with weeping. "Will you destroy everyone who does not agree with you? Because this man had strength that you have never had? The God he follows…only a true God could inspire such love. Do you hear me? Only the true God! The only true God! So slay me too if you dare."

Diocletian startled away from her, eyes wide—for just one

moment—with dismay. Then he turned from her with a low growl. "Take her away!" he shouted at the guards. "Take them all away!"

He strode out of the courtyard, Galerius and Maxentius close on his heels, and the guards dragged Alexandra and her two soldiers behind them. The stunned crowd slowly dispersed, and soon only Constantinus, Agapius, Sabra, and Menas remained, keeping their silent vigil in the rain.

"Agapius," Constantinus said at last. "Take Sabra to my ship. Menas and I will follow."

Sabra clung to Agapius. "You can't leave him here," she sobbed. "Please, Constantinus, you can't—"

"I will not leave him," Constantinus said fiercely. He abruptly turned his face aside, and passed a hand over his eyes. "Nor Casca. Trust me. Now go."

Agapius gently guided her away, and Sabra staggered along the path, feeling at every moment as though she had to command her heart to keep beating and her lungs to keep breathing.

"Not much further," Agapius murmured.

They found Constantinus's *trireme* in the harbor, and as they made their way up the ramp, a young soldier came forward to meet Agapius.

"Servius," he said. "Take her. I have to go back."

Agapius handed Sabra over to Servius and then called for three more soldiers to come with him. They jogged back down the ramp and disappeared. As soon as he had helped Sabra to sit on a low bench near the prow, Servius turned away to order another soldier to bring some wine. Sabra sat on the bench, her teeth chattering, shaking from head to foot. Servius found a rough woolen blanket and wrapped it around her, and then handed her the cup of wine.

She sipped at it, but it was bitter and unmixed, and it only made her stomach churn. "I can't," she said, her voice thick with tears. She handed the cup back to Servius. "I can't."

The rain had finally stopped when she saw the slow

procession arrive. Six soldiers of Jurian's *ala* came first, bearing the linen-shrouded body of their commander on a simple pallet, unable to hide the grief etched on their stern faces. Six others followed behind them with Casca's body, and Sabra watched, numb and exhausted, as the soldiers carried their burdens below decks. Last of all came Constantinus and Menas, carrying the execution stone with Excalibur still lodged within it.

They set the sword and the stone down beside the mast.

Once he had secured the stone to the mast with a rope, Constantinus crouched a moment with his hand resting on the hilt of the sword. Then he straightened and stood staring out at the sea, pale, with tears or rain clinging to his lashes. Shoulders lifting in a heavy sigh, he finally turned to face the helmsman.

"Put out for Ioppe," he said. He glanced back at Sabra and added softly, "We'll go to Lydda."

EPILOGUE

Lydda, Palaestina — May, A.D. 303

On one of his many campaigns through Palaestina some years ago, Constantinus had discovered an unfinished shrine in Lydda, commissioned almost one hundred years prior by the Emperor Septimius Severus. Constantinus had claimed the shrine for his own and saw to its completion, but he had never dedicated it to any god or power. It was there that the solemn procession from Ioppe brought the bodies of Jurian and Casca for their final internment, and Sabra thought it was strangely fitting that, after so many years, after so many journeys, Jurian would finally return to the place of his birth.

Constantinus had Jurian's body entombed beneath the shrine's white marble altar, below a high clerestory window. Casca was buried in a small alcove on the right, flanked by simple pillars, unadorned, unpainted.

Now that all the rites had been fulfilled, and the sharp pang of grief and loss had subsided to a dull ache, Sabra stood before the main altar, her mind slowly revolving through memories and decisions for the future. The soft light of the spring sun shone down through the narrow windows, and Sabra closed her eyes, drinking it in as if she had been starved for it.

"Have you decided where will you go?" Constantinus

asked, coming to stand beside her.

Sabra opened her eyes and looked up at him. "I don't know," she said slowly. "I do not fear returning to Alexandria now. That danger has passed, I think, and I would be glad to see Kat again."

Constantinus nodded. "It is a wise choice. And I know my niece would be grateful for your company." He was silent for a short time, and then he said, "Will you take Menas with you, or will he return north?"

"I think he will come with me," she said. "I have not asked him, but he seems determined not to let me out of his sight." She smiled. "I think he made a promise."

"And what of Agapius?"

Sabra lifted her shoulders. "He may return to Alexandria," she said. "But he told me that he wishes first to travel to Aelia Capitolina, to see the place of the Crucifixion."

"My mother is there, by all accounts," Constantinus said. "Perhaps he will meet her. I would dearly love to know what she is doing there—she won't reveal anything in her letters."

"What about you?" Sabra asked. "Will you come to Alexandria before you go north again?"

"I think I must," he said. "Constus has died. It is only fitting that I pay my respects, and I must be sure that Aikaterina is well provided for. And then…I am not sure where I will go after that." He picked up something that Servius had brought to the shrine, the *draco* of Jurian's *ala* with its banner of scarlet, the copper dragon's head glinting in the pale sunlight. "Perhaps I will take this north, along with the sword. I know that is where Jurian always intended Excalibur to stay, and besides, my heart is keen to be back in Britannia."

Sabra nodded and turned a little, her gaze falling on Casca's tomb. Constantinus followed her gaze.

"Can you forgive him, for what he did?" he asked. "His hands were stained with blood."

Sabra glanced up at him, and for once there was no lingering darkness in her heart, no whispers of guilt and hate and shame, only a deep peace, and joy.

"So were mine," she said. "Who are we to place boundary stones around the mercy of God?"

A small smile touched Constantinus's lips, but he said nothing.

"I went to Nicomedia to save him, but I came too late," she said after a long while. The words brought a fresh burn of grief to her throat, but she took a deep breath and stared up at the high vaulted ceiling, the alcoves empty of any statues. "You have not dedicated this place to any of the gods."

"No," Constantinus said. He fixed his eyes on Jurian's tomb for a long moment. "It is better as it is. I must...consider many things." He fell silent again, and then added, "For now, I think it will belong to a Man of Highest Distinction."

Sabra swallowed back the ache of tears in her throat, and nodded.

"You and I," she said. "We must carry on, it seems. But," and she nodded toward Jurian's tomb, "thank you for this—to have a place to return, and to remember, is worth so much to me."

Constantinus inclined his head. "I hope you return often," he said. "But for now, we should be going. The tide will be turning soon, and the ship is waiting."

Together, they left the small shrine, and as they stepped into the sunlight, Sabra took a deep breath and glanced over her shoulder at the great stone facade, the rosy marble bright in the afternoon sun.

"*Vale*, Jurian," she murmured. "Until we meet again."

A NOTE FROM THE AUTHOR

The oldest historical reference to Saint George can be found in the *Historia Ecclesiastica* (VIII, 5) written around A.D. 324 by Eusebius of Caesarea:

> *Immediately on the publication of the edict against the churches in Nicomedia, a certain man, not obscure but very highly honored with distinguished temporal dignities, moved with zeal toward God, and incited with ardent faith, seized the edict as it was posted openly and publicly, and tore it to pieces as a profane and impious thing, and this was done while two of the emperors were in the same city—the chief of all, and the one who held the fourth place in the government after him.*
>
> *But this man, first in that place, after distinguishing himself in such a manner suffered those things which were likely to follow such daring, and kept his spirit cheerful and undisturbed till death.*

Tradition identifies this unnamed "certain man...very highly honored" as Saint George who "kept his spirit cheerful and undisturbed till death."

DID YOU ENJOY *STORM OF FIRE AND BLOOD*?

Please help others discover this book by taking a moment to leave a review of the novel on Amazon.com

LEXICON

ADELPHE — Greek word for *brother*.
ADSUM — a colloquial expression meaning, "Here I am."
ADYTON — the innermost sanctuary of a Roman or Greek temple, which could only be accessed by the priests of the temple.
AELIA CAPITOLINA — The name given by Emperor Hadrian to the city of Jerusalem in A.D. 130. Hadrian had intended to gift the city's rebuilding to the Jewish people until he was advised that doing so would encourage the Jews to revolt. Instead he instituted a pagan Roman colony there, calling it "Aelia" after his family name and "Capitolina" after Jupiter Capitolinus. He was responsible for building a Temple of Jupiter on the site of the old Jewish Temple, and the Temple of Venus over the site of Calvary.
AGASO — a stablehand, a slave who takes care of the horses. Pl. *agasones*.
AGORA — a Greek marketplace for buying and selling goods, as well as a public meeting place.
ALA — literally "wing," this was a 500-horse division of cavalry in the Army of the Roman Empire.
AMICUS — friend.
AMMA — mother; the title given to the Desert Mothers, female Christian ascetics living in the deserts of Egypt, Syria, and Palestine in the 4th and 5th centuries.
AMPHORA — a clay urn or jar used to carry oil, grain, wine, etc. Also a unit of measurement.
AQUILA — the eagle, the symbol of Rome. Roman Legions marched beneath an Aquila standard.
ARA — an altar.
ARAR — a type of cypress tree, the fragrant wood of which (*thuya*) was popular for decorative carvings in northern Africa.
ATRIUM — the front room in a Roman house. It had an opening in the ceiling (*compluvium*) where the rainwater would drain in.
AUGUSTUS — in the four-fold division of the Empire called the Tetrarchy, the two higher-ranking emperors were called *Augustus* (Diocletian in the East, and Maximianus in the West). *Augusta* — the title reserved for the Emperor's wife.
AVUS — grandfather.
BARBARIUS — barbarian. Pl. *barbarii*.
BIBLIOTHEKA — Greek word for library. The Library of Alexandria was one of the greatest libraries of the ancient world, until it was

destroyed in the mid-7th century.

BIRRUS BRITANNICUS — a hooded wool cloak commonly worn in the northern regions of the Empire.

BRACCHAE — short pants that reached about the knee; worn by Germanic tribes in the north and adopted by Legions stationed there. *Bracchae* were also worn by cavalry troops.

CAESAR — in the Tetrarchy, the two subordinate tetrarchs were called *Caesar* (Galerius in the East, and Constantius Chlorus in the West).

CAMPUS — a field, often used for military drills and training.

CAMULODUNUM — an ancient Roman fortress that has been traditionally identified with Camelot.

CARCER — prison cell; the Romans did not typically have prisons as we think of them, but temporary holding cells like the Tullianum.

CARDO — a north-south road in a Roman city.

CARA — dear one; a term of endearment. *Carissime* — dearest.

CASTRA — a Roman Legion camp or permanent fort, or the military quarter of a city. *Castra aestiva* — a summer camp, a temporary fortification during the summer campaign season.

CATACOMBS — underground burial sites. By the laws of Rome, these had to be situated outside the city limits. During the persecutions, these became places Christians would hide and practice their faith.

CATAPHRACTARIUS — a heavily armored cavalry soldier, generally considered the precursor to the medieval knight. Pl. *cataphractarii*.

CELLA — shrine, the inner chamber of a Greek or Roman temple which might hold the cult statue of the deity worshiped there.

CENTURIO — centurion; a professional officer in imperial Rome who might lead a *centuria* in a Legion. In Diocletian's time, the size of a *centuria* was fixed at 80 men.

CHI-RHO — the first two Greek letters of the name *Christos*, one of the most recognizable symbols of Christianity.

CHITON — Greek; a form of sewn garment with or without sleeves, and worn draped with a girdle or belt. Called a *tunica* in Latin.

CHLORUS — a Latin name meaning "the pale."

CHRISTOPHOROS — Greek for *Christ-bearer*; Menas' title and Christian name.

CODEX — a book constructed of sheets of paper, vellum, or papyrus. The *codex* gradually replaced the scroll as the dominant form of long writing in the ancient world, and its rise is often linked to the spread of Christianity, which opted for the *codex* format for the Scriptures. By A.D. 300, the *codex* was as common as the scroll.

COLONIA — a Roman outpost, often a place where Legionaries went to retire.

CUBICULUM — a small room in a Roman house that typically served as a bedroom, but could also be used as a meeting room.

CULINA — a Roman kitchen. Related to the word "culinary."

CUSTOS ARMORUM — in the Roman military, the soldier tasked with managing the registration and supply of weapons and armor.

CYRENICUS — "of Cyrene." Like the honorific given to military generals indicating sites of their major victories.

DECURIO — a cavalry officer who commanded a unit of ten horsemen.

DEIPNON — the Greek word for a formal evening dinner.

DENARIUS — a Roman silver coin.

DIDYMAION — the site of an ancient oracle of Apollo in Didyma, Anatolia, much like the temple of Delphi in Greece.

DOMINE — lord; used as a title of respect for those in positions of authority, like "sir"; *domina* — lady

DOMUS — a house, typically one occupied by the wealthy or upper classes; also, the part of an imperial palace dedicated to the Emperor's residence.

DRACO — a Roman cavalry standard characterized by a dragon.

DRACONARIUS — the Legionary charged with bearing the *draco*.

DRAKONOTOMACHOS — Greek for dragon-fighter

DRAUGR — an undead being like a wight or revenant.

DUX — a high-ranking officer of the Roman Legion who commanded frontier troops.

EKKLESIA — church.

EPISCOPUS — a bishop.

EQUES — horseman; specifically, a Legion cavalryman. Pl. *equites*.

EUCHARISTIA — Greek for "thanksgiving." The name given to the sacred mystery of partaking in Christ's body and blood in the rites of Christian worship.

EX CALCE LIBERANDUS URSO — from stone to be freed by the bear. The prophetic inscription which gives Excalibur its name.

FABRICA — in the Roman army, the wood and metal workshop.

FALAKROS — "bald one," a taunt made more amusing because Nikolaos himself is bald.

FAUCES — in a Roman house, the narrow corridor from the front door to the *atrium*.

FERETRUM — a bier.

FIDE — in faith. One of the oldest types of engagement rings, this is the ancient precursor to the Claddagh ring, characterized by two hands clasped in promise.

FILIA — daughter. *Filia regis* — daughter of the king, i.e., princess. *Filia praefecti* — daughter of the governor.

FLAGRUM — a scourge with two to three leather straps knotted with small pieces of metal and attached to a wooden handle. Pl. *flagra*.

FORUM — an area of a Roman city set aside for public discourse. People would gather in the *forum* to transact business, discuss new ideas or politics, or hear public addresses.

FRATER — brother.

GAPA — an old Germanic word meaning "gape."

GERMANIA SECUNDA — the northern region of Germania, formerly called Germania Inferior.

GLADIATRIX — female gladiator. Pl. *gladiatrices*.

HARUSPEX — a priest who practiced haruspicy, or the study of animal entrails for divination.

HIO – the Latin word for "gape." (So, *hias*—you gape)

HIPPODROMOS — hippodrome; an oval stadium used for horse races.

HORTUS — a garden.

HYPOCAUSTUM — a system designed to heat Roman rooms by circulating hot air through spaces or pipes under the floor and sometimes within the walls.

ICHTHUS — the Greek word for "fish." A symbol of early Christianity because the Greek letters form an acrostic of "Iesous CHristos THeos Uios Soter" meaning "Jesus Christ, Son of God, Savior."

IMPERATOR — emperor. A title reserved for the Augusti in the Tetrarchy.

IMPERIUM — imperial power or sovereignty, the right to command a state.

IMPLUVIUM — a depression in the atrium floor to collect rainwater.

INTERDICTIO IGNIS ET AQUAE — "interdiction of fire and water"— a form of banishment that deprived the exile of the necessities of life (food, shelter, water) within the boundaries of the Roman Empire and forbade his return to his homeland.

JOL — the Yule. *Jolfaedr* — Yule-father, a title of Woden. *Jol-clog* — the Yule log.

KALENDS — the first day of the month.

KOUROS — a statue depicting a young man, typically life-sized and nude, and most often occurring near sanctuaries and temples dedicated to Apollo. Pl. *kouroi*.

KYRIE — lord; the Greek equivalent of *domine*. *Kyria* — lady.

LATRUNCULI — a two-player board game similar to the modern game of chess; commonly considered a game of military tactics.

LECTICA — a portable bed of Eastern origin; a popular form of transportation for the wealthy.

LECTUS FUNEBRIS — a funeral bed. See also *feretrum*.

LEGATUS — the *legatus legionis* or Legion Legate was the highest ranking officer in a Legion. He often acted as a civil ruler, especially along the frontier.

LIBELLUS — a detailed program to accompany the gladiatorial games and other entertainments.

LICTOR — a bodyguard.

LIMES — borders, boundaries; especially fortified borders.

LORICA SQUAMATA — scale armor worn by Roman Legionaries, and favored by the *cataphractarii*.

MANE — wait!

MEDICUS — doctor, healer.

MILES — soldier. Pl. *milites*. Miles Gloriosus — *The Swaggering Soldier*, a play by Plautus.

MONACHA — a female hermit, one who lives apart from society. The root of the word *monastic*. Pl. *monachi*.

NATIVITAS — the Nativity, the feast of the birth of Jesus Christ.

NECROPOLIS — "city of the dead"; a massive burial site where the dead were housed in mausoleums or tombs.

NOBILISSIME—most noble.

NUMMUS — a Roman bronze coin, also known as a *follis*. Pl. *nummi*.

NUMMULARIUS — a money-changer, banker.

NUX SYLVESTRIS — the Latin term for a hazelnut.

NYMPHAEUM — a grotto, typically with a fountain, dedicated to the nymphs.

PAGANUS — a pagan. Pl. *pagani*.

PALLA — a long rectangular piece of fabric worn as a veil or wrap by Roman women.

PAPPAS — a Greek word meaning "father"; this was the common title for all bishops in early Christianity, but gradually became associated in particular with the bishop of Rome.

PATER — father.

PAX — peace.

PENDRAIG — Pendragon, the red dragon, a title which later becomes associated with King Arthur.

PERFECTUS PRAETUMIDUS — a play on *praefectus praetorio*, this means "the perfect puffer" or "puffed-up one," or something equally insulting.

PERIPTEROS — a style of temple in ancient Greece and Rome that was completely surrounded by columns.

PERISTYLUM — an inner courtyard that served as the main social area of a Roman house. It was often decorated with statues, columns, a fountain or a pool, and fruit trees.

PHAROS — Greek; refers to the great Lighthouse of Alexandria, built in the Ptolomaic Kingdom (280-247 BC) and one of the Seven Wonders of the Ancient World.

PHYLAKE – Greek word for a prison.

PORTA PRINCIPALIS — the main gate of a fort or city.

PORTCULLIS — a metal or wooden gate that could be raised and lowered on chains to secure a fort.

PORTUS — a Roman port. Alone, it refers to the port outside of Rome.

POSCA — a bitter mixture of vinegar and wine popular among Legionaries and sailors. This was probably the drink given to Christ on the Cross.

PRAEFECTUS — a provincial governor in the Roman Empire; *Praefectus Augustalis* was the title given to the Prefect of Egypt, who ruled in the personal name of the Emperor. *Praefectus praetorio* or Praetorian Prefect was a high-ranking official in the Empire, originally as commander of the Praetorian Guard, but later holding more of an administrative function. *Praefectus alae* is the title given to the commander of an *ala* of cavalry. See *ala*.

PRAETORIUM — the building where the Legion Legate would live with his family, and where Legion business was conducted.

PRONAOS — the area of a temple between the outer colonnade of the porch and the inner shrine. See *cella*.

PROTECTOR — a cadet regimental commander. A rank in the Imperial army designed for training officers for command.

PSITTACUS — a parrot.

PUGIO — dagger with a wide, leaf-shaped blade.

PURPURA — the purple coloring used to dye the imperial *toga purpura* and the border of the *toga praetexta*, among other things.

ROSTRUM — a raised platform used for public speaking.

SACRATISSIME — most sacred.

SALVE — hello.

SAPSARIUS — a Legion field medic.

SEAX — an ancient Germanic weapon, longer than a dagger but shorter than a sword.

SELLA — a Roman chair that had no back; the *sella curulis* was a symbol of authority and power.

SIGNUM — a sign. This had many meanings, from the eagle emblem of the Emperor to the *signum crucis* or "sign of the Cross" that early Christians used to recognize each other.

SPATHA — a Roman sword that became popular in the first century AD. It was longer than the *gladius*, which it replaced, and could be used by either the infantry or cavalry.

STOA — a wide colonnaded walkway. This is the root of the word *stoic*.

STRATIOTA — Greek word for soldier.

STRIGA — a long tent that served as barracks for common soldiers.
SUBLIGACULA — underclothes.
TABERNA — a tavern or public eating house popular with travelers.
TABLINUM — a small office in a Roman house usually situated between the *atrium* and the peristyle.
TERRA NOVA — new land; a Christian metaphor for heaven.
TERTIA VIGILIA — the third watch of the night, roughly from midnight to 3 AM.
TESSERARIUS — the commander of the night watch.
THERMAE — public bath houses, which were centers of Roman social life throughout the Empire.
TOLLE ME, EMITTE ME — "take me up, cast me away." This is the mysterious inscription on the two sides of Excalibur's blade.
TOR — a large hill or rocky mound jutting up from an otherwise level region. This Tor is a reference to the Glastonbury Tor.
TRIBUNUS — A high-ranking Legion official, usually second-in-command to the Legion Legate. These were usually young men in their late twenties, who often aspired to a senatorial career.
TRIBUNUS (MILITUS) ANGUSTICLAVIUS — a military tribune chosen from among the *equites*; there were five in each Legion, identified by a narrow purple stripe (*angusticlavia*) on their tunic.
TRIBUNUS ET COMES ORDINIS PRIMI — Tribune and Companion of the First Rank. During the Roman Empire, a *comes* was an official member of the Imperial retinue.
TRICLINIUM — the dining room in a Roman house, often arranged so the men would eat reclining, and the women sitting in chairs.
TRIREME — a warship of the Roman navy.
VALE — goodbye.
VESTIBULUM — an entryway. Origin of the word *vestibule*.
VIA FOSSA — called Fosse Way, it was one of the principle Roman roads in Britain, leading from Dumnoniorum in the southwest to Lindum Colonia (Lincoln) in the northeast.
VIA JULIA MARITIMA — a Roman road along the coast of modern-day Wales, leading from Maridunum to Venta Silurum.
VIA SACRA — sacred way; a road leading to a temple or shrine.
VICUS — a village or small provincial town, often developing near a Roman fort or garrison. Pl. *vici*. Origin of the word *vicar*.
VITIS — the symbol of office of a Roman centurion, used to conduct military drills or to inflict punishments.
VIVA, ET AMA — Live, and love.
YNYS AFALLON — Isle of Apples, the ancient name for the Isle of Avalon.

ACKNOWLEDGMENTS

I am chiefly grateful to all those forgotten and "liturgically suppressed" saints in Heaven such as Saint George, Saint Christopher, Saint Catherine, Saint Blaise, Saint Anastasia, Saint Eleutherius, (Saint) Constantine, Saint Helena and countless others depicted in the *Sword and Serpent* saga. Through the mercy of God, I have no doubt of their intercessory assistance (and perhaps delight) in our little stories about them.

Thank you to all the readers who purchased and read the first two novels *Sword and Serpent* and *The Tenth Region of the Night*—especially those who wrote kind and encouraging letters, emails, and reviews.

After hiring several graphic artists, we could not find the perfect image for this book cover. Mitchell DeSouza is a sparring partner of mine at my Brazilian Jiu Jitsu gym and also a tattoo artist. I explained my predicament and he offered to create something that included "a sword, a serpent, a storm, and fire," based on the title. I thank my friend Mitchell DeSouza and his assistant Jose Luis Virviescas for producing the "Fire Storm Serpent" graphic for the front cover *Storm of Fire and Blood*. "Oss."

It has been a delight to work with S.K. Valenzuela and J. Leigh Bralick over the years to perfect the plots, pace, and personas within the *Sword and Serpent* creative universe. They have woven the original woolen threads of Georgius, Christophorus, Nikolaos, and Sabra into a finely crafted tapestry. One side of the tapestry presents itself as flawless, but the underside reveals the countless hours of changes and corrections: reweaving and re-reweaving. Like Penelope, you weave by day, unravel by night, and yet weave again in the morning. Rightfully could it be said for each of you: *Lanam fecit*.

And speaking of Saint George, I salute all the captains, men, and young men of the Troops of Saint George. Saint George is the forge of men. *Ora pro nobis*.

These books are written in a devoted way for my wife Joy and our eight children: Gabriel, Mary Claire, Rose, Jude, Becket, Blaise, Elizabeth, and especially for Margaret Grace Carol, to whom this book is dedicated.

Taylor Marshall
Feast of Saint Margaret of Scotland
November 16, 2017

A special thanks to our Storm of Fire and Blood Launch Team who read this novel before publication and also helped us with promotion. Thank you for your time, input, and enthusiasm.

Godspeed,
Taylor

Sister Tarcila Abaño, Sharon Abrahamson, Thomas Achatz, David Agreda, Rawad Al Feghali, Armando Alderete, Claudia Alderete, Anil Alexander, Theresa Allen-Caulboy, Bernardo Altamirano, Ignacio David Alvarado, Joseph Anuga, Sheila Appling, John Arellano, Paul Arias, Robert Atkinson, Doug Austreim, Sarah Badger, Isabella Baeten, Robert Baeten, Kevin Bailey, Hartley Bancroft, Jennifer Barton, Eliot Bassett, David Bates, Orland Daniel Batongbakal, Madeline Bauer, Christopher Beckett, Melanie Behnke, Jill Bender, Elaine Bennett, Suzanne Berendt, Jane G Bernal, Kathryn Bevis, Timothy Black, Robert Blanchard, Jocelyne Blanchette, Angela Bloch, Brett Bloch, David Blyth, Robert Boatwright, Kenneth Bolin, Michael Bonin, Rick Bookwalter, Eric Boutin, Max Bradicich, Steve Branch, Anne Bremer, Mary Brennan, Patty Broome, Bill Brown, Pam Brubaker, Pam Brubaker, Edward Bucnis, OFS, Paul Burdett, Ronald Burg, Robert Burgess, Patrick Burke, Lesley Camaioni, Linda Campagna, Kathleen Campos, Jacqueline Candello, Diane Cannon, Marjorie Carr, Pat Carvalho, Lisa Cash, Jessica Castillo, Celines Ceballos, Susan Cenci, Tarisai Chiborise, Karen Clabby, Andrew Cody, Annie Coffey, Francisco Colino, Robyn Collyer, Brock Cordeiro, Jeff Corey, Emily Cowley, Walter Crabtree, Rossa Croce, Kristy Crosby, Kaitlyn Croyle, Sean Cunningham, Andrée Daugereaux, Matt Dawson, Chris Dawson, Viola De Velasco, Father Chris Decker, Michele Deering, Leonard DeFoggia, Susan De la Rosa, Annika DeMaster, Andrea Deranek, Regina DeSpain, Mike DeWitt, Jenny Dibley, Andrea Dick, Michael DiCosoma, Kimberley Dierdorf, Jim Disimoni, Julie Dodge, Linda Doran, Therese Dougherty, Matej Dragoner, Dylan Drego, Carol Dubeansky, Marie DuMabeiller, Brian Dvorak, Shawna Dziedziak, Paul Eades, Bryan Eagan, Rick Eagan, Samuel Edwards, Sarah Eichler, Donna Ellwanger, Jennifer Ely, Christina Enkler, Sophia Estabrooks, Andrew Fakult, Gregory Fast, Catherine Felicien, Adrian Fernandez, Butch Fernando, Linda Fiessinger, Joseph Firoozmand, John Fitsimmons, Maggie Flood, Mary Anne Florich, James Florio, Gill Fowler, Christina Fox, Patricia Fraide, Karen Frederick, Howard Fulks, Laura Fusco, Linda Gabriel, Maria Garcia, Bryan Gardner, Connie Garlitz, Daniel Garrison, George Gehring, Alice Gess, Carol Getty, Sanda Gheorghe, Tadeu Giatti, Renee Gibula, Nancy Gierszewski, Valerie Giggie, Jessica Goh, Thomas Goh, Cecilia Gonzalez, Janet M Green, Jon-Mark Grussenmeyer, George Gussy, Rich Gustafson, Frank H, Tamara Haas, Cindy Hamer, Paul Hammond, Emily Harder, Katie Harder, Annmarie Hart, Christine Hebert, Faye Heffele, Anne Heffernan, Matthew Heffron, Rosanne Heiliger, Teresa Hemphill, Roy Henderson, Phil Henneman, Grainne Hennigan, Marla Hernandez, Aida Hernandez, Michelle Hinckley, Darlene Hinman, Eunice Hnitko, Eunice Hnitko, Scott Hoey, Linda Hoffstetter, Neil Holder, R.W. Holleman, Kevin Hollyfield, Stanley Holmes, Patty Homegun, Father Geoff Horton, Theresa Hubbell, Hugh Hubble, Sean Hudson, Richard Hudzik, Jason Hull, William Hynd, Maria Incer, Nancy Jackson, Bernhard Janssen, Emily Jeffries, Lauren Jenkins, Darryn Johnnie, Walter Jones, Lauren Jones, Kathryn Jones, Kelvin Jukpor, Aaron Junge, Jacob Jurkoic, Mary Kalslen, Sylvia Kendall, Keith Kennedy, Mary Kessler, Cora W Ketchum, Renee Kimball, Luke Kippenbrock, Patricia Koranda, Jim Kornegay, Sunita Kottoor,

Theresa Kowalczyk, Meredith Krebel, Katie Kuchar, Wendy Kutanzi,
Andrea Kvasager, Christina Kylochko, Frances Lafferty, Katherine Lamb,
Max A Langley, Ian Larch, Margie Larson, Lillian Marie Laruan, Miguel Lasaga,
Peter Lassiter, David Lawless, Paul Leader, James LeBert, Beth Ledbetter,
Disna Lee, Thomas Lee, Pierre-Louis Lefebvre, Alex Lessard, Heather Leuci,
Laurie Lewandowski, Catherine Loft, Richard Losch, Jeanne Lugert, Tina Lujan,
Edel Lukens, Taylor Mac Manus, Eileen Maggio, Michael Maker, Alex Maldonado,
Cyndy Maletta, Crystal Mallner, Father Bill Malloy, Susan Mark,
Mary Claire Marshall, Thomas Charles Marshall, Lukas Marshy, Christina Martin,
Silvio Mattacchione, Rachel McAdams, Julie McCabe, April McCullough,
Jay McCurdy, Steven R. McEvoy, Erin McGahuey, Thomas McIntyre,
Michael McKay, Seth McQuillan, Spence McSorley, Larry McWilliams,
Brandie Meisner, Alex Melhorn, Barb Melvin, Catherine Mena, Kim Mercanti,
Marisa Merkle, Douglas Metz, Judi Mielke, Loretta Miller, Angela Miller,
Andrew Miner, Kevin Mitchell, Catherine Mohs, Alfred Monteiro, Mark Moran,
Andy Morgan, Philip Morin, Olivia Morris, Susan Mule, Mary Murphy,
Cameron Murray, Andrew Musano, Eric Myers, Pat Nacol, Katerina Naiser,
Chris Nash, Catherine Nelson, Joan Nelson, Joseph Nguyen,
Zachary and Kathleen Nietling, Dalia Nino, Amber Nold, Linus Nworie,
Michael Nyoagbe, Timothy O'Neil, Jade Ola, Andrew Olson, Gracela Omamalin,
Patricia ONeill, William Orsborn, Maria Ortiz, Gerald Osborn, Aileen Osias,
Joseph Paragone, Patricia Pasquarelli, Dr. Joe Pastorek, Amy Pavey, Ring Peace,
Vicky Pelegrin, Emilio Perea, Pamela Pettibone, Mitzi Phalen, George Piccone,
John Picone, Bradley Poole, Natalie Porter, John Pramberg, Donna Prather,
Les Preston, Amanda Pritchard, Sharon Pry, Caitlyn Pszonka, Gordon Rafool,
Claudia Ramirez, Connie Ramirez, Dominic Rankin, John James Rayel,
Dawna Reandeau, Landon Reffitt, Kevin Reginald, Ashwith Rego,
Joan Marie Reiley, Daniel Reisinger, Anthony Renzette, Michael Rhyner,
Joyce Riske, Amanda Robben, Lisa Roberts, Collin Roberts,
Carlos Abraham Rodriguez, Gil Rodriguez, James Rogers, Alfredo Roldan,
Izalco Ruiz, Nowellyn Ryan, Gary Ryan, Emad Saad, Elizabeth Joy Sadiarin,
Dave Sadlowski, Audry Salvador, Amy San Filippi, Gemma Sanchez-O'Brien,
Deacon Greg Sass, Francesco Sasso, Jeremy Sauer, Lori Sautter, Ryan Sayles,
Joe Scaffidi, Angela Schade, Angela Schade, Olivia Schmidt, Rick Schrader,
Melissa Schulze, Aaron Schweitzer, Sam Sebastian, E E Segura, Theresa Selenske,
James Senecal,John Sengenberger, Ellie Severino, Mary Sevier, Loretta Shalosky,
Robert Shea, Elizabeth Sheehy, George Shook, Marianne Sibal, Jason Sim,
Walter Simons, Jean Simonson, Jeffrey Singer, Lacie Smaldone, Alyssa Smeltzer,
Peyton Smith, Valerie Smyder, Julian Sommers, Laio Souza, Karen Spaziante,
Christopher Spiller, Charles Spivak, Susan Stalter, John Standifird, Beatriz Stapleton,
Kristopher Stickney, Theresa Stiner, Richard Stockard, Kolbe Stover, Eleanor Stowell,
Father Cayetano Maria Sulit, Derek Swallow, Nettie Taylor, Bernadette Thorley,
David Thrower, Lawrence Todd, Matthew Toenjes, Deborah Tofflemire,
Anna Tognaci, David Trana, Nicholas Trandem, Jeffrey Traughber, Charles Trujillo,
Jeremy Trull, Janine Tryban, James Tucker, Forrest Tucker, Karly Tuttle,
Marcel Urban, Jeremy Urban, Lima Vadakara, Téo van der Weele,
A Van Male, William Van Riper, Jaime Vanchura, Ant Vassallo, Giona Vazhappilly,
Clare Vining, Charles Volz, Dr William von Peters, Veronica Walsh,
Victoria Walter, Catherine Walton, David Warner, John Wasko, Daniel Waterfield,
Gregory Watson, Chris Watts, Misty Weber, C. Thomas Weigel, Jim Welling,
Thomas Whitfield, Steve Whitters, James Wilson, Debbie Womack,
Michael Woodruff, Michael Woodward, Darek Wyrzykowski, Esterio Yap,
Sean Yuan, Aidan Zaballero, Marilyn Zayac, Sherry Zeisel,
Thomas Ziolkowski, and Amy Zizzi.

Made in the USA
Monee, IL
26 September 2020